First published in Great Britain in 2018 by

ZAFFRE PUBLISHING
80–81 Wimpole St, London W1G 9RE
www.zaffrebooks.co.uk

A CIP catalogue record for this book is
available from the British Library.

ISBN: 978–1–78576–418–9

Also available as an ebook

3 5 7 9 10 8 6 4 2

Typeset by IDSUK (Data Connection) Ltd
Printed and bound in Great Britain by Clays Ltd, Elcograf S.p.A

Zaffre Publishing is an imprint of Bonnier Zaffre,
part of Bonnier Books UK
www.bonnierzaffre.co.uk
www.bonnierbooks.co.uk

THE
ASH
DOLL

JAMES HAZEL

ZAFFRE

This book is dedicated to Grace, who once asked if I was a bald man with glasses. For the record, I am not (at least, not yet).

'Do not repay anyone evil for evil. Be careful to do what is right in the eyes of everyone. If it is possible, as far as it depends on you, live at peace with everyone. Do not take revenge, my dear friends, but leave room for God's wrath, for it is written: "It is mine to avenge; I will repay," says the Lord.'

Romans 12:17–19

'Eye for eye . . .'

Exodus 21:24

Chapter 1

1 November 1989

Rose scrambled up the last few feet of hillside where the incline banked sharply, and mossy turf gave way to a stone ledge running across the cliff. The light was fading and the air was cold and damp. She hurried over the crest but knew that she had to watch her step. As the path narrowed, only a series of rotting fence posts joined with wire separated her from the waves crashing on the scree below.

There was a small gathering of people ahead of her where the path widened out before it disappeared altogether as the cliff ended abruptly, falling away at an almost perfect right angle where it would eventually meet the flatter coastline. As she approached, one of the figures broke from the group and hurried to meet her.

'Thank goodness, Rose,' the woman gasped. Rose recognised her as the tall widow who kept the flower shop in the nearby village of Tome, but the name eluded her.

'I came as soon I could,' Rose explained, sensing the panic in the flower-woman's voice.

'Not a moment too soon.'

The flower-woman ushered Rose through the group who parted for her, their grim faces barely registering in the dusk.

There were a few she recognised from the town and even a couple she could put names to. Being two months into her post with the local constabulary, she felt she really ought to know all of them, but Rose was damned if she could tell one face from another in this light.

'What took you so long, Officer?' growled a voice obscured beneath the hood of a raincoat. The garment would have swamped a basketball player, let alone the dumpy character wearing it. She ignored the insinuation and allowed herself to be led to where the wire fence cut across them and a yellow sign warning of the dangerous sheer drop swung precariously in the wind.

Near the edge, a cracked wooden sign bearing the name of the cliff jutted out of the ground at an angle: DEVIL'S POINT.

'Who found her?' asked Rose to the flower-woman.

'Vern was leading his history group up here.'

'What was a history group doing up here at this time of night?'

'Well, it's more of a ghost walk, if you ask me. The cliff is supposed to be haunted by the ghost of a Celtic sailor who—'

Rose raised her hand irritably and the woman had the good sense not to continue. Rose lowered the wire and stepped over it; it was astonishing how brittle the safety perimeter was.

She stopped and stared ahead. Behind her, the dying sun was plunging into the horizon, its final burst of energy igniting the foot of the night sky with a deep crimson gloss. Rose swallowed hard. Standing on the edge of the cliff, her hair caught in the breeze, was a young girl of no more than ten. She faced outwards towards the sea, her hands outstretched, looking for all the world as if she might suddenly sprout wings and dive into the grey abyss.

She looked back, as if the flower-woman might be able to offer some explanation. She was met with an array of blank faces.

'Hello?' Rose called gently, careful not to startle her.

At first, the girl did nothing but, when Rose called again, she turned her head and Rose caught a glimpse of a pale, tear-stained face.

'Sweetheart, I'm a police officer. You're standing very close to the edge. Can you step back towards me?'

The girl didn't move. Rose edged forward. The girl was perilously close to the brink – a strong, unexpected gust might be enough to send her over.

'You're safe, honey. You just need to turn around, slowly and carefully.'

The wind whipped around her face as Rose lowered herself to the girl's level. She was seven or eight metres from Rose but, given the proximity of the danger facing her, she might as well have been a thousand miles away. Her heart racing, Rose extended her hand.

'Can you tell me your name?'

The girl shook her head, almost imperceptibly.

'Can you tell me where you're from?'

Another slight shake.

Rose was about to move towards her when someone spoke from behind. The small man hidden in the oversized raincoat.

'Officer, look.'

Rose followed the outstretched hand to the girl's midriff, and down to where a ragged skirt flapped across her thin, bare legs. At first Rose thought it might be dirt. It had rained hard the night before and the ground was muddy in places.

But the rust-coloured patches running from underneath her white dress to her heels weren't mud.

'Honey,' she whispered, 'what happened to you?'

Chapter 2

Present Day

SIMEON: HEY ARE YOU THERE?

SIMEON: HELLO?

USER3412:   SORRY, I'M HERE.

SIMEON: BEEN THINKING ABOUT NEXT WEEK A LOT.

USER3412:   WHAT ABOUT NEXT WEEK? WE'RE GOING TO CHANGE THE WORLD ☺

SIMEON: I NEED TO TALK TO YOU.

USER3412:   IT'S TOUGH I KNOW. BUT WE'VE COME SO FAR. DID YOU REMEMBER THE MEETING PLACE? WE WON'T NEED IT BUT HOPE IT HELPS. KNOWING IT'S THERE AND STUFF?

SIMEON: IT'S MORE COMPLICATED THAN THAT. I'M NOT SURE ANYMORE.

USER3412:   SIMEON, RELAX. EVERYTHING WILL BE FINE. THIS IS WHAT WE BOTH WANT RIGHT? THE TRUTH. WE ARE MARCHING TO AN APOCALYPTIC TUNE.

SIMEON: NOT SURE I GET WHAT THE TRUTH IS ANYMORE. IT'S ALL GOT VERY CONFUSED IN MY HEAD. LAST NIGHT I HAD THIS DREAM THAT WE WERE IN A THEATRE LOOKING OUT TO AN AUDIENCE, TELLING THEM OUR STORY. THEY WERE ON FIRE.

	ALL OF THEM. I COULD SMELL THEIR FLESH BURNING. FUCKED UP RIGHT?
USER3412:	OK. THE BALANCE, SIMEON. REMEMBER IT'S ALL ABOUT RESTORING BALANCE. IF WE DON'T DO THIS THEN WHO WILL? REMEMBER – SNE, HNE, SNE.
SIMEON:	NO. I'VE MADE UP MY MIND.
SIMEON:	U THERE?
USER3412:	WHAT DO YOU MEAN?
SIMEON:	I MEAN ABOUT THE TRUTH.
USER3412:	THIS IS JUST YOU HAVING DOUBTS WHICH IS NATURAL CONSIDERING THE CONSEQUENCES OF WHAT WILL HAPPEN NEXT WEEK WHEN THE WORLD FINDS OUT THE TRUTH.
SIMEON:	I HATE MYSELF.
SIMEON:	HATE WHAT I'VE BECOME MAYBE. I KNOW WHAT WE'RE DOING AND I KNOW WHAT HAPPENED HAPPENED, BUT THAT DOESN'T MAKE US RIGHT. WHO GUARDS THE GUARDS IF WE DO WHAT WE WANT?
USER3412:	IT DOESN'T WORK LIKE THAT.
SIMEON:	WHAT DO YOU MEAN?
USER3412:	SIMEON, WE'VE BEEN DOING THIS FOR 2 YEARS. IT'S NOT LIKE YOU CAN JUST SAY HEY FUCK IT AT THIS POINT CAN YOU? DID YOU TALK TO THE MAG'S LAWYER?
SIMEON:	I MET HIM A COUPLE OF TIMES.
USER3412:	WHO IS HE?
SIMEON:	HIS NAME IS PRIEST.
USER3412:	AND?
SIMEON:	WHAT?

USER3412:   WHAT'S HE LIKE?

SIMEON: KIND OF LIKE A GUY THAT'S GOOD TO HAVE ON
            YOUR SIDE AND A REAL BIG DEAL IF HE'S ON THE
            OTHER.

USER3412:   NOT GONNA FUCK WITH HIM THEN?

USER3412:   SIMEON? U THERE?

SIMEON: WE SHOULD GO TO THE POLICE.

USER3412:   AND THEY'LL DO WHAT EXACTLY?

SIMEON: YOU KNOW WHAT.

SIMEON: I GUESS WHEN WE STARTED I BOUGHT INTO THE
            AGENDA. I GOT WHAT WE WERE ABOUT. CUTTING
            OUT THE ROTTEN CORE AND EVERYTHING. YOU
            WERE MY INSPIRATION. I THOUGHT I CAN DO
            THIS – THIS MAKES REAL SENSE. DON'T GET ME
            WRONG. THEY SHOULD BURN FOR WHAT THEY
            DID BUT IS THIS THE WAY? IS THIS ME?

USER3412:   CALL ME.

SIMEON: I'M SORRY. SOMEONE HAS TO END THIS.

USER3412:   DON'T BE A FOOL, SIMEON. IF WE DON'T DO IT
            THEN THEY WIN. THAT'S ALL THAT WILL HAPPEN.
            THEY WILL WIN.

SIMEON: YOU DON'T KNOW THAT.

USER3412:   WAIT.

USER3412:   I DON'T WANNA HAVE TO DO IT THIS WAY,
            SIMEON, BUT I OWN YOU.

USER3412:   YOU DON'T GET TO LEAVE. NOT NOW.

SIMEON: I'M SORRY.

SIMEON: ***SIMEON HAS LOGGED OFF***

USER3412:   FINE. BUT DON'T SAY YOU WEREN'T WARNED.

USER3412:   ***USER3412 HAS LOGGED OFF***

Chapter 3

Vincent Okoro sat with his arm draped across the back of the front bench of court thirteen, which creaked under the weight of his muscular frame. The trial bundle was spread across his lap but his interrogation of it was limited to idly flipping through the pages, only giving cursory attention to the text. Anything else would have been pointless: he knew the contents intimately.

He was vaguely aware of the hum of people around him. Behind, two men and a woman sat nervously shuffling around, not quite sure how to find a comfortable pose on the ancient wooden pews that served as seating in the Royal Courts of Justice. To his left, an usher draped in ill-fitting robes was moving papers around with great purpose, although the end result eluded Okoro. High above him to the back of the court, a scattering of journalists were engrossed in the soft lights from their smartphones and tablets, trying to find something productive to do before the trial started.

It was a disappointing turn-out. Given the media attention the case had enjoyed for the past two years, he had hoped for more of a journalistic presence on day one of *Elias* v. *The Real Byte Limited*. But then it was early. The start time was an hour and a half away. Not even the claimant and her team of blood-sucking lawyers had arrived in court, although rumour suggested they had been milling around the public cafe earlier filling their time with croissants and anecdotes.

Still, an hour and a half to go – and no sign of Priest, or their first witness.

Okoro sighed heavily, and threw the bundle back under the bench. He turned around and was surprised to see behind him another figure who must have ghosted into court.

'Hello,' Georgie Someday said brightly, her green eyes peering curiously at him.

'How long have you been there?' Okoro asked.

'Three minutes. I didn't want to disturb your reading.'

'I've read it before. Where's Priest?'

'He rang to say he's on his way.'

'Is he with Simeon?'

Georgie grimaced. 'He didn't mention that.'

Okoro found himself sighing again, but with more vigour. Simeon Ali – his crucial witness – could make or break this case. Without his evidence, it could well be a very short and humiliating trial.

Maybe the lack of journalists at the back wasn't so bad after all.

'Go and phone Priest,' Okoro instructed. 'Find out where he is and get confirmation that Simeon is turning up on time this morning and looking like the million-pound witness he is.'

Georgie nodded, brushed a strand of ginger hair out of her face and scurried out.

'Morning, Okoro.' A gruff voice directed Okoro's attention to the claimant's side of the courtroom where a hunched figure was lining bundles up on the front bench.

'Hagworth.' Okoro acknowledged his opponent with a curt nod, which the old silk returned before getting back to the job of trying to make his bundles stand upright – a task that Okoro surmised was being hindered by his shaking hands and milky eyes.

'Fine morning,' Hagworth muttered.

Okoro shrugged. 'I thought there might be more press.'

'There are some reporters busying themselves in the lobby. *Parasites*. But enough to give you some publicity, if that is what you desire.'

Okoro grunted in a way that was intended to be non-committal. Dickie Hagworth QC was one of the most experienced libel lawyers in private practice but that didn't stop him from being an objectionable snob.

'A fine suit,' Hagworth observed.

Okoro looked down and inspected his eighteen stone of muscle bulging out of an Armani three-piece. He looked back up, not sure what to say. Hagworth rarely said anything for no good reason.

'You certainly look the part, Okoro. I hope you don't take the loss too hard.' The QC smirked and picked up another bundle.

Okoro leant forward, the bench creaking under the movement, and rested his chin on his hand thoughtfully. Then he said, 'It's going to be tough for you back at the gentlemen's club, Hagworth. Trying to explain how you got beat by a black man.'

In front of him, Hagworth's line of files collapsed, sending papers scattering across the courtroom floor.

Chapter 4

The morning sun glistened off the frost-covered grass as the procession slowly trailed over the brow of the hill, the church behind them and the vista falling away ahead. Crows lined the fence like sentries, watching the proceedings with avid curiosity. The ground was damp and the day smelt of fresh dew. Only the distant rumble of traffic reminded the gathering that the burial ground was only a few miles outside of the city.

The hole was already dug, ready to accept the casket, which was now lowered into the ground. At the far end, the vicar read the familiar set of words, shivering slightly in the cold. Charlie Priest stood at the back, hands thrust deep into his pockets, trying not to be recognised, but it wasn't easy. At six foot three with broad shoulders and a strong, athletic build, Priest wasn't good at merging into the background. With bright blue eyes and drifts of soft brown hair, he cut a rugged and striking sight. Several people had already turned around to look, nudging each other and whispering. They knew who he was. Through the crackle of their hushed chatter, Priest caught one electrifying word drifting on the breeze: Mayfly. He was the man who Kenneth had hired to find his son's killer. The man who had undone everything for the Ellinders.

The ceremony had been mercifully short. Two tuneless hymns and a generic eulogy read to a modest gathering of family and well-wishers. Kenneth Ellinder's life had been reduced to fifteen simple minutes before his remains were swallowed by the earth.

When a bearer threw the first handful of dirt over the coffin, Priest turned to go. He had paid his respects and discharged what would have otherwise been a nagging burden. He had felt his phone vibrate several times in his inside pocket; no doubt Georgie trying to ascertain his whereabouts at Okoro's request. The Priest & Co. in-house counsel would be furious, but the trial wasn't starting for another hour and a half and Okoro always over-prepared. Besides, Priest's job was done. Everything had been meticulously organised. All he had to do was wind Okoro up, put Ali on the stand and watch the media lap up the hype.

He was halfway down the hill when he felt a hand on his arm.

'Charlie,' said a voice that was neither pleased to see him nor overtly hostile.

Priest turned round and there she was. 'Jessica.'

She stood on the elevation at his level, the breeze gently playing with her hair, her eyes fixed on his. For a moment he just stared, searching. But he couldn't read her. This mysterious woman who haunted his dreams stood so close that he could smell the sweetness of her skin, a sensation that was both familiar to him and, at the same time, despairingly alien.

'Say something,' she said.

'I'm sorry for—'

'*Not* that.' She broke her gaze and let her eyes drift into the middle distance. 'Where were you?'

Priest didn't know. So much had happened. He had first met Jessica Ellinder the previous year, at his office, with her father. Reluctantly, Priest had agreed to investigate the apparent murder of Jessica's brother, Miles. The case had almost been the undoing of him and had ended with him exposing her family's links with a secret neo-Nazi cult.

Jessica was the only positive thing that had come out of that case. They had agreed to meet – Priest had *wanted* to meet. But he never turned up.

'Charlie. Where *were* you?' she repeated.

'I'm sorry,' he offered, but he knew it wasn't enough.

She nodded. He didn't need a psychology textbook to tell him that she was disappointed, and angry, but whether that was because she had wanted to see him again or because she wasn't used to being stood up was beyond him.

He looked down and pushed the earth around with the toe of his shoe, his inadequacy enveloping him. How could he explain it to her? Whenever he tried to sound out the reason in his head, it sounded pathetic, but the root cause was a mantra that had arisen from the ashes of his past: *whenever I touch something special, it just seems to wither in my hands*. In a world where nothing seemed real, Priest had found that people, especially lovers, eventually faded away. At least this way, Jessica would always stay real to him.

'How are you?' Priest asked, feebly.

For a horrible moment, he thought she might do what he felt he deserved and slap him across the face, but instead she released her hand from his arm, as if she had just realised, with embarrassment, that she was still touching him.

'I'm doing better than perhaps I should be,' she conceded.

'Maybe we could start again?'

'From which point? The point at which I was shown a picture of my brother impaled on a spike, or before that?'

He faltered, although he felt justified in doing so. 'Starting again doesn't necessarily have to mean going back to any particular point. Perhaps it's about rebuilding what we have.'

'Which is what exactly?'

'I have absolutely no idea.'

At last, a statement he was sure of. He shouldn't have stood her up, but maybe there was hope – maybe he could atone. He carried out a quick mental calculation. The trial started in ninety minutes. He had to travel halfway across London to the Strand and negotiate the plethora of cameramen lining the High Court entrance, which would take him to the point where the trial was scheduled to start, but Okoro's patience would have worn thin way before then.

Inside his jacket pocket, his phone resumed its familiar, angry buzz.

'Meet me tomorrow night,' he said, his heart in his mouth. 'Come over to mine. We can shut ourselves away from the world for an evening. I'll attempt to cook you something. Do you like lemon sole?'

'You're asking me out on a date? At my father's funeral.' There was no trace of humour in her voice.

Priest shuffled his feet again. On reflection, he did seem to have set a record for inappropriate passes.

For a full agonising minute, she said nothing, but continued to stare at some imperceptible spot behind him. For every excruciating moment that passed a feeling of hopelessness set in until, finally, she nodded.

'You'd *better* be there, Priest. Or God have mercy.'

Chapter 5

Georgie Someday had never been one to panic. To her mind, she was more of a fretter. The difference was subtle but important. A panicker abandons logical thought in favour of irrational dread. A panicker assumes the worst, but fails to formulate any sensible strategy for dealing with it. A fretter, on the other hand, uses anxiety positively. A fretter calculates all possible outcomes and designs coping strategies for as many as conceivably possible.

Having said that, standing in the Royal Courts of Justice Great Hall, clutching her phone, with half an hour to go before the trial was due to start and still no sign of Priest or the defence's star witness, Georgie was experiencing a sensation she thought was, in truth, much closer to panic than fret.

She put her phone away and removed her glasses to clean them for the eighth time before passing back through security and out onto the Strand. People bustled past, pulling coats tightly around them, ignoring the glare of television cameras lining the entrance-way to the High Court. Close by, she overheard a solemn-faced presenter standing rigidly in front of a camera:

'Operating globally with a combined turnover of over fifty-five million pounds, the Elias Children's Foundation is one of the largest charities in the UK established for the benefit of child victims of war, domestic violence, abuse, neglect and exploitation. Its operations include an African education programme, disaster and emergency response schemes, HIV and AIDS prevention and care programmes, and programmes aimed at stopping the exploitation of child soldiers for terrorist purposes. It's not for profit but don't let that label fool you – this is big business.

'I'm outside the High Court today because the charity's founder and CEO, Alexia Elias, is suing small independent online magazine, *The Real Byte*, for libel following an article about her they published in 2014. You may remember that in 2009 a scandal broke out at the Elias Foundation when it was discovered that a small branch office had been funnelling charity funds to an organisation known as the Free People's Army, a terrorist cell operating in northern Turkey.

'Following extensive investigations by the Charities Commission, that office was closed down, with Turkish police arresting several Elias Foundation employees.'

She decided to hang around. Although the way the reporter kept brushing her hair back vainly was beginning to grate on her, she was interested to know how accurate the reporting was. So far, not too bad.

'In 2014, *The Real Byte* published an article alleging that not only was Alexia Elias fully aware of the Turkish scandal involving her charity, but she had received bribes from terrorists totalling four hundred thousand pounds to keep quiet about it. This is day one of a four-week trial here at the High Court in which Alexia Elias hopes to clear her name . . .'

Georgie went back inside, nodding at the security guard on her way in. What might make more interesting reporting, she thought, was if *The Real Byte* solicitor, Charlie Priest, her employer, didn't turn up in the next half an hour accompanied by the magazine's main witness. It was this thought that was making her stomach churn.

'Come on, Charlie,' she said to herself through gritted teeth. 'Now's not the time to be late.'

Until 2012, Simeon Ali had been an Elias Children's Foundation employee working at their Turkish branch. Georgie had never met him. As far as she was aware, Charlie had only met him a few times. He kept a very low profile and with good reason – Alexia Elias and her husband, Dominique, were powerful figures with powerful friends, and connections that went right the way to the top of government. There were plenty of images of Alexia sitting in conferences – a broad smile across her face – drinking tea with Cabinet ministers doing their rounds across social media. A lot of influential people had backed the Elias Foundation and its charismatic CEO. A lot of people had put their hands deeply into their wallets. In Georgie's view, the charity had survived the Turkish scandal because of some very good spin. During the press conference in the immediate aftermath of the scandal, Alexia Elias, surrounded by PR managers and lawyers, had produced the performance of a lifetime:

'We are hurt, and we are betrayed, but we will not succumb to evil, nor we will shrink in the face of oppression. We will rise up, in union, and remember why we are here, who we are and what we stand for.' Then, with a tear in her eye: 'We are the Elias Foundation, and we shall not be beaten by a tiny group of weak-minded traitors. I will use every resource available to me to right this wrong.'

After assuring the press that the corruption had been isolated and contained, the weeping CEO had stepped down to embrace her husband in a moment of rehearsed solidarity before giving way to her press officer to mop up any question from the awe-struck crowd.

The suggestion that Alexia had been lying when she said she knew nothing about the scandal until it was too late was unthinkable. The idea that she had been a part of it was heresy.

Nonetheless, a trace of doubt remained, and Alexia Elias was not without her critics. So far, though, the voice of dissent was small, confined to people who had been labelled conspiracy theorists: dismissed as part of the same group who supposedly believed the Rothschild family controlled the world and Hillary Clinton was an alien. Although perhaps the non-believers weren't as insignificant as some first thought: *The Real Byte*'s advertising revenue had doubled following the media's coverage of the libel action.

There were two things in Priest & Co.'s favour: the first was that the magazine's insurers were funding the trial, albeit with considerable reluctance, and the second was that Alexia had openly taken the moral high ground and decided to only sue the magazine itself and not Tomas Jansen, its owner, personally, which would have complicated matters. Jansen might have even needed separate representation.

But even with a third party paying the bills – for now – there was considerable risk. Insurers would always find a reason not to pay, or only partially pay out, if they backed the wrong horse. For *The Real Byte* and Priest & Co., the stakes were about as high as they could get.

She tried ringing Charlie one more time, this time leaving a message. She hoped it made it clear she was anxious to hear from him without completely betraying the panic that had now gripped her.

Damn, damn, damn!

She glanced back to court thirteen but decided it would be best not to report back to Okoro until such time as she had some positive news. As she did, she saw an older gentleman lope across the lobby looking rather harassed. This, she surmised, must be Dominique Elias, Alexia's husband. His witness statement had struck her as being rather curt. He loved his wife and regarded her as the very personification of integrity and professionalism and of course he would have known if she had received bribes of that level. All very businesslike and matter-of-fact.

Her mind had wandered, and it took a few seconds to register the voice in her ear.

'Miss Someday? Hello?'

Georgie spun around and found her personal space had been filled by a young woman with long, blonde hair which looked bleached, beaming at her. She was tucked inside a black coat and was clutching an iPad. She was pretty. With such a sparkling smile, she might even be called striking were it not for a certain air of detachment visible through her eyes. Georgie groaned inwardly.

'Yes?' she asked.

'Elinor Fox – independent. You're with Priest & Co., aren't you? Could I ask you about the trial?'

'You mean you're independent or you're from the *Independent*?' replied Georgie, folding her arms.

The dazzling smile faltered slightly and Georgie rejoiced in its retreat. 'The former.'

'Sorry, I can't talk to journalists.'

Fox continued, undeterred, 'How are your clients bearing up?'

Not too badly, was the honest answer, *considering that the future of their magazine depends on winning this case*. The Real Byte was a small outfit which had stumbled on a big exclusive and were paying the price. The magazine's executive editor, Tomas Jansen, was born and graduated in Denmark and had started *The Real Byte* five years previously when the demand for quick, accessible online news was starting to increase exponentially. He had written the Elias article, with some input from his managing editor, Gail Woodbead. Their small team was completed by Karl Jones, the magazine's technical director. Those three – and a handful of external contributors – comprised the entirety of the magazine's human element.

Elinor Fox was apparently still speaking. 'Miss Someday?'

'No comment,' Georgie said.

'Not even one little quote?'

'Not one. Thank you.'

Fox pinched her face together in what appeared to be a sympathetic gesture but which was obviously a manifestation of huge disappointment and utter contempt.

Then Georgie saw something flit past her vision. She scanned the air around her, then saw a bee land behind Fox. She stiffened and moved around the reporter, who looked puzzled.

'Sorry,' said Georgie, motioning to the insect. 'I'm allergic to bee stings. It's called anaphylaxis.'

A voice crackled over the PA system – 'All parties in *Elias* v. *The Real Byte Limited* to court thirteen. That's all parties in *Elias* v. *The Real Byte Limited* to court thirteen, please' – and Georgie took the opportunity to go back inside, giving the bee and the reporter a wide berth.

Once inside, she looked around, realising that she would have to explain to both Okoro and the clients that they would have to proceed without Charlie and Simeon for now. *Just don't shoot the messenger. Wait! Is that . . . ?*

A figure bounded up the court steps and threw his keys and a phone into the security box. He looked up and waved at her. She pointed to her watch and Charlie Priest waved her away, as if they had all the time in the world.

He collected his things from the box once it had passed through the scanner then started to usher her across the lobby to court thirteen. 'Did you miss me?'

'Vincent will be *very* angry,' Georgie advised.

'No doubt. How's Dickie looking?'

'Richard Hagworth QC?'

'Yes. Dickie.'

'He looks OK, I guess.'

'Oh, come on, Georgie. I've seen Ikea tables with more movement in their joints. Now, where's Simeon?'

Georgie stopped.

'I thought he was with you?'

Chapter 6

Charlie Priest knew a lot about disaster management in litigation. Rule number one was to preserve the illusion that no disaster existed. Nothing was more fragile than the short period of time between parties shuffling into court and the moment the chambers door swung open and the judge manifested himself or, in this case, *her*self. Trials were made and broken in that vacuum where time stood still. The slightest breeze could be enough to dislodge the nerve of a witness or an advocate; a case that took years to prepare could be undone in seconds.

So Priest ignored the burning sensation developing in the pit of his stomach and announced his entrance into the courtroom by letting the ancient wooden door deliberately crash against its frame, which drew a turning of heads from the occupants of the front bench. Even the journalists lowered their phones to see who had disturbed the calm.

'Dickie.' Priest nodded to the QC as he joined Okoro. Hagworth neither returned the gesture nor rejected it but stared curiously at him from behind a pair of round glasses perched on his crooked nose.

Unimpressed, Okoro hadn't moved other than to look up from behind the bundle he was holding. He gave Priest a look that suggested, in no uncertain terms, that he regarded his unpunctuality with considerable annoyance. When Priest reached across to place a file on the table Okoro whispered in his principal's ear.

'Where in the name of Jesus have you been, Priest?'

'Funeral.'

'A what?'

He placed a reassuring hand on Okoro's shoulder and turned to the three bemused faces sitting behind him. Shaking each hand in turn he addressed the oily-haired man sitting on the edge of the bench.

'Tomas, how are you doing?' Priest asked, smiling.

'We were expecting you a little earlier but—'

'Just checking a few things for you but all done now. Gail, hi. Karl, love that tie. Listen, Tomas, have you heard from Simeon?'

'No.'

Tomas shifted his weight while Gail leant across him anxiously. Priest had thought when he first met *The Real Byte* team that, despite the obvious discomfort Tomas felt in his own skin, he might have been having an affair with Gail Woodbead. She was a good foot taller than him and had the air of a retired headmistress but there was an obvious tension between them, the kind that lovers might share. So perhaps it was unsurprising that, in this critical moment, Tomas now exchanged a worried look with her. Karl Jones, *The Real Byte* technical director, was slumped back in his seat and might not even have been a noticeable occupant of the bench were he not taking up most of it. His frame was oversized, cumbersome, bulging in places that weren't supposed to bulge. The fat pulled at his jowls, giving him a frog-like appearance. He also insisted on lugging an enormous holdall bag with him everywhere, which now sat at his feet, although goodness knows what was in it.

Priest nodded and breathed in hard, a thousand possibilities surging through his head.

'Did you speak to him last night?'

'No,' said Tomas, anxiety creeping into his voice. 'I thought he was meeting you before court.'

'We agreed he would be here at nine thirty and we would meet in the foyer. You've not seen him?'

'I haven't. This is disturbing news, Mr Priest. Our case—'

Priest put his hand on Tomas's arm to steady him. 'Slow down, Tomas,' he urged. 'They're watching you.'

He nodded subtly. Over the executive editor's shoulder, he saw Alexia Elias nudge Hagworth and gesture in their direction. Fortunately, it took Hagworth the equivalent of three moon cycles to manipulate the sagging muscles in his neck and make his head turn, by which time Tomas had understood the point and had lowered his voice.

'When did you last speak to Simeon?' Tomas asked.

'A few days ago. Everything was fine, and everything *will* be fine, I'm sure. We have his statement and he won't be giving evidence until this afternoon, possibly not even until tomorrow. I'm sure there's a perfectly reasonable explanation.'

Priest heard the words tumble out of his mouth but even he was unconvinced by them. This was the principal risk that he and Okoro had considered. Throughout, Simeon Ali had demonstrated a deep-rooted desire to ensure that the court, and the world, was presented with the truth, but he had proved to be an aloof character, insisting that almost all communications were carried out by email or Skype. They had met a few times, at a train station outside of the city in the summer, and even then, the meetings had been like a clandestine encounter straight out of a Sherlock Holmes novel.

'He seemed so sure of himself,' offered Gail, leaning further across Tomas. 'I can't believe he's lost his nerve at this moment.'

'He was convinced somebody was watching him,' said Tomas. 'We should have done more to ensure his attendance, Mr Priest.'

'Short of bundling him in the back of my car and holding him hostage I'm not sure what,' Priest remarked, ignoring Tomas's intonation.

'I take it you've rung him?' asked Gail.

He glanced over at Georgie who had just lowered her phone. She shook her head.

'Straight to voicemail,' she explained.

'Let's not worry just yet.' Priest smiled and turned back to whisper confidentially into Okoro's ear. 'Did you hear all that, old man?'

Okoro replied in a low growl, 'As I understand it you want me to win this case without my star witness, relying purely on hearsay evidence from non-independent witnesses. Is that right?'

'Yes and I pay you bloody well for it, too,' Priest hissed back. 'But I realise it's a tall order so why don't we try an alternative approach under which you buy me time and I go and find our witness?'

'That's fine because, doing it my way, Dickie's going to have a bloody field day.'

Chapter 7

Priest's exit from court thirteen was far less grand than his entrance and would have been entirely unnoticed had it not been for Alexia Elias's grey eyes watching his every step.

Outside the courtroom, he passed several robing rooms, finding vague amusement with the sign pinned to one of the doors – MEMBERS OF THE BAR ONLY. As a solicitor-advocate, Priest was perfectly entitled to pop in and use one of the wire coat hangers to store his overcoat, but the thought couldn't have been further from his mind. Firstly, because he did not own an overcoat and, secondly, because Charlie Priest generally hated other lawyers. Those that he didn't were merely the exceptions that proved the rule.

As he passed myriad portraits of stony-faced judges he couldn't name and didn't care about, he tried to reflect on the present situation. Simeon's no-show was bad news but it wasn't his firm's one hundred per cent win record that troubled him. It was the grey eyes of Alexia Elias that had tracked his quiet withdrawal from court. There had been mounting media pressure backed by a plethora of very high-profile individuals against *The Real Byte* and, indirectly, its lawyers. The Turkey scandal aside, the Elias Children's Foundation had benefited tens of thousands of children across the globe. Its brand stood for everything that was good in humanity. This trial meant everything for both sides.

Litigation disaster management rule number two: if you have to call Mother Teresa a whore, make sure it's a charge that sticks.

In the Great Hall, he paused. People were milling around everywhere. Mostly worried-looking parties and pompous-looking counsel, mixed in with the occasional tourist photographing the court's cathedral-like architecture. As he looked down to the entrance a familiar feeling of disconnection began to creep over him. The Great Hall was still there in all its Victorian glory and the people were still bustling around the security checkpoint, but Priest no longer felt that he was a part of the scene, it was as if he had stepped backwards and found himself looking in to the stage rather than out of it.

For a moment, he wavered between worlds, like Alice staring down the rabbit hole, contemplating the leap. But in his mind, Alice didn't look like Alice. She looked like Jessica Ellinder.

'Charlie?'

He felt a tug on his arm. The rabbit hole vanished. The image of Jessica dissipated. A pair of startling green eyes stared at him.

'Charlie? Are you OK?'

He shook the feeling of drowsiness off. 'Fine. Everything's fine. Thank you.'

'Were you having one of your disassociation moments?' asked Georgie.

'Of course not. I only get those when I'm stressed.'

Priest waved the notion away before it occurred to him that he had never discussed his dissociative disorder with his assistant solicitor. He hadn't really discussed it with anyone. Not that he was ashamed of the condition that caused breakdowns in his perception of reality, but he didn't see the value in talking about it. Besides, he counted himself lucky. There are generally six recognised classifications of dissociative disorder but many sufferers of one of the most common – depersonalisation disorder – have their lives utterly wrecked by the condition, living in a permanently emotionless, unreal world. Priest had experienced that early on, but the symptoms had faded with time. Now he was able to function ninety per cent of the time without giving the slightest hint of his vulnerability, except on occasions where, like now, he felt his grasp slip slightly.

He shook the feeling off, refocused. It didn't feel like the onset of an episode. Just a glitch in his own personal matrix.

'How do you know about it, by the way?' he asked, meaning the disorder. When she didn't immediately answer, the detail suddenly seemed unimportant. 'Moreover, why aren't you in court? I pay you to be in court, not diagnose complex personality illnesses.'

'Vincent said I should go with you,' Georgie said firmly.

'What about the clients?'

'He said you might need more looking after than them.'

'No, he didn't. Okoro would never say that.'

Georgie at least had the decency to look slightly sheepish. 'That may have been my interpretation of what he said.'

Priest smiled and she smiled back. She had an infectious smile. He remembered seeing it for the first time when she had walked into the interview room and presented a CV bursting with commendations, awards and an Oxford first. Priest's policy was to only ever ask one interview question. None of the pro forma questions and aptitude tests candidates were subjected to in the recruitment processes of the supposed elite practices – the so-called Magic Circle firms. Priest found the best measure wasn't something Freud had conjured up. It was his gut.

'If you were me, how would you conduct this interview?'

Priest had laid out his only interview question to another fresh-faced candidate and sat back, waiting for the usual diatribe of executive bollocks which might include repeating large sections of the About Us section of the Priest & Co. website or, if he was lucky, a Google-assembled analysis of the reform of conditional fee arrangements in personal injury work.

To his surprise, Georgie Someday had met his gaze and spoken without a hint of sarcasm.

'I wouldn't. Asking me questions isn't going to tell you anything about me you won't get from your receptionist. That's why your candidates have to turn up an hour early.'

Priest had faltered. She had smiled awkwardly and, without being able to stop himself, he had smiled back. Awkwardly.

Later, as he had poured over the headnote of a Court of Appeal authority, Maureen, his chain-smoking receptionist, had poked her head around the door and directed a series of gruffly constituted words in unambiguous tones at him which had landed Georgie her training contract.

'You better bloody hire that girl, Priest,' she had said. 'Your tea's in the kitchen.'

'You seem distracted,' Georgie observed as they negotiated through the jumble of lawyers and clients cluttering up the High Court entrance. 'You know: even more than usual.'

He dismissed her. 'No, no. This is just as it is, Someday. Follow me.'

She took him by the arm and was about to lead him away from the court when a voice stopped them. Priest turned and saw a small man hunched up against the side of the court, a cigarette stuck to his lip. His hair was grey and wiry and his skin had the purple stain left by years of alcohol and fags.

'Excuse me?'

He immediately regretted having spoken so when it became clear that the man who had addressed them was Dominique Elias. He must have slipped out at some point for a smoke after the cameras had packed up.

'I said, I wonder if you get a kick out of what you do, Mr Priest?' Elias croaked.

Priest hesitated and felt Georgie tug on his arm, but something stopped him from doing what he should do and move on.

'Sorry, Mr Elias. I can't talk to you. Professional rules. You know how it is.'

Elias ignored him. 'How do you think it's going to be after this, Mr Priest? When the judge throws you out of court? Did you ever stop to think about the children we look after? All that charity money wasted on legal fees that could have gone to helping kids who need our help. How many of them do you think have died because of you and that poxy online operation you're representing?'

'None.'

Elias made to say something but stumbled into a fit of coughing. When he'd finished, his face was red. One eye was a little bloodshot. 'You have a lawyer's conscience, I see.'

'No,' said Priest, calmly. 'I just have a better understanding of moral causation than you.'

'Hm. And what do you know about moral causation?'

'*Your* side brought the claim, Mr Elias.' Priest was relaxed – in fact professional rules prevented him from talking to Alexia, since she was a party to the proceedings, but Dominique wasn't, so the conversation wasn't illicit. *There is no property in a witness.* 'Remember: you picked the fight.'

'Didn't have much choice, did we? *Your* client published that filth.'

There was more; Dominque was about to say something else but he stopped. Something had caught his eye, further up the road on the other side of the High Court entrance. He winced, squinted as if he saw someone he vaguely recognised. Then slunk back against the wall. Priest followed his eyeline but it was impossible to tell from the group of people mingling outside who had distracted him.

Assessing that the exchange was at an end, Priest doffed an imaginary cap. 'Good luck in court, Mr Elias.' He turned and led Georgie away, sensing Elias watching them all the way. When they reached the Tube entrance, he noticed Georgie was still holding on to his arm.

Chapter 8

The little girl sits in front of the wall, staring at the cracked bricks; her hands resting on her lap. There is a window above her, too high to reach unless she climbs on a tower of boxes and, even then, she can only just peek through the opaque glass and see the top of the church spire. The basement is behind her, she is so close to the wall. The floor is made of stone but there is some carpet spread across the far side: the unwanted ends, a mishmash of colours. It is dusk, neither the sun nor the moon has dominance in the sliver of grey sky she can see through the window.

A woman paces behind her, muttering. She is angry, rightly so. The girl had managed to nick the corner of her mouth with her nails, drawn a little blood. The girl hadn't meant to hurt the woman. She had just wanted to feel the woman's skin, see if it stretched like hers, was warm like hers.

The woman is ranting, but the girl only hears it in waves of muffled white noise.

'Again . . . I didn't want any of this, you bring it upon yourself . . . do you know what happened? Do you . . . you aren't mine, not mine . . . I don't see why I should put up with you, everything was fine before . . .'

The girl closes her eyes but she can still see the wall in front of her, and its crevices, like the lines across the woman's furrowed brow.

'He hates you, you know . . . those things he does with you, don't think they are acts of love . . . nothing like that . . . I know love when I see it and . . .'

Suddenly the ranting stops. The girl stirs. It's cold – it's never warm in the basement. Even in summer, the sun only shines directly through the little window for a few hours and what little warmth finds its way into the room is soon absorbed into the bare walls. In the winter, the window leaks and the rain trickles down the brickwork, flowing through the grooves, and collecting in a puddle at the foot of the wall. If it rains all day, the pool is so big it spills over into the sunken recess in the floor. The girl is waiting for the day when the water fills so high that the recess is like a lake into which she can dive.

The white noise has stopped. The girl risks opening one eye. Maybe the woman has gone. Maybe this time she might be left to sleep. She is left alone for long periods of time, her meals thrown down the stairs from the house above like a dog's. But she doesn't mind – it's better than when the woman rants at her, sometimes hits her. And that's better than when she has to get dressed for him. That's the worst.

The girl's relief is short-lived. The woman is still there, but closer suddenly. In her ear. This time the words form clearer in the girl's head – not fully formed but almost complete.

'She brought you here, that bitch of a mother of yours, you know. You were a child, ugly and fat. I didn't want you but he saw something in it for him – a profit, of sorts . . . then she killed herself, your mother. That's how little she thought of you – delivered you here into his hands then hanged herself on a tree a week later . . . poor wretch, how pathetic . . .'

The girl remembers nothing, but senses the woman isn't lying. Why would she lie? Why would they compound her misery with deceit when everything they do is already so wicked?

The girl doesn't move. Knows better not to. The woman hovers nearby, her breath on the girl's neck. The girl listens, smells the woman's perfume, a sickly, arresting smell. That is the smell of the outside world, thinks the girl. The sickly, arresting smell of freedom.

The girl shivers.

Satisfied, the woman withdraws without warning, leaving the girl to calm her beating heart. This time, she leaves the lights off and the girl is left in semi-darkness.

Chapter 9

Georgie held on as the Tube rattled along. The carriage was hot and airless – most of the seats had been taken and she was squashed up against the corner, conscious that every time the train lurched around she fell on to Charlie's shoulder.

Five stops down the train pulled in to Bethnal Green and Georgie looked up at Charlie. 'Is it this one?'

Charlie frowned. 'No. I don't think so.'

'It's Mile End next.'

'Mm.'

Georgie waited. A few people had alighted and an old man had hauled two bags of shopping into the aisle and had stood opposite them. The signal for the doors shutting toned, which is when Charlie leapt up.

'Actually, it *is* this one.'

She barely made it as the doors slammed shut behind her.

'Come along, Someday!' Charlie called back over his shoulder.

'Where are we going?' Georgie puffed as she took two steps for every one of his to keep up. They weaved in and out of busy commuters but somehow he seemed to just keep marching straight ahead as people parted around him like the Red Sea. Georgie, on the other hand, was constantly ducking and sliding past the crowds – less Moses and more of a fairground dodgem.

'Tomas was never very forthcoming when it came to revealing the original source of the article, was he?' Charlie called back, ignoring her question directly.

'Simeon is a bit of an enigma,' Georgie agreed.

'Tomas's original idea was to run a justification defence based on the documentary evidence he had amassed about the Turkey scandal without Simeon.'

'But nothing directly connects that to Alexia.'

'That's right. Some of it's helpful. There are chains of emails that link to Alexia eventually but nothing that nails the point. It's all circumstantial, Hagworth will say. Anyway, after I told them I wouldn't take the case Tomas contacted me and said, albeit reluctantly, that the source for the original article was Simeon Ali, who worked for the Foundation at the time of the scandal and was based in Turkey. He'd since moved to London.'

'And you think that Simeon wasn't involved with the siphoning of funds to the Free People's Army?'

They skipped up the last few steps and out into the street at such a pace that Georgie lost track of which station they had just come from.

Charlie crossed the road and rounded a corner into a residential street lined with tall Victorian terraces set back from the pavement and fronted with black iron railings.

'I recognise this road,' said Georgie, turning a full circle and taking it in.

'That's right,' Charlie agreed, heading about halfway down before turning into one of the pathways and pressing a doorbell.

'This is your sister's house,' Georgie said, recognition suddenly hitting her.

'That's right.'

'Why . . .?'

The door swung open and Sarah Boatman tumbled out. She seemed surprised and, with a bag over her shoulder already, Georgie guessed that she was just on her way to work.

'Charlie?'

Charlie cleared his throat. 'Good morning.'

'I'm just . . .'

'I only need a second.'

*

Georgie stood in Sarah's hallway looking at the pictures on the wall. Most of them were of Tilly, Charlie's six-year-old niece, in various situations, invariably with a grin spread across her impish face.

There were a few of Sarah holding her as a baby. Sarah's hair was a different colour in every photo but each time she looked nowhere near as tired and run-down as a new mother should be. She had the Priest family blue eyes and Charlie's smile. Her husband, Ryan, was noticeably absent from the photographic montage. Georgie had never met Ryan – she had only met Sarah a few times – but she was aware of Charlie's deep-rooted dislike of his brother-in-law which he did very little to hide. Luckily, it didn't seem as if Ryan was home. Tilly, presumably, was at school.

She shuffled closer to the kitchen so she could make out the voices a little better – not that this was in any way a form of eavesdropping but there were some particularly stunning landscape shots further down that caught her attention.

'Do you mind awfully if I have the spare keys to Bristol Road?' she heard Charlie ask.

'Why?' Sarah sounded wary.

'Because I'd like to gain access.'

'Charlie, I'm sure there are loads of people out there who find you endearing but to me you're really quite annoying.'

'Thank you.'

'The property's let, remember?' Sarah pointed out.

'It appears the tenant may have absconded.'

Georgie distinctly heard Sarah exhale heavily. 'What have you got yourself into this time, Charlie?'

'Nothing you need to worry about.'

'Don't patronise me or so help me God—'

'I didn't mean it like that,' Charlie placated. 'I mean – it's nothing. Really. The guy just didn't show up at court this morning, that's all.'

'The thing on TV about the Elias Foundation? Wow, I really hope you know what you're doing.'

'Fortunately, I know a really good PR agent if it turns out that I don't.'

'You're going to need more than a good PR agent if you lose that trial, Charlie. They're talking about it everywhere – *I'm* even getting shit about it from clients.'

Georgie took a few steps further towards the door and strained to listen as Charlie asked, 'From who?'

'As if I'd tell you that.'

'Why wouldn't you?' asked Charlie, seemingly offended.

'Because you'd do something stupid like sue them.'

'If they were lucky.'

'Mm. Keys are behind you, in the top drawer.'

'I am most obliged for your assistance, oh magnificent sister.'

'Piss off back to court, Charlie.'

She heard the rattle of the drawer. Turned quickly and tried to look as though she was casually strolling up and down the hallway and not listening intently to every word when Priest emerged from the kitchen.

'Come on, Someday,' he said, leading her to the door. 'Thanks, Sarah.'

Georgie looked back over her shoulder. Sarah leant against the door frame, arms folded. As Georgie turned, Sarah caught her eye.

'Georgie?'

'Yes?'

Sarah hesitated before shifting her weight and turning to walk back into the kitchen.

'For God's sake, look after him.'

Chapter 10

At the stroke of ten the chamber's door to court thirteen opened and Justice Peters swept in, nodded curtly to the congregation in front of her and sat down, rigid and businesslike, in the high-backed leather chair.

She looked older than Okoro remembered from the last time he had been before her. Her hair was tied back but it was greyer than at the preliminary hearing six months earlier. Back then she had berated Hagworth for not having properly complied with the disclosure order and hadn't been particularly impressed with Okoro either, even though he *had* complied.

At least she was consistent. She hated *everyone*.

'Good morning,' Peters grumbled without a trace of warmth. She looked up at the advocates for the first time and picked up a bundle from in front of her. 'Mr Hagworth—'

Slowly, Hagworth rose to his feet.

Okoro glanced behind him but the door at the back of the court had been shut. He risked checking his phone – nothing. Although *The Real Byte* was the defendant, they would present their case first, as was customary in a libel trial. The statement complained about would be assumed defamatory unless the contrary was proven. Okoro only had three witnesses – Tomas Jansen; Gail

Woodbead, who had had some input in writing the article; and Simeon Ali himself. Tactically, it would make the most sense if Ali went first. Indeed, the trial might be over quickly if Hagworth couldn't produce anything in cross-examination to damage Ali's credibility.

Putting Tomas on the stand first was going to cause some confusion. Okoro braced himself for the interrogation.

Hagworth began, 'Your Honour, may it please you, I represent the claimant in these proceedings, Alexia Elias, who seeks damages and other relief against the defendant, an online magazine with a small following—'

'Yes, yes, I know all that.' Peters waved at Hagworth irritably. 'I have your skeleton argument. Can we not just get on with it? Mr Okoro?'

Okoro got to his feet with caution, every second he delayed might be precious. Behind him, he heard *The Real Byte* staff shuffling around. Panic was starting to set in, despite Priest's warning to them about remaining poker-faced. Across the courtroom, he sensed Alexia staring at him expectantly. He couldn't see her face, but he knew exactly what expression she was wearing. One of mock sympathy. Without Ali, *The Real Byte* was as good as bust and she knew it.

'Your Honour,' he said, tentatively. In the pause between his words, he heard nothing. Not the rustling of papers, not the creaking of the benches. Not the sound of breathing. The courtroom held its breath.

Sensing Okoro's hesitancy, Peters looked up.

'Well?' she said.

*

Sarah's rental property was ten minutes' walk south in a non-descript urban nucleus comprising mainly of Chinese takeaways, pawn shops and places where you could, apparently, secure a loan of up to five thousand pounds in less than three minutes; that was assuming you were prepared to accept an APR figure that was the same length as the shop's telephone number.

Priest led Georgie down the street past a group of men huddled together at the entrance to a William Hill. They were examining a ticket carefully. From what Priest could gather, a particular greyhound had crossed the line first and a dispute had developed between them as to who owned the winning ticket. Priest guided Georgie across to the other side of the street.

Further down they walked under some badly constructed scaffolding. Someone wolf-whistled behind them from a third-storey balcony but Georgie seemed oblivious, engrossed as she was in asking Priest more questions about the arrangements that had been made for Simeon.

'So Simeon lives at a house your sister owns?' she asked.

'It's actually one of a few we have together but Sarah keeps the keys and deals with the paperwork. I'd just lose them if they were under my control. When our parents died, they left us a small portfolio.'

'What about—' Georgie blurted out but then, flushed, covered her mouth quickly. 'Oh, I—'

'You mean *what about William*?' said Priest, referring to the eldest Priest child, who was currently serving an endless sentence in a maximum security psychiatric hospital just outside London. Eleven years ago, he had pleaded not guilty by reason of insanity to a string of murders that had earned him notoriety as one of the country's most prolific serial killers. In a decision that was as controversial at the time as William's crimes were outrageous, the Old Bailey had absolved him of responsibility but passed down an indefinite hospital order. William Priest would never see the outside world again.

'Yes. Sorry. I didn't mean to . . . you know.'

He smiled, although the memory of William's trial still haunted him, particularly the last walk out of court. After they had escorted William away, Priest had walked out into the sunshine to a sea of cameras and microphones, but that didn't bother him. What bothered him was the bereaved; the families of the dead. He could deal with the angry ones, the ones who shouted abuse, cursed him. They were fine, understandable. What drove him to the brink were the quiet ones; the ones who didn't say anything, just looked at him with wide, questioning eyes. Ghosts' eyes. 'It's OK. To be honest, it's Sarah who disallows any mention of Wills. I kind of like the guy, apart from the killing and the madness.'

By the look on her face, he surmised that Georgie wasn't quite sure whether she was supposed to laugh or not.

'So,' she prompted instead, 'Simeon.'

'Ah. So, eventually, I got to the bottom of what *The Real Byte*'s defence was. Now, as you know, there are only a limited number of defences to libel.' Priest paused, waiting for her to fill in the gaps.

'Justification, fair comment, qualified or actual privilege.'

'Spoken like a true legal nerd. Here, the only plausible defence is to establish that what was said was actually true, meaning that it's necessary to demonstrate that Alexia actually not only knew about her organisation's links with terrorism but also received bribes to keep quiet about it. This is what we call justification, as you know. What I quickly identified, however, was that Simeon Ali rather regretted his little whistle-blowing expedition, so he was reluctant to come forward and reveal himself as the source of *The Real Byte's* article when called upon.'

'So you got him a safe house as part of the deal?'

'Essentially.'

'Are we allowed to do that?'

'Technically, we're not doing anything wrong, but it would give Hagworth the opportunity to attack Simeon's credibility if he found out that we were safe-harbouring him, at our cost. That said, Simeon genuinely feared for his life – what else were we supposed to do?'

They slowed as Priest glanced at the building numbers. This was definitely Bristol Road but exactly where the flat was, he was infuriatingly unsure about. Indeed, he wasn't sure exactly where any examples of the Priest portfolio were – that was Sarah's domain. He checked his watch. The trial would have started and Okoro would be on his feet. Hopefully, Peters would allow him to put Tomas Jansen up first, but she was an awkward old bird, so there was no guarantee of any indulgence from her. They carried on. Behind them, Priest heard a car slowing down.

Georgie continued, 'In what way do you mean his life was in danger?'

'You don't become instrumental in cutting off funding for a group like the Free People's Army without making some seriously dangerous enemies along the way. These are people even Okoro is worried about and, as a former prosecutor for the International Criminal Court, Okoro doesn't scare easily.'

'So, Simeon not turning up for court is . . . ?'

'Inconvenient. Let's leave it at that.'

Priest stopped outside a shop no wider than a doorway. A sign above it advertised laptop and PC repairs for a very reasonable price that would be waived if lost information could not be retrieved.

'It's this one,' he announced.

'He lives in an electronics store?' Georgie sounded sceptical.

'He lives *above* an electronics store.'

He indicated up, directing Georgie to a single window above the shop looking out across the street to a run-down Methodist chapel.

'How do you get through to the flat?' she asked.

By way of an answer, Priest opened the door to the shop and walked in. Inside, a narrow counter ran up the left-hand side of the small galley. The wall on the opposite side was plastered from floor to ceiling with little bags containing computer parts: virtual memory, motherboards, sound cards, hard drives, unspecified bits of random circuit board. At the end of the counter, a scrawny man in his early sixties stared at the carcass of a desktop computer through thick-rimmed glasses.

'Hello,' said Priest. 'It's Graham, isn't it?'

'No. It's Gary.'

Priest faltered, then recalled that this had happened the last time he had met Gary. *I simply cannot get this guy's name into my head.*

'I'm sorry. Gary.'

'You're Priest,' Gary said, looking up only momentarily from his examination. Evidently, he recalled their last encounter.

'I'm looking for the tenant.' He nodded at the ceiling.

'Haven't seen him for the last couple of days.'

'Can you be a bit more specific on when you last saw him?'

'It's in the back. Look for yourself.'

'I'm obliged.'

Priest skipped past him with Georgie following, through a set of beads hanging from a door frame. He recalled that this led to a small set of stairs to the flat above.

'He seems friendly,' she remarked as they reached the top and faced the door to Simeon's flat.

'I keep calling him Graham by mistake. That's going to grate on you after a while.'

Priest knocked loudly. He still had a policeman's knock. Generally, he disliked sounding arrogant at someone else's door but that and the pension were legacies from ten years in the Met. It was fruitless anyway. Simeon understood the importance of the trial. If he hadn't turned up, he was hardly going to open his door readily.

He was mulling over some theories. One, Simeon had bottled it because either he was lying all along and his conscience had got the better of him or, more likely, his paranoia had stripped him of the necessary confidence required to show his face in public. Two, he had been paid off by the defence. Three, something more sinister had happened.

He dwelt upon the third possibility. Simeon had drawn some attention to himself by coming forwards, but the Free People's Army was a relatively small and poorly resourced operation, especially now its illicit funding had been stopped. It was based in Turkey with modest aspirations of jihad compared to its more ambitious cousins working for Daesh. In other words, the reality of the threat was significantly less than Simeon's perception of it.

There was no doubt that Alexia Elias and her husband had a lot to lose from this trial personally. They were well resourced but, if *The Real Byte*'s story was true, would they cross the line to avoid discovery? It was not totally inconceivable that Simeon's disappearance was precipitated by their actions. But then why leave it this late in the day to pay Simeon off?

He knocked again. They waited. A little clock in the back of Priest's mind ticked a further minute on. There might not be a trial left to save if they didn't get to the bottom of this quickly. He slipped the key into the lock and released the latch.

A wall of hot air hit them. If Simeon had quit the property, he had left the heating on full blast before he left. They ventured in. Priest fiddled with the thermostat on the wall.

The flat was uninspiring. A dimly lit hallway from which sprouted a small kitchen to the left that stank of rotting food and sour milk and a sitting room to the right comprising a leather sofa that had seen better days, a flat screen TV and a few bookshelves. Further back, the flat ended abruptly with a bedroom and bathroom opposite, complete with seventies avocado-coloured suite. Priest made a mental note to encourage his sister to modernise the older rental properties.

'Simeon,' Priest called, although it was obvious he would receive no reply.

Georgie had made her way to the bedroom.

'There's a few clothes here,' she reported. 'And a suitcase – looks fairly new.'

'Who absconds without taking a new suitcase with them?'

'Indeed.'

Priest pushed the bathroom door open but again there were no useful clues. A toothbrush holder welded to the sink and a month's supply of unused toilet paper. A towel left on the floor, but everywhere was dry. The bathroom didn't seem to have been used recently.

'This kitchen's a mess,' Georgie shouted from down the hallway. Priest joined her and was inclined to agree. There were dirty dishes piled high in the sink; half-empty tins of tuna on the side. The tap was running slightly. Priest flicked the handle and the water trickled momentarily before stopping.

'If he's done a runner then he did a good job of making it look as though he intends to come back,' Georgie said.

Priest clicked his tongue. She was right. Everything looked just a little wrong. The plates were piled in a way that was too perfectly aligned, the towel in the bathroom had been placed in just the right position so he had rubbed the door against it, the clothes were too many to suggest abandonment but too few to amount to a convincing collection.

'This has been staged for us,' he said slowly.

'By whom?'

'No idea – maybe Simeon himself. Did you see the chair in the living room?'

'Yes. The grooves in the carpet were far too big to be unnoticeable.'

'I agree. It's been moved but in a way that was intended to make it obvious that it had been moved.'

'Spooky.'

'I've seen something like this before,' Priest muttered. 'You used to see these kinds of set-ups at scenes of domestic violence. We'd get called out but by the time we got there the wife already had a broken nose from tripping on the stairs or whatever lame excuse she could come up with and the husband had gone about making the house look like he hadn't kicked seven bells out of her. It was the same atmosphere. Everything was too still, too serene to be real. Like a film set.'

'Why would someone do that here?'

'I don't know. There are so many questions, but right now only *one* that matters: where the fuck is Simeon Ali?'

Chapter 11

Vincent Okoro had experienced his fair share of advocacy melt-downs. Even the best counsel was prone to them. It comes from thinking about the situation too much. Like walking along a tightrope and then becoming suddenly very conscious of the drop, which usually precedes falling.

Mrs Justice Peters was glaring at him down her absurdly curved nose and Okoro had the sudden feeling that he was back in his old headmistress's office explaining why, yet again, his homework was late.

'I asked a simple question, Mr Okoro,' she said coldly. 'Mr Hagworth raises the point that your main witness's statement contains various allegations that are rightly to be regarded by this court as hearsay. I am asking whether a hearsay notice was served and, if so, whether I might peruse a copy?'

Okoro fumbled around in the bundle. He knew the notice had been served – Priest would never have missed a point like that – but where the damn thing was he couldn't recall. *Where the hell is Georgie when you need her?* The bundle seemed alien to him all of a sudden.

'A copy is here at page a hundred and nine, Your Honour,' said Hagworth, positively brimming with the glee of having to come to Okoro's aid.

'Thank you, Mr Hagworth. Ah, yes. I see. It would make sense for Mr Ali's evidence to be dealt with first, would you not agree, Mr Okoro?'

'I think not, Your Honour,' Okoro replied. 'The defence wishes to call Tomas Jansen first. He is, after all, the executive editor of *The Real Byte* and thereby best placed to give the court the benefit of some insight into the magazine's intentions behind the article, which will enable the court to put Mr Ali's evidence in better context. He is also the article's primary author.'

Peters's eyes narrowed and Okoro was reminded of a large crow peering over the fence at a rabbit carcass. 'Am I not able to understand evidence unless you are spoon-feeding me context, Mr Okoro?'

'Of course, Your Honour. But—'

'Good. Then we may hear from Mr Ali first.'

'I fear greatly, Your Honour, that this may not be possible. As it is, Mr Ali is not present in court.'

Peters nodded before consulting the papers in front of her and making a fuss of producing a particular document. Okoro started to wish the ground might swallow him. He glanced around at *The Real Byte* staff behind him and cast what he hoped was a reassuring glance. He received cold stares of apprehension in return. To his right, he noticed Alexia Elias smiling to herself.

'The notice of hearing,' announced the judge, adjusting her spectacles and studying the document, 'is dated over nine months ago. Your witness knew where he had to be and when, didn't he, Mr Okoro?'

'He did. But it appears that, nonetheless, he has not yet arrived.'

Hagworth was on his feet and, as Okoro feared, looking to capitalise on the defence's misfortune.

'Your Honour, the conjectures against my client are poorly pleaded but, if sustainable at all, are only so on the evidence of Mr Ali. If he can't be bothered to turn up to court to attest to the truth of his statement and make himself available for cross-examination, then I invite you to bar the defendant from relying on his evidence, tentative and ill-conceived as it was anyway.'

Mercifully, Peters looked indecisive. 'I'm not sure that's the right approach, Mr Hagworth.'

'Your Honour, my client has been defamed. The defendant raises only one defence – that of justification. They can only establish that if they can adduce cogent evidence of Mrs Elias's alleged wrongdoing. The allegations are serious and, if proven, potentially ruinous for Mrs Elias. She, her husband and a very reputable and important charity have already been irreparably damaged by these misconceived allegations based on the flimsiest of evidence which we are now told cannot be substantiated. It really is an outrage that Mr Okoro now seeks to reorganise his witnesses to cope with the gaping hole in his case. The claimant should not—'

'Yes, yes, Mr Hagworth, I get the point,' Peters mumbled. 'What have you to say, Mr Okoro?'

Okoro stood up and tucked his fingers firmly into his lapels. As it happened, Hagworth's intervention had given him the opportunity to think things through. Two years' work would stand or fall on what he said next. He heard the bench creak behind him, the journalists poised in the public gallery breathe in, and felt the weight of responsibility crushing his shoulders. Why was it so damned hot in this courtroom?

Peters waited expectantly. Three of the slowest seconds of Okoro's life ticked by before he took a deep breath and said: 'Your Honour, it was understood with Mr Ali that he would attend court this morning. My instructing solicitor is making urgent enquiries as to his whereabouts. While it is an inconvenience, I suggest that justice would be better served by a short adjournment than a rearrangement of the defendant's witnesses to enable Mr Ali's intentions to be established. We can then avoid wasting any further of the court's time.'

'That's extremely unsatisfactory.' Peters folded her arms and glared at Okoro. 'What do you say, Mr Hagworth?'

'I concur wholeheartedly with Your Honour's sentiments. Extremely unsatisfactory. My application is for the trial to continue, for Mr Okoro to present his evidence and for the defence being barred from relying on Mr Ali's witness statement.'

'What if Mr Ali turns up on Monday?' asked Peters, but in a way that suggested she was offering Hagworth the opportunity to stick the knife in, rather than testing the parameters of his submission.

'Well, that would be unfortunate but our laws are based on the here and now and not what may or may not occur. In the same vein, if the claimant, my client, had failed to issue these proceedings within the one year limitation period then we would be relying on the mercy of the court to allow this action to be prosecuted. In the absence of a very good reason, we would not expect the court to allow us salvation. The claim would die. Similarly, what explanation has the court been offered for Mr Ali's absence? None. Why therefore should Mr Okoro be allowed a second bite of the cherry?'

Peters looked over at Okoro and raised an eyebrow. A sinking feeling started to eat away at him. He supposed the captain of the *Titanic* must have experienced a similar sensation when he realised that there was an iceberg stuck in his ship's hull. He rose again.

'I understand my learned friend's point, Your Honour, but the situation here is not the same as the one he hypothesises over. In the case of a claimant missing the limitation period, the fate of her claim was at least in her hands. If she failed to get proceedings up and running before the claim became statute barred, then she is the author of her own misfortune and should not attract the court's sympathy. Here, the circumstances are outside of the defendant's control. The reason why we cannot offer the court an explanation for Mr Ali's absence is because we do not know why he has absented. The interests of justice suggest that, in such a case, the defendant ought to be given the opportunity to ascertain where Mr Ali is and, if necessary, issue a witness summons for his attendance.'

'He would then be a hostile witness, Mr Okoro,' Peters pointed out.

'Then so be it. Why should *The Real Byte* be stripped of the opportunity to treat Mr Ali as hostile, if that is what he has become? The advantage of starting on Friday is that there is a natural point to start again on Monday. The claimant would hardly be prejudiced. Besides, I'm sure Your Honour would benefit from a reading day.'

It was a risk, since the implication was that Peters wouldn't have already read the five bundles of evidence that lined the shelf behind her.

Another three painfully slow seconds passed.

Peters looked up at the array of anxious faces staring at her. Then she picked up her papers and banged them on the desk decisively.

'We're adjourned until Monday,' she said with great displeasure. 'If your witness isn't in court by then, Mr Okoro, then his evidence is barred.'

Chapter 12

Priest led the way back through the laptop repair shop, passing Gary who barely looked up, and back out onto the street.

'What now?' Georgie asked.

He looked up the road. There was a row of cars parked on one side, mostly with their wheels up on the pavement. On the other side, the fracas between the betting shop men had developed and one of them was accusing the other two of stealing his ticket. People making their way past were steering well clear.

Bollocks! Where have you gone, Simeon?

'Our IT friend must know more than he's letting on,' Priest mused, although deep down he felt that Gary wasn't going to be any more helpful than he already had been. He turned back towards the shop but stopped when Georgie called out.

'Charlie, wait.'

He turned around and saw the door of a blue VW Beetle open and a woman a little older than Georgie step out onto the pavement. It didn't seem like a particularly significant event, although the woman was quite attractive. He looked at Georgie for an explanation.

'She's a reporter,' she warned as the woman started to stride purposefully towards them. 'She collared me outside the court earlier.'

'Hello there!' the woman called before reaching Priest and extending her hand. He groaned inwardly. *I don't have time for this.* He took her hand for the sake of civility but tried not to look at her. Perhaps if he didn't make eye contact she might go away.

'Elinor Fox,' the reporter said, smiling. 'I'm covering the Elias trial. You're the magazine's solicitor, right?'

'Listen, Miss Fox,' Priest began, 'I'm really sorry but right now I'm a little tied up. Could we—'

'I hear one of your witnesses hasn't turned up at court and I was just wondering if I could help in any way?'

Priest took a moment before answering, allowing the words to digest. *Help in any way?*

'A kind offer,' he said. 'But not one that I can possibly take up. Besides, you're missing all the action in court. It's far more interesting in there than it is out here.'

Priest felt irritated by her presence – he couldn't go back into the shop and interrogate Gary with her hanging around waiting to print whatever he said, but equally he knew better than to be overtly rude. *Litigation disaster management rule number three: never annoy the press without good reason.*

Fox was still talking. 'Look, I know everyone's a little wary of the papers but I'm trying to get to the bottom of the Turkey scandal. I'm not interested in you or *The Real Byte*. I just want to publish the truth about Alexia Elias.'

'Then wait until the case has finished.'

'Which witness hasn't turned up? It's Simeon Ali, right? The whistle-blower?' She was probing further, stepping closer to him so he had to take a step back towards the shop.

'How did you know we were here?' Georgie asked Fox.

'I got a tip-off that Simeon lived on this road. I guessed this is where you'd start looking.'

'Have you been here before?'

Fox smiled, non-committal.

He caught on to Georgie's line of questioning. 'I take it you don't know where Simeon is, Miss Fox?'

Fox cocked her head to one side. 'If I did, why would I be here?' She nodded to the electronics shop. 'I take it he's not at home.'

He thought about probing further, but something told him Fox was genuine when she said she didn't know where Simeon was. And why would she? 'Look, we can't talk to you,' he said. 'You might as well give up on that. I'm too long in the tooth to be talking to the press.'

'Oh, come on.'

Priest noticed the change in her voice – it had softened – and he couldn't resist looking at her. She was biting her lip, half smiling, staring at him intently. For a moment, Priest thought he recognised her but the notion disappeared as quickly as it had come.

'I can help,' she assured him, taking another half-step forward. She reached to her side, then looked down. 'Damn. I left my bag in the car. Can I just get a quote from you? Something really simple?'

Priest glanced across at Georgie. She was standing at the side of the pavement, arms crossed and looking distinctly unimpressed.

'As I've said. I can't help you.'

'Honestly, it won't take a minute. Let me just grab my iPad.'

Fox was heading back to her car but with her head turned, her smile unfaltering. Georgie stepped forward.

'Maybe we should just go.'

He nodded. 'She's *very* enthusiastic.'

They turned to cross the road, but, before they reached the kerb, Priest looked back. Fox was standing behind her car with the boot open and Priest might have turned away again had he not caught sight of her face.

He stopped and felt Georgie collide with his back.

'What?'

Fox looked up, ashen. In the moment it had taken Priest to fully turn around, her entire complexion had transformed. The colour in her face had drained away, the smile extinguished. Their eyes met and she mouthed something inaudible.

'What is it?' Priest asked her. Georgie's eyes darted between them, confused.

'There's . . .'

Fox slammed the boot shut. Staggered back on to the pavement, her hand now covered her mouth.

Priest exhaled in frustration. He strode back towards her, met her eyes again but saw nothing but bewilderment, and something else. Something malignant.

He followed her outstretched hand, pointing to the back window.

He peered in.

A cold sensation flooded through him – a feeling akin to being suddenly drenched in icy water.

'What is it?' Georgie whispered, alarmed.

Priest straightened up. 'It's not a *what*,' he said quietly. 'It's a who. Simeon Ali.'

Chapter 13

In a pebble-dashed semi-detached house at the end of a non-descript suburban street, the owner was sitting in a room surrounded by computer screens.

There were three in all, working from a server gently humming in the corner of the room. It was all new equipment, bought at great expense to a custom specification. The server had been difficult to install; the owner liked to keep the heating as high as possible, cold was an irritant, so the server needed two large fans positioned either side of it to keep it cool.

It had been a difficult morning, weaving in and out of the crowds, dodging the cameras outside the High Court. And what good would it do? The trial was listed for four weeks, and at the end of it, would there be justice?

Maybe not in court, but the owner would see to it anyway. Trial or not, there would be justice.

Justice *and* retribution.

There was little to do but wait, so the owner was drawn to the computer screen, idly filtering through the search history, wincing at the terms that had been inputted, wondering if the computer realised what sordid material it had produced.

At the bottom, a familiar term: 'The Girl of Devil's Point'. The owner clicked on it but knew what would come up. A conspiracy blog written by some useless pervert who supposedly collected strange stories and commented on them. As if he knew anything. The owner scanned the blog but there were no new comments – there hadn't been for months. Just the original story and a few mindless remarks from various users. 'Spooky' and 'that's fab'. Morons, the lot of them.

The blog's author had moved on, apparently realising that no one was interested, and started a new page about 'The Green Children of Woolpit'. The owner read on, vaguely interested, although already familiar with the legend. *In the twelfth century, two children are found in the Suffolk village of Woolpit with green skin speaking a language no one understood.* That was it, basically.

The owner clicked back to the blog about the girl of Devil's Point. Who was she? Where did she come from? What happened to her?

The blog was full of stupid questions and no answers.

The owner turned around and looked at the wall behind. It was covered with photographs from top to bottom, some squeezed together so tightly that only an inch or so of wall was visible. The owner picked one of the photographs and stared at it. It showed a boy of ten standing in front of a house on a hillside, the sun at his back and, in the distance, the sea. The owner found it a very calming image.

Although, like the green children of Woolpit, it wasn't real.

The owner replaced the photograph and retrieved the novella, flipped through the pages, held it tentatively, like it was charged with something dangerous. The owner had read the novella countless times, but there was always a little detail emerging, a new hidden message in the text. The writing was exquisite.

It had taken the owner a long time to figure out that the novella was more than a simple story. It was a portal, a window into a secret past. A key.

The owner read from the passage again:

When she wakes, she finds the sheets are wet with God knows what. She blinks. A little sunlight, enough so she casts a weak shadow.

The girl rubs her eyes. She has no concept of time; it is raining outside. She can smell the mildew on the walls; she doesn't know what it is but she hates it.

She stumbles to a table nearby. There is a wooden doll. She picks it up. The doll has yellow hair in pigtails and a red dress. She is smiling at the girl, but the smile is worn and almost faded completely. There is a key at the back, so the doll plays music. The girl winds the key and the tune strikes up.

Ting, ting, ting.

The doll is her friend. The feel of the doll in her hand – the slight vibration created by music – comforts her. Sometimes, the girl talks to the doll; tells the doll all her secrets, the things she's thinking. The things she could do in the outside world.

She tells the doll that she hates the man and the woman and wishes they were dead.

But the thought throws the girl into panic. The basement is all she has known. The man and woman are the only people she has, unless you count the wooden doll. Maybe the girl doesn't want to see what the real world is like. Maybe it's worse than this.

There is a toilet in the corner of the room. She hears the pipes creaking at night, like poltergeists laughing at her in the dark. She wonders if she could flush herself away – where she might end up. The sea perhaps? The ocean?

The girl shakes the thought out of her head.

It is futile.

She is already dead.

Chapter 14

Priest rubbed his hand down his face and stared again at the body slumped in the boot of Elinor Fox's VW.

The reporter seemed to have lost her voice when she had lifted the boot for Priest to check Simeon's pulse. It was a pointless act – Priest had attended enough murder scenes to know a corpse when he saw one. The cause of death wasn't obvious – no wounds or blood – but Simeon's face was horribly contorted. His jaw was locked open and dislocated at an angle. His eyes bulged out of their sockets, the yellowy skin around them stretched taut across angular cheekbones; the image vaguely reminded Priest of Edvard Munch's iconic painting, *The Scream*.

He straightened up and, turning to Fox, said, 'My witness is dead in your car, Miss Fox. Any comments you may have on that state of affairs would interest me greatly.'

Fox was fiddling with her hands, occasionally running them through her hair. She looked shocked, and as any good actor will tell you, shock is one of the simpler human reactions to mimic convincingly. Priest wasn't sure what he thought of her just yet.

He watched her closely as she mumbled a reply: 'I don't know how he got there.'

'OK.' Priest nodded and pulled his phone out of his pocket before turning back to the car.

'Wait!' Fox spluttered, moving forward and taking his arm. 'What are you doing?'

He looked over his shoulder at her and got a good look at her eyes. They were wide and alert with dilated pupils – *startled prey*.

'There's a dead body in the boot of your car,' he explained slowly. 'I thought I might let the police know. What do *you* think?'

'Well, can't we just talk this through first?' Priest noticed her hand was shaking as much as her voice. Georgie had moved away from her, as if she might catch some contagious disease. 'I mean . . . I don't know anything about this.'

'So you've said. In which case, you'll have nothing to worry about.'

'What?' she bleated. 'It's *my car*. Are they going to believe me?'

'We're going to find that out pretty soon,' said Priest, examining his phone. *Although given that my ex-wife is the Assistant Commissioner of the London Met and most of her colleagues hate me, I suspect we're both in for a rough ride over this one.*

'Oh my God, oh my God, *oh my God*.' Fox had started pacing around frantically. She fumbled in her coat pocket and pulled out her own phone and started tapping away on the screen. 'I'll have to phone my boss.'

Georgie grimaced. 'Your boss?'

'I have deadlines to meet,' Fox said with venom before turning her back on Georgie and putting the phone to her ear.

Priest had found what he was looking for in his own contact list and was about to hit DIAL when Georgie took his arm.

'Charlie, I don't trust her.'

Priest looked Fox up and down.

'Her reaction seems genuine enough,' he said, trying the words out to see how they sounded to himself more than anything.

Georgie looked around nervously. 'Poor Simeon. I just can't comprehend it. What do we do now?'

Priest scratched his chin, pained. Then came to a decision.

'Report back to Okoro and tell him to make a paper application for a restricted reporting order and a longer adjournment to be heard on Monday morning. Tell him the restriction on reporting is particularly important. A media frenzy isn't going to help.'

'Oh, come on, Charlie. The first thing she'll do is post a picture of the body on Twitter. She's probably phoning in the headline right now.'

Priest looked over. Fox was strutting up and down the pavement speaking into her phone. An old man walking a dog passed her and received an angry glare after she stumbled into him.

He waited and took a moment to think. *The elephant in the room right now is the 'm' word. Nobody stuffed into the rear of a hatchback died from natural causes. But the Elias Foundation, as desperate as they are, surely aren't capable of . . .*

He thought about Simeon Ali. A man he had only met a few times. A man who had seemed sincere – a quiet and thoughtful individual who had displayed an air of sadness in the slow and mechanical way he spoke, the long pauses between statements as he gathered his thoughts. A man who knew right from wrong, but never wanted or asked for any of this.

Priest clenched his fist.

A man who deserved so much more than this undignified end. An unnerving thought struck Priest. *I wonder how much of this is my fault?*

'She'll do whatever she's going to do, Georgie,' said Priest in the end. 'Go and deliver the news to Okoro but tell him not to pull the plug on the trial. Simeon might be dead, but we're not. We're going to find out what happened to him and if that means tearing the Elias Foundation apart from the inside then that's what we're going to do.'

Georgie nodded. He noticed a tear in her eye – he hoped she would be OK. It was a curse of her intellectual maturity: sometimes he forgot she was only twenty-five, and whereas a body in the boot of a car wasn't exactly an everyday occurrence for him, he did at least have ten years' experience of being a CID officer in a major crime unit to draw upon.

So Priest offered her the most encouraging and positive gesture he could think of, which turned out to be a rather lame pat on the shoulder followed by the words: 'Chin up.' *Oh, very good, Nelson. Another rousing speech.*

'What are you going to do?' she asked, offering him the courtesy of a smile as he took his hand away.

He looked back down at his phone and the glowing red button marked DIAL. 'I'm going to phone an old friend.'

Chapter 15

Priest sat back in an extraordinarily uncomfortable office chair as best he could and watched Detective Chief Inspector Tiff Rowlinson read through his statement. It was less than ten degrees outside but Rowlinson's windowless space situated in the middle of the eighth floor of Holborn Police Station was curiously warm. Priest had removed his jacket but hadn't ruled out the possibility that Tiff kept the temperature deliberately high to make his guests feel prickly. So far, Rowlinson hadn't said anything but the wry smile spread across his face suggested that he found great amusement with Priest's latest predicament.

Finally, he put the statement down and stared across at him.

'I leave you alone for five minutes and now look what you've got yourself into.'

Priest clicked his tongue. 'How long have you been on secondment here?'

Rowlinson had been part of the South Wales Police Major Crime Unit before he had been brought across to fill in while the Met reshuffled its budget-struck pack, again. They had previously worked together when Priest was a detective inspector (Rowlinson had started his career in London at a similar time to Priest, although he was a few years older). Indeed, Rowlinson represented about the only friend Priest had retained after he had left the police and the pair had found themselves forged together again last year when investigating a series of gruesome murders that turned out to be the work of a secret neo-Nazi cult known as the House of Mayfly. It was a case that had scarred them both, in different ways.

'A few weeks. Part of the Met's efforts to learn from other forces and possibly also because half the staff here are off with some strange sickness bug.'

'Or stress,' Priest suggested.

'Yes, and that.' Rowlinson cupped his hands behind his head and leant back in his chair. 'I interviewed your new friend Elinor Fox earlier, by the way. She's a looker, if ever I saw one.'

'I hadn't noticed.'

'Are you still single, Priest?'

'Tiff – you know it would never have worked out between us,' Priest said. He wasn't in the mood for humour and Rowlinson's enjoyment of the situation was irritating. Rowlinson laughed – he had a good-natured laugh, Priest considered. Not like his own, which was more like an old car stalling.

'Her story holds up,' Rowlinson commented. 'The car's parked outside her house in Blackheath. She keeps the keys on the side in the kitchen. It's normally locked but occasionally she forgets. She left home at seven and parked her car around the corner from the High Court. What puzzles me is how she knew to find you on Bristol Road.'

Priest shrugged. 'She said something about a tip-off, but Simeon's address was in the trial bundle. Maybe she managed to get a copy from somewhere. Hagworth leaves his papers lying around all over the place.'

Even as he said it, Priest wasn't convinced, but Rowlinson seemed satisfied and was carrying on. 'Anyway, she never checked the boot, save when she collected her kit bag after an hour at the gym last night at around eight. So whoever dumped the body in the boot, assuming it wasn't her, had several opportunities between eight last night and seven this morning.'

'You don't think she's got anything more to do with this other than owning a convenient place to dump a body?'

'She's a person of interest.' Rowlinson nodded his head – the smile had waned a little. 'But she seems genuine. Questions are: who killed Mr Ali? Why? And why dump the body in Fox's car?'

'Cameras?' Priest asked, hopeful.

'Nah. CCTV blackspot. Typical.'

'Sarah's going to kill me. She's down as the landlord of the flat where Simeon was staying.'

Rowlinson sighed. 'I'm going to need to talk to her.'

'I know. Go easy on her.'

'You have my word. And she's not a priority. A few days' time, I'll get round to it. Besides, the flat's not a crime scene as far as I can tell and I can't get Forensics there until tomorrow. So for Christ's sake don't go poking around there.'

Priest nodded, appreciative. 'How was Simeon killed?'

Rowlinson stretched his arms out and yawned, before leaning across the desk and idly flicking through Priest's statement. Priest guessed he was trying to work out whether their friendship extended to giving him more information than he already had – but they'd been through a lot together and Rowlinson had Priest to thank for closing the file on the man who had mutilated himself in a wood in South Wales last year, Rowlinson's own Mayfly victim. A debt was owed and Rowlinson knew it.

'There will be an autopsy early next week. I don't know when exactly. Spending cuts mean I can't get hold of a duty pathologist until the weekend to oversee moving the body but the budget won't allow for an overtime funded examination, and it's too late to do it today, not even in a case like this.'

'But the early indications are . . . ?'

'Looks like he was asphyxiated. We found traces of cling film in his mouth. There were no defensive wounds, but there's a needle mark in his neck. Eyes were bloodshot, classic sign of suffocation. We'll know more when we get a tox report.'

'This is a murder investigation then?'

Rowlinson rubbed the bridge of his nose. 'Yep. More damn paperwork.'

'She's going to print everything, you know that, right?'

'Fox? She's a journalist, not much I can do about that. We live in an age of open justice and all that bullshit.'

'Couldn't you agree an embargo with her?'

'No, someone from Corporate Communications tried, but there's not much we can do, short of getting an injunction.'

He had to agree. The authorised professional practice for police media relations didn't apply since Fox's information had come as a result of her direct involvement with the event that precipitated the investigation, not because she was a journalist. Rowlinson's hands were tied. It was only a matter of time before Simeon's death, and the murder investigation, would be public knowledge.

'Anything else I can help you with, Tiff?'

Rowlinson sucked in some air. He seemed to be contemplating something, then: 'No, you're done for now. Try and stay out of trouble, won't you?'

Priest got up, stretched. 'Later, alligator.'

'And Priest?' Rowlinson called him back as he made to leave. 'Not that I want to sound corny, but – don't leave town.'

*

Priest turned right outside Holborn Police Station with the intention of making his way back to the office in order to contact Tomas Jansen, who was probably climbing the walls. Priest had telephoned him on the way to the station to relay the news. Jansen had been cold, and it had irritated Priest that his first thought was where this left the trial. He didn't express any sympathy for Simeon.

'What do we do now, Charlie?'

'I don't know yet. I'll contact you after I've spoken with the police.'

'The trial?'

'Can wait. For now.'

Priest heard footsteps running up behind him and his name being called; he turned around warily.

'Mr Priest?'

'Miss Fox.' The reporter was coming towards him, a cigarette in her hand. Her hair looked ruffled, most likely the result of being constantly played with, and a dark line of dislodged mascara under one eye suggested she had been crying at some stage.

'It's Elinor,' she told him.

'They let you go then, Elinor,' said Priest, trying a smile. The effort wasn't reciprocated.

'On the condition that I stay in London and don't contact anyone else involved in the Elias case.'

'Whereupon you promptly walked out of the station and accosted the defendant's solicitor.'

Fox slipped her arm into his, used the other to take another long drag of the cigarette. They walked down to the end of the road; he let her dictate the pace. She was clearly anxious, the shake in her hand hadn't got any better, but some of the over-confident reporter mannerisms he had seen when they had first met on Bristol Road had returned.

'Who were you speaking to on the phone after we first found Simeon?' Priest asked when they reached the crossroads. Busy commuters ghosted past them, weaving in and out like worker ants. The traffic was backed up and a set of temporary lights had been installed around several open holes surrounded by cones.

'I told you. My boss, Max.'

'You're freelance. You don't have a boss.'

She took another drag. 'Everyone has a boss, Mr Priest. Even freelancers. Don't you?'

'Not for a while.'

She smiled, but not with her eyes. 'Lucky you. What about a girl?'

'Not for a while,' said Priest, less certainly. Fox still had her arm linked into his. Priest suddenly felt very conscious of it – and of her stare. He looked around and wondered what Jessica would think if she were standing on the other side of the road, watching him.

'Assuming that your boss knows about what happened, I imagine Simeon's death is now public knowledge?'

She looked at the floor and found something interesting to move around with her foot. 'They can't stop me. I haven't signed a confidentiality agreement.'

He decided to change track. 'What's your interest in the Elias case?'

'I think there's more to it than your libel action,' she said in a ponderous tone. 'And given the body in my boot I feel pretty vindicated, don't you think?'

'What about *The Real Byte*?'

Fox shrugged. 'They're run by Tomas Jansen. I don't know much more than that – nothing about the other staff.'

'You know Jansen?'

'*Everyone* in journalism knows Jansen. Or at least they've heard of him.'

He looked away for a moment. 'How so?'

'He gets up people's noses, as do many tiresome socialists. The people versus the establishment and all that – it's all been done before and much better.'

He looked back at her. 'You don't approve?'

She smirked – it was a very childish gesture and conjured up a picture of freckles and pigtails in Priest's mind. 'It's not that *I* don't approve. I'm just saying that there is a growing tide of wariness for Marxist clichés.'

'Which you are a part of? Or not a part of?'

She laughed, a little more grown up this time. 'Mr Priest – I am the embodiment of neutrality.' She winked at him and suddenly the little girl was back.

'No doubt,' Priest mumbled.

Fox smiled, pleased. 'I don't know what to do next. They've kept my car.'

'Where do you live?' Priest already knew, but didn't want to let on.

'Blackheath.'

She looked at him hopefully. He noticed that she had averted her eyes back to the ground where she began playing again with whatever it was under her foot. He hesitated, processing all the little contradictions he had observed. The hard-nosed investigator and the little girl, all fighting for supremacy in her head. *No doubt that she's shaken, though.* The slight tremor in her hand confirmed it. *What harm can it do?*

Against his better judgement, Priest relented. 'I'm parked around the corner. I'll give you a ride home.'

Fox's face lit up. She tightened her arm through his and let him lead the way.

*

It took them about thirty-five minutes to negotiate the queues of black cabs, buses and those other city itinerants foolish enough to drive a car south-east through London to Blackheath. When they arrived, the sun had managed to penetrate the cloud covering and Blackheath Park was bathed in a pallid autumn light.

They had talked sporadically during the journey. For most of it, Fox had been playing with her hair, but she seemed calmer now and they had mostly talked about her life as a freelance journalist – how she came into it after getting an article on abortion published in a local newspaper. Eventually, she indicated for him to slow down.

'It's just through there.' She pointed to where a secondary road pulled away to the left through a regiment of large oak trees. Priest hit the indicator.

'Nice place,' he remarked, staring up at the swaying trees as the old Volvo rumbled underneath.

'My parents helped me buy it. Otherwise, I couldn't afford to live here, not when every pound I earn comes from writing.'

Hidden away from the main road, they came to a small row of terraces that fronted an orchard. Through the trees, Priest could see the park and, in the distance, a white-stoned church silhouetted by the low-hanging sun.

'It's the far one.' Fox motioned towards the end of the building – a four-storey house, but one that was barely wide enough for the front door and single window on each floor.

'You mentioned your boss – Max,' Priest reminded her, pulling the Volvo up at the gate.

'He's more of an agent, I guess. I go out and get the stories and he sells them on. I get commission and the chance of a desk job. It's a shit deal but there aren't many avenues for those of us that aren't prepared to fuck our way into a newspaper.'

'Raw deal.'

'Alexia could have done it, you know.'

'What?'

'Murdered Simeon.'

Priest did a double take. 'You really think so?'

'She wouldn't have done it herself, of course. She wouldn't get her hands dirty. She'd have hired someone.'

'I'm not sure . . .'

'Really? How much would it have cost her? Fifteen thousand? Twenty at the most? A drop in the ocean for her.'

'Probably cost about that, yeah.'

'Worth thinking about it.' She winked. Priest was forced to agree, but there would be time to think about that later: for now there was something else preying on his mind.

'Look, I can't stop you from doing anything, but it would really help me if Simeon's murder was kept out of the papers for now.'

Her eyes lit up. 'Are you asking me for a favour?'

'No, that would be unprofessional. I'm just saying – it would help.'

She smiled – a little impish. Priest wasn't sure he liked it. 'How about I give you a head start?'

'How long?'

'A fair amount of time, but of course the public has a right to know.'

He thought about pressing it, but now wasn't the time. Besides, what difference would it really make? It was all going to come out soon anyway and trying to get his own injunction against Fox would leave the door open for Hagworth to walk all over the main case. No – he didn't have the leverage, so he'd have to settle for Fox's 'head start'.

'What will you do now?' he asked her.

She shrugged and put her hand on the door handle but didn't open it. 'Probably have a bath with at least two bottles of Pinot Grigio. You, erm –' she turned and looked at him '– want to join me?'

He smiled back. Passed her his business card. 'Mind how you go, Elinor.'

She feigned a disappointed face. She got out of the car, didn't shut the door immediately but leant over it, her coat falling open just a little and showing a blouse loosely buttoned over a pink bra. A little taste, Priest surmised, of what he would be missing.

'Can I tag along with you tomorrow?' she asked, biting her lip while she waited for the reply.

'What makes you think . . .'

'I know you're not going to leave it to the police to look into Simeon's murder. Two heads are better than one, don't you think? After all, we both have a vested interest in the outcome.'

'I might salvage the trial and you might get off the hook?'

'Something like that.' She swept her hair away from her face. 'I don't want to stalk you or anything, I just want to tag along. I had a stalker once, at university. He used to send me flowers and cards and stand outside my bedroom window at night. It really wasn't very nice, so I'm not going to do that to you.'

She winked. There was something very elfin about her petite features that Priest liked. *Maybe I was a little hasty to turn down her offer.* Then he remembered his date with Jessica tomorrow night: the thought evaporated and he felt ashamed for even contemplating it.

'I'll think about it,' he said.

She straightened up as he turned the car around. Pulling off, he glanced at her in the rear-view mirror. She stood curiously still, watching him as he drove away.

Chapter 16

Priest awoke the following morning to the sound of pan pipes drifting in from the open bedroom window. He lay sprawled across the bed, partially clothed, and tried to open his eyes but they didn't respond.

He remembered coming back home yesterday with his head spinning and a disturbing sensation of numbness in his fingers and toes. He had spent most of the evening in the lounge trying to make sense of it all until he felt the icy impression of his body detaching itself from its grip on reality. He perceived himself walk out of the room and collapse on the bed in what an onlooker might have assumed was a drunken stupor, if they did not know any better. There he had lain, face down on the covers, conjuring up images of Elinor Fox's cleavage and the top of her pink bra until the picture was disturbed by a very angry-looking Jessica.

Now, in the emptiness between sleep and full consciousness, Priest struggled to regain traction.

The pan pipes emanated from a street performer outside the Royal Opera House, from where he was regularly regaled with music of varying quality and origin if the window was open. Priest liked the pan pipes the best; for reasons that he did not understand, they reminded him of his mother.

One of the many ghosts who inhabit my head.

The feeling of emptiness was familiar and depressing, but Priest reminded himself that he was lucky. He could still function, most of the time, and the feeling came and went. Some sufferers of depersonalisation disorder are left devastated, the breakdown in their perception of reality leaving them in a permanent state of disillusionment; they watch, helpless, as their bodies move around in front of them, like a horror film in which they are the star. Some even question whether they are in fact alive. Priest knew that sensation, but the worst of it was behind him – for now – although he still experienced both depersonalisation – the sense that the individual is not real – and derealisation – the perception that the world isn't real – temporarily, and although unpredictable and terrifying, the hallucinations and out-of-body experiences never lasted for more than a few hours a day at most.

Like many DPD sufferers, Priest hated his condition. He had wasted months, years, obsessively ruminating – why could he *think* but not *feel*? What had happened? What if things had been different? What could he have achieved? Why him? Priest didn't believe in souls, but it was the closest he had come to admitting that the body and the mind were two separate entities, and that the former could not function if the latter took leave.

And if his mind *had* departed from his body, *where the hell had it gone*?

He suddenly became aware that his phone was ringing from another room. With a great effort, he hauled his muscular frame out of bed and sauntered through to the lounge where he found his phone next to the fish tank. The lionfish seemed uninterested in him today; their amber and beige striped tentacles waved nonchalantly at him from the other side of the plastic castle Sarah had bought for him last year. The newest addition, Hemingway, was particularly aloof.

'Well good morning to you too,' he grunted at them.

His phone had stopped ringing but there was a message:

'*Charlie, it's me,*' said Jessica's recorded voice. '*We never agreed a time so I'll come over to yours at seven. I'll assume that's fine unless I hear otherwise from you.*'

He hung up and found himself in a state of unrest. He had acted rashly by inviting her over, but he was prone to ill-conceived impulses. Having said that, he hadn't expected for one minute that she would accept. Now he wasn't sure what to do. He sat down on the sofa heavily and closed his eyes. He tried to think about what he would say to her, what he *shouldn't* say to her – but there she was, hijacking his thoughts, her flawless body straddling him on her bed. With a smile, she unhooked the top of her silk dressing gown from her shoulders and unpeeled it as she began to writhe on top of him, her soft moaning as melodic as the dulcet pan pipe music he had awoken to.

And Elinor Fox's pink bra didn't feature once.

*

Georgie Someday occasionally regretted living with a professional escort.

That was what Li called herself – a professional escort. Georgie appreciated the importance of labelling but, whatever you called it, it was still sex for money in her book. Li could make an easy living working for herself if she wanted to, but she was more than happy to hand over a percentage of what she earned to her pimp, a mysterious woman whom Georgie had never met named Mrs White. In return, Li's clients were carefully selected for her – mainly married-middle-class men with big incomes and little risk.

Today was one of those days. Georgie had been up most of the night – first spending an hour reading every article she could find on the web written by Elinor Fox (of which there weren't many) and then reading everything she could about the Free People's Army. Finally, the early hours were spent with a very thick volume of Keats, and Wagner on repeat.

Another night with the light on. Georgie hated the dark.

Now she was barely awake and her head was pounding from lack of sleep. The sound of Li and one of her clients wasn't helping. Georgie hated the ones who dropped in early in the morning having told their wives that they were going to the gym or something equally feeble.

Fortunately, it didn't last that long.

After Georgie and Li had graduated they had shared a flat with three other friends, including a greasy-haired psychology graduate named Martin Penton-Smith. At first, Georgie had been attracted to Martin. He wasn't particularly good-looking, but she could relate to his geekiness, and the little bit of herself that she had recognised in him. He liked his own company more than that of others – she could relate to that. He had seemed nice. He had seemed harmless.

Georgie hadn't gone to the police. How could she? She had gone to his room willingly. They had been alone. She had sent out the wrong message. She was angry with him – she had never felt hate like it – but she was just as angry with herself.

She opened the wardrobe door and examined its rather drab contents. At the back, three stacks of files and papers – her two-year long investigation into Martin – sat gathering dust. She hadn't opened the files for a month. She'd forced herself not to look, not to let the obsession overcome her. And the files disgusted her – she couldn't let it go and, even now, they called to her like Sirens across the water. This was the price she had paid for not going to the police – this was her punishment, her private vendetta.

Not that she had dug up anything of interest, even after hacking his computer. He liked porn, but what boy of his age didn't? His emails were dull. His social circle was small. His friends were uninteresting. He was an only child and his mum and dad paid for his accommodation.

It seemed like the only thing of note that Martin Penton-Smith had ever done in his life was rape his flatmate.

Georgie closed the wardrobe and caught her breath.

To distract herself, she inspected her phone and found an email from Charlie; he was on his way to the office to think things through – would she join him? Georgie thought fleetingly about Elinor Fox and the way Charlie had been so quick to dismiss her suspicions, like he had been, she recalled, with Jessica Ellinder.

She briefly glanced at herself in a small mirror on the dressing table. Her face was too freckly to wear make-up, her mother had told her. Georgie knew of course that wasn't true but it suited her to think it was and it saved a lot of time in the morning. She quickly tied her hair back and pushed her glasses further up her nose.

If I was lying, would you protect me, Charlie? Am I pretty enough to be given the benefit of the doubt?

She felt a flush of shame and scolded herself inwardly for being unkind. After all, Charlie had been right about Jessica and she had been wrong. *I must be more trusting.*

She wrinkled her nose in the mirror before scurrying out past Li's room, hoping she wouldn't run into her client on the way out. Maybe she would burn the Martin papers tonight. They told her nothing anyway.

Yes. Georgie would buy matches on the way home.

*

Priest felt vaguely guilty about pulling Georgie into the office on a Saturday but, until Peters said otherwise, the trial was reconvening on Monday and there was no guarantee she would give them another grace period, dead witness or not. Consequentially, time was of the essence.

He calculated that she would be there in half an hour relying on the Tube and then a brisk walk through Holborn. Time for a quick cigarette on the rooftop garden of his penthouse. He rarely smoked nowadays – he avoided most intoxicants – but recently he felt the need for something tangible to anchor him; something other than late night Hammer horror films and dreamless sleep. Dreamless except for Jessica. Moreover, something about seeing Fox cling to the cigarette in her hand when they had met outside the police station yesterday had reawakened an old craving within him.

So, wrapped in a coat and scarf, Priest took out a menthol cigarette, sat down underneath the shade of a white-tipped amelanchier tree and lit up. He'd barely taken a drag when his phone rang for the second time that morning. This time he managed to hit ANSWER before the voicemail overrode him.

'Hi, Sarah,' Priest said.

'Are you smoking?'

How the hell do you know that? 'No.'

'You're outside at nine o'clock in the morning on a Saturday,' she said with certainty.

'That doesn't mean I'm smoking.' Priest took a drag.

'Whatever. I was just ringing because I wondered if you were OK.'

He groaned inwardly. *I hate it when you take on Mum's role.* 'Sarah, I'm fine. Really.'

'You just seemed a bit on edge yesterday – you know, when you randomly turned up with Georgie and demanded the keys to Bristol Road without explanation. It's not a safe house, Charlie. Who have you got in there?'

'Sarah . . .'

'And you looked even more unkempt than normal. I mean, you generally look unloved, like one of Tilly's rag dolls she's forgotten about and keeps under the bed for months.'

'Well, you know what they say, Sarah.' Priest looked along the strip of flower bed dug around the edge of the square patio, dotted with purple crocus heads protruding cautiously out of the soil in anticipation of spring. 'Some flowers thrive on neglect.'

Sarah huffed. 'How ridiculous. And all this fuss over a tiny two-bedroomed flat. Listen, one of my girlfriends is really keen to meet you. Apparently, she's spent a lot of time studying your website photo and she messaged me last night and I thought, *Wow! My brother would . . .*'

'Sarah, not this again,' Priest sighed.

'No, really . . .'

'Wait.' Priest found himself stood up all of a sudden. 'Wait – what did you say?'

'I said I've got this friend . . .'

'No, before then – about the flat.'

'I said *all this fuss over a tiny two-bedroomed flat*,' Sarah repeated, puzzled.

'Oh, Jesus.' Priest bolted across the patio towards the stairwell. 'Thanks, Sarah. Got to go. Love you.'

*

Gary had owned the electronics shop on Bristol Road for eight years and in that time he had barely turned a profit. He fixed PCs and laptops and, by all accounts, he was pretty good at it, but he didn't make any money. Fortunately, having won the best part of four million pounds on the National Lottery in 2008, he didn't need to. Gary fixed computers because Gary enjoyed fixing computers.

Gary's good fortune meant that his shop only opened between ten and three and he picked and chose who he worked for – customer service was relatively unimportant and Gary could decide whether he was helpful and welcoming to new customers or downright rude and hostile.

Right now, faced with an attractive blonde who had identified herself as a freelance reporter, Gary was on the fence. On the one hand, he hated reporters and didn't like the line of questioning about the guy who lived in the flat above him – the one owned by that awful lawyer – but on the other hand, with her curvy body and flirtatious smile, she was joyous to behold.

'You don't happen to have a key, do you?' asked the reporter, flashing him another gorgeous grin.

'Told you, miss. It's not my flat,' Gary replied.

'When was the last time you saw the occupant?'

'Like I told the police when they asked the same thing, keeps himself to himself. I don't even know his name. But I thought he might be in some kind of trouble.'

'How so?'

'There was a lot of scurrying about. You know, sometimes you can just tell these things.'

The reporter looked thoughtfully at the doorway that led to the flat. 'How does he get in when the shop's closed?'

'There's another door round the back. I don't know when he comes and goes.'

'Thank you,' she said brightly. 'You've been most helpful.' Gary grunted something in reply and turned back to the corrupt hard drive spread across the counter. 'You don't mind if I take a quick look through there, do you?'

He opened his mouth to reply but he was rudely interrupted.

'Tell you what, how about I open up for us?'

Gary groaned. The awful lawyer was standing in the doorway holding a key.

Chapter 17

Priest unlocked the front door and led the way into the cheerless hallway. Georgie followed him in. He'd managed to ring and divert her to Bristol Road before she got to the office. Elinor Fox came in behind, seemingly unperturbed at having been caught trying to flirt her way into the flat.

'What were *you* doing?' Georgie fired at her.

'Doing what an investigative journalist does: investigating.'

'They call it snooping elsewhere.' Georgie turned her back on the reporter and sidled up to Priest with her arms folded.

He stared at the back wall. 'How many rooms do you see?'

Georgie scanned the end of the hallway. 'Lounge, kitchen, bathroom and a bedroom. Four.'

'Right,' Priest murmured, making his way to the rear of the flat where he started to run his fingers across the back wall. 'Whereas Sarah distinctly told me there were *two* bedrooms.'

'The geek downstairs told me that Simeon used the rear entrance to come and go, too. Yet there isn't one,' offered Fox, mimicking Priest's inspection of the wall.

'Not one that we can see, anyway,' said Priest and, with that, put his fist through the wall.

He felt Georgie jump in alarm as his hand went right through the plasterboard to the other side. He withdrew it and felt a draught of cold air escape the new opening. He peered through; could see only darkness but there was definitely a space behind the wall.

'Stand back,' Priest grunted. 'This might get rough.' He raised his foot. The idea was to take the wall out bit by bit if he had to. Turned out he didn't. There was the sound of a latch mechanism operating somewhere in the wall and suddenly a hitherto unseen door on the far side of the wall fell open. Priest looked over at Fox, who was standing next to it.

'Ingenious,' she mused, closing the door again, whereupon Priest saw the outline seal shut. A minuscule overhang the same colour as the wall lined the edge of the door so, when it was shut, it was completely invisible, until pressure was applied to a particular spot which Fox showed them and the door rematerialised before swinging open.

'Lucky guess,' Georgie mumbled.

Priest said nothing before entering the secret room beyond the hallway and finding himself in a dark, enclosed space. He used the light from his phone to find a switch on the wall and suddenly the second bedroom manifested itself, complete with back door leading to the street below.

'Simeon must have installed this himself,' Priest concluded. 'A secret room only he knew about.'

The two women joined him as he started to look around. The room was approximately four metres deep, no more, with furry, maroon wallpaper and a threadbare carpet. There was a bed, with a stained mattress but no covers. A wardrobe, a desk and an empty bookshelf. Everything smelt musty and old – Priest imagined this was what Egyptian tombs must smell like when they were unsealed after thousands of years.

'Yes, wonderful things,' he murmured.

'Howard Carter, on the opening of King Tutankhamun's tomb,' Georgie completed. Priest nodded. 'Why create a single room and not apparently use it?'

'To hide something,' Priest suggested.

The bed hadn't been slept in and Priest found the wardrobe devoid of anything except the same archaic stench that pervaded the rest of the room, only stronger.

'Only someone who already knew the layout of the flat would have realised that this room must exist,' said Fox.

'So?'

'So, *you* were meant to find this room first, Charlie.'

They checked under the bed and in the corners of the room but without finding anything of significance. The door to the rear was locked but, looking through the window, it appeared to lead to an external stairwell that allowed access to the side street.

There remained one feature that all three of them appeared to notice at once. A small drawer underneath the desk. Priest felt the handle: a flimsy piece of wood affixed to the front, off-centre. A thought struck him. He had nowhere to go next. No plan. No clue. If this drawer was empty, it was back home or to the office and, for now at least, he would be beaten.

Come on, Simeon. Tell me something.

Priest slid the drawer open. It was despairingly empty.

'Damn,' he breathed, letting go of the handle.

They all seemed to exhale at once before Georgie asked, 'What next?'

Priest shook his head. *Fuck it!* 'I'm not sure.' He stared down at his hands – they were always the first to go – first the feeling in them then, by abstract dislocation, they would become foreign objects, swirling untouchably in a sea of hazy mist. At its most extreme, he could hallucinate – see things that weren't there, talk to people who didn't exist.

He needed to get out of this room and its oppressive reek, but something stopped him. Fox had leant over, touching his arm as she did and pulling at the little drawer until it dislodged from the slide runners and clattered to the floor.

'Sorry,' she said, wincing. 'I didn't mean to . . .'

She stopped mid-sentence, no doubt because she had just seen what Priest had. He bent down and carefully picked something out from amongst the broken wood and held it up to the light for them to see.

'It must have been stuck to the underside of the drawer,' Georgie said.

Priest nodded in agreement and turned the photograph over. Nothing on the other side. Only the black and white image of a young boy of maybe ten standing off-centre with his hands placed on top of each other across his middle. He was standing outside on a grassy incline fifteen feet or more from the camera, but looking into the lens with an expression of complete neutrality. In the background, Priest could see a house further up the incline with boarded windows and a damaged roof – beyond that, the picture quality did not allow any further scrutiny.

'Who is he?' asked Fox.

'I have no idea,' Priest admitted.

'It looks like a recent photograph,' Georgie added. 'Probably printed black and white for effect.'

But what kind of effect? A memory of some words uttered by one of Priest's law lecturers echoed in his head – *assume every piece of evidence is inauthentic until proven otherwise.*

'I've got to go,' Fox announced all of a sudden, but not before she'd whipped out her phone and taken a picture of the photograph. Priest didn't have time to hide it.

'Hey!' Georgie exclaimed. 'That's evidence.'

Fox ignored her. Backed out of the room with an apologetic semblance. 'A girl's got to make a living. Ciao for now.'

Georgie was about to get up and follow her, but Priest held her back. 'Let her go, Someday.'

She turned to him, incredulous. 'We can't just let her publish everything.'

'We can't stop her either. She said we'd get a head start. That's the best we're going to get.'

Georgie huffed in frustration. 'Fine, but it's still disgraceful.'

Priest held the picture up to get a better look. 'Tell Leveson about it. Right now we've got more important things to think about. Like working out who our little friend here is and what's he doing stuck to the bottom of a dead man's drawer.'

*

Lawrence Baker parked the delivery van outside the pebble-dashed house and checked the address. *This is it, all right.* He jumped out of the cab and rang the doorbell. There was one of those wind chimes dangling from the porch, tingling eerily in the breeze. Lawrence hated those things – they were the sort of thing that he associated with haunted houses.

Lawrence didn't pay any attention to the figure that opened the front door. He rarely noticed details like that – as long as he got paid, the client could be Jack the Ripper for all he cared.

'Hey,' said Lawrence. 'You asked for a removal guy?'

He peered inside the house behind the figure. Not much going on there. No evidence of moving house, no boxes piled up on the side or a sofa stuck in the doorway like usual. Lawrence tensed up – *This better not be a time waster.*

'It's through here,' the figure said, disappearing into the house. Irritated already, Lawrence followed and found himself in a hallway and then a lounge area. The heat was unbearable.

'Crikey, is your heating broken?' Lawrence puffed. 'It's like a sauna in here!' When he didn't get a reply, Lawrence said impatiently, 'What is it then? What do you want moving and where?'

The figure drifted across the room, which had a sofa and TV in it, and a small cabinet in the corner. And something else.

'It's this.'

The figure motioned to the safe in the corner. Reinforced steel and with a circular dial, it was a hell of a bit of kit. Lawrence sucked his teeth and inspected it, tapping the surfaces and finding them rock solid.

'Shit. I dunno. Where do you want it shifting?'

'There is no address, I'm afraid, but here's a map.'

Lawrence took the map and studied it. Looked again and winced. *The bloody Norfolk coast!*

'You've got to be kiddin' me,' Lawrence said, handing the map back. 'This ain't for me, I'm afraid. You'll need to find some other mug.'

'Triple rate. In cash.'

Seriously?

Lawrence scratched his head. He thought about his gambling debt and the money he owed to the loan sharks. He was in it up to his neck.

'All right,' Lawrence said at last. 'Triple rate. When d'ya want it moving?'

The figure smiled. 'I'll call you. I need to fill it first.'

Chapter 18

'What do you think of our reporter friend?'

Priest pushed a bottle of ketchup across the table towards Georgie and watched as she unscrewed the cap and made a fuss of dolloping it over her fried breakfast. If he didn't know better, he would have said she was buying time to consider her answer.

'Fox? I'm not sure I trust her.'

'Not sure I do either,' concluded Priest. He started picking apart his own breakfast, separating the egg from the beans. He could see Georgie smiling in his peripheral vision. It was late, but the Hairy Hand Special was served all day at his favourite cafe. 'What's so funny?'

'You compartmentalise all your breakfast items so they don't touch.'

'Yes,' he said, although the reason for her amusement eluded him.

'You have to have every item separated so nothing touches each other and your mushrooms don't contaminate your hash browns.'

'And your point is?'

Georgie stuffed a spoonful of black pudding into her mouth and said through chewing, 'I thought I was the only person in the world who did that.'

He looked at her plate, the mirror of his. Everything had been ordered in roughly the same way. He shrugged and moved the fried tomato towards the edge of the beans. Without looking up he produced the picture they had found of the boy outside the house and placed it on the table in front of her.

'What made you think this was a recent photo?' he asked.

Georgie replied in between chews. 'He's wearing an Apple Watch.'

Priest turned the photo back his way. *Well I'll be damned.* 'Well done, Eagle Eyes.'

'We could run a reverse search through Google,' she suggested. 'Solly will know how to do that.'

'I'll take it to him, just as soon as I've finished this incredibly greasy meal.'

'Who makes the black pudding? It's delicious, although probably very bad for you.'

'The hairy hand.' Priest motioned to the hatch in the wall. 'You don't see it often but that's where the food comes from.' They were the only two people sitting in the cafe which, judging by the cleanliness of the tablecloths, was perhaps understandable. It was the extraordinary black pudding made by the hairy hand that lured in those in the know.

'Who would have thought it? I must stop shaving my palms if I'm to cook like this,' Georgie garbled, taking another bite.

It was a long time since he had sat in this same seat opposite Jessica and she had turned her nose up at the Hairy Hand Special, much to Priest's amusement. It was refreshing to see Georgie's enthusiastic reception of it.

Although, it begs a question. Priest recalled the voicemail message Jessica had left him earlier: she was coming round to his flat at seven tonight. *And she's expecting me to cook a meal. I promised lemon sole, my speciality.* Priest felt a sudden surge of anxiety. Once again, his inadequacies as a human being were about to be exposed in all their glory for her to see.

*

Priest took the Tube to Kew Gardens Station and skipped past the market stall holders who were boasting about the quality of their fruit and veg in loud Cockney accents. He headed towards the Thames. Rows of houseboats lined the bank, most of them sunk deep in the low tide riverbed sludge. Solly's home was one of these: a short gangplank led to a fifteen-foot houseboat with an upper deck peppered with plants and gnomes and a single deckchair and table at the stern looking out towards the estuary.

Simon Solomon, Solly to those who knew him, was a short, elusive man of almost indeterminable age with a mottled complexion and black hair that looked as though it was permanently wet but, unassuming as he was to look at, his planet-sized brain and talent for numbers had endeared him to Priest as the team's financial genius. He had qualified as an accountant, but his hobbies included computer coding, studying quantum mechanics and avoiding all non-necessary human interaction.

Priest rang the bell. After a while, Solly answered, wearing the same tweed suit he wore for work.

'Priest,' he said, without surprise or interest. 'My contracted hours don't begin until nine o'clock on Monday morning.'

'Yes, I know. I just wondered if you could do me a small favour.'

'Well, I don't know.' Solly shuffled his feet uncomfortably. 'It's not that I'm not committed to the cause, Priest, but I rarely accept guests into my home. Have you decontaminated yourself?'

Priest waved his hands around in front of him in a gesture that he had intended to appear unthreatening but which appeared to have the opposite effect. Solly stepped back, alarmed. 'Sorry, it's an intrusion, I know, but it's a matter of life and death, Solly.'

'Well,' said Solly thoughtfully. 'Since the stakes are that high, I suppose I ought to make an exception, but you will have to remove your shoes.'

'Gladly,' said Priest, relieved. He took his shoes off and moved forward but Solly stopped him.

'And your jacket.'

Priest hesitated, but realised Solly meant it. He slipped his jacket off and hung it on the gatepost. He made to move forward but Solly stopped him a third time.

'Sorry, Priest. It's not that I am trying to be difficult but I do have house rules. I'm sure your house is just the same.'

'It's a *little* more flexible, if I'm being honest, Solly. Can we go in now?'

'Of course we can. Just as soon as you remove your belt.'

Priest motioned uselessly with his hands. 'My belt?'

'Yes. I have a particular concern about foreign metals, I'm afraid, and that buckle looks like it hasn't been cleaned in years.'

He nodded, exasperated. Took his belt off and hung it next to his jacket. *Only faith and hope now hold up my trousers.* 'Anything else?'

'I think that will suffice. This way, please.'

Solly led Priest through a door into an area that appeared to be a dimly lit living room complete with a black and white TV from the eighties and, curiously, a life-sized stuffed bear.

'Fuck me, Solly. What's that?' Priest indicated the bear.

'Oh, that's Mother.'

Priest thought about whether or not he wanted to ask any follow-up questions. Time was short and he had to get back and prepare for Jessica's visit, so in the end he decided to let it drop.

He produced the photograph and handed it to Solly. 'Can you reverse image search this?'

'No.'

'Really?'

'I can of course carry out a reverse image search for you on this photograph but I cannot reverse image search this, as you put it.'

'Isn't that the same thing?' asked Priest, his patience beginning to slip away.

'It will most likely achieve the same outcome, if that's what you mean.'

Priest suppressed the urge to grab Solly by the throat. 'Could you? For me? It's rather urgent.'

'Wait here.'

Solly disappeared through a door in the back which led to goodness-knows-where. There can't be many possibilities on a fifteen-foot houseboat. *A torture chamber, maybe? Oh, how silly! He does his torturing in the front room.*

Priest's phone buzzed and he found he had received a text from Jessica:

'*Did you get my message about tonight?*'

He tapped a quick response:

'*Yes. See you at 7 at my place.*'

A kiss to finish? A smiley face? Damn it, what?

In the end, he settled for a 'thumbs-up' emoji. The lameness of it made him wince, even before he hit SEND. He closed his eyes. Saw her face: her thin lips, pale skin, high cheekbones. Hardly any make-up, her features made their own mark. She was classically beautiful – her chestnut hair, and bright irises threaded with amber brought her an ethereal quality. She was everything he had ever wanted: fiercely intelligent, radiant, elegant; and everything he deserved: cold, brusque, ruthless.

He stared at his phone. Waited for a reply – anything, but it didn't come. When he looked up, shaken from the daydream, Solly was waving the photograph at him.

'No joy, I'm afraid, Priest. Which means this was an original image and not one readily available on the internet.'

His heart sank. What hope had they of identifying the boy? The photograph might be nothing to do with the Elias case – they could be on a complete tangent, wasting valuable time. They had to have something usable by Monday or there was no chance Peters would allow an adjournment. Then *The Real Byte* would be ruined, Alexia Elias would come out a heroine and Simeon would still be dead, needlessly. *Fuck it.*

'Thanks anyway, Solly,' Priest said, making for the door.

'Well, I'm sorry I couldn't be more help.'

Solly opened the door – a gust of cold air hit Priest, compounding the anxiety eating away at him. *What do I do now?*

He started to gather up his personal belongings and put his shoes back on. 'See you later, Solly.'

'Yes. Bye, Priest. Curious, though, wasn't it?'

He stopped and turned to look at Solly. 'What's curious?'

'Why the unknown boy is standing outside Alexia and Dominque Elias's former home.'

Priest waited a few moments, letting Solly's assertion sink in and mix around with the rest of the confused musings cluttering up his head.

'Say that again,' Priest requested.

'It's quite simple,' Solly explained. 'I'm surprised you didn't pick up on it, Priest.'

'Go on.'

'Well, I recognised the house in its ruined state immediately but I couldn't place it at first until I checked the Elias papers – I have an exact replica of my office at the front of the boat, including all documents, of course – and there are pictures of Alexia in one of the disclosure bundles. She is standing outside her former home in Norfolk. The property is the same, undoubtedly.'

'Show me.'

Solly rolled his eyes like it was all too much trouble and then scuttled off back through the rear door. He emerged a few moments later with an open folder, which he handed to Priest.

'Here.' He indicated to a printout of a series of messages between Alexia and various members of Elias Foundation staff.

'I don't see . . .'

Solly directed Priest's gaze to the thumbnail picture of Alexia's face which preceded each section of dialogue supposedly sent from her phone. Priest strained to look further. Most of the picture was taken up with Alexia's smug-looking expression but, yes, in the background . . . the side of a house, on a grassy incline.

'Does Alexia ever give a description of where she used to live in her witness statement?' murmured Priest.

'In fact she does,' said Solly, clearly pleased with himself. 'In anticipation of you wanting that information I wrote it down on this piece of paper. I also took the liberty of checking with the Land Registry – the house is owned by Alexia.' Solly passed Priest the papers. 'You can keep the pad,' he added. 'I'll have no further use for that once you have touched it.'

*

Georgie had contemplated taking a bus home but elected to walk instead. The sun was breaking through the cloud covering and bouncing off the reflective glass of Holborn's commanding office blocks. Nonetheless, she had pulled her coat tightly around her shoulders – sun or no sun, it was still cold this time of year.

When she finally got in, Georgie found Li in the kitchen frantically moving between three different boiling pots on the hob. The sides were cluttered with various packets that looked like they had been opened by a rabid dog. The thick covering of vapour hung to the ceiling.

'Hi,' Georgie said, taking in the scene.

'Hi!' Li called back. 'I'm doing a stir-fry. Would you like some?'

'Is it a stir-fry or a nuclear missile test?'

Li laughed manically. 'I'm not sure it's going to be very good. I've never done stir-fry before.'

Georgie inspected the chaos and picked up a half-used tin of kidney beans. 'There seems to be an awful lot of ingredients for a stir-fry.'

'What?' Li shouted over the sound of water hissing off the hob as she hauled a pan to the sink.

She could see that Li didn't need distracting from what was already a total shambles, so she asked Li to call her when it was ready and headed to her room. It was a mixed blessing. No doubt the entire contents of the fridge would have been poured into the meal but Li's attempt at cooking indicated that she wasn't expecting a client this evening.

She sat down at her desk and turned on her laptop. She had work to do – file notes to type up, mainly. The week leading up to the Elias trial had been manic and she had hardly had a night's sleep, let alone an opportunity to put her records in order.

She tried to work. She pulled up several unfinished documents, moved some files around on her desktop, flipped through her scribbled notes, but she couldn't concentrate. At the back of the cupboard, to her right, the Martin Papers called to her.

Damn it, shut up!

There would be no harm in just taking a peek, surely? Taking the papers down and sifting through them, like she used to. Rearranging the order, indexing them. Maybe she'd missed something? There had to be more to his life than just the dreary, parochial existence she had found. Something that made him more three-dimensional, but what was she looking for? A worthier nemeses? Was that it? *What does that make me?*

She had told herself this morning that she would burn the damn papers tonight, but she'd forgotten to buy matches.

She got off her chair, opened the cupboard and removed the first file. She spread the papers out on her bed, gently running her fingers over the pages, knowing intimately what each one contained.

Nothing. It contains empty space.

'Georgie?'

She looked up, startled. She hadn't heard Li come in.

'Sorry – what?'

'Stir-fry's kind of ready. Hope you like vegetables that are well done.'

Chapter 19

By six o'clock that evening, Priest had examined the contents of his wardrobe several times but found nothing more appealing than the dark jeans, white shirt and suit jacket he already had on. *I'll stick with that.*

He was experiencing an unfamiliar sensation. One that he supposed might be associated with his nerves. *Put me in front of a circuit judge and tell me I have five minutes to prepare a case I've never seen before and present it, and I'd be fine. So why are my hands trembling slightly about the prospect of an evening with a woman I've already slept with?*

It was a question he thought he might know the answer to but it scared him to admit it.

He inspected the lionfish tank. Orwell and Hemingway were hiding behind Sarah's plastic castle. 'Probably best you two stay there,' he mumbled. 'Doubt this is going to be easy to watch.' Colonel Stinky, who he had let Tilly name, had taken a keen interest in Priest's preparations and was drifting around at the front of the tank. Either that or he was hungry.

He watched them for a while, as he often did in times of deep rumination. *We've been through a lot together, these fish and I.* In his darkest moments, after William's fall from grace, when Priest's connection with life was at its most fragile, the lionfish had been there; a calming, non-judgemental energy. He found it relaxing just to be near them. Hell, they were a lot better company than most people.

He was flipping through a playlist on his iPod trying to decide what music Jessica might like when the doorbell rang. *Shit, she's early.* He quickly settled on a live Crowded House album that he judged to be inoffensive and went to open the door wishing sincerely that he had never suggested this whole ridiculous idea.

But it wasn't Jessica Ellinder who greeted him on the other side.

'*Elinor?*'

She was wrapped up in a long cream-coloured coat, with an impish expression on her face, her head cocked to one side. That was something she did, he had noticed. Cock her head in that purposeful way.

'Can I come in?' she asked in a tone that was verging on childlike.

Priest hesitated – he had no wish to be rude but equally no desire to be hospitable, either. Notwithstanding the mild inconvenience she presented in view of Jessica's imminent arrival, he had hoped not to be reminded of the Elias case disaster, if only for a few hours.

'Actually, it's not entirely convenient right now—'

She pushed past him anyway and wandered into his kitchen. *Fuck it, come on in, why don't you?*

'I'm sorry.' She spoke to him over her shoulder in what she clearly must have realised was an overdramatic stance. 'I didn't know what else to do.'

'How did you get my address?' he asked, walking around the kitchen island to avoid having to talk to her back.

'I'm an investigative journalist,' she said by way of explanation.

He was mildly irritated by her already. 'How can I help you, Elinor?'

'Aren't you going to offer me a drink?'

'I don't have time for this.'

She shrugged; made a face like it was his loss and slipped off her coat. She was wearing a low-cut knee-length red dress that would have made her look overdressed at most presidential balls, let alone Priest's kitchen. He had anticipated asking her to leave. Telling her that her visit was compromising for her and she ought to cut it short before . . . *before what?* But, staring at the way that dress caressed her slim figure, he couldn't find the words.

'I just want to talk,' she said softly. 'This whole thing – finding that dead man in my car – I feel . . . violated. It was like my university stalker all over again. You understand, don't you?'

'Don't take this the wrong way,' said Priest. 'But, I don't know you and I've got no idea whose side you're on.'

She laughed and took a step closer to the island, leant over and rested her chin on her hands playfully. Priest resisted the temptation but he knew if he looked down – as she surely wanted him to – he'd see that pink bra again.

'I want to see Alexia Elias go down just as much as you do,' she said.

'Why? What has she done to you?'

'I just have a very strong moral sense.'

'Not a common disposition that. For a reporter, I mean.'

'OK, fine.' She straightened up and shrugged her shoulders. 'When I was young, my school was collecting money for the Elias Foundation and my mother refused to give me anything to take in. I guess at the time I was too young to recognise how out of character this was but over the years I noticed that she always avoided that charity. Once I overheard her talking to Dad about them, saying the Eliases were crooks, criminals even. I was shocked. She's always been such a forgiving, gentle person and yet here she was with nothing but disdain for a children's charity. Dad, too. He hid it better but I could tell they both had a problem with it. So when I was looking for a story to cover, the Turkish scandal was in full swing and that all came together. I started looking into it – I even went to Ankara and spoke to people there. And I believe that Alexia Elias is up to her neck in it.'

'You've got evidence?'

She faltered, brushed her hair away from her face. 'No, but *you* do. Or did . . . until . . .'

'Until Simeon turned up dead in the back of your car.'

Fox looked down, drew in her lips. 'That's right.'

'So, this is some kind of quest for justice?' said Priest, unconvinced.

Fox narrowed her eyes; the flirting was evidently over. 'You're better than that, Charlie. Don't lower yourself to using cynicism as a defence. We both have a common goal. Why don't we join forces?'

'I let you tag along to Simeon's flat, didn't I? What more do you want?'

'Whatever you do next, I want to be there.'

'How do I know I can trust you?'

'Seen the news lately? Not exactly overwhelmed with talk of a dead witness in a high-profile libel case, is it?'

She had a point. The latest round of North Korean economic sanctions and some boy band split were the only current news topics of interest. So far, nothing about the libel trial, or Simeon's murder.

'Look,' she said, 'if not collaboration then at least cooperation. What do you say?'

She cocked her head to one side again – she never seemed to blink.

'What exactly do you mean?' asked Priest.

'Information sharing. You know, you show me yours and I'll show you mine.' She delivered the line with so much saccharin that Priest found himself cringing. He realised he needed to end this. Jessica would be here soon – he had better things to do.

'I'm really not sure.'

She huffed, feigning disappointment. 'That's too bad. I guess you'll just have to work out who the boy in the picture is, all on your own.'

Priest waited but she didn't expand. She just kept leaning over his kitchen table looking at him with her large, brown eyes and running her fingers with her hair. In any other situation, at any other time, in any other place, Priest felt his self-control might not have been so robust. As much as he didn't want to admit it, the prospect of reaching out and touching the soft white skin of her bare arms was tantalising. *Would it really matter if I did?*

'You know who it is?' he asked.

'Yes.'

'How?'

'I've been investigating the Elias Foundation for years – I told you. There's no secret they can hide from me.'

'Alexia and Dominique Elias are childless,' Priest pointed out.

She smiled again. She had perfect teeth, he noticed. 'Nothing escapes you, does it?'

'Who is it?'

She laughed, but didn't move. Just watched him, like a predator, as Priest leant back against the side, arms folded.

'As if I'm going to tell you that easily,' she whispered.

'Then how does this game work?' Priest spoke through gritted teeth. A man was dead, and she was teasing him.

'It's simple,' she said. 'I've written the name down on a piece of paper and I've put it in one of my hands. You've got to guess which one.'

She offered her clenched hands to him across the island, just out of reach. Priest studied them but he was beginning to feel angry. He didn't like being toyed with, and Fox clearly couldn't give a damn about Simeon. He should end this. *But if I can guess right . . .*

'Did I mention that you have to do this by touch alone?' she breathed.

Priest checked the clock on the oven – half an hour until Jessica arrived. Fox had leant further across the kitchen island with her fists outstretched and her head raised, lips apart, eyes wide. He couldn't reach her from here. What she wanted was obvious.

Priest didn't think about it any further. He knew if he did he would come to his senses. He walked around the back of the island. She watched him part of the way but didn't turn around when he was out of sight. Instead she straightened her neck in a very feline way, and waited.

He stood behind her and saw how the dress fitted perfectly across the arch of her back, showing off the slenderness of her figure, and finished just above her knees. He leant across. Brushed his hands past her waist – she reacted to his touch, stiffening. He ran his fingers down her arms; watched as the tiny hairs began to rise. She exhaled roughly and whispered in his ear, 'Be gentle with me.'

Priest cupped his hands around hers, ran his thumb across her knuckles, pressed against her, breathed in her scent; the sweet smell of her perfume across her neck. His groin reacted as she pushed back, rubbing her body on his until she turned her head towards him and their lips almost touched.

'Enough playing games,' she rasped. 'Don't you have a bed in this flat of yours?'

Priest smiled, moved his hands back up her arms. 'Mm. I do.'

She laughed. 'Oh, thank fuck.'

'We won't be needing it, though.'

'What have you got in mind?'

'Nothing.'

Priest let go. Extracted himself from her. She made to say something but there was no sound – her eyes flitted sideways in confusion.

'What?' she stuttered.

'There's no need,' he said, holding up the piece of paper he had dispossessed her of. 'I guessed the right hand.'

Her face changed in a beat from sickly sweet to rage. 'You . . . !'

What she had planned to say next was unlikely to be a complimentary remark about Priest's sleight of hand but he would never know the exact words because she was interrupted by a deliberate cough coming from the corner of the room.

'Am I interrupting anything?'

Priest looked up, feeling it was now his turn to be startled. Jessica stood leaning against the wall, arms folded. She didn't look angry, or even surprised. If anything, she appeared insouciant.

'Jess—'

'The door was open so I let myself in. Please accept my apologies for being early,' she said, without a trace of humour.

Elinor straightened her hair but didn't look at the other woman. Instead she fixed Priest with a virulent stare.

'This isn't over,' she said, before marching out of the flat and slamming the door behind her. Priest hastily stuffed the paper Elinor had had into his pocket. Jessica was looking at him, not saying anything. *Probably need to choose my next words carefully.*

'It's not what it looks like,' he said, realising how banal that sounded before the words even left his mouth.

'And what do you think it looks like?' she asked.

Priest clicked his tongue. 'Probably didn't look good.'

'That's something we can agree on.'

'I can—'

'Save it,' she interrupted, turning away. 'It was a mistake coming here anyway.'

The door to Priest's penthouse slammed for a second time.

Chapter 20

Georgie sat crossed-legged on her bed, opposite Li, a bowl of burnt stir-fry in her hand.

Li passed her a pair of chopsticks. 'I thought it would be fun if we used these.'

Georgie took the chopsticks and examined them carefully before trying to pick at a piece of carbon-coated chicken – if indeed it was chicken.

'Good thinking.'

Li wedged a heap of food into her mouth and chewed laboriously. 'Wow. It's not that great, is it?'

No, it's awful. But right then Georgie felt nothing but affection for her flawed housemate and her useless cooking, so she scooped as much as she could on the chopsticks and tried to make it look as though she was enjoying it. 'Li, it's delicious. Really good.'

'You're a fucking awful liar,' Li laughed through mouthfuls.

They ate in silence for a short while; Georgie was conscious that her floor was strewn with the Martin papers. She hoped Li couldn't work out what they were but by the way she kept peering at them out of the corner of her eye, she doubted it.

'You want to talk about it?' Li said in the end.

Georgie looked at the half-eaten bowl; her appetite dissipated almost immediately. She knew Li was right – she did need to talk about it. But she had never said it out loud, never admitted what had happened to anyone. Her guilt and shame had kept it buried. Until recently, she had pretended it had happened to someone else, and her obsession with Martin had been . . . what? On that person's behalf?

'It was a long time ago,' Georgie said quietly.

'So? What difference does that make?'

A fair point. 'It wasn't . . . you know. It wasn't like I hadn't asked for it.'

'What do you mean?' snapped Li, and Georgie was taken aback by her tone. '*It wasn't like I hadn't asked for it.*'

'I just mean . . . Oh, for heaven's sake, Li.' Georgie felt as though she was welling up. 'We were on a night out. We all came back, we were all a little tipsy. I wanted him to kiss me. I wanted him to touch me. I just . . . wasn't ready for him to touch me *in that way*.'

'And you told him no?'

'Yes, I told him no. I was very clear.'

'It's not your fault, sweetie.'

Georgie wiped away a sudden tear. She put the bowl down beside the bed. *Why did you have to bring it up?* But to her surprise, Li was suddenly next to her, holding her, stroking her hair, like her mother used to when she was little. It was ridiculous, but in those few moments of comfort, Georgie forgot herself and sobbed gently in Li's arms.

'You still sleep with the light on, don't you?' asked Li gently.

Georgie nodded. She was terrified of the dark – terrified of what had happened in the dark and what could happen again.

It was completely irrational, she knew that. But she still slept with the light on anyway.

'It's OK,' Li whispered. 'It's OK. It wasn't your fault, Georgie. You mustn't ever think otherwise.' And then Li said in a hardened voice that Georgie barely recognised. 'We can put this right, you and me, can't we? We can put this right.'

*

In darkness, the owner sat in a grey high-back chair in the corner of the pebble-dashed house.

There was a scratch mark on the owner's arm that ran from elbow to hand. An angry, red gauze over split skin.

The owner waited and, when the time was right, flicked on a reading lamp that sat on a large metal safe to the side of the chair and picked up the red folder.

The key was weighty. Some of the pages were torn and dog-eared but they were all neatly packaged in clear plastic wallets, arranged back to back. The owner turned towards the middle. Some of the owner's favourite entries were there where the diary's author veered into an abstract world of dreams and imagination.

The owner hovered over one particular entry and read it, although it was already intimately familiar.

The girl sits cross-legged, staring up at the door. She wears the expression of a child much older than her eleven or so years. A long, endless look through large doe eyes that have seen too much and cried too little. A look that makes you wonder: is she the haunted, or the ghost?

She moves quickly, like the wind changing direction. She slides a bruised arm under the bed and pulls out a book.

The front cover is worn, the pages are creased. The colours are old and faded like the memories the girl has of her time in the basement. She has trouble remembering things now. She tells herself that there is no room in her head to remember things; there is only hate.

She reads the title of the book and her head clears a little. Fairy Tales for Girls. The girl doesn't know much about life outside the basement but she knows that the book is from a different time to now; she finds this a curious comfort.

She turns the page and for a short moment her mind is filled with images of freckled princesses and fairy godmothers waving wands, genies granting wishes and handsome princes climbing castle walls to rescue fair maidens. She cannot read many of the words but some of them are known to her. Apple. Castle. The wolf.

Dream.

Snow.

Evil.

The girls are all the same in the book. They all have long, flowing hair, bright blue eyes and waists so slim that they dissolve into nothing at all. The girl checks her own waist. She cannot reach her fingers all the way around so they meet comfortably like the woman tells her she ought to, but the distance is short and, if she breathes in, she is more or less there.

The woman is not like the fairy godmother in the book, the girl knows this. Sometimes the woman pretends to be. She tells the girl she is not her mother, and the girl is not her responsibility and she wants to help the girl. But she never does. The next day, the woman is cold and distant.

Sometimes, the girl can hear the woman and the man talking.

There is a vent at the foot of the wall the size of a letter box. There must be some system of pipework in the wall connected to another room because, when the wind is still, the girl can hear the man and woman's muffled voices drift through to the room. If she places her ear right against the vent, she can just about make out their conversation.

The girl shuts the book – the vent is calling to her. She can hear them. She gets down on all fours like a cat stretching in the sun. Listens. The sound is faint and she has no idea where it comes from – it might as well be from another world.

'You're drinking too much,' says the woman's voice, unsteady.

'What does it matter?' the man replies.

'You're a liability.'

He coughs and splutters. Calms. Rasps, 'There's no one for miles. What we do in here is our business.'

She snorts. There is silence for a while, except a shuffling sound, like paper being moved around. Then she says, 'Someone will come looking for her one day, you know.'

'No. They won't.'

'How can you be so sure?'

The girl holds her breath. They mean her – they're talking about her. It is the first time she has heard them talk about her, acknowledge her.

Her heart skips a beat.

'Because her bitch of a mother had no one, and now she's dead,' he says. 'No one knows the girl exists. And she doesn't. Exist, I mean.'

'She's real enough when I go and see her.'

'Well then let her out!' he shouts, angry. The girl pulls away, startled. 'Open the door and watch her leave if you're so fucking bothered.' There is silence for a short while. 'No. Not that easy, is it?'

There is silence for a moment. The girl strains to hear.

'There are others, aren't there.' She says it quietly. Her voice is laced with venom.

He is indignant, retorts instantly: 'What do you mean?'

'You know what I mean. Others.'

'If you're unhappy, leave. You're free to walk out, anytime.'

She says softly, 'You're sick.'

He chuckles. 'Really? You get your own reward, it isn't just me.'

'What do you mean by that?'

'You know what I mean.' There's something unpleasant about his voice. The girl feels that she is short of breath, her throat tightens. 'You like watching.'

'You sick fucking . . .'

He interrupts her. His booming voice wipes out her protest and, although the girl doesn't fully understand what he means, she knows that he is right.

'You like watching. You think I don't know, but you sit at the top of the stairs and look round the corner like a little fucking peeping Tom. You like watching. If I'm wrong, then let her go.'

The girl takes a short intake of breath in the reticence that follows.

Then, satisfied, he snarls, 'No. Didn't think so.'

The owner exhaled. Scratched across the gauze and cut deeper into the wound. Soon it would be time. Years of waiting were drawing to a close.

Soon, the world would know the truth.

Chapter 21

It was Sunday morning and London was covered in a thin layer of frost. Apparently, the shoppers outside of Priest's penthouse hadn't been deterred by the cold and were scurrying around from shop to shop, bags and kids in tow, cramming their baskets with the latest fragrance from Chanel or a new gadget from Apple; all of which would be out of fashion by the time they got home.

Priest was thinking. He pulled himself away from the window and went into the bathroom. Studied himself in the mirror and was drawn to the bags under his eyes, which were as dark as his mood.

When Jessica had stormed out of his flat last night, a realisation had dawned on him. He wanted to be with her. He had had a taste of the rapture she had enveloped him in and he wanted more. Now he felt adrift, like a boat with its anchor line cut, helplessly bobbing on the water.

Fuck, fuck, fuck!

He struck the mirror with his fist, hard. The glass exploded instantly, crystal-like shards rained down on to the sink, then to the floor underneath. A jagged section remained stuck to the wooden frame; half of his distorted face stared back.

He inspected his hand. The skin was broken around the knuckle, and it throbbed painfully. He spent some time cleaning up the mess, wrapping the shards of broken glass in old newspaper before binning them.

He went upstairs to the rooftop garden, oblivious to the cold, and lit a cigarette. His phone rang. *Fuck off, whoever you are.* He answered it anyway.

'What?' he coughed through the cigarette smoke.

'Priest – you OK?' It was Okoro.

'Fine. Woke up with a headache, that's all.'

Okoro made a noise, like he didn't believe him. 'I'm sitting here trying to draft out some submissions for Her Honour Judge Peters's indulgence tomorrow morning explaining why we want an adjournment and I don't have anything positive to say other than we think Simeon Ali is dead.'

'We don't think he's dead. He *is* dead.'

'Peters is a bitch, Priest. She might just say if he's dead and our case hinges on his evidence then that's it – pack up and go home. *The Real Byte* to pay Elias's costs, subject to whatever the insurers have to say. She might even question if a fair trial can take place.'

'I'll appeal her.'

'Sure you will,' said Okoro. 'But do you think our clients have the stomach for that? Doubt the insurers will want to back it.'

Priest swore again under his breath. He knew Okoro was right. And what was an adjournment going to achieve anyway? Delay the inevitable – Elias had already won. He could see Alexia Elias's smug face in his mind's eye.

'Simeon was murdered,' Priest exhaled. 'The defence want time to understand the circumstances surrounding his death and to evaluate the merits of their position in light of it. Go with that for now.'

Okoro sighed in a way that suggested he was unimpressed. 'All right. I'll try that.'

Priest hung up, pressed the half-smoked cigarette into an ashtray on the patio table and went back down to the kitchen. He rummaged around in the cupboards and found a tin of pea soup, which he poured into a pan and started to heat on the hob. It would suffice for breakfast this morning.

He sat down with the soup and took out the piece of paper he had extracted from Elinor last night and placed it next to the bowl. On the other side, he placed the photograph of the mysterious boy. He had read Elinor's note over and over again last night. Just two names, father and son. Now, he was convinced that she was probably right, although he remained sceptical of her intentions. The boy shared the same reptilian jawline and sunken eyes as his father. Even the mulish way he stood bore a similarity.

Alexia and Dominque Elias had never had children. Not together. But this boy was sure as hell Dominique's product.

'Hello, Julian,' Priest muttered. 'Now where do you fit into all of this?'

*

Okoro took a generous gulp of coffee and stared at the blank computer screen, dejected. His fingers hovered over the keyboard but he felt devoid of inspiration. It was all very well pleading for an adjournment but, even if Peters was feeling charitable and gave it to them, *The Real Byte* would be ordered to pay Elias's wasted costs. Hagworth's brief fee alone would exceed fifty thousand.

The insurers aren't going to like that.

Simeon Ali had been murdered, but that wouldn't necessarily stop the wheels of justice from turning. Not unless it was Alexia Elias who had murdered him, or someone acting on her instructions. That situation was not without precedent. In a 2006 case, the Court of Appeal granted an application to strike out a defence on the basis that the defendant had murdered the claimant.

But the notion that Alexia Elias was somehow involved with Simeon's murder was surely preposterous.

The door to Okoro's study opened and a bright-eyed teenage girl appeared. Her hair was braided in tight cornrows and she wore a grey Nike vintage crew shirt and black leggings. Faith Okoro had her father's penetrating stare but otherwise she had inherited her mother's sharp looks which meant, much to Okoro's chagrin, that her ambition of being a part-time model to fund her medical degree was very achievable.

'Mama says are you going to be working all day because she's forgotten what you look like?' said Faith, trying to hide her grin.

Okoro heard Winifred's voice drift across from the living room. 'Tell him I will just get myself a new man!'

'Mama says—' Faith began.

'Yes, I heard what Mama said.' Okoro held up his hand. 'Another man. Tell her good luck finding one.' Faith raised an eyebrow. 'OK, fine. Tell her I'll be another hour, two at most.'

Faith shook her head. 'Your funeral. Is it the trial, Daddy?'

'Just a few problems, that's all. It's a big case – news was all over it on Friday.'

'Nothing that you and Charlie can't put right, surely.'

Okoro looked at her thoughtfully – like him, Faith always had an agenda, even if it was nothing more complicated than mischief, and the sparkle in her eye was clear enough to him. 'No doubt.'

'Hm.' Faith smiled. 'Perhaps when it's all over Charlie can come and have dinner with us for once.'

'Faith—' Okoro said warningly.

'He can sit next to me and . . .'

'That's enough,' Okoro jested and he made to lecture her but was interrupted by his phone ringing. He checked the caller display and groaned inwardly. 'I've got to take this.'

She blew him a kiss and withdrew from the room.

Okoro put the phone to his ear. 'Hagworth,' he sighed.

'Okoro?' Hagworth's voice crackled over the line – Okoro had an image of him sitting in a tartan chair listening to the wireless while trying to work out how to make a phone call. 'Okoro, is that you?'

'Yes. What do you want?'

'I wonder whether we could talk without prejudice, old chap?'

Old chap? Who the hell does he think he is? 'Whatever.'

'Your people are in a spot of bother, don't you think? I take it Mr Ali isn't turning up?'

Okoro sneered. *Here he comes – as predictable as ever.* 'There's still time,' Okoro growled, stalling.

'Of course it upsets my client greatly to be in this position – we would have much rather have won fair and square, after disproving Mr Ali's evidence. But surely there's nowhere for you to go now, is there?'

'There's always places for me to go, Hagworth. Your client's witness statement looks like a crock of shit for one thing.'

'Oh, come on, Okoro. No one wins a libel trial by cross-examination alone. You're good, I'll give you that. But you're not *that* good.'

Okoro realised he was scribbling on a pad next to him, ripping up the paper with his pen. 'What's your offer, Hagworth? Get it over with.'

He could hear Hagworth chuckle down the line. 'Well, look. Horse-trading isn't my usual style – I haven't managed to speak to my client about this. In fact, I haven't been able to get hold of her since Friday so don't take this as an offer but a point to discuss with your clients. All I ask is that your clients make amends by publishing a retraction and apology, you pay our costs and we settle damages at, say, a mere hundred thousand. What do you say?'

'I say we'll take our chances,' Okoro said, seething.

'Oh dear, no, Okoro. We both know you're obliged to take instructions first and I suspect, in light of the circumstances, your clients are feeling particularly vulnerable. In more ways than one, wouldn't you say?'

Okoro stopped tearing the pen through the pad. *What did he just say?* 'What do you mean by that?'

'Take instructions, Okoro. I'll be on this number.'

Hagworth hung up and Okoro was left holding the phone, the dial tone buzzing in his ear – the dull white noise seemed to epitomise the bleakness of the situation, and was punctuated only by the sound of Okoro's pen snapping in his hand.

Chapter 22

Priest backed the Volvo out of its space outside his apartment block, hit the accelerator and spun out into the main road narrowly missing a black cab, whose driver hit the brakes and the horn with equal rancour.

Sorry, pal.

He took the bus lane most of the way through Holborn despite the cameras and headed west. It was Sunday morning and the traffic was light – mostly taxis and white vans interspersed with the occasional family saloon or people carrier. This time of the week, the pavements were more congested than the roads.

Waiting at the lights he punched Jessica's number into his phone. There was no reply at the other end save for the answerphone, which kicked in after a couple of rings. *She cut me off!*

'Jessica,' he said into the phone cautiously. 'I just thought that we ought to talk. Call me.'

He knew she wasn't going to call him – not today at least. *I wouldn't call me if I were her.*

The light went green and a trickle of cars filtered through onto Charing Cross Road. *No wonder this city grinds to a halt so easily when people are so bloody slow to react to a green light!*

He found Georgie's number and rang that. Unlike his previous call, this was answered with considerable enthusiasm.

'Hi, Charlie!'

'Georgie? Are you dressed?' He hadn't meant that to sound sleazy but it came out wrong and he heard a moment's hesitation at the other end of the line. 'I mean, are you up?'

'Yes! Been up for hours. I don't sleep well.'

'Me neither. Grab your coat – I'll be outside your flat in a few minutes. We're going for a ride.'

*

Georgie had been partially truthful. She was up but she had still been sitting in bed reading when Charlie had called. What occurred next was a furious transformation out of a pair of Charlie Brown pyjamas (a present from her mum she could not bear to part with) into a pair of jeans, white top and a brown body warmer. She grabbed her phone and stuffed a purse into one of the body warmer's pockets. According to Li, it was a hideous garment that made her look like Dora the Explorer but its redeeming feature was an array of deep pockets which meant she didn't need to carry a bag.

She was standing outside her flat waiting for Charlie in six minutes flat. The Volvo pulled up onto the kerb and she hopped in the passenger seat; a wave of heat from the inside of the car hit her. When she closed the door, she felt suffocated by it.

'It's like a sauna in here,' she said.

'The heating's broken,' Charlie explained. 'Just open the window a bit.'

Georgie found that the window was operated by a crank mechanism below the door handle.

'Why don't you use the other car?' she asked, poking her head out the window to inhale fresh air. 'You have an Aston Martin.'

'This was William's car. He could have bought whatever he wanted but he preferred this for some reason I'll never understand. I promised him I'd look after it until he gets out so I keep it running so it doesn't rot in a garage somewhere.'

Georgie looked at him uncertainly. 'William isn't likely to get out soon, is he?'

Priest laughed. 'Doctor William Priest is one of the most prolific serial killers London has seen since Jack the Ripper. He's also clinically insane. He's never getting out.'

'Then why . . . ?'

'Because I promised him I would.'

Georgie breathed in but decided against asking any more questions about Charlie's personal life. It always seemed like trespassing. Instead she stole a sideways glance at his profile – watched his strong jawline and unshaven face for a moment while he concentrated on the road, eyes dead ahead. *You won't ever break that promise, will you.*

'Where are we going?' she asked.

'I discovered that the boy in the photograph we found at Simeon's hideout is Julian Greenwood. He's ten years old and the son of Dominique Elias. He's standing outside Dominique and Alexia's former home.'

Georgie gasped. 'How did you find that out?'

'That's a long story but I had a bit of help.'

'Dominique and Alexia can't have children, if you listen to idle gossip.'

'*Alexia* can't have children. This is Dominique's kid. I've no idea who the mother is yet.'

Georgie shifted in her seat. She wondered whether *the help* Charlie was referring to was Elinor Fox. If it was, then she didn't trust the information.

'So, we're going to the house in the picture?'

'It's in Norfolk. So sit back and relax.'

There was a buzzing noise and they both felt around their pockets. It turned out to be Priest's phone. He answered it and kept driving with one hand. Georgie did a quick sweep of the road in front and behind for police although that didn't seem to have occurred to Charlie. She caught only one side of the conversation:

'Hi, Tiff . . . I'm doing great . . . Me? Not much. Just going to the gym, actually . . . No of course I wouldn't be looking into Simeon's death, that's your job . . . Of course I'd tell you if I had anything . . . Honestly, Tiff, you'd be the first to know . . . No . . . I can't talk to the claimant, Tiff, you know that. Professional etiquette and all that bollocks . . . Really? How long? Interesting . . . I'm sure we can meet tomorrow, just text me a time later . . . OK, see you.'

Charlie clicked his tongue, something Georgie had noticed he generally did at the point of some revelation or other manifesting itself.

'What?'

'That was Rowlinson,' Priest reported. 'He was trying to get hold of Alexia Elias to talk to her about Simeon's murder. Turns out the husband hasn't seen her since Friday although he doesn't seem too bothered; apparently she's prone to going AWOL when she's stressed.'

'A bit strange, though, don't you think?'

He pulled a face. 'Maybe.'

'Do you think Alexia is somehow involved in Simeon's death?'

He appeared to give the question considerable thought before he remarked, 'I think she has an awful lot to gain from it.'

They headed north to the M11; the old Volvo rattled over the motorway sleeper line as they pulled out of the slip lane undertaking a convoy of lorries. There was no satnav, just a wooden-panelled glove box, an analogue radio and various other bulky dials and buttons. The temperature was set to cold but the ventilators were still pumping out hot air as if the engine were the very bowels of Hell itself.

Georgie wriggled out of her body warmer.

'There's a map behind my seat,' Charlie told her.

Georgie felt behind him and pulled out an AA Road Map from 2002, complete with dog-eared corners and faded cover. She opened it. For a moment, she froze. *This belongs to William.*

'You're looking for a village called Tome.'

A few moments later Georgie, recovered, settled on the right page. 'Found it.'

'Can you direct me once we get off the motorway?'

'Duke of Edinburgh Gold Award,' she quipped. 'Take the next exit.'

*

Gail Woodbead sat in front of her iPad scanning the internet but so far there was nothing about Simeon's murder. She didn't like to, but she had to give the police credit – they were doing a good job of keeping it out of the papers.

She had slept at Tomas's house for the past two nights – it was easier that way; there was so much to do, so much to talk about. And Andros, her husband of fifteen years, didn't seem bothered. His initial jealously of Gail's relationship with Tomas – which had meandered between professional, social and tactile familiarity over a number of years – had faded.

Tomas lived in a three-story townhouse; he had a couple of spare rooms, one with its own bathroom. He had never married, although there had been girls from time to time. And boys, too. But nothing long term – Tomas's work was too restrictive and the various partners Gail had seen come and go soon realised they would only ever be second best.

As for Gail, the child Andros craved – the one he probably deserved – had so far eluded them and when she had entered her forties an unsaid truth had passed between them: time was nearly up. It was no wonder that he'd hardly batted an eyelid when she went to Tomas's house – it felt like he'd already given up.

She looked across at Karl Jones, sat at a computer screen in the corner of Tomas's living room. He looked like he hadn't slept a wink in days but somehow he was still playing *World of Warcraft*. It was a ridiculous game, but she felt slightly envious. At least Jones had his escapism. She wished she could replicate it for herself. Somehow, by immersing himself in a pixel-generated fantasy world, Jones had managed to forget that the magazine – and all their careers – was on the brink of extinction.

Or maybe he just wasn't clever enough to work it out.

Gail had been *The Real Byte*'s managing editor for five years. She had been sucked into Tomas Jansen's infectious enthusiasm, his rebellious ideology, his own unique brand of socialism. From Anonymous to the KKK, nothing escaped *The Real Byte*'s satirical eye; the blunt commentary had cult following on the internet, but they all knew that Alexia Elias might be the end of them.

Gail closed her hands around a mug of coffee, feeling the heat scald her. She was tired; the trauma of the last twenty-four hours was starting to take its toll.

'Are you still playing that fucking game?' Tomas complained, entering the room with a bowl of something that resembled pasta.

Karl looked round, annoyed. He was rarely with them now, preferring instead to spend time at home but that was hardly surprising. He was a recluse most of the time anyway. Tomas had half-heartedly included Karl in the invitation to stay over but no one had expected him to accept, or take Tomas's advice. *Never take the same route anywhere, never stay in the same place too long, always stick together.* Although exactly what threat Tomas was trying to avoid had never been made clear to Gail. Both Karl and Tomas seemed to be suffering from a severe case of skunk-induced paranoia.

'It takes my mind off this mess we're in,' Karl replied.

'Fucking kids' stuff,' mumbled Tomas.

'Shut up, Tomas,' Gail snapped. 'At least it keeps him quiet. I wish you would find something to occupy *your*self and stop pacing round like a caged lion.'

'A caged lion is exactly what I am.' She caught his eye, but suppressed the urge to shout at him. *Back down, Gail.*

'Then phone Priest,' she offered, quiet. 'Find out what's going on.'

'If he had something then he'd let us know,' Tomas growled, taking a seat opposite her and throwing the bowl of pasta on the table. He leant forward, hands between his legs.

'You're too trusting of the lawyer, Tomas,' she murmured, returning to the iPad screen.

'He's not let us down so far.'

Gail sighed, swiping her hand across the screen with forced vigour. Priest wasn't *that* good. He talked the talk well, but it would take a miracle to rescue the magazine now. A deal with an American publishing house had fallen through because of the trial already. The advertising revenue was short term; it would soon dry up. They were on borrowed time. Tomas might seem to be taking the pressure well on the surface, but she had seen him crack before. She knew his temper would one day get the better of him. The man was like a pot of perpetually simmering water, liable to boil over at any time.

Gail shivered at the thought.

A few minutes of silence passed before Tomas erupted again. 'I can't stand this! Why doesn't he ring? Simeon was murdered, our *friend* was murdered. We should be publishing this, not living in fear of it.'

'Is that all you can think about?' said Gail. '*Publishing* what happened to Simeon?'

Tomas looked at her with distaste. 'You know what I mean.'

She was about to rebuke him when Karl interrupted.

'Do you think the Free People's Army did it?'

Tomas shot him a scathing look. 'Are you a fucking moron?'

Karl turned back to the game, dejected.

Gail shook her head. 'If they did, Karl,' she muttered. 'I guess we'll be next, won't we?'

Chapter 23

Priest pulled the Volvo off the main road down a single-track lane. The car scraped past the overgrown conifers lining the driver's side – the open fields on the other side were enclosed by a low, stone wall and speckled with forlorn-looking sheep. Half a mile back they had meandered through the small village dismally named Tome – it had been nothing more than a few thatched houses, a pub and an unloved church.

'Rural England at its most sickeningly quaint,' Priest remarked under his breath.

He caught an occasional glimpse of the grass escarpment on the other side of the hedgerow which disappeared into the horizon. The Google Earth picture he had checked before they had set off had shown the house to be off this track, but he hadn't been able to identify the access way. He took his foot off the pedal; the car seemed to sigh with relief.

'I thought I saw something,' said Georgie. She was straining across the back of the driver's seat. Priest touched the brake and tried to follow her gaze but all he saw was greenery. 'Pull over.'

He did as instructed and they got out to investigate the seemingly impenetrable wall of green. The contrast between the cold air and the sauna-like atmosphere inside the Volvo was staggering. Priest hastily retrieved his jacket from the back seat. Georgie was pulling on her brown body warmer. It looked functional but hideous.

'It was up there,' Georgie called over her shoulder. Then all of a sudden the hedge seemed to swallow her.

'Georgie?'

Priest went to the space where Georgie had been, but she had vanished. *What on earth?* Priest was about to call out when a hand appeared, took hold of his collar and he suddenly found himself on the other side of the hedge looking at Georgie's grinning face.

'Have you ever seen Jim Henson's *Labyrinth*?' she asked.

'A thousand times. I lent it to Tilly – she loves it. We often watch it together.'

Priest looked up at the house nestled at the crest of the slope. He produced the photograph from his jacket pocket and examined this against the view. It was the same house, all right.

'Julian Greenwood was standing somewhere over there.' Priest indicated to where the incline softened and an unkempt pathway wound its way into the distance. They started to walk upwards.

'If this was Alexia and Dominique's house, why does the picture show Dominique's illegitimate child standing outside it?' asked Georgie. 'You said you thought he lived with his mother.'

'Somebody's trying to make a point,' said Priest. It was something he had presumed from the moment the photograph conveniently fell out of its hiding place, but he'd yet to articulate it out loud.

'You think Julian was taken here against his will?'

'Not necessarily.'

'But he was here, right?'

'Have another look at the photograph.'

Priest handed the picture to her. She studied it carefully, held it up so it was level with the horizon. Moved it around to reconcile the images. Waited for her to work it out. He didn't have to wait long.

'Oh, I see,' she said. She stood roughly in the spot where Julian stood in the photo, measuring the location against a distinctive cluster of clay stone protruding from the grass. 'On the photograph, Julian's shadow pitches forward, towards the camera, suggesting the sun is behind him.'

'Whereas?'

'Whereas the treeline obstructs the lower part of the skyline. At this distance, if the sun was low enough to cast a shadow at the angle in the photo, it would be obscured by the trees. It would be almost overhead by the time the light broke over the treeline.'

'Very good.'

'But couldn't the photograph have been taken in autumn or winter?'

'Nope. They're evergreens, meaning the picture is a fake.'

Georgie handed the photograph back and they resumed their trek up the hillside.

*

When they reached the house, Georgie did her best to hide the fact that she was slightly out of breath. She was slim (like an eel, as her father used to say to tease her), but she wasn't one for going to the gym and she preferred pizza to the protein shakes and bird seed that Li ate all the time. *I swear I'm a fat girl trapped in the body of a gymnast.*

By contrast, Charlie looked like he was strong enough to run up the hill with the house on his back.

'I wonder why the house wasn't sold,' Georgie mused. 'It looks abandoned.'

'Mm. Looks like it could make someone a good project.'

Georgie stood back and stared. The dwelling was typical of Norfolk – a sizeable grey stone-clad rectangular box with boarded-up white windows and as many chimneys as bedrooms. The walls were suffocated with vines that reached as high as the red-tiled roof. The facade was filthy – the vines had weaved into the house itself, trespassing through the boards across the windows and out of the cracks in the walls: the impression was of a house in an advanced state of dilapidation. It reminded Georgie of a much grander adaptation of a cheap holiday home her parents had rented for a weekend when she was a child. They had said that the coastal air would be good for her pale complexion but she had spent all the time in her bedroom writing a play. *The Penitent Goldfish: A Romantic Comedy*. She had never finished it.

They were on high ground. Behind the house, the terrain slipped away and became marshland before finally reaching the murky strip of North Sea a mile or so away. There were fishing boats in the marshes, resting on their side, but Georgie couldn't tell whether they were wrecks or just waiting for the tide.

'What now?' she asked.

Charlie didn't reply at first. He tried the handle of the front door, which came off in his hand. It looked as though he was considering putting his shoulder to it but then he felt around the void left by the broken door handle. Evidently, he found a latch. The door creaked open.

'Now we take a tour,' he said.

Inside, the hallway comprised bare floorboards and peeling, cream wallpaper. Birds had been nesting in the little alcoves above them and the floor was covered in their mess. A mildewed smell hung in the air. Georgie felt her heart rate quicken as she stepped over the threshold into the gloomy entrance, flinching as the floorboards groaned underneath her tread.

They found a lounge area shrouded in darkness. A musty suite covered in sheets was slowly disintegrating in the corner and a dresser sat across the back wall. There were a table and four chairs in the dining room in front of a set of faded curtains. It was eerily quiet: just the occasional gull calling in the distance.

'It's like they just got up and walked out,' Georgie said, opening the dresser drawer and finding a scattering of stained cutlery.

Charlie tried the light switch but there was no power.

'What are we looking for?' asked Georgie.

'I've no idea. There must be something. Simeon wanted us to come here.'

'You think he faked the photograph?'

Charlie didn't reply, and Georgie didn't press it. They examined each room methodically but it was the same story – dust, grime, frail furniture and bird shit. Upstairs was equally uninspiring. The master bedroom featured a blackened mattress that looked like something out of a horror film but, other than some curious scorch marks on the walls, nothing of any apparent significance.

'Clear your mind,' Priest advised. 'Don't look for clues, don't look for evidence. Look for anomalies. Anomalies can become clues and clues can become evidence. In that order only. Work it like a crime scene, from left to right.'

She was tense, the stillness of the house was oppressive, but she was determined not to let her anxiety show. 'That's how you do mazes: working along the left wall, you always eventually get to the middle.'

'Same principle here, Someday.'

Georgie agreed. She knew that while she had trained in the law she had only been properly taught about evidence and investigation when she joined Priest & Co. At university, they taught you it was all about the law. In the real world, it was almost always all about the evidence.

After an hour or so, they reconvened in the hallway.

'It's just an empty house,' Georgie said, disappointed. 'The only thing of interest is the furniture they left behind.'

'Mm. Is it?' Charlie was distracted, feeling the underside of the pinewood desk that sat askew next to the lounge entrance.

Georgie shrugged. 'Yes. It is.'

She turned away, towards the front door. Light was filtering through the broken window, offering only partial illumination. The gulls were louder now, circling excitedly outside. She wondered how long it would be before sunset. She bit her lip. Whether Charlie was with her or not, this was not a house that she wanted to be in when it was dark – it had a fetid feel to it. Like it was alive. A sleeping giant on a hill, waiting for the sun to go down before it woke.

Shivering, she kicked a bundle of twigs and feathers – residue from one of the abandoned nests – and watched as one of the feathers took flight and was abruptly caught in a draught. It twisted and keeled in the air, swept along in an invisible current all the way to the front door.

Curious, she nudged another feather in the same direction with identical results. She bent down and traced the conduit of air back through the hallway opposite to where Charlie was fiddling with the desk, letting the draught flutter against her hand. She stopped when she reached a dust-ridden Welsh dresser.

'We need to move this,' she said, putting her shoulder against the dresser.

'What? Why?'

'Just help me.'

Charlie pulled the dresser sideways, taking Georgie, on the other side, with it. She scrambled to regain her footing before they examined the space left behind.

'I wonder where that goes,' Charlie mumbled.

The door in the wall was smaller than the others, about half the height. When Charlie tried the handle, they found it locked.

'Maybe it's just a cupboard or . . .'

Georgie never finished. She jumped as Charlie took aim and kicked the door at its weakest point. The latch splintered as if it was made of balsa wood and the door swung open revealing a set of stairs descending into the gloom.

'You could have warned me before you did that,' she said.

'Sorry.'

Georgie stared – she couldn't see anything beyond the first three or four steps, the rest was consumed by blackness. A feeling of unease at the darkness below clawed at her chest. The air wafted through, carrying with it a strange smell. An odour that made Georgie's stomach clench.

'I can't go down there,' she whispered. She was nauseous but whether it was the smell or the dark, she wasn't sure. *Probably both*. The room was spinning, the door drifting in and out of focus. She was vaguely aware that Charlie had activated the torch on his phone. Intense light showed that the stairwell turned at a right angle ten or more steps down.

'Stay here,' he instructed. She nodded, knowing that she couldn't have done anything other than stand rooted to the spot even if her life depended on it. *The smell . . . I've smelt that somewhere before . . .*

She watched as Charlie took the stairs one at a time. The light of his torch probed further and further downwards. *If this house is alive, then here is the giant's throat.*

A minute passed in which Georgie felt as though she was going to be sick.

Then Charlie emerged and her head was flooded with relief just to see him, but it was short-lived. He looked spooked, pale and restless.

'Let's go outside,' he said. 'I need to make a phone call.'

Chapter 24

Tiff Rowlinson sat back in the green leather armchair he had been offered and surveyed his three interviewees carefully. They all looked like rabbits caught in the headlights, although the woman was marginally more composed. He got a bad vibe from the leader, Tomas Jansen. He sat unnaturally upright and maintained too much eye contact. They would tell you at the NPIA – the National Policing Improvement Agency – that these were classic signs of a liar, although Priest would have said that was a pack of shit. *We're all liars*, he would say, *just some of us are better than others*.

He was damn right, at least on that point.

'Tell me about Simeon Ali,' he said to no one in particular. He was interested to see if Jansen would act as spokesman.

'What do you want to know?' asked the Dane, right on cue.

'He was a Turkish immigrant who came here to speak the truth,' Gail Woodbead offered. 'He was introverted, timid and kind-natured. He has no family here that we know of. I have no idea what he left behind in Turkey. He was a good man and we trust that you will find his killer and bring him to justice.' She seemed irritated at Rowlinson's presence, which also aroused his suspicion.

He raised an eyebrow. 'Were you and he in a relationship, Mrs Woodbead?'

She snorted loudly. 'Is there something more constructive you can ask?'

Rowlinson raised his hand defensively. 'I meant no offence. But I'm starting from a disadvantage here. I don't know any of you. So the questions might get a little personal, but we're all on the same team here, right?'

'We're all on the same team, DCI Rowlinson.' Jansen nodded convincingly.

Rowlinson noticed that the larger man – Karl Jones – couldn't sink any further into the sofa if he tried.

'Where were you all, please, between midday and four last Thursday?' Rowlinson asked, watching for a reaction. The pathologist had put Ali's death at having taken place between one and three on Thursday afternoon; Rowlinson had given it an hour either side to be sure. 'Let's start with you.' He nodded towards Karl Jones who looked like Rowlinson had stood up and slapped him.

'I was . . .' Karl stared at the floor, presumably he was suffering from a sudden case of amnesia.

'We were all together,' said Gail sharply. 'In conference with our lawyers. The trial started on Friday. We were there from twelve for the rest of the afternoon.'

'Your lawyers are Priest & Co.'

'That's right. We were with Charlie Priest, Vincent Okoro and Georgie Someday the whole time. I hope that removes us from suspicion, Inspector?'

'You were never a suspect, Mrs Woodbead. These are just routine inquiries, but thank you all the same.'

Rowlinson swept a vein of blond hair from his eyes and scribbled down a note about their alibi.

'Can you think of anyone who would want to kill Simeon Ali?' he asked, again to no one in particular.

'Do you mean apart from Alexia Elias?' said Jansen. Rowlinson didn't like the way he narrowed his eyes and screwed up his face.

'Alexia Elias wanted to win her trial against you. Is that a motive to murder someone in cold blood?'

'You tell me, Inspector. She has an awful lot to lose.'

Rowlinson sucked on the end of pen thoughtfully. He was about to ask another question when his phone rang. He looked at the caller ID and answered.

'Priest – what do you want?'

'You mentioned that Alexia Elias hasn't been seen for a few days.' Priest's voice at the other end of the line was uncharacteristically quiet. Rowlinson sat up.

'What of it?'

'I've found her.'

*

Earlier that day, in the pebble-dashed house, the owner had reflected on the previous day's work.

Killing Simeon Ali had been easier than expected, although the owner had never killed anyone before. Simeon was the first. It was not something that the owner could even have contemplated until recently, but needs must, and Simeon had betrayed the owner. He had brought his demise upon himself. He had been given fair warning.

Luring Simeon to the house had been easy. Passing Simeon a glass of water laced with Rohypnol and watching him drink it had been easy. Suffocating Simeon with cling film while he was passed out on the owner's sofa had been draining, leaving the owner exhausted. There was no physical reaction of significance – Simeon's body went limp quickly. But the owner had nearly fainted from the rush of adrenaline.

Killing Alexia Elias had been even more satisfying. Again, the owner had been amazed at how easy it had been to entice the fraud to leave her London residence alone and scurry north to her former home. *How ridiculously naive!* There, the murder had produced a rush that surpassed that which he had experienced when killing Simeon. It appeared that killing someone while they remained conscious was a far more intense experience. It had taken all the owner's strength to finish the job.

The owner had spent many months considering the best way to kill a person. Considering first, that the most efficient way would be to tie wire to a fixed point, loop it around the victim's neck and pull it tight, severing the head with one hard tug. The Indonesian gangsters had perfected that technique in the massacre of communists in 1965, but the concept presented too many logistical complications for the owner, not least of which included the amount of blood and mess that would be made.

In the end, the owner had settled on asphyxia. What better way to destroy a body than to starve it of its most basic necessity, oxygen? The soul is extinguished in the same way that fire is. Although killing had only been the start of the fraud's punishment.

Initially, Simeon's decision not to participate in the exposure of Alexia had been a disappointment. On reflection, the alternative plan was far more fulfilling and had given the owner the opportunity to put into practice the results of months of research and, to tell the truth, the owner may have secretly wanted things to have played out this way.

They would find her soon. The lawyer had purportedly found the picture of Julian standing in front of the old house and would surely make visiting the property a priority. It was important that the lawyer made the discovery. The owner wanted him to see what happens to fraudsters and traitors, dispositions that he was only one step away from. But then, surely he already knew?

The owner breathed deeply, counted to ten. Then returned to the diary.

The door creaks open. The girl smells that sickly, arresting smell. She stiffens, unable to move. She knows what is about to happen: he hasn't been down for days.

She looks over at the wooden doll but she is hiding under the table. Good. She doesn't want the doll to see her.

The girl closes her eyes and thinks of the church spire, just visible beyond the trees. Standing on the boxes, she can see out across the valley and to the top of the church. She finds comfort in this simple image, just an upside-down ice cream cone above a tree. But it makes her calm. It gives her hope.

'Sweetie,' the woman calls. 'Sweetie. Are you dressed, sweetie?'

The girl does not reply but stands and opens her eyes, although the woman cannot see them. She trembles, feels hands around her shoulders and through her hair. Her pigtails are detangled and her hair straightened. It is long, like the princesses in the book, so it covers her back. Make-up is applied to her face, around her eyes, over her lips and cheeks. The girl hates make-up. A bow is tied in her hair and she is

*instructed to stand with her legs wide apart against the wall
and look ahead, into the horizon.*

*'Don't blink, sweetie,' the woman urges. Her grin reminds
the girl of the witch who delivers the apple to Snow White.
'He doesn't like it when you blink.'*

*The girl does as she is asked. She waits. Until the door opens
and the woman leaves. Even when she is alone, she stands
with her arms apart and her fingers straight and tense.*

*She waits, until the door opens again, and as he comes in,
she lets out a small gasp of stale air.*

The owner placed the diary back down and went into the bathroom. Stared into the mirror. The face that stared back was sal-
low and weathered. The owner had observed that most people
grew into their skin, shedding the early pastiness of youth and
burgeoning into adulthood so that their later selves appeared as
mature copies of their former selves. Not so the owner, whose
features had not so much matured but warped into an unrecognisable parody of his younger self, a transformation compounded
by the nose and cheeks, which had been surgically reconstructed
following a car crash four years ago.

The owner felt less like a person who had grown up, and more
like a snake that had shed its skin, only to find that what existed
underneath was an entirely new animal.

No matter. Whatever was on the outside was of little importance. The owner's soul burn fiercely. Soon it would be time. For
justice, for balance to be restored. For redemption. For retribution.

*And when the whole world knows the truth, there will be no
place to hide.*

Chapter 25

The basement of Alexia and Dominque's former home was a miserable red-bricked cavity with a raised section at the bottom of the stairwell which looked out onto a sunken area filled with grey water. It wasn't clear where the flood had come from but Priest wondered if it was the reason why the house had been abandoned.

Rowlinson's team had rigged up an array of floodlights at the bottom of the stairwell that enabled the four SOCO technicians to bustle around Alexia Elias who was laid horizontally across the raised section, her legs dangling in the murky water. Priest stood at the back on the platform next to Rowlinson. There were three people in salopettes wading through the water, including the crime scene manager and the duty pathologist, a wiry man in his late fifties named O'Connell. The water was up to his waist.

'Wherever you are, Priest, dead people spring up,' Rowlinson observed. He was leaning against the wall chewing on something and watching the techs working.

'I'm just lucky I guess,' Priest replied.

They were standing at the foot of the stairwell in a safe zone delineated with chalk. Rowlinson looked at the body. 'What do you think about the face?'

'Unpleasant.'

'Somebody's sent us a message. Or sent *you* a message, perhaps?'

'Uh-huh.'

Rowlinson paused, then said, 'How did you know it was her?'

'That horrible cardigan and she was wearing the same watch in court. It's a Jaeger-LeCoultre. Probably worth ten grand.'

O'Connell had climbed out of the water and knelt down next to the body. He gently turned Alexia's head and for a moment Priest caught a glimpse of her distorted face. *I've never seen anything like that before.* Beside him, Rowlinson was still chewing.

'Tell me,' said Rowlinson. 'How did you find her?' Priest didn't reply but passed Rowlinson the photograph they had found at Simeon's flat. The DCI took it and held it up to the light. Nodded slowly. 'Where did you find this?'

'Simeon's flat.'

'You mean *your* flat, that Simeon Ali rented from you.' Priest didn't reply but watched as O'Connell lifted Alexia's head to allow further pictures to be taken. *One thing's for sure, this improves our chances of getting an adjournment on Monday.*

'Jesus, Priest, I told you to fucking communicate with me.'

'I rang you, didn't I?' Priest pointed out. From the look he received back, he suspected Rowlinson hadn't appreciated his flippancy.

'Where's your bag carrier?'

'Georgie? Giving one of your uniforms a statement outside. I told her to wait in the car after that.'

'The DSI will want me to interview you formally this time around, Priest. You know that, right?'

'Have you come across my ex-wife yet?'

Rowlinson snorted. 'I have bumped into Assistant Commissioner Auckland on two occasions since the beginning of my secondment. On both of those occasions, she pulled a facial expression that suggested she had either eaten something that disagreed with her or, curiously, she wasn't particularly pleased to see me.'

'She probably remembers your appalling best man speech.'

Despite the macabre circumstances, Rowlinson managed a chuckle. 'I'm afraid that my words were rather spoilt by the drink. As I understand it, the objection was my reference to the blonde twins you met on duty when you were still a wooden top and your stiff interrogation of them in the . . .'

Rowlinson tailed off as O'Connell stood and addressed them.

'She's been dead for at least twenty-four hours. First signs of rigor just starting to show,' he said in a guttural voice that Priest suspected had been shredded by decades of cigarette smoke.

'Was she killed here or moved here?' Rowlinson asked.

'Killed here, I'd say. I'll know more when I get her on the slab.'

'What killed her?' asked Priest.

O'Connell looked across at Priest incredulously. 'Pardon me, sir, but who the fuck are you?'

Priest feigned looking hurt. 'I found the body.'

O'Connell looked over at Rowlinson. 'Isn't he a person of interest, then?'

'He's very interesting. Maybe you could answer his question so we can get out of this shit-hole.'

O'Connell hesitated but eventually relented. 'Asphyxiation. There's cling film in the corner of her mouth.'

'Same as Simeon Ali,' said Rowlinson under his breath.

Priest inhaled, deep and slow. Given the connection, it was now clear that they were looking at the same killer. *But what had somebody gained from killing both Alexia and the man who was going to testify against her?*

'What about her face?' Rowlinson asked.

O'Connell wiped his nose on his sleeve. 'Those pictures, Harry.'

One of the SOCO team dressed head to toe in a white coverall passed Rowlinson a set of polaroid photographs of Alexia Elias's head. Rowlinson passed them to Priest, who shuffled through, whistled. From a distance it wasn't clear what had happened but the close-ups showed a terrifying image.

During his time as a major incident detective inspector, Priest was used to seeing the aftermath of violence – more than most senior officers see in an entire career. Widely regarded as an expert on serial killers and having had specialist training in the States, he thought of himself as generally unshockable.

Now, looking at Alexia Elias's mangled face, he concluded that he may have to recalibrate that idea.

'*What the fuck?*' he breathed.

Alexia's mouth had been stitched shut. The thread was thick and blue and the needlework was untidy, leaving a row of engorged sores either side of her mangled lips. Her ears looked like they had been burnt away, as had great chunks of her hair leaving nothing but two fist-sized crusts on either side of her head that resembled molten rock.

There was more. Her eyes were unidentifiable – the shape of the sockets remained roughly intact but the upper part of her face was a bloody mess; a solidified pulp, red and purple like a grotesque mask. A wedge of hair, her chin and nose were the only human aspects of her head left alone and it was only because of these patches of normality that she was recognisable at all.

'What do we think did this?' asked Rowlinson quietly.

'I'm not completely sure, yet,' mumbled O'Connell. 'But best guess at this stage is a blowtorch.'

Chapter 26

For the first hour of the journey back to London, they drove in silence.

When they eventually joined the motorway, Priest glanced over at Georgie. She was leaning against the passenger door, arms folded, staring gloomily out of the window. By the time they had given their statements and watched as Rowlinson's SOCO team had carted Alexia's body away, the sun was hanging low in the sky and their figures cast long, spindly shadows across the driveway.

By the time they left, the putrid smell of death was still in the air at the bottom of the incline.

Priest thought about what words he could use to tell Georgie that everything was going to be OK, but a sentence wouldn't form properly in his head. Even if it had, he doubted he could deliver it with enough conviction. It would have been an obvious lie.

He finally settled on, 'How you doing?'

She sat up. 'Fine. I'm fine. Honest.' She turned and half smiled, although not with her eyes. Priest nodded in return. In that moment he realised: she would never relent. She would never allow what she was feeling to be bigger than her. It was as if all her emotions were carefully compartmentalised into little boxes that could be kept closed at will.

How he envied her.

'You want to get something to eat on the way back?' he suggested. He wasn't hungry and he doubted she was, but it seemed like something he ought to offer.

'I don't mind.'

Priest pulled off the motorway a few miles further on and found himself leading her into a service station cafe beside a small arcade glimmering with flashing lights and pitchy sound bites. They stood in the queue with a couple of thinly filled sandwiches in wrappers on a tray. Priest watched as a black cat leapt from one gambler to another. He closed his eyes, but he could still see the flashing lights at the back of his eyelids. When he opened them, the cat was gone.

Shit, I shouldn't be driving.

He could feel the onset of a turn creeping up on him. *The ghosts are closing in on me.* He remembered the first time it had happened. He was in the park on a summer's day, sitting on the grass, fifteen years old, a bottle of whisky by his side, stolen from his father's study. He could still taste the dreadful first-time burn of the liquid in his throat. People were laughing around him, friends kicking a football, calling out to him to keep goal. But he wasn't listening. He was staring at his hands. Or at least he was staring at *a* pair of hands, which appeared to be attached to his arms but were moving independently. He seemed detached from them. All of a sudden, he was nothing more than a shadow, watching as his body lurched up from the grass, staggered a few yards and vomited into a rose bush.

He glanced over at Georgie. She was examining a chocolate bar. Her hair fell over both shoulders, the artificial light accentuated her soft features. She was lost in her own thoughts, unaware of his observation of her.

'Are you getting that, or not?' he asked.

'Hmm?' She shook herself out of the apparent daydream and offered him another smile, this time with her eyes. It seemed to be her default reaction to him.

'One chocolate bar isn't going to hurt, kid.'

Priest took the bar off her and threw it onto the tray. An old couple further up the queue had managed to count out their bill in pennies. Finally, they shuffled a little further up.

'What happened to her eyes, Charlie?' she asked. When he looked at her for an explanation she went on to say, 'I overheard some of the SOCO men talking about her eyes.'

He sighed and scratched the back of his neck. He felt light-headed, like the slightest breeze might be enough to topple him over. 'Someone took a blowtorch to her face. Burnt her eyes out and most of her face as well and the ears. Then stitched up her mouth.'

'Before or after they killed her?'

Good question. He recalled that O'Connell had offered no opinion about it. 'Don't know. I'll find out from Rowlinson when the post-mortem is due.'

'The three wise monkeys,' Georgie muttered.

He took a moment to register what she had said. 'What?'

'See no evil, hear no evil and speak no evil. Her eyes, her ears and her mouth were all removed.'

Georgie's voice echoed around Priest's head. He closed his eyes and saw the ugly parody that was Alexia Elias's face staring at him. The sound of blood thundering past his ears was deafening and in the background he could see an image of a woman in a red dress walking away from him, auburn hair tied up, her delicate neck partially revealed underneath. *Jessica . . .*

'Hello?'

He opened his eyes. The image drained away. The cashier behind the till was looking at him oddly.

*

Georgie fiddled with her keys and, after what seemed like an age, managed to get her front door open. The hallway was dark but light filtered through under the crack in the door to the right. The muffled sound of classical music drifted past her, a haunting, unhappy melody. *Elgar . . . ? No, more baroque.* She hit the light switch. There was a blue ribbon tied around the handle to the door of Li's room, meaning she had a client with her. One that evidently liked classical music. *Oh, of course, Albinoni – Adagio in G Minor. Strange choice, considering.*

She felt a wave of disappointment – she rarely sought company, preferring to deal with trauma in her own quiet way, but tonight she wanted to talk to Li. About a lot of things. She wanted to tell her about what had happened today, that someone had had their face burnt off with a blowtorch, how she had been there when they had found the body. How the policeman had questioned her account, tested it, probed it for inconsistency. Looked at her sceptically. She wanted to talk about Charlie, about his condition. About how infuriatingly capricious it made him.

Most of all, she wanted to talk to Li about what she had meant when she had said the other night that, 'we can put this right'. Georgie was not vengeful. Is that what Li had meant? That they should get revenge on Martin?

Georgie tiptoed past Li's room and turned on the light in the kitchen. She would stay in here until the client had gone – it was the furthest away from Li's room and Georgie hated hearing the things Li did with her customers.

'We need a cat,' she said out loud.

Yes, a feline companion to make our duo a trio.

She retrieved a bottle of water from the fridge and collapsed into a kitchen chair. Without any real interest in watching, she found the remote control and flicked on the television bracketed to the wall. She channel hopped for a few moments, then stopped. Sat up.

No!

The sound was off but the headline scrolling underneath the BBC News reporter was screaming in Georgie's head: ELIAS FOUNDATION LIBEL WITNESS FOUND DEAD IN CAR BOOT.

*

Priest stumbled through the bedroom door, barely aware of his surroundings and with only the vaguest notion that it was his flat he was tearing through. The bed looked warm and inviting, in stark contrast to the swamp-like basement where the hideous, dead creature had been dumped.

The smell of rot stuck to him. He couldn't get it off.

He half fell onto the bed, sat up against the headboard and scrunched his knees up. He was breathing loudly but he hadn't run anywhere. Had he? He sat still, unable to extinguish the worry that he was bleeding from somewhere but he didn't know where from. The detachment from his body was the ultimate paranoia trip.

There was a commotion in the room next door and Priest froze, every muscle in his body tensed. Someone was in his flat. More than one person. They were here, right next door, getting closer. He couldn't move, even when the door crashed open and took a chunk of skirting board with it, he couldn't move.

Priest saw a man with dark, messy hair and a woman, young and pretty with long slender legs, fall through the open door and scramble onto the bed next to him. They hadn't noticed him, so engrossed were they in each other, their mouths locked together, their arms entwined. Priest knew that he should leave, get off the bed at least, but he couldn't. The man was familiar, the woman too, and yet their animalistic groping suggested they didn't know each other, as the man clumsily straddled her, removing his shirt and starting to unbutton her top.

'I only came round to get my photograph back,' the woman gasped, pinching the skin across the man's biceps.

'It wasn't *your* photograph, and I know what you *really* came for, Elinor,' the man grunted, and his voice sounded like it belonged to Priest.

He felt his erection fighting to be released, a bead of sweat formed on his brow. He felt ashamed, getting off on watching the couple.

The man had unwrapped the woman and she sat up, her long, blonde hair ruffled and glinting in the light as he kissed her chest, felt around her back and removed her bra, ran his tongue over her nipples as she moaned softly.

'Why didn't you fuck me the other night?' she whispered.

He didn't answer, instead he tucked his fingers into the sides of her jeans and pulled them off, pants as well. Priest felt a surge of energy as he lost control and the man on his bed buried his head between her legs.

Chapter 27

Priest awoke with a headache that could have ended the world. The sound of morning commuters filled the room through the open window, although the curtains were still drawn and the light was artificial, emanating from a reading lamp next to the bed. He sat up tentatively and rubbed his forehead, trying to squeeze the pain out of his brain but it was still there when he let go.

His recollection of the night before filtered through his mind like the blurred images of an old projector. The recall of a turn was very much like trying to distinguish a vivid dream from a memory in the hazy lacuna between sleep and consciousness; the split second of time that passes just after waking, where it's not clear what's real and what isn't.

Oh, bloody hell, what have I done this time?

Priest was the only occupant of the bedroom, but the sweet aroma of bacon wafted through from the kitchen. As the events of the previous night started to unfold in his head, a knot in his stomach tightened. He put on a pair of joggers and an old T-shirt and padded towards the smell of food. He thought at first that she might have come back and forgiven him and he would open the door in front of him and find Jessica in his kitchen, sitting at his breakfast bar with tea ready for him . . .

He opened the door, already knowing it wasn't going to be like that.

Elinor Fox was wearing one of his shirts and nothing else. She was busying herself over the hob with a frying pan, the one that he had salvaged from Dee's house just before the divorce. The frying pan was special because it represented the only thing he had taken away from his first marriage, save for the legal fees and bad memories. Now someone whose intensity surpassed even his ex-wife's had her hands around the handle.

Fuck.

She turned her head and looked at him, a deliberate and rehearsed move. Her hair was straight and didn't look as though it had been affected by a night's sleep or the rough sex that he now recalled she had enthusiastically participated in.

'Good morning.' She smiled and winked.

Lost for an appropriate salutation, Priest returned the smile weakly and took a seat at the breakfast bar behind her.

'Bacon sandwich?' she called over her shoulder. 'I was going to make you a full fry-up but you didn't have any eggs. Or sausage. Or mushrooms. Or anything other than bacon, really. How do you eat?'

Priest pinched the bridge of his nose. 'I get by mainly on protein drinks and Pot Noodle.'

'Proper bachelor, aren't you?'

The display on the oven was blurry but he was fairly sure it read '07:12'. The Elias case was listed for ten but Okoro would want to meet at least an hour beforehand and the clients would be nervous. He needed to be out in an hour at the most and he had papers to get ready and phone calls to make. He'd lost most of the previous evening and time was now alarmingly short.

'Actually, I'm not that hungry,' he heard himself say.

She turned around and leant back against the kitchen worktop. 'Something else you'd rather be doing than eating?' she asked, nodding at the table suggestively.

'The Elias case,' he replied.

'Of course. How silly of me.' She turned back abruptly to the frying pan and threw the half-cooked bacon in the bin. It seemed a pointless act but one which apparently gave her a great deal of satisfaction. 'There. All gone.'

Priest turned his hands up in a confused gesture. 'Thanks for doing that.'

'How did Alexia Elias die?' Fox asked suddenly.

'How do you know she's dead.'

She frowned, genuinely perplexed. 'You told me last night. You remember last night, right?'

Priest closed his eyes. *Shit, what else happened that I can't remember?*

'She was shot,' Priest said. He watched her closely but she didn't flinch. If she knew the truth, she didn't let on.

'What?' she gasped convincingly. 'Is it connected with Simeon's murder?'

'I don't know. Could be coincidence.'

She didn't seem persuaded by that one. 'I doubt that.'

Priest had run out of things to say. He usually felt comfortable with silence but Elinor Fox's penetrating stare was starting to have an effect – he felt deconstructed by it.

'I'd better be getting ready for court,' he said, pointing vaguely in the direction of the bedroom.

'Sure thing,' Fox said brightly and before Priest could say anything she slipped off his shirt and stood with her back arched slightly over the work surface, her naked, model-worthy body was like a marble statue as she offered him the shirt.

'You'll be needing this, then.'

*

Priest fought his way through the throng of people that had assembled outside the entrance to the Royal Courts of Justice. From what he could gather most of them were reporters from various news agencies but, whereas day one of the Elias trial had attracted only a modest interest, most of the nationals were now represented.

He had received a text from Georgie warning him that Simeon's death had hit the headlines. It didn't surprise him. The 'head start' Elinor had promised him had lasted longer than he had anticipated anyway.

He kept an eye out for the journalist. He had left her in the flat out of exasperation and, although she had warned him she would still be waiting for him when he got home, he suspected she would be heading straight for court as soon as he had left.

No sign of her amongst this lot, though. He hadn't given her a key but told her to make sure the door was on the latch when she left so it locked behind her. *Good job I don't keep rabbits.*

After turfing out the contents of his pockets onto a plastic tray and risking a touch-up by the burly security guard, Priest found Tomas Jansen alone in the High Court cafe, brooding over a cup of black coffee. He ordered a cup of Earl Grey and pulled up a chair opposite Jansen.

'Where are the others, Tomas?'

'In court with Vincent.'

'Any sign of Hagworth?'

Jansen shook his head. His eyes were red and his skin blotchy – he seemed only a shadow of the fearless journalist Priest had met eighteen months ago. 'Not yet. What will happen, Charlie? Is this it? Do we win?'

'I'm afraid it's not that simple.'

'Alexia Elias is *dead*. *She* was bringing the claim. I don't understand.'

'The cause of action falls to the conduct of her executors,' Priest explained. 'The judge will grant us an adjournment – she *has* to now. The executors will apply for an order that they are indemnified by Alexia's estate and they'll decide whether they want to carry on.'

'And if they do?'

'Then we'll cross that bridge. But not now, Tomas. A lot's happened over the last few days. Too much to process right now.'

Jansen nodded slowly and drained the last mouthful of coffee before replacing the cup. Priest noticed an unmistakable shake in his hand, and something else too. A flash of anger when Priest had told him that the trial wasn't over automatically. He'd tried to conceal it, but it was there: in his eyes. The thought that, right now, Tomas Jansen had the most to gain from Alexia's death was preying on his mind.

'A policeman came round to see us yesterday,' he said, staring out behind Priest.

'DCI Rowlinson?'

'Yes. I think that was his name. He asked a lot of questions about where we were when Simeon Ali was killed.'

'It's routine,' said Priest, picking up his tea. 'Elimination is the first part of any investigation.'

'You used to be a policeman.'

Priest passed off his accusatorial tone as a symptom of the stress he was under. 'That's right.'

'What happened? Why did you stop being a policeman?'

Priest thought about the moment when he had thrown his ID on the superintendent's desk and walked out for the last time. He'd worked in a bar for six months after that – cleaning glasses, pulling pints of bitter and throwing out troublemakers. The most educated barman in London, his old boss had said. *What was that guy's name, now?*

'The police and I had a disagreement,' Priest said eventually.

Jansen smiled – he seemed to appreciate people who didn't answer questions directly. Must be his profession. 'And what was the nature of this disagreement?'

'They thought I knew what I was doing. I thought they were wrong.'

Jansen laughed. 'That's good, Charlie. Very abstract. You'd have made a fine journalist, as well as a lawyer.'

'What did you tell him?' asked Priest. 'Rowlinson.'

'I told him we were with you the whole time, and Vincent and Georgie.'

Priest nodded. 'I see.'

'Interesting, though, don't you think?' said Jansen. He rested his chin on his hand, stared at Priest's tea thoughtfully. Priest surmised that he was being deliberately enigmatic – playing the insightful amateur detective, although for what reason he wasn't sure.

'How so?' he asked.

'Well. We weren't all there, were we, Charlie? Not all of the time, at least.'

*

Priest led Tomas into court thirteen and sat him down three rows back from the front. Gail was already there, as was Georgie who cast him a determined smile as he set out a laptop in the row behind Okoro.

To his left, Hagworth was trying to get a folder open. To Priest's surprise, Dominique Elias was sitting behind Hagworth, hands clasped together on the table, eyes straight ahead.

A door opened at the front and Justice Peters swept in, her hair tied up in a bun and a Bible-length copy of the Civil Procedure Rules tucked under her arm. Everyone in the court-room rose as one; even the media rabble gathered at the back sensed her authority and stood. She slammed the book down on the table and indicated that they should find their seats, although Hagworth had barely yet managed to stand.

They sat and waited while Peters made notes. Eventually, she looked up.

'Can we clear the public gallery, please.'

At first nobody moved. Peters waited a few moments before addressing the assembled journalists directly.

'*Can we clear the public gallery, please.*'

There was some reluctance, but as the court usher opened the door, they eventually filed out. Peters waited until the door was shut and the grumbles had faded before turning to the advocates.

'Mr Hagworth,' she said. 'I gather that your client is dead.'

Hagworth was still standing. 'I very much regret so, Your Honour.'

'Mr Elias.' Peters looked beyond Hagworth at the forlorn figure hunched over the bench behind him. 'The court offers you its sincerest condolences.'

Elias nodded, a curt non-committal acknowledgement.

'And, Mr Okoro, I gather your witness is also dead.'

Okoro rose to his feet. 'That is correct, Your Honour.'

Peters shook her head. 'How very unfortunate. It seems to me that we have little choice but to adjourn this case. Now, which of you is going to apply for a restricted reporting order?'

Chapter 28

Priest stared at the board but his next move wasn't obvious. He had a modest battalion stationed in eastern Europe which could be fragmented and used to advance across Asia but that would be the last of his reserve troops; he had already lost Africa and most of America, North and South. Options were few and far between.

'I do so enjoy our games of *Risk*, brother. Don't you agree?' said William. Over the years, Priest had noted his older brother's voice had deteriorated to a throaty rasp. Eight years of confinement in a maximum security psychiatric hospital had physically diminished William Priest almost beyond recognition; although his mind, when focused, seemed as sharp as ever.

'Mm.' Priest continued his appraisal of the dire situation he was in.

'My God!' William suddenly exclaimed. 'I had forgotten to enquire about the fortunes of your trial, Charles. I saw on the news that a key witness had been killed in suspicious circumstances, something that I hope was not to your detriment. Although of course your mood and the mere fact that you are here on a weekday suggests it was.'

William hadn't always talked like this. He had always been well spoken – all of the Priest children were highly articulate – but Priest had noticed a definite shift in William's register to make him sound like something out of a Sherlock Holmes novel, although he couldn't tell whether that was purposeful or not. Most likely it was. William was far more prone to drama than his younger siblings.

'The claimant also died in equally suspicious circumstances, so we called it a one-all draw.' *Something that, so far, Fox hadn't distributed to every news station in London, but how long would that last?*

William sat back, pleased. 'Well, if anyone can haul the case out from the legal mire into salvation then it is you. How did the two individuals die, might I ask? I trust their deaths are connected.'

'Cling film,' Priest replied. He placed his last reserve in Australia and moved a unit across the European border into William's territory.

William emitted a low growl of disapproval. It was the only area of the board where he was vulnerable. Behind him, the warden coughed nervously.

'Cling film, indeed,' William muttered, counting out the dice. Priest outnumbered him three to one this time. 'How fascinating. A very personal way to kill someone, don't you think? Like strangulation. You have to really *hate* your victim to strangle them, you know. Same with cling film – you just have to accept that they'll be thrashing around in your arms for three or four minutes, maybe longer with someone of greater stamina. Although I find that physical stamina is less important than a person's desire to live.'

*Find. As in present tense. Not ready for parole yet, old chum.
Not that you'll ever be eligible for it.*

'Have you ever tried it?' Priest asked. The brothers tapped their
fists together in a tradition that dated back to their childhood and
rolled. William talked almost absent-mindedly as he moved the
dice around.

'No. I did once design a contraption that latched around a
man's neck like a dog collar and could be expanded by means
of a rubber ring and pump concealed in the frame. It could be
operated remotely, by an electronic signal transmitted from a
device I had stitched into my trousers.'

'Did you ever have the opportunity to test this contrivance
of yours?'

Priest watched, vexed, as William tipped over his units with
his finger as each dice cast in turn went in the older brother's
favour.

'I regret not. Pity, too. I had a fine-looking Fleet Street banker
in mind as a guinea pig.'

Behind William, the nervous-looking warden shuffled his
feet and coughed again. Priest looked up sharply and whatever it was that the warden was about to say evaporated in his
throat. He looked young, barely out of school. Priest didn't
recognise him – presumably then he was new and ill-used to a
serial killer's musings.

'Well,' Priest began as he checked through what cards he had
left, 'sorry to disappoint but the first victim had a needle mark
and no defensive wounds.'

'Oh, how boring. That's like microwaving a roast dinner.
But, in the absence of a physical confrontation, the killer could

be either male or female, don't you think?' William cast him a knowing look, although Priest had already considered the point. 'Were there any mementos taken? Underwear, fingers, an eyeball, perhaps?'

'Afraid not. But the second victim had her face mutilated.'

'Oh?' expressed William, interested. He reached across and passed Priest the dice and they rolled again. The novice warden shifted his weight uncomfortably, watching all the time and occasionally glancing at the CCTV flashing above them. *Fat lot of good he would be if Wills kicks off.* 'No doubt the killer left the first victim alone, other than the grievous act of killing itself, of course?'

'That's right.'

'Hm.' William had counted out the dice and flattened Priest's assault, leaving his reserves depleted and his last continent exposed. 'Oh, bad luck, by the way, Charles. Truly, the statistical improbability of my last victory was quite evident. There's nothing wrong with your strategy, brother. You're just out of luck.'

'Tell me about it,' Priest mumbled under his breath, although not completely inaudibly.

'Now, in what way was the face abused?'

'Ears and eyes blowtorched and the mouth stitched up,' Priest said grimly.

'Indeed. Quite a show. How was the needlework?'

'Amateurish, and the burning was messy, too.'

'Well, you're well under way given that you can eliminate anyone who is either a surgeon or a car mechanic.' Priest looked up. William was running through his own cards and rearranging reserve troops. In all likelihood, he hadn't intended his comment to be funny at all.

'Thanks, Wills. That's helpful.'

'You're welcome. And by the way, Charles, is it the murder that's upsetting you at the moment or the blonde girl you slept with last night? What's her name? Something that starts with a vowel, I dare say.'

Priest felt wrong-footed; he made to reply but faltered, much to William's apparent pleasure. Then he looked down, realising the presumption would have been based on William's detection of some physical evidence, and there it was: a long strand of blonde hair attached to his jacket sleeve. He picked it off and dropped it on the floor.

'I sense she's trouble, brother. Do be careful,' William cautioned.

'And how have you reached this conclusion?'

'She cooked breakfast for you this morning wearing your shirt. A little presumptuous after a first liaison, no?' Priest felt he was half a second behind his older brother at every turn – it was a feeling he had endured since he was three years old. William went on, gleefully aware of his advantage. 'There's cooking fat splashed on your shirt and the faint smell of bacon about you. You never cook yourself breakfast at home, you don't have time, so she must have done it for you, in your shirt, and of course she would have known you never eat a cooked breakfast unless it's from that dreadful cafe of yours if you had spent more than a night with each other, as surely you would have mentioned it.'

'Maybe I've changed my habits,' Priest suggested, although he knew it sounded unconvincing and was received as such.

'Rubbish. Serengeti leopards and all that. Now don't be such a bore: back to the murders and the destruction of the second victim's eyes. To stop her seeing something or to punish her for something she had already seen?'

'Not sure yet.'

William had reallocated troops to the western front of his Asian stronghold and was lining up to advance into Europe. Victory was now more or less just a formality but Priest decided to keep the game going – visiting time was an hour and he still had five minutes left. He doubted William had much concept of time but stealing five minutes off him seemed unsavoury.

'Very well. Here, roll.' William handed Priest the dice. 'Was the damage to the face done pre-or post-mortem?'

'Don't know yet – waiting on the autopsy.'

'Ah!' William cried. 'How frustrating! Your best guess?'

'Post.'

'How so?'

'Just the logistics of it. Pathologist said there's evidence of only one killer and there was no apparatus around to hold her down so I'm guessing she was killed and then her face mutilated. Besides, if it's the same killer then the first victim had to be paralysed first and the work on him was far less extravagant.'

'How fascinating – so someone really is making a point.'

'Apparently.' Priest rolled the dice again but the outcome was predictably unfortunate.

'I trust you've thought of the three wise monkeys? Perhaps that is the point?'

'I have.'

'Good. And who found the bodies?' William asked, concentrating on the board.

'That was me.'

'I see. Well, you wouldn't be the first Priest to find himself next to a corpse. Let's hope you didn't do it, then.'

William laughed and removed another of Priest's units. He was still chuckling five minutes later when Priest forfeited the game.

Chapter 29

As was so often the case when Priest visited his brother, he found himself sheepishly reporting for a dressing-down at his sister's house straight afterwards. He knew she disapproved of his continuing relationship with William – she was so bitterly disappointed and angry with his inability to let him go. So when he had finished his infidelity at Fen Marsh Secure Hospital, he would unburden his guilt by immediately seeing her. He supposed he needed her condemnation, somehow. Her scorn would wipe the slate clean and they would go around the merry-go-round again.

As it turned out, today Sarah was in a jovial mood, bustling around the kitchen with considerable zeal making lunch for Tilly and tea for Priest, although no doubt she knew full well why he was there.

'I don't have any Earl Grey,' she told him, biting her bottom lip. 'I did buy you a box once to keep here but it stank out the cupboard.'

'It's fine, Sarah. Just whatever you have will be great.'

She grinned and handed him a mug, which he took gratefully. 'It's this or cold water.'

Priest played around with some papers on Sarah's breakfast bar while she returned to Tilly's lunch. He saw a couple of payment reminders and some drawings Tilly had done. It was the holidays, apparently, and he could hear the sound of his niece playing some imaginary game with considerable enthusiasm from the room next door. Underneath the pile he found her school report, which he flipped through. Tilly was doing well. Mostly A's for effort and the little book was peppered with encouraging remarks about her attitude and ability to listen, although she had a propensity to get carried away with her projects and argue with her teachers. A notable Priest trait. Pleasingly, there seemed to be very little evidence that her useless father's genes had impeded her development. She thrived not because of him, but in spite of him.

'Tilly, lunch!' Sarah called.

Tilly trotted through, her ungovernable mass of strawberry-blonde hair bouncing everywhere like it had a life of its own. She climbed up on the seat opposite Priest to retrieve her plate of sandwiches and pointed at him accusingly.

'Uncle Charlie!' she exclaimed. 'Your bottom smells.'

'Tilly! Enough! Out with you!' Sarah ushered her out of the room but before she could escape Priest leant over and whispered, 'Not as much as yours, munchkin.'

She ran off cackling. After a few more moments of clattering around the kitchen and an intense negotiation with the dishwasher door, Sarah sat at the breakfast bar, her own mug of tea in her hand.

'What's troubling you, this time?' she asked, her chin resting on her hand and her bright eyes staring at him unblinkingly.

'Ah, work stuff,' Priest sighed. 'The libel trial isn't going well.'

'Hope you're not thinking of losing. How's our Bristol Road tenant?'

'Dead.'

'Dead!' Sarah spat some of the tea back into the mug in surprise. Priest found himself the subject of her scrutiny yet again and watched as the realisation dawned on her face. 'The news . . . I didn't put it all together.'

'Yes,' he said, pursing his lips and hoping she wouldn't shout too loudly. 'The dead witness from the libel trial was our tenant.'

Sarah nodded, her mouth slightly open and her brow furrowed. Then, 'You bloody idiot.'

'I accept without reservation your concern.'

She shook her head and took a hefty gulp of tea. 'We're not going to be able to relet it for ages, are we?'

'Probably not.'

They sat in silence for a while. *She's taking this pretty well, all things considered. Must be getting soft in her old age . . .*

'What happened?' she said at last. 'The news said the police were treating the death as suspicious.'

'You should never trust the news. There will be an autopsy and he will have choked on a grape or something. Then it won't be headline news anymore. Police might want to talk to you. All routine. Nothing to worry about.'

She watched him carefully. *She knows I'm lying. She must know.* If she did, she chose not to push any further and her appraisal of him concluded with a sympathetic shrug of her shoulders. She swallowed down the rest of the tea. 'If you say so.'

'Tilly's doing well at school,' Priest remarked.

'Are you sleeping with anyone at the moment?' she replied. The question caught him off guard – as was presumably the intention – and he felt the sensation of blood rushing up through his face. He remembered Elinor, and what they had done. She hadn't been in touch. No texts, no emails. She just fucked him and . . . where the hell was she now?

Jesus, what a mess I've made there.

Sarah said drily, 'I'm going to take your uncomfortable silence as a *yes*.'

Priest struggled to work out how best to reply. In the end, he settled for shrugging and pulling a face that he hoped looked non-committal.

Sarah nodded. 'I won't buy a hat just yet, then.'

'It's complex,' he conceded.

'As everything about you is. My brother: the human onion. The layers just keep peeling away one after the other.'

She laughed and Priest felt a little of the uneasiness slip away, although he also found himself checking his phone for messages again. Maybe Elinor had regretted the whole thing, disappeared back to Blackheath and that would leave him free to try to patch things up with Jessica? *Patch things up with Jessica. It sounds so easy.*

'I've got to get back to the office,' he said, getting up. He fumbled around in his jacket pocket and threw a set of keys across the table at her. She picked them up and studied them. 'The keys you lent me to Bristol Road. The police have Simeon's set so you can have these back.'

'Thanks.' She thumbed through the set idly. 'How long will it take to find out what happened to him?'

'A few weeks, I guess. There's a lot to do.'

'Mm. What's this?' Sarah asked, holding up a small key that formed part of the set.

'I don't know,' Priest admitted. 'It's your flat.'

'No, this isn't part of the set of keys to Bristol Road.'

Priest felt a cold shiver ripple down his spine. It was the way she was holding the little key up to the light, as if it was a long-lost ancient relic. He sat back down.

'What do you mean?'

'I mean . . .' She flicked through each of the keys in turn. 'Front door, back door, windows, gas meter and . . . this.' Priest looked at the alien key – it was small and simple and with the number six faintly printed on the head. 'It must be the tenant's.'

'How so? These were in your drawer.'

'Only recently,' Sarah recalled. 'The agents contacted me about a week ago and said the tenant had asked for a duplicate set because the back door key kept getting stuck. They gave him their set and they sent this set back to me.'

Priest's eyes widened as a surge of adrenaline flushed through him. There is a turning point in every case – a point when a piece of evidence emerges from the thick fog of obscurity, rising to the surface like a beacon pointing the way. *Is this that point?*

'Sarah,' he said, putting his hand around the set of keys. 'On reflection, could I have these back?'

Chapter 30

Georgie sat in the passenger seat of Charlie's Volvo playing with the key between her fingers. They were parked two hundred or so yards from the flat Simeon had rented but on the opposite side of Bristol Road. It was busier than when they had been here the last time, although Georgie recognised the rowdy gang of idlers huddled together outside the William Hill, each cradling a can of lager.

Charlie had a phone to his ear and was waiting for someone to pick up at the police station. When they eventually did he rolled his eyes and cast her an exasperated look.

'Hello? Yes . . . Could I speak with DCI Rowlinson, please . . . It's Priest . . . No . . . It's just Priest. He'll know who I am . . . If you could just . . . Well . . . Yes, I'll hold.'

He fiddled around with the touch screen and placed the phone on the dashboard in front of them. 'Hands-free,' he explained.

'Do you think Simeon knew what was going to happen and ditched this key on purpose?' Georgie asked.

'That's possible, I suppose. If it's important then it seems like a strange mistake to have left it on another set.'

Georgie studied the head and the faded number six printed onto the metal. 'It looks like a locker key,' she commented.

'I thought that, too.'

'That's why we're here, isn't it? To see if we can find out where this key goes?'

Charlie didn't get a chance to answer before Rowlinson crackled over the phone. The audio quality was poor but there was a distinct echo chasing Rowlinson's voice.

'Priest,' Rowlinson said. 'Who's died now?'

Charlie leant across to make sure his voice captured every element of ironical intonation. 'Do you mind awfully if I have a poke around my flat? I rather think the heating might have been left on.'

'No, can you fuck, Priest. SOCO have only just left.'

'I thought you said the flat isn't a crime scene.'

'And I thought I told you that doesn't mean you can go poking around in there!'

'Jesus Christ, Tiff. Have you any idea how pissed off Sarah's going to be when she finds out your boys have been wading through there?'

'Why do I get the distinct feeling that you're not taking this seriously, Priest?'

Charlie laughed. He had an endearing laugh, Georgie thought, and he only laughed when he meant it. You knew where you were with that.

'Look,' said Rowlinson. 'You can have the damn thing back by the end of next week but for now it's being treated as a crime scene until I say otherwise.'

'Fine, but can you keep it low profile? A murder really does reduce a dwelling's marketability, you know.'

Rowlinson made a noise that suggested he didn't like being mocked. 'I'll see what I can do. How about I ask SOCO to redecorate while they're in there?'

'That would be swell.'

He hit the END CALL button before Rowlinson had a chance to respond, then turned to Georgie.

'And now we know that the flat's empty, save for the police officer stationed in the coffee shop over there watching for anyone poking around who shouldn't be.'

Georgie looked in the direction Charlie pointed, past the gaggle of drunks to the Starbucks approximately half the distance between them and the computer shop underneath the flat on the opposite side.

'How do you know there's someone there?' she asked.

'SOCO have just left. They won't leave someone actually in the flat. They'll put someone there to watch over it for the next twenty-four hours.'

'So murderers *do* return to the scene of the crime,' Georgie murmured.

'Almost always. And Georgie—' Charlie put his hand on her shoulder. She wasn't expecting it but she reacted instantly to the warmth of his hand. She turned and he was staring at her intently, his eyes shining like blue lights and for a moment she thought that . . .

'I need you to create a small distraction,' he said.

She blinked twice. 'Sorry? You want me to *what*?' *Is he serious?*

Without warning he released his hand and jumped out of the Volvo. Realising he was quite serious she hurriedly undid her seat belt and climbed out of the car.

'Just a few minutes,' he told her. 'That's all I need.'

She looked at him, perplexed. 'How do you propose I distract a police officer on a stake-out?'

'Oh, you'll think of something.' He was about to walk off but, seeing her hesitate, turned back around. 'It's best not to overthink plans like this. Just see what comes to mind when you get there. If you spend the next hour planning something, you'll realise how ridiculous this is.'

'What?'

He had already started a brisk walk down the road towards the Starbucks. Over his shoulder, he called back to her: 'I'll cross here.'

She watched motionless as he waited for a break in the traffic before striding across the road. In moments, he was on the other side and making his way towards the computer shop. Georgie looked about desperately but couldn't fathom any sort of plan; her mind was completely blank. For want of some better idea, she started to walk up the pavement on the other side across from Charlie, half running to keep up with his pace and closing in on the drinkers who had started to idle up the street. On the other side of the road, Charlie had turned and subtly gave her a thumbs-up sign.

Oh, my God, he's quite serious.

Georgie felt a rising sense of panic grip her. *He's going to get caught going into the flat and it'll be all my fault!*

One of the drinkers stumbled but kept himself upright by clinging on to his companion who objected by pushing back, causing the one who had tripped to fall into the third, smaller man. They fell about each other in a chorus of profanities and curses, including some words that Georgie had never heard before. In any other situation, it might have been comical.

She stopped. *Oh, damn, damn, damn!* She was standing next to a bin tagged onto a lamppost, covered with faded and torn stickers from club events two years ago. The bin was full, a half-drunk glass bottle of Coke jutting out of the top.

Georgie looked at it. Then at the drinkers up ahead, almost level with the Starbucks.

I can't do it.

She looked across. Charlie was almost at the computer shop – no sign of him slowing down. She caught a glimpse of a WPC peering out of the Starbucks window. Had she recognised Charlie? *If she sees him going into the flat she'll report it to Rowlinson . . .*

She checked for CCTV; couldn't see any. She had seconds left to react.

Bugger it!

Georgie took hold of the Coke bottle and hurled it as hard as she could in the direction of the drinkers before darting behind a bus shelter.

She peered through the gap between the metal frame of the shelter. She had hoped the bottle might smash on the pavement, causing the drinkers to react. Instead, the bottle ricocheted off the back of the smaller man, causing him to tumble into the others, yelping angrily. *Sorry!*

Despite the projectile's misdirection, the effect was more or less as intended.

When the smaller man had regained his balance, he put his fist into the stomach of the nearest man to him. That man immediately went to ground, which drew a screech of incomprehension from the third man.

'Fucking bastard just bottled me!' barked the smaller one, nursing his back.

'You fucka'!' cried the innocent victim, pulling himself up from the floor. 'You're a dead man!'

Innocent lurched forward and clattered into Smaller while their bemused companion tried to make sense of it. The brawl was enough to draw out the irritated WPC from her surveillance point.

'That's enough!' she shouted, fumbling around on her belt for a can of CS spray.

Georgie cringed, decided not to look anymore and pulled her head back around, leaning against the side of the bus shelter, eyes closed. The commotion intensified. She heard the desperate plea for assistance from the WPC into her radio. And the horn of the car that swerved to avoid the fray. One of the others, presumably Innocent, had sent Smaller sprawling into the middle of the road.

She opened her eyes. Ahead, several other people had stopped what they were doing to watch the scuffle unfold. There was a hissing sound, presumably the WPC discharging her CS spray into someone's eyes, and the sound of an agony-induced yelp.

Georgie decided it was best to close her eyes again. She recalled reading an article about CS spray some time ago. The pain of the chemicals was similar to the sensation of boiling water being poured over your eyes, apparently.

Oh dear.

There was a loud slap on the side of the bus shelter beside her. She jumped and let out a squawk of shock.

'Sorry,' said Charlie.

She looked at him, baffled. He craned his neck around the bus shelter to watch the brawl.

'Good work, Someday,' he breathed.

'Hope it was worth it,' she said, breathless.

He pulled out a leaflet and handed it to her. 'The Budget Gym on Grace Street,' he announced, clearly pleased with the discovery. 'It was on the pinboard in the kitchen. SOCO probably didn't think it was important.'

Georgie didn't see the significance at first. 'And this is helpful because . . .'

Charlie turned the key and the Volvo's engine coughed into life. 'Because they have lockers, Someday.'

Chapter 31

Priest pulled the Volvo out of the parking space and U-turned so he was heading back down Bristol Road. He noticed Georgie fidgeting in her seat; she was trying to see what was going on behind them but the bus shelter was blocking the view.

As they reached the T-junction at the bottom of Bristol Road, two Metropolitan patrol cars, blues lit up, cut across them, tyres screeching over the tarmac.

'Do you think it'll be all right?' Georgie asked.

'I'm sure it'll be fine.'

'Yeah, you're right.' Georgie looked down in what was presumably an attempt to reassure herself.

After half a mile of silence, Priest asked, 'Was that a bottle of Coke I saw you lob at that man?' Georgie didn't respond but looked across at him sheepishly. Priest nodded. 'Good throw, kid.'

'What do you think will happen with the trial?'

They wound their way through the traffic to the Budget Gym, with the little key burning a hole in Priest's inside pocket. At last, he could sense they were getting somewhere.

'Well,' he sighed, pushing back against the car seat to stretch his aching back, 'I suspect Dominique won't want to give up the fight easily.'

'But now both sides have lost their main witnesses. Surely a fair trial isn't possible.'

'Perhaps, but I don't fancy running a human rights argument in front of Peters. For one thing, I suspect she's not actually human.'

'The executors might think twice if they think that the estate includes dirty money,' Georgie speculated.

'That's assuming *The Real Byte* article was actually true,' Priest pointed out.

'And what do you believe?'

Priest smiled and pulled past a set of roadworks before offering her an answer: 'I think you should never let the truth get in the way of a decent libel trial.'

*

The Budget Gym on Grace Street was aptly named. The front comprised two enormous windows either side of a revolving door plastered with signs indicating monthly membership fees as low as nine pounds.

Access to the gym was offered by way of the revolving door but, once inside, there seemed to be no clocking-in system. They were presented with a large room, a concrete floor and a mirror that ran the length of one wall. There were three men at the back gathered around a bench press. They had been discussing something but looked up at Priest and Georgie as they entered.

'Do you go to the gym?' Georgie asked. Priest sensed she was nervous.

'Nope. Hate the damn places.'

'How do you stay so . . . big?'

'I eat a lot of red meat,' he said, watching as a young girl with a pierced nose and blue hair appeared from behind a counter at the back.

Priest walked towards her, Georgie sticking close, aware that the three men had stopped what they were doing and were watching them with interest. The tallest man was white, the other two were black. All three looked like gym regulars.

'Can I help you?' asked the blue-haired girl, crossing her arms. She looked at Georgie and fixed her with a hostile stare.

'Do you have any lockers?' said Priest.

The blue-haired girl looked puzzled. 'Yeah, we got lockers. I've never seen you in here before, though.'

'Friend of mine is a member. He gave me his key to retrieve something from his locker. I'd like to get it, please.'

There was a moment's silence before the blue-haired girl started to laugh. 'What the fuck? Why doesn't your friend just come and get it himself?'

He leant across the counter. 'He's indisposed.'

'Hey!' one of the men in the corner shouted. 'This guy causing you problems, Mims?'

Priest looked across. The three men moved towards them, led by the smaller man, the one who had shouted. He had a towel draped over his shoulder and a dark tattoo around one eye that made him look like a cyborg. Priest felt Georgie shrink behind him.

'I'm looking for the lockers,' Priest announced, drawing himself up to his full height and making sure they got a good look at him. He was maybe a stone lighter than the biggest of them and alarmingly outnumbered but he wanted them to see he was unperturbed.

Mims didn't say anything. She just stared at the locker key. 'Is that number six?' she asked warily. 'He's got a locker key, Benny. Number six.'

Priest watched as the one called Benny advanced on them until he was close enough to prod a stumpy finger in his chest.

'What you want, big man?' Benny demanded.

'The lockers,' said Priest evenly. 'Just the lockers.'

It was three on one and Benny didn't seem like he was in the mood for talking. Then there was Georgie to think about. She had backed away so she was as close to the nearside wall as she could get but one of the gang had positioned himself between her and the door. She looked across and Priest registered the fear in her eyes. He remained calm, relaxed, made sure that Benny wasn't in his face but without backing down – a situation he had been in plenty of times before, although it had tended to be as a policeman rather than a lawyer. Everything was now a finely balanced dance – one foot wrong and . . .

'Gimme the key,' Benny instructed. Then, when Priest didn't answer, he roared the same request, 'Give me the fucking key, prick!'

Priest glanced across at Georgie – her face was ashen. Then back at Benny, into his small bloodshot eyes.

Doesn't look like there's much choice.

It was over in a matter of seconds without anyone, save for Priest, understanding how. Benny was sent sprawling backwards, Priest's open hand striking his chest with such force that Benny's lungs were evacuated of air in a fraction of a second. Predictably, the closest of Benny's accomplices lunged forward in retaliation. Priest ducked underneath his attacker's uncontrolled punch, wedged his knee between the confused man's legs to use as leverage and sent him flying into the third accomplice, who toppled over like a skittle into a squat cage.

Priest surveyed the damage. Benny was winded and unlikely to be a problem for the next few minutes. The one he had tossed over his shoulder was nursing a gash in his head. The third man lay in a crumpled heap inside, his head resting on the weights, motionless.

He turned back to the blue-haired girl who was stood with her mouth wide open.

'Lockers, please,' Priest said more assertively than last time. She nodded without speaking, or taking her eyes off him, and pointed to a door in the back. 'I'm most obliged.'

He stepped over Benny who seemed to be having problems breathing and got to the door before he realised Georgie wasn't following him. He turned round and saw she was also suffering from the same open-mouthed condition as the blue-haired girl.

'Are you coming?' Priest asked.

A second later she nodded and skipped over Benny to follow him through to the locker rooms. Priest shut the door behind him and turned the key on the other side.

'You think they'll be back?' asked Georgie.

'I suspect one of them might.'

'I must have missed the kung fu module on my Legal Practice course.'

'You'd be amazed what universities offer these days, Someday.'

He led Georgie through to a changing room that looked like it hadn't been cleaned in months and smelt like a weed factory. There was a single bench in the middle of the room, a couple of yellow-stained sinks and a row of lockers on the far wall. Someone had covered the smoke alarm with a plastic bag.

'Six – it's here, and the key's out.'

Georgie was pointing to the last locker on the top row. Priest wasted no time before trying the key. It didn't seem to fit. *Damn!*

'The other way,' Georgie said, reaching out and turning his hand in hers so the key was the other way up. He turned and she was right next to him, the panic he had seen earlier had drained away.

The latch clicked and the locker swung open.

They peered inside. Priest reached in and removed the locker's only item.

'A burner,' murmured Priest.

There was a loud bang emanating from the door behind them and a cry of rage as the handle was violently shaken from the other side.

'Best go out the back,' Priest suggested. 'Think we've outstayed our welcome.'

Chapter 32

The rear exit to the Budget Gym deposited Priest and Georgie into a tight alleyway that looked as though it hadn't seen a living soul since the plague, a consideration spoilt only by the wheel-less bicycle frame dumped behind a mound of rubbish on the opposite wall.

Georgie made a small noise as if she had eaten something disagreeable – presumably in response to the smell of the rubbish decomposing outside the gym's back door.

'What's all that?' she asked, turning her nose up.

'I don't know,' Priest breathed. 'But if we stand around too long it might try and communicate with us.' He looked up and down before turning right, away from the rubbish. 'This'll get us back to where we're parked.'

As they hurried through the alleyway, Priest examined the phone they had extracted from Simeon's locker. It was a Nokia, but an older model – not even touch-screen. Priest held the POWER button and, after a few seconds, the low-res screen lit up and the Nokia logo briefly appeared. The battery was low and the phone was struggling to find a signal.

'What do you think?' asked Georgie.

They reached the end of the alleyway and Priest stopped as he waited for the phone to load whatever data was on it. He was surprised the phone didn't have a lock on it, given what lengths Simeon had gone to in order to hide it. But then again perhaps that was the point and Georgie was right: *Simeon wanted someone to find this phone.*

'I think we're finally on to something,' he replied.

'Does it have internet access?'

'It barely has a colour screen, but maybe.'

After what seemed like an age, the phone finally stopped whirring and Priest was able to navigate the menu. He clicked through to the text messages but it wasn't easy to assimilate: the incoming messages were saved individually with a separate folder for outgoing, meaning he had to keep swapping between menu items to read the dialogue.

'There are texts from someone in his contacts he calls "USER3412",' Priest muttered.

'What about?'

'I don't know, it's difficult to follow. It's also difficult to work out when the messages were sent. I can't see how to look at the metadata, although I suppose there must be a way.'

They started to walk a little further up the road. There was a pub with outdoor seating and a group of old men brandishing pints of dark ale. It was hardly the weather for it but Priest supposed they had formed an immunity to the cold since the smoking ban.

Eventually, he managed to put together some of the messages in sequence.

SIMEON: NOT SURE I GET WHAT THE TRUTH IS ANY MORE. ITS ALL GOT VERY CONFUSED IN MY HEAD. LAST NIGHT I HAD THIS DREAM THAT WE WERE IN

A THEATRE LOOKING OUT TO AN AUDIENCE,
TELLING THEM OUR STORY. THEY WERE ON FIRE.
ALL OF THEM. I COULD SMELL THEIR FLESH
BURNING. FUCKED UP RIGHT?

USER3412: OK. THE BALANCE, SIMEON. REMEMBER IT'S ALL
ABOUT RESTORING BALANCE. IF WE DON'T DO THIS
THEN WHO WILL? REMEMBER – SNE, HNE, SNE.

SIMEON: NO. I'VE MADE UP MY MIND.

'Restoring balance,' Priest said aloud. *And what do the initials SNE, HNE and SNE stand for?*

From out of nowhere, Priest felt a sharp blow to his side. At first he thought he might have been shot but then he realised someone had clattered into him at full pelt and the impact had sent him flying across the pavement. He heard Georgie scream but it was too late – Priest careered into the old men and their pints, bringing the table down to the sound of breaking glass and splintering wood.

To cries of anguish, the old men fell backwards, taking their beers with them. Priest felt a sharp pain in one of his arms but he ignored it, righting himself as quickly as he could to see what had hit him. He was ready for another blow, fists clenched, his body deluged with adrenaline, but none came. Just the fading sound of footsteps on the pavement and the curses of the old men.

'He took the phone!' Georgie yelled, pointing up the street in panic.

Priest took a moment to register what she was saying but then, realising his assailant had neatly dispossessed him of Simeon's phone, he heaved the broken table out of the way before sprinting up the street.

Priest's upper body strength and weight meant he was not the fastest of runners but knowing he was so tantalisingly close to the answer urged him onwards; the distance his attacker had created was already starting to slip away. He was wearing a dark hoodie and tracksuit bottoms, under average height, much smaller than Priest but his success in bringing the lawyer to the ground had been more luck than judgement – another day and another angle and the phone thief would have just bounced off him.

With a furious cry, Priest put his head down and powered forward, taking one stride for every two of the thief's. *Oh, no you don't!*

At the bottom of the road, the thief took a left, crashing into a line of mopeds outside a college and sending them toppling like a line of dominoes in Priest's path. He cleared the first two in one leap but caught his front foot under the third. A teenager was standing on the pavement opposite waving his arms in the air frantically and screaming in Spanish.

'Fuck it!' Priest snarled.

Realising he didn't have time to free his foot, Priest kicked the bike as hard as he could. Pain shot up his leg but it was enough to send the moped spiralling across the street to a torrent of Spanish abuse. The next few strides on his right leg were agony but since he was still upright he guessed he hadn't broken anything. Ahead, the thief had restored some of his lead and was heading downhill, narrowly avoiding a black cab pulling out of a junction.

Hampered by whatever damage he'd done to his right leg, Priest resumed pursuit, shouting the sincerest apology he could muster to the Spanish bike owner on the side of the pavement.

The thief turned right where the road ended. Priest could feel his chances of catching him increase with every step. They were running along a thin strip of grass with the backs of terrace housing filing sideways to the right. To the left, at the foot of the embankment, ran a dual carriageway; three lines of fast-moving traffic on either side of the island. It was the start of rush hour and a horde of commuters were looking to get out of the city, oblivious to the chase taking place just a few yards away. Only a low, metal barrier separated Priest and the thief from the thunderous interchange.

'Hey!' Priest shouted. He doubted he could be heard above the sound of the traffic but releasing his anger this way felt good. 'Hey! Stop!'

The thief checked over his shoulder, the first time he seemed to sense that he was losing the race. Priest didn't catch a look at his face. He guessed he was about five and half seconds behind, maybe less, using the street lights as a guide.

The next pass and he was four seconds behind.

'You're too slow, my friend!' Priest taunted, drawing another nervous check over his shoulder from the thief. 'Give it up!'

The top of Priest's legs burnt, his right shin felt like it was twice its normal size but it was just white noise, sensations he was vaguely aware of happening but too distant to be concerned about. Nothing mattered, except getting that phone back.

You're not stopping me from finding Simeon's killer!

Priest passed another lamp post. Three seconds behind now.

Without checking over his shoulder again, the thief suddenly veered off course, half falling and half running down the embankment towards the dual carriageway. There was no hard shoulder and his descent was met with a flurry of alarmed car horns, but he managed to keep his footing and was now running on the tarmac just outside the lane marking towards the on-coming traffic.

Ah, shit!

Priest followed roughly the same path, taking the embankment at an angle but the grass was wet and he had to slow his pace to avoid tumbling over. If he lost control now, he'd be sent sprawling into the carriageway. Some cars had seen what was going on and pulled over to avoid the thief but the density of traffic meant that most cars stayed in the inside lane, only giving the runners a couple of feet of room.

Every car that passed brought with it a slipstream of air, knocking Priest off balance and threatening to pull him further into the road. The thief didn't seem to be coping particularly well either and was checking the top of the embankment, perhaps recalculating his plan. He was right to do so: with so many cars unable to see them until the last minute, the race was going to come to an end shortly, one way or the other.

Ahead, an articulated lorry in the lane nearest to them loomed closer. A deep horn blared but the middle lane was blocked and the lorry could do nothing but advance forward. There would be a few inches either side of the thief to spare when it passed and even less for Priest.

For a moment, the thief seemed to have abandoned the roadway and was heading back up the embankment but at the last minute he feinted right before leaning sharply left, in front of the lorry. The sound of the horn, brakes and rubber losing traction on the tarmac was ghastly. Priest caught sight of the driver's panicked face as he slammed his foot on the brake and the back end of the vehicle fishtailed around, spilling into the middle lane and sending a cluster of smaller cars scattering across the carriageway and into the central reservation. One of them hit the high kerb and reared up for a few seconds on two wheels before crashing back down and sliding in front of the lorry like it was on ice.

The traffic behind had jammed up; the chorus of horns was deafening. The lorry had come to a complete stop, its tyres hissing angrily. The car that had nearly flipped had ploughed into the central barrier but the driver was already scrambling out, nursing his head. Behind the lorry, Priest could see most of the other vehicles had managed to hit their brakes in time. Miraculously, what collisions there were seemed fairly minor.

Out of breath and exhausted, he scanned the front of the lorry but there seemed no sign of any damage. He looked to the other side of the carriageway – the traffic had ground to a halt on that side too. Then he saw the distant shape of the thief scrambling over the crest of the embankment on the other side of the road and disappearing into the haze beyond.

This time, Priest didn't give chase.

Chapter 33

As a rule, Charlie Priest didn't spook easily; but as he approached his front door there was a knot in his stomach.

Maybe she went home? Surely, she must have gone home.

Since his misadventure on the dual carriageway, Priest had forgotten about Elinor. Now, with his head throbbing and his thighs burning, leaving her alone in his flat seemed like one of the most moronic things he had ever done.

But then maybe the urge he felt to run when she threw off his shirt and stood there naked in his kitchen was founded on something deeper rooted than regret, or disgust, or shame, or whatever other petty doubts harassed him.

Maybe it was the same thought that had haunted him for years: *What am I really capable of if I can't remember what I'm doing?*

He opened the front door and peered inside. The blinds were drawn and the kitchen was in semi-darkness, the only form of illumination came from the hallway beyond, but that could be how she had left it. In the distance, he could hear the familiar rumble of comings and goings in Covent Garden and the street musicians playing their endless tune.

He crept in and shut the door behind him. Looked around. There was no obvious evidence of disturbance. In the lounge, the lionfish were resting in the far corner of the tank.

You guys know the truth of it. Good job you can't talk.

Fragments of memory soaked back into his thoughts as he checked the bed where they had been together. It occurred to him that it might have only been oral sex but it was of little consolation in the end, and probably wishful thinking.

He looked through each room carefully, dared to believe that she might not actually be there until he saw a sliver of light lining the bottom of the en-suite bathroom. He put his ear to the door. His heart sank like a stone as he heard the telling swish of water.

Priest pushed the door open. She must have been aware; the creak was loud enough and echoed round the tiled bathroom. But she didn't look up from her position, half submerged in the green bubble-filled water of his bath.

Bugger.

'Welcome home,' she sang. She was staring vacantly at the end of the bath while soaking a flannel and wringing the water onto her chest, dislodging the foam, making sure her breasts were visible.

'What are you doing here?' He intended to sound unwelcoming but the sight of her nakedness caught him off guard. Her body was lissom and toned. Her hand was resting on the pit of her stomach, the tips of her fingers disappearing into the water between her legs.

She looked at him, puzzled. 'I'm bathing. Isn't that obvious?'

Priest looked away, but he knew it was too late – she had seen him looking, noticed his eyes scanning her body. She revelled in his embarrassment, moving her hand further into the water.

'Don't you want to join me?' she teased.

'There's a towel on the side.'

'You've changed your tune.'

'Elinor, look, we crossed a line that maybe we shouldn't have crossed. I'm sorry.'

'*Sorry?*' She reacted, incensed, but whether it was feigned or real, Priest wasn't sure. 'You're sorry about what? That I'm still here or for fucking me in the first place?'

He held up his hands, too tired to fight. 'I simply mean that, given our involvement with the Elias case, it might not be sensible to . . .'

'It's funny how you didn't take that view yesterday.'

Priest realised she was right. He knew how it looked. How could she ever understand that? A lot of the time, he didn't even understand it himself.

'I'm sorry,' he repeated. He looked at her, tried to hold her gaze, ignore what she was doing with her hands.

She snorted, narrowed her eyes. 'And *who* is the problem?'

Priest faltered – caught his breath. *Are we really doing this?* The problem was Jessica, but even without that issue, everything about Elinor Fox was wrong. From the fake smile to the sickly voice, she screamed danger. But still, he couldn't stop himself reacting to the sight of her body in his bath.

He opened his mouth, choosing his words carefully, but she cut him off.

'The redhead? From the other day?'

Priest nodded, bit his lip. It seemed like an easy way out. *Although Jessica would hate it that anyone had referred to her auburn hair as red.*

Elinor Fox paused, appraising him sceptically.

'Thought so,' she murmured.

He saw something flash across her eyes. Didn't like the way she played with the word across her lips. He was about to say something, but then the look was gone.

'Leave,' she said, closing her eyes and resting her head back.

I'm pretty sure this is my *bathroom.*

Priest turned, partly relieved the conversation was over.

She called back to him as he opened the door. 'By the way, do you know how Simeon died?'

'Asphyxiated.'

She'll find out soon enough anyway.

She nodded, took the news like it was perfectly natural. She took her hands out of the bath and rested them on the sides. The performance was over.

Priest waited a beat, then left, shutting the door behind him.

He felt hot and tired, with a throbbing in his groin that disgusted him. In the lounge, he collapsed into a sofa and sat, one leg crossed over the other, his foot swaying gently to the muted rhythm of the musicians on the street below.

He waited and, sure enough, after a few minutes he heard movement. She swept into the lounge, her soaking-wet hair tied back hastily. Priest stiffened, waiting for her to say something.

She crossed the room towards him, a nascent smile playing at the corner of her mouth. Dragged her nails across the fish tank. Priest felt a sudden hollowness in his chest – a quivering buzz of anticipation.

'These are . . . lionfish,' she said, gazing at the tank.

'That's right.'

She watched them for a while, following Hemingway's movement across the tank with her finger.

'This one is smaller than the others.'

'That's Hemingway.'

'Why do you have them?'

'My sister bought me the larger one, Orwell, years ago, as a present. I stepped on one once in a South African bay, almost killed me. She bought that tank, had it installed as a surprise. Best present I've ever had. My niece loves them, so I added to the collection.'

'Now they're your only friends?' She turned to him. 'How touching.'

Priest nodded, but he felt the weight of her look and of his internal conflict. There was nothing to like: she was arrogant, scheming, amoral. But her body, her lips, her long legs and the way she tossed her hair over her shoulder, knowing exactly what the effect was – it all spoke a different language, one he didn't understand, but his groin easily translated.

He wanted her to move away from the lionfish. Whenever he watched them, he just thought of Tilly, and how she loved them. Elinor's presence by their tank felt somehow threatening. She walked towards him, leant over, took hold of her coat draped across the back of the sofa and whispered. 'You'll be back for more, won't you?'

Without waiting for a reply, she took her coat and whisked off. Moments later, he heard the front door slam.

Priest exhaled, relieved. He thought about calling Jessica. Hearing her voice would make him feel better, even if it was only to hear her tell him to piss off. But it could wait. Something had caught his eye, a flutter of movement, falling off Fox's coat as she had picked it up.

He checked the sofa where he thought it had fallen and, yes, there it was. *Well, I'll be damned.*

He picked up the hair that had fallen off Fox's coat. Studied it. It was long and unmistakably blue.

Chapter 34

The back garden to the pebble-dashed house ended abruptly at a rickety fence that ran across the rim of a grass basin, through which a railway line had once run. The tracks had long since been removed, although the odd sleeper could be found rotting on the side. The basin was overgrown with nettles and weeds.

About a quarter of a mile down, the wooden footbridge crossed the basin, although this had also fallen into disuse and was boarded up at both ends. Metal signs had been affixed to the boards warning of the consequences of trespassing.

The only people to use the abandoned railway line were kids looking for trouble, and even that was rare.

The owner sat in the basin crouched behind a mound of earth looking at the rabbit two hundred yards away in the crosshairs. The creature had dared to show itself a few minutes before, oblivious to the danger it was in.

The rifle had been hard to come by but it was a beautiful weapon. A Mosin-Nagant bolt action sniper rifle fully restored and operational, imported at great expense from Russia. It was standard issue for Soviet soldiers at the beginning of the Second World War and had been adapted in the thirties as a high-precision assassination device. After months of negotiation, the weapon had been delivered four weeks earlier and, in that time, the owner had become a competent shot.

This was fortunate. The rifle's acquisition had initially been for the purposes of self-preservation but, with the change of plan coming about as a consequence of the traitor's actions, the gun would play a central role in the solution.

On this occasion, however, the rabbit had experienced an episode of extreme good fortune; something had disturbed the creature's grazing and it had scurried off to safety.

Displeased, the owner packed the rifle away in its carry-case and skulked up the basin side, through the garden and into the house. The owner placed the rifle on the kitchen table and proceeded to inspect the safe in the lounge.

It had occurred to the owner many years previously that the safe was a potential killing machine, although it was only recently when watching a rerun of the film *Apollo 13* that the cause of death had become clear. The owner had previously assumed that the cause of death would be hypoxemia, oxygen deficiency, but instead it would be CO_2 retention, as was the problem for the *Apollo 13* astronauts.

Survival times were important to the owner. *The rule of threes is of particular importance: three minutes without air, three hours at extreme temperatures, three days without water, three weeks without food.*

Infuriatingly, there were difficulties calculating the prospective survival time in the safe given the number of academic disagreements regarding the value of certain variables.

The safe was a perfect cuboid, one point six metres in height, depth and width, giving just over four thousand litres of air. Air comprised around twenty-one per cent oxygen and less than half a per cent carbon dioxide. On average, a human generates thirteen litres of carbon dioxide and consumes fifteen litres of oxygen per hour, although other claims put this as high as eighteen litres an hour. There was some difference of opinion noted in the owner's research about a fatal level of carbon dioxide but all accounts agreed that anything over six per cent was considered toxic. However, being optimistic about the chances of survival inside the airtight safe, the owner had used eight per cent as a definite lethal level, which equated to approximately three hundred and twenty litres. At a production rate of thirteen litres an hour, the owner calculated that a human would last around twenty-four hours before they would die from hypercarbia, or carbon dioxide poisoning. At a rate of eighteen litres per hour, the survival time dropped to eighteen hours.

The owner knelt down and fiddled with the dial on the safe until a click was heard and the locking mechanism snapped open.

The owner pulled the door open with caution and peered into the safe.

There was no movement. To confirm the position, the owner reached in and felt the body inside, finding it cold and lifeless.

The owner closed the safe door; the corpse would be disposed of later.

Curious, though, that despite having a smaller lung capacity, the Alsatian had lasted no longer than a human should.

The owner resolved to revisit the calculations.

Chapter 35

The dawn sun was partially covered by mottled clouds through which brilliant shafts of light burst over the high-rises lining Chancery Lane. Priest meandered through the sea of commuters and round the occasional early-morning tourist before turning off to a quieter street that connected to the Nook. The cafes and coffee shops were full, serving fried breakfast and orange juice. Despite the cold, a few business types were sitting outside smoking roll-ups and planning the day ahead. One of them threw Priest a cheery wave, although he didn't recognise him. Overhead, a police helicopter banked sharply. The cafe patrons had to raise their voices to be heard over the chunter of the rotors but otherwise the intervention was ignored.

He bounded up the Priest & Co. office steps and crashed through the front door expecting to find the reception deserted. Instead he was met with an unimpressed scowl from behind the front desk.

'Remind me,' said Maureen drily. 'The name escapes me.'

'Charlie Priest, your beloved employer, at your service.' Priest bowed in an exaggerated way.

'That's funny, for one minute I thought you said *Priest*, the guy who owns this place, but it can't be.'

'You're in early, Maureen.'

'Someone has to keep this place going while you're off gallivanting around the city looking for trouble. I hear your star witness is dead. Case going well?'

Priest headed towards the stairs. 'Cup of tea would really go down very well, Maureen.'

She inhaled sharply, replaced her headphones and resumed typing. 'Kitchen's next to your office, Charlie.'

'You're most kind.'

She smirked then, apparently just recalling something, fumbled around under the desk. She produced an envelope. 'This was hand delivered for you,' she said, handing it over.

'By whom?' He inspected the envelope, marked with his name and postal address, preceded with the words STRICTLY PRIVATE AND CONFIDENTIAL – ADDRESSEE ONLY.

Maureen shrugged and resumed typing. 'A courier. Didn't catch his name, I'm afraid.'

*

Priest was soon joined in his office by Okoro and Georgie, the former wearing a cream Ralph Lauren sports coat with a navy handkerchief protruding from the breast pocket; the latter wearing a cardigan that looked as though it had been rejected from a jumble sale.

'It seems to me,' said Okoro, taking a seat opposite Priest, 'that this case has turned into a bit of a mess, for both sides.'

'Yes,' said Priest, motioning for Georgie to also sit down. 'Although I think that might be a slight understatement.'

'Hagworth contacted me over the weekend and suggested we hold settlement talks,' said Okoro. 'He seemed rather triumphant at that stage, presumably because he was labouring under the misapprehension that his client was still alive.'

'Doubt he wants to talk now.'

'I have a message to ring him back from yesterday.'

'Don't rush to talk to him.' He flicked a switch underneath the desk and fired up a PC. Dual screens whirred into life. 'He can bloody well stew for now.'

'There's nothing to talk about anyway,' said Okoro, leaning back in the chair. 'We don't even know who the executors of Alexia's will are yet. This case is going to be well and truly dumped on the back burner.'

'Maybe,' said Priest vacantly. *The legal aspect of it, perhaps, but there's a much bigger picture here.* He ripped open the envelope Maureen had given him and found a note inside written delicately with a fountain pen—

Cafe Olivero, Chancery Lane 10 a.m.

'Something interesting?' Okoro asked with a raised eyebrow. Priest realised he had been staring at the note.

'No,' he said, stuffing the paper into his pocket. 'Nothing interesting.'

Georgie piped up: 'Tomas emailed me – the case is obviously preying on his mind; the email came in at quarter past four this morning. He wants a conference with all of us to work out where we go from here.'

'OK. Georgie, set up a conference for tomorrow afternoon, but late, I've got things on after lunch. I take it you filled Okoro in regarding the burner we found.'

'She did,' Okoro said before Georgie could answer. 'Let me get this straight: you took out three men in a gym and then chased someone down a dual carriageway?'

Priest nodded, like it was no big deal. 'Unfortunately, I lost the phone, but not before I saw some interesting dialogue between our friend Mr Ali and someone called USER3412.'

'Simeon Ali was being pressurised into giving evidence,' Okoro mused.

'Come on, now,' said Priest, turning to one of the computer screens and watching Okoro out of the corner of his eye. 'It's not as if we didn't suspect that.'

'Doesn't make him dishonest,' Okoro pointed out.

'True. But it does still make him dead.'

Okoro whistled, leaning back further in the chair which was already struggling to accommodate his massive frame.

'So what now?' asked Georgie.

'Now,' said Priest, 'we do exactly what you suggested, Miss Someday.' Georgie looked blank. 'We apply to strike out Alexia's case on the grounds that a fair trial is no longer possible.'

'That's not going to work,' Okoro remarked.

'You're probably right but it will put the frighteners up Hagworth and put pressure on whoever is going to run the case in Alexia's absence to fold. Ask Solly to prepare a cost schedule for negotiation purposes, and give the insurers an update with a deceptively positive spin on it.'

Okoro stretched, yawned. 'Will do. I'll get working on the papers.' He heaved himself out of the chair, which seemed to trigger Georgie to stand up as well.

'What do you want me to do?' she asked. She had that look in her eyes Priest had seen before – *the thirst*. She wanted to find out what was going on just as much as he did and she wasn't going to let anything get in her way. Georgie and her Oxfam cardigan would travel to the ends of the earth itself if she thought it was the right thing to do.

'You're coming with me,' Priest told her. 'We're going to a cafe and I'm going to buy you a coffee.'

An email from Maureen popped up on the screen nearest to Priest. *DCI Rowlinson in reception for you.*

'Is that it?' asked Georgie, unsure.

'That's it.'

Chapter 36

Tiff Rowlinson took the seat opposite Priest and looked around the office. His hair was swept back, every strand perfectly aligned, although what sorcery was used to keep it that way Priest couldn't fathom. He carried a pilot's bag, a little worn around the edges, which he placed carefully down next to the chair.

'Can I offer you a hot beverage?' Priest asked.

'Afraid I don't have the time, but thank you,' Rowlinson replied. 'Nice place.'

'It suits our needs, although the rates are upsetting. I'm sorry, as you know I'm really awkward at small talk, can we cut to the chase?'

Rowlinson sighed before reaching down to the bag, from which he produced an iPad. He started flicking through it while continuing to talk.

'We're working with the theory that Ali and Elias had the same killer,' Rowlinson said. 'The murders were carried out with precision by someone who knew what they were doing. Not a professional – assassins don't use their hands to suffocate people – but not an amateur either. Post-mortem is happening shortly.'

'How are you getting on sussing out a motivation for said murders?'

'Honestly, not great.' Rowlinson rubbed the back of his head. He looked stressed: there were bags under his eyes and lines on his face Priest hadn't seen before. 'We keep coming back to your trial, of course; but something tells me that's not the whole story. There's something more complicated going on.'

'I agree entirely.'

Rowlinson looked up from the iPad for a moment and held Priest's gaze. 'It would help if, confidentially, you could tell me whether Alexia Elias was actually taking bribes from terrorists or not. That would cut out a whole layer of investigation and I don't know whether you caught the Home Secretary's recent ramblings but the Met's in for another round of cuts.'

'Tiff, if I could help on that front then . . .'

'Oh, come on, Priest! I'm doing my own fucking photocopying at the moment!'

Priest held his hand up in what he intended to be a conciliatory gesture. Rowlinson's outburst was a surprise – the detective was always calm under pressure.

'The simple fact is this: I don't know,' Priest concluded.

Rowlinson ran a slightly quivering hand through his hair. 'What do you mean, *you don't know*?'

'I'm running a libel trial. Defamation cases are concerned with evidence, not truth. If those two things happen to align then it's nothing more than a happy coincidence.'

'Or an unhappy one.'

Priest said nothing.

Rowlinson carried on. 'Well fine, I'll put it in *your* language then. What were the chances of the court coming to the view that Simeon Ali was telling the truth, were he still alive?'

'Sixty per cent, maybe fifty-five. But it's not going to help you, Tiff. I'm working to a much lower standard of proof than you. I have to show that, on the balance of probabilities, *The Real Byte*'s article was justified, in other words there was a fifty-one per cent chance or more it was true. If I had to prove everything beyond all reasonable doubt, I'd have packed up eighteen months ago.'

'I really hate lawyers, Priest,' Rowlinson grumbled.

'I know.'

'Let's try you on something else then.'

Rowlinson swung the iPad around to face Priest and propped it up using a stapler from the end of the desk. The image was a paused video – Priest couldn't make out what.

'Yesterday, there was an incident on the A3, the dual carriageway that runs in and out of London.' Rowlinson pressed PLAY and Priest realised the view was from the inside of a vehicle travelling in the middle lane. His stomach knotted and he bit the inner part of his lip – he knew what was coming. 'The picture's from a prison officer's dash cam. Dangerous game those boys are in so the Prison Service give them two pieces of travel advice: never take the same route home and always have the dash cam on. The file was recently uploaded to YouTube. Now if you just watch this for a few moments . . .'

The prison officer's car overtook a green Focus and advanced on an articulated lorry in the lane running parallel with the grassy incline. Priest could just make out the backs of the terrace houses filtering past before the hard shoulder ended and the road cut inwards so it was abutting the verge. In a heartbeat, the image changed as a flurry of brake lights preceded the road disappearing and the prison officer's car spinning out of control.

'I didn't know you'd been promoted to the Traffic Unit, Tiff,' Priest remarked.

'Very amusing. But what interests me is this . . .' Rowlinson fiddled with the horizontal white bar at the bottom of the screen until the prison officer's car was backing up the road. Then he stopped and moved the image forward frame by frame.

'See here?' Rowlinson pointed to what was unmistakably two figures running up the side of the road against the oncoming traffic. Priest groaned inwardly – he had been closer to catching the phone thief than he'd thought.

The lead figure darted across the road in front of the lorry – he made the other side in just four frames before the picture distorted into chaos. Rowlinson froze the screen. The second runner was looking out past where the first runner had vanished. The image was grainy; Priest thanked his lucky stars that Rowlinson didn't have a very compelling case for identification. He was just guessing, albeit correctly.

'I think this is you, Priest.' Rowlinson pointed at the figure standing on the side of the road.

'I agree he's a handsome chap, Tiff, but that could be anyone.'

Rowlinson withdrew the iPad and placed it back into his bag. 'You know what, I'm not even going to ask you what the hell you were doing.'

'Surely it's the obvious copper's question, even though it's not definitively me,' Priest averred, although he suspected Rowlinson didn't find his cynicism the remotest bit funny.

'You know why I'm not going to ask you, Priest? Because, if I did, you'd lie to me again and there's only so much I can handle.'

'Look, Tiff, we're on the same side—'

'Are we?'

Priest didn't reply. He could see Rowlinson had already made up his mind, so he let the question hang in the air. In time, Rowlinson nodded, as if his silence had implied an answer, before picking up his bag and vacating his seat.

'You need you to remember who your friends are, Priest,' Rowlinson said on his way to the door. 'There's only so many times I can cover for you.'

*

Gail sat at Tomas's kitchen table staring at her iPad, but not taking anything in. The kitchen was filthy, nobody was taking responsibility for cleaning it. Dirty pots and pans were piled high on the side, alongside a half-eaten salad and the remains of a Chinese takeaway from two nights ago.

The mood was sombre, no one was talking. Karl had gone AWOL again. Gail's inbox was cluttered with messages. She had contacts in mainstream media; they all wanted a slice of the action, an exclusive on the trial. But they didn't know the half of it.

Alexia Elias was murdered. Someone took a blowtorch to her face.

She checked her phone but there was nothing from Andros. They had argued that morning.

'Why aren't you here, with me?' He had every right to ask.

'It's a few days, a week at most. Tomas says we need to stay together.'

'Why? What the fuck is he so afraid of?'

'Andros, people are *dying*.' Her voice was a hiss; she barely recognised it.

'All the more reason why you should be here, with me. I'm coming over there, now.'

She had persuaded him not to. Promised to come home tonight, even though she had no intention of doing so. He had relented, begrudgingly. They hadn't been close in years, they both knew they were at the tail end of a dwindling marriage.

But that wasn't the reason why Gail preferred to stay at Tomas's.

'What are you doing?'

She looked up, startled. Hadn't heard him pad through. He wore joggers, a white T-shirt, bare feet. His hair was a mess, and there were heavy shadows under a pair of eyes cobwebbed with tiny red veins. Tomas Jansen looked washed out.

'Reading,' she replied quickly. 'Seeing what's out there and what's not.'

'Don't mope, we should be celebrating. The wicked witch is dead.'

He opened the fridge but not before casting her a dangerous look. It said, *Don't defy me: be happy.*

'I didn't want to win like this.'

Tomas snorted, took a pint of milk from the fridge and drank straight from the bottle. Then, he walked round behind Gail, stood there, looking over her shoulder. She didn't move, just soaked up the tension he was giving off. The hairs on the back of her neck prickled.

'You want to ask me something, Gail?' he said softly.

Gail felt her throat tighten. *It suited you to have Alexia dead,* she wanted to say. It wasn't as if Tomas had never been violent. Or at least that's what she thought. There had been Bella, Tomas's ex-girlfriend, and those bruises on her arms. But no proof, and Bella herself never said anything.

She couldn't be sure. But she would stay here to find out. *If you had anything to do with this, I'll know.*

'I guess we can all relax now, then,' she said, sensing his agitation behind her.

'No. Priest says it's not that simple.'

'You must be disappointed.'

He didn't respond at first, but leant over her. She flinched, but resisted the urge to push him away, although he was close enough that she could smell his cheap aftershave and morning breath.

'What do you mean?' His voice was faint, and it occurred to her: *how can someone be so close, yet so distant at the same time?*

'It didn't work for you. Alexia dying. That's all.'

'For *us*, you mean.'

'For the magazine. *Your* magazine.'

'What are you trying to say, Gail?'

'Just that.'

She held her breath, wondered if he could hear the same rush of blood she could hear surging through her brain. She sensed Tomas shifting his weight. Then, everything was still. She closed her eyes and wondered: *Is this man capable of murder? Could he kill me?* Whether it was the short pause, or Tomas's unnatural stillness at that moment, or her memory refocusing, homing in on Bella and her bruises; she wasn't sure. But she had made up her mind: *Yes, he was capable.*

'We're in this together, Gail.' His breath was hot, stale; his hand was on her back. She felt a bead of sweat form above her eyebrow, an itch enveloping her scalp. 'Aren't we?'

Her throat was dry, and her reply was half choked. 'We are. But if we lose, I'll survive. I doubt you can say the same.'

'We'll go down together, won't we? Isn't that the plan?'

'*Your* plan, Tomas.'

'You're not making any sense, Gail. We wrote the article together.'

'*You* wrote it. My additions were unimportant. It was *your* article.'

What if she was right? What if she pushed him too far? *Capable of killing to save his magazine? Yes. Capable of killing me? Here, now?*

'What about Simeon?' she asked.

'What about him?'

'Do you know . . . ?' She half turned, met his eye. *Do you know what happened to him?* It was unthinkable, and it made no sense. Tomas had motive for killing Alexia, but Simeon?

'You're in over your head, Gail.'

She leant in, every nerve fought against it but she was determined to show him she wasn't scared. 'No, Tomas. I'm fine . . . But you? You're burning up. I can *smell it.*'

He slammed his fist on the table in front her, enough to lift the iPad into the air a little. Gail jumped, her heart lurched, her muscles contracted. But the blow she anticipated never came. Tomas had moved, he was already on the other side of the kitchen, putting on his coat.

'I'm going out,' he said coldly. She didn't respond, just looked at him. 'Don't leave without letting me know.'

He slammed the door behind him. Gail looked down at the iPad, made to swipe the screen lock-out, but found her hand was shaking too badly.

Chapter 37

Priest sat looking pensively at the vapour rising from his cup of Earl Grey tea as it swirled into wraith-like shapes before disappearing into nothing. Much like the thoughts circulating in his head, never quite forming completely, rendered useless by their ephemeral existence.

There had been something about the way Tomas had leant across the table in the Royal Courts of Justice cafe when he was describing Rowlinson's visit and the question about the timing of the conference the day before the trial.

'We weren't all there, were we, Charlie? Not all of the time, at least.'

That's certainly true. I wasn't there for all of the time.

Priest had absented himself for part of the conference, claiming he had to take a phone call but in truth he had felt a wave of disassociation sweep over him and needed a blast of fresh air to ground him. How long had he been gone? An hour? Longer?

Rowlinson isn't going to be impressed.

He added another heap of sugar to the tea.

At five to ten, Cafe Olivero on Chancery Lane was packed full of men and women, mostly on their own, cradling tall glasses of frothy lattes and burying their heads in laptop screens. Arty folk, thought Priest. Long coats and stripy scarves, even though it wasn't cold. People who might describe themselves as 'bohemian' in a lonely hearts column.

Do they still have lonely hearts columns?

The door opened and Priest looked up. He caught a flash of red hair through the crowd and put his hand up to wave. A couple of students pointing excitedly at a stack of papers made way for Priest's visitor to half stumble through the small space and join him at the table.

'I come in here all the time!' Georgie exclaimed. 'I didn't know you did, too.'

'I don't,' Priest replied, looking over her shoulder. Georgie had left the door open, much to the annoyance of those sitting close by. A hefty woman wearing a denim jacket made a fuss of closing it.

'It's not even cold,' she complained.

'They want the smell of the coffee to be kept in.'

'Oh. Who are we meeting?'

The door opened again. A tall figure stood at the entrance, scanning the cafe. He wore a long, grey overcoat. He was maybe sixty, with emaciated features and sunken cheeks, heavy eyes and the air of an undertaker about him.

'That man, there.'

Georgie looked round as the figure glided effortlessly across the room. Whereas Georgie's trek to the table had been more of a haphazard negotiation, the crowd seemed to part automatically for this man to take a seat next to her.

'Georgie, this is Jack Oldham. Jack, meet Georgie Someday, my associate.'

Jack offered his hand, which Georgie took. 'Charmed,' he said, looking her in the eye.

'You're the Chairman of the Trustees of the Elias Foundation,' Georgie said, confused.

'And you are the brilliant young lady that Priest here has told me so much about,' Jack replied, letting go of Georgie's hand and offering her a strained but genuine smile.

Georgie turned to Priest, 'Should we be . . . ?'

'You didn't think I was going to take down a children's charity without being able to prop it back up again, did you?' Priest asked, raising an eyebrow. He could see she was starting to catch on.

'So . . . ?'

'I first met Priest when this whole affair started,' Jack offered. 'We knew that Alexia Elias was bad news but the Board didn't have any firm evidence to oust her; she had become too powerful.'

'Because Alexia had set the charity up in the first place, she had made sure that constitutionally her position was safe,' Priest explained. 'The Board's only option was a derivative action to wrestle control from Alexia through the courts.'

'And for that we needed evidence,' Jack added. 'At least, much more evidence than we have currently.'

Georgie pointed at Jack, although it was clearly an inadvertent gesture. 'So, you're on our side?'

'She's as quick as you described, Priest,' Jack laughed.

'What about *The Real Byte*?'

'Probably best we don't think about that too much,' Priest replied. 'The Solicitor's Regulation Authority are unlikely to be impressed, let's put it that way.'

'There's a greater good,' Jack said, casting her a confidential look. 'To the outside world, Alexia Elias was a saint. Only a select number of the Board knew what her true colours looked like.'

'So you knew about the bribes?' Georgie asked Jack. 'I thought the charity was supporting Alexia in the libel action.'

'That's our official line, yes. There really is no other option. As I say, though, some of us know the truth. That woman has been using the Foundation as her own personal bank for years. I strongly suspect she took the bribes as well, but I can't prove it. Only Simeon could have done that.'

'She'd been *stealing* charity money?'

'Let's just say that vast sums of money – and we are talking hundreds of thousands of pounds – over a long period of time have eventually found their way to various trust funds that are in her personal ownership.'

'But you couldn't . . . ?'

'Unseat her, no. As your boss says, legally that would have been very difficult without cogent evidence. The problem is that Alexia is – *was* – very adept at covering her tracks.'

'And whenever someone looked like they were thinking about taking a stand, they were paid off,' added Priest.

'I'm afraid that the corruption is institutional,' said Jack sadly. 'Rotten to the core.'

'But *The Real Byte* article was the perfect opportunity to start a war,' Priest continued for him. 'We knew Alexia wouldn't have much choice but to sue and we were fairly confident that we'd win, up until we found Simeon in the back of that reporter's car, but even if we lose, we've kicked around enough mud; some of it will stick. This is the beginning of the end.'

'Except that someone murdered her,' Georgie pointed out. The confusion in her face had evaporated. She had caught on, as Priest had predicted.

'Indeed,' said Jack. 'Hence why I called this meeting. What are our options, Charlie?'

'Under the Elias Foundation constitution you can appoint an interim CEO from the Board while you sort everything out. I'd suggest you put yourself forward. Will there be enough backing?'

'Yes. There are enough good eggs at board level. The problem is the paid staff, but once we have control of the charity we can sort them out in no time.'

'Good.' He turned to Georgie. 'It's starting to get a little tricky to orchestrate this without some help, Someday. That's why I've brought you in to the inner circle. We going to be flouting a few professional rules. Feel free to say no.'

Georgie beamed excitedly. 'I absolutely will not say no.'

'I thought as much. You can start by preparing the paperwork for Jack. He has a board resolution to pass, quickly.'

'That would be most helpful,' said Jack. 'What can we do in return?'

Priest produced the photograph of Julian Greenwood and placed it in front of Jack, who leant over and adjusted his glasses to study it.

'This is Julian Greenwood,' Priest explained. 'Standing outside Dominique and Alexia's former residence in Norfolk. We found this picture taped to the underside of a desk in Simeon's flat after he died. He had gone to great lengths to hide it.'

'I see,' Jack muttered, picking up the photograph and looking at it more carefully. 'This is Dominique's boy, isn't it?'

Priest nodded. 'Yes, but the picture's fake. Julian was never there and the photo has had work done to it to make it look old.'

'Why?'

'I don't know but I suspect someone is trying to tell us something. I'm just not sure what.'

'This is most concerning.' Jack replaced the photograph on the table, removed his glasses and rubbed the bridge of his nose. 'It isn't widely known that Dominique has a child.'

'Who is the mother?' asked Priest.

'I don't know. My understanding of the story is that the child is the product of a one-night stand. The mother got in touch after he was born and, surprise, surprise, she was paid off, probably out of the charity's funds.'

Priest scratched his head. A group of businessmen had entered the cafe and everyone around the entrance had begrudgingly moved up again, adding to the claustrophobic feel of the place.

'Can you find out what you can about Julian Greenwood?'

Jack sucked his teeth. 'I'll see what I can do.' He got up. 'I have to go. I will need to call a board meeting immediately. Nice to meet you, Georgie. Charlie.' He nodded at them both before making his way back across the crowded cafe to the door.

Priest took a sip of the Earl Grey; it was lukewarm and very sugary. He looked at Georgie. It had been a risk, telling her everything. The things that even Okoro didn't know. But her sense of justice burnt strongly, and she was staring at him warmly. The risk had paid off.

'How do you feel about all this?' he asked her.

'Like I missed a really important staff meeting at the start.'

Priest got up. 'I'm sorry, but it had to be this way.'

'I understand. Where are you going now?'

Priest glanced through the sea of coffee-drinkers and out of the window to Chancery Lane. The sun was out but it had begun to rain and people were scuttling into shops to avoid getting wet. Priest remembered the blue hair he had found at his flat and the look Jessica had given him before she had stormed out.

'A personal errand,' he declared. 'Meanwhile, I want you to do some internet searching for me.'

Chapter 38

The reception area of Ellinder Pharmaceuticals International (EPI) was a cavernous space overlooked by an open mezzanine floor and adorned with marble flooring and plush red furnishings. The reception desk puffed outwards in a semicircle and spanned the whole rear section in perfect symmetry. Foot-high letters embossed along the desk announced the name of the group. People milled around a cafe to the left of the reception desk, engrossed in laptops and tablets. The smell of disinfectant hung in the air.

EPI's share price had crashed the week after the arrests the previous year, as news had filtered out that the head of the deadly secret society known as the House of Mayfly, and her closest partisan, both bore the name Ellinder. The group would forever be tainted by a dark stain. Jessica had picked the worst moment in the group's history to take over as CEO. Slowly, a recovery was under way, underpinned by the sale of several overseas subsidiaries. A complete meltdown had been prevented, largely thanks to Jessica's skilful diplomacy and some good fortune: enough high-profile individuals had been implicated in the Mayfly scandal to just about overshadow EPI's association with what had happened.

While EPI had taken an horrific blow, the wound was apparently not fatal.

Priest approached the desk and a man in his twenties with shiny black hair and a pinched face lathered in orange-toned blusher smiled mechanically.

'Can I help you, sir?'

'I'd like to speak with Jessica Ellinder, please,' Priest declared with feigned conviction.

The receptionist raised a thinly plucked eyebrow. 'Of course. Do you have an appointment?'

'No. I do not.'

'You just popped in on the off chance?'

'Yes. Clearly.'

The receptionist hesitated before consulting his computer screen. Several clicks later he announced that Miss Ellinder was in a meeting but he was happy to let her know that Priest had dropped by *on the off chance*. Priest declined the offer and asked to use the toilet, whereupon he was, with considerable disdain, directed to the right.

'Thank you, you've been most helpful.'

The toilets were located in a sizeable alcove off the main area and out of the receptionist's line of sight. The male and female toilets were opposite each other but ahead a set of glass double doors led to a stairwell. A sign advised that entry was for authorised personnel only and that all visitors should report to reception. To make the point firmer, the door was locked and entry was controlled by a keypad, for which Priest did not have the code.

At least I know she's in and, like all egotistical corporate machines, the executive floor will be at the top.

Priest checked over his shoulder but he was hidden from view, unless someone wanted to use the facilities. He investigated the door; there was also a fob system but the keypad offered hope. Maybe it was an older mechanism awaiting removal or a backup for people who forgot their fobs. It didn't matter. Priest took out a small rattle-can filled with LCD screen cleaner and quickly sprayed the keypad. The fine powder settled, although to no obvious benefit, before Priest took a photograph of the pad with his iPhone, making sure the flash was on.

He studied the photo. Ideally, he would have used fluorescent spray or aluminium powder but he tended not to carry those around these days. The spray wouldn't show the prints clearly but, under intense light, a slight mark was visible on four of the numbers: one, three, five and nine. He just needed to work out what order they should be in.

Priest clicked his tongue and repeated the numbers in his head before tapping in a combination. The door emitted a satisfying click and he pushed it open.

Nineteen fifty-three. The year Ellinder Pharmaceuticals was founded. Easy.

There was a spiral stairwell on the other side encased in a cylinder of glass going both up and down – a transparent conduit impaling the heart of the building. Priest looked up. At least fifteen storeys and no lift.

Bollocks.

He took the stairs two at a time and by the time he reached the executive floor his thighs were burning. That wouldn't have mattered in itself were it not for his progress having been frustrated by another locked door – this time with no keypad.

More bollocks.

He stood to catch his breath, with one hand leaning on the stairwell banister. It was a long way to come to be foiled by a glass door. He looked through to the corridor behind the door, both sides of which were punctuated with doors through to offices with walls garlanded with HSE posters and performance graphs stuck to cork boards.

There was a man standing near the door, playing with his phone. When Priest tapped on the glass to attract his attention, he turned, startled. He had a juvenile face and greasy hair.

Ah, excellent. An apprentice.

Priest pointed to the black fob reader on his side of the door. It took the apprentice a few moments to register what Priest was insinuating but eventually he sidled over and opened the door cautiously.

'I'm not supposed to let anyone through this way,' he explained.

'No, quite right, too,' said Priest, putting a trusting hand on the boy's shoulder. 'Can't be too careful, can we?'

'You don't have an ID badge, sir,' the apprentice pointed out.

'Also, correct. Hence why I needed your assistance to open this door.'

'I see,' said the apprentice, although his expression suggested that he had been presented with a dilemma.

'Could you tell me where I can find Jessica Ellinder's office, please?' Priest asked, gently leading the apprentice down the corridor with his arm.

'Well . . .'

'It would be most helpful. As you no doubt have surmised, I am unfamiliar with the building, this being my first day and all.'

'Oh.' The apprentice looked uncertain. For a moment, Priest thought he might have overcooked it, but then the apprentice seemed to perk up. Perhaps Priest's explanation had registered with him as plausible. 'You're new here? Like me. I started last week.'

'And yet already you conduct yourself in the manner of a veteran executive!'

'I just help out in the archive room mostly. I had to take tea to the board meeting earlier. Miss Ellinder's office is down here but she's in the meeting with the rest of them at the moment. Are you OK to wait in her office?'

Priest smiled. 'That would be most agreeable.'

*

Georgie felt like someone had taken her head off and replaced it the wrong way round.

In one respect, Charlie's secret collaboration with the chair of the Elias Foundation Board of Trustees was welcome news. She now understood that there was a bigger plan and the ethical problem posed by Priest & Co.'s involvement with the potential downfall of the Foundation had been straightened up.

In another respect, the news was a chilling reminder of the precarious walk across the burning tightrope they were all facing.

She had got over the fact that Charlie had only just told her. He was in charge and if he thought that she should have been in the loop earlier then he would have let her in.

Who am I kidding? She sat at her desk at work waiting for her camomile tea to cool, staring at a blank Word document on her desktop monitor. *I'm thoroughly annoyed.*

She couldn't think about that right now, though. For one thing, people were dying. Horribly. She started to draft out the board resolution Jack would need to pass to appoint himself as interim CEO when a text popped up on her phone. She saw it was from Li. *Hi, babe. Thought we could get pizza tonite and talk about you know what. Got some ideas! Xx*

Georgie smiled and replaced the phone on the desk. It was a sweet thought, although she couldn't think of anything worse.

Chapter 39

Priest found that Jessica Ellinder's chair was surprisingly comfortable. At first sight, he had thought it might be too hard for his liking but the leather was deceptively soft and the height and back only required minor adjustments to make him feel at home looking out across the desk to the only door in.

The office was less resplendent than the CEO of a multimillion pound group might command; he suspected this wasn't her father's office but her old one. She had been catapulted into leadership following his death but he doubted she would have found the prospect of taking her father's office appealing.

So other than a row of filing cabinets, a desk, a couple of chairs and an old fax machine – *who the hell uses fax nowadays?* – the room was sparse. Most notably, it was devoid of any items of a personal nature. No pictures of beaming family members propped up on the desktop, no certificates on the wall, no little trinkets or silly executive toys, or even any artwork. This could have been absolutely anybody's office, or nobody's.

He thought about opening one of the drawers and rummaging through when the door burst open. Jessica swept in and at first didn't register her visitor until the door shut behind her. Then she stopped dead, her mouth gaping.

'What on earth . . . ?'

She looked breathtaking, and whatever speech Priest had planned suddenly died on his tongue. She was wearing a cream pencil skirt cut just above the knee and a deep-blue silk shirt with half-sleeves, ruffled, so he couldn't tell if she had rolled them up or it was the design. He glanced down to her bare legs. She had the most perfectly shaped calves he had ever seen. He noticed how tanned she was; her skin was a warm, olive tone. It hadn't been as evident when he had seen her at her father's funeral. He swallowed, and a thought shuddered in his head: *has she been on holiday with someone else?*

'Hello,' Priest said weakly.

Jessica dumped the papers she was holding onto the edge of the desk. For a moment she looked as though she might cry.

'How in God's name did you get up here?'

'Jessica, you ought to know that the security arrangements here are really not tenable, especially for a drugs company.'

'Get out.'

'Now, hold on . . .'

'*Get out!*'

Priest had intended to stay seated but found himself out of the chair with arms raised in a gesture of conciliation.

My God she's beautiful.

'Hear me out,' he pleaded.

She folded her arms and looked away, disgusted. 'Why?'

'Let me explain.'

'Explain which bit? The little tart you were bent over or the breaking and entering?'

Priest scanned desperately for something to anchor the conversation with. He suspected the building had security guards and he didn't fancy the idea of being thrown off the top of a fifteen-storey office block. He thought he might try an old lawyer's trick to get a judge to listen.

'How about you give me one minute to persuade you that you've misunderstood and we should start off where we were before and if I can't then I go quietly?'

She folded her arms, which he took as the start of his minute of reprieve.

'I know it doesn't look good. I know from where you're standing, I look like a fucking creep. I also know that I can be . . . a little awkward sometimes.'

She leant her head to one side as if to reply with, *You don't say.*

'I have a condition . . .'

'Yes, you suffer from depersonalisation disorder. I know.'

Once again, the words that he had prepared were ripped out of his throat. Not only did she know about his condition, she also knew the exact type. His mind raced: *how does she know that?*

'That's right.' He felt as though he was three feet tall and she was towering over him. 'Just out of interest, how do you know that?'

She stepped forward, and her command of the situation tightened. My father did the business on you, Charlie. He was a very careful person. He also knew *your* father. Did you expect him to keep your medical history secret from me?'

'No,' he admitted. It seemed obvious now. 'Probably not much point in using that as an excuse then.'

She sighed, but there was a tiny movement across her lips. 'No. No point at all.' She had almost smiled.

'How about an apology instead?'

The smile didn't materialise. Instead, she pushed past him. Up close her face was as he remembered: high cheekbones, authoritative, flawless skin, bright devilish eyes and minimal make-up.

'You can give me my desk back first,' she said, positioning herself behind it, but not sitting down. 'Then we'll talk.'

Priest pulled a face, the balance of power had shifted. If she was going to kick him out, she would have done it by now.

'How are things here?' He motioned around the room, meaning the Ellinder Group.

'Not good. The strength of the balance sheet is keeping us afloat, and the patents on new drugs are valuable. But we have around six months to stop the haemorrhaging before we start to question our viability. I'm selling subsidiaries like they're going out of fashion.'

'That good?'

'Why did you come here, Charlie?'

She had said it softly. It hadn't been intended as a threat or a challenge. It mattered to her. Priest's head was burning. He looked at his hands. It wasn't that they didn't look real, they just didn't look like *his*. He was ashamed, but there was more to it. He was *afraid*. Afraid he had blown it. After William's crimes had been made public, Priest had spent years in an emotional wasteland, tortured by the ceaseless paradox that depersonalisation disorder created: he felt *nothing*, yet that lack of feeling had driven him to the edge of despair. Now, time had softened the disorder's debilitating effects but he was still haunted. The ghost of the condition wouldn't go away. For the first time in years, for over a decade, Charlie Priest had felt something, a possibility.

A fleeting chance. This woman could make him happy, and the ghost could be laid to rest.

But he might have squandered the chance.

His stomach churned.

'I can't exorcise this overwhelming feeling,' he said, meeting her gaze. 'I've tried, but it won't go away.'

She seemed suspicious, defensive. Impenetrable. 'What feeling?'

'That there is a bond between us.'

He let that hang in the air. Sensed a chasm opening up in front of him – a black hole, into which all of his energy was being pulled. He was drained. The adrenaline of the trial had been sucked dry. Alexia's ruined face haunted him. Simeon's death weighed heavy on his conscience and he had been so close, holding what might have been the answer, Simeon's phone, only to have it cruelly snatched away by a faceless thief.

'There is no bond between us,' he heard her splutter in that deep, melodic rasp of a voice. Anger enveloped him, rising in his chest and spreading outwards.

'I'm sorry,' she repeated. 'There is no—'

He took half a step forward. Without warning, he curled his hand around the back of her neck and pulled her into his embrace, put his mouth to hers and tasted the sweet tang of her lips. Her eyes widened with alarm and there seemed to be a moment when she realised what he was doing and brought her hand hard across his face, breaking the contact with such shock that Priest thought he had blacked out.

'How dare you!' she bellowed.

He was about to retreat, the horror of what he had done seeping through his fury. Then she hit him again. The third time she lashed out he caught her wrist, held it, his chest heaving.

Then she threw herself at him.

At first, Priest thought she was attacking him before he realised her mouth was biting down on his neck and she had hooked her hands around his waist, until he fell back against the wall.

She kissed him, long and clumsily, her tongue finding his immediately, sending a surge of lust down through his body to where she was desperately scrabbling at his trouser belt. He tucked his hands around her backside and spun her around, pushing her against the wall and she gasped as he pulled her skirt up, finding the top of her tights and tearing them away.

'Did she give you want you wanted?' she hissed in his ear, throwing his belt to the floor.

'It wasn't what it seemed,' he grunted, her insinuation fuelling the disgust and shame that enveloped him. He took her leg, pulling it around the small of his back, opening her up for him. She had him in her hand, stroking his shaft but it wasn't enough – he wanted more, he wanted *her*. He pulled her hand away, pressed himself against her.

'No, wait,' she begged.

'I want you.'

'I'm not ready for this.'

He exhaled loudly with frustration, pulling her head back so he could suck on her neck. 'Jessica . . .'

'I need you to know that if you do this, then it doesn't make me yours. I don't belong to you.'

She was fighting for breath, barely able to breathe out the words as he kissed her again. She pulled his hand over her breast. He fumbled for the buttons on her shirt, tugging the first open, then the second before running his hand across her bare chest, reaching the point of no return.

'Fine,' he gasped, exasperated. 'You don't belong to me.'

She relaxed, closed her eyes. He positioned himself between her legs, entered her, and she moaned with what Priest knew was a desire as raw as his own.

Chapter 40

The owner finished masturbating and lay still, panting, stretched out on the damp bed sheets. There was a portable gas fire in the corner turned up full blast and the room was enveloped in oppressive, hot air. In the distance, jackdaws squabbled on the abandoned railway line.

The owner had seen the headlines, they were everywhere: ELIAS FOUNDATION LIBEL WITNESS FOUND DEAD IN CAR BOOT. But why wasn't the source of the story ever mentioned? It was infuriating that credit wasn't given to those who deserved it. The limelight was always stolen by less talented, egotistical fuckwits.

The owner shuffled over to a dryer part of the bed. Looked at the wall. It was plastered from floor to ceiling with photographs. The owner reached for the diary under the bed. Knew exactly where it was. This was the favourite bit. The owner knew the words by heart, had memorised them with religious devotion. The diary had been more than just a revelation: it had changed everything. A key, one that had unlocked a secret world. The diary, the key, was the owner's personal Torah and this section was the most sacred: it described the moment of escape from evil.

The Exodus.

He removes his finger and, although it is a relief, she knows that the pain won't subside until the morning. She hadn't dressed up today: he was in too much of a hurry. That had been both good and bad.

'There,' he says, as if everything is normal and she had enjoyed it. The girl doesn't cry. He doesn't like it when she cries.

It is light today, and the television had been left on. She turns her head, bites her lip. It is a news programme – a man talking to the screen and words she couldn't understand passing underneath him. The sound is off. While he had finished, the girl had thought of the man from the television.

He leaves in a hurry, mutters something about being late. He is careless, knocking into a table and cursing under his breath. He is swaying like he does sometimes. And that smell. Always it was worse when he came with that smell; it reminds her just a little of the sickly, arresting smell of the woman's perfume.

The door closes behind him, the latch clicks and she waits for the bolt to shoot home, sealing her into the airless basement. The girl doesn't mind the bolt. Sometimes she can just about imagine a world where she can close her eyes and move the bolt just by thinking about it, like the film she had seen with the green man who gets his words mixed up. Another world she isn't sure actually exists.

So, she waits. And waits.

But the bolt doesn't move.

At first, she thinks she must have missed the moment when he locked the door, but she can see through the little gap between the edge of the door and the frame. There is nothing but clean air filtering through.

The girl sits quietly and counts to ten. Then sings 'The Alphabet Song' in her head. Still nothing. The door is unlocked.

She can't move. She is hurting inside and there is some blood, but it isn't that. She is petrified. What if she gets into trouble because the door is unlocked? What if they think she is trying to escape?

Gingerly, she gets up and inspects the door. Maybe she can somehow lock herself in, then they'd never know.

She listens at the door, puts her ear right up against it. She can't hear anything. Just a gentle hum from upstairs. She hears that noise every now and again but she doesn't know what it is.

She runs to the table, grabs the wooden doll and turns the key. The doll strikes up her tune obediently.

Ting, ting, ting.

She goes back to the door, taking the doll with her. Listens again. Still nothing. She tries the handle. She had never tried the handle before. Never. It was the only bit of the room she had never touched, except the ceiling and the light.

It turns surprisingly easily and, for a moment, she wonders if it is even connected to the latch but, sure enough, she hears a little click and the door moves a bit. She jumps back. The doll is still singing. There is a gap in the door just wide enough for her to look through.

Only she can't see much. Just more bricks and . . . are those stairs?

She pushes the door, just a little, to widen the gap. Still, she can't see much. She looks down at the doll. 'What should I do?'

The doll winks at the girl.

She only intended to open the door, sneak out to the other side and see if she could somehow work it so the lock clicked after she had shut the door on her side again. She opens the door further, just enough to squeeze through. She is dirty and there is blood trickling down her leg. It is difficult to move. Everything hurts.

But then, all of a sudden, she is on the other side. Like the little girl who walks through the wardrobe, past the furry coats and finds herself in a wondrous, snow-covered land.

Except there is no snow. Just a narrow staircase going upwards.

She stops, holds her breath. It occurs to her that she had to have been outside of the room at some point, when she was younger. The woman said she had been delivered by her mother when she was little.

But now she is here, she can't go any further. She belongs in the room. The girl doesn't know if she can even breathe the air outside of the room. Is it OK, or would her head explode like in the film that had scared her where they went to Mars?

Then she remembers the church, and the tree. She can just see the top of the church from the window, its spire towering above everything else, except the tree. She remembers what she had said to herself about the church.

That God is in there, waiting for her.

She looks at the doll. She thinks the doll is crying but isn't sad that the girl was going. The doll is pleased for her, proud of what she is going to do.

She looks up the stairs into the void. Then decides something. 'Come on, Ash Doll,' she whispers. 'We can go together.'

Chapter 41

After they had finished, Jessica unravelled herself from his embrace, pulled up her tights and started to tidy herself up; all the time avoiding his eyes.

Unsure, Priest zipped himself up and perched on the end of the desk watching her. From an expensive-looking bag on the floor, she had produced a small mirror and went about busying herself with her hair, although there wasn't much wrong with it from Priest's perspective. One side was a little ruffled from where he had slid his hand through it in the moment of climax – the point at which she had opened her eyes, albeit briefly. In that moment he thought he had seen something – evidence of the bond she had so vehemently denied.

Now the moment had passed and the CEO of Ellinder Pharmaceuticals had reappeared. The barriers were back up.

'I have a meeting in fifteen minutes,' she announced.

'You want me to leave?'

She replaced the mirror and retrieved a lip balm. This was applied sparingly – as if the need for it in itself represented the most reluctant of concessions – and then also replaced.

'I have a meeting in fifteen minutes,' she repeated.

Priest scratched the back of his head, nonplussed at the suddenness of her metamorphosis from the lustful vixen who had clawed at his back to the cold, detached woman who was now holding the office door open, waiting for him to leave.

'OK,' Priest conceded. 'Can I at least see you again?'

He walked to the door, stopping just short. He wanted to kiss her but everything about the way she was poised warned against it.

'Yes,' she said eventually. 'I'll call you.'

*

Back in his office, Priest found Georgie in a state of considerable excitement.

'Look,' she said, guiding him to her computer monitor and sitting him in her chair. She leant across him and fiddled with the mouse. She had her hair tied back and was wearing a sleeveless blouse; her freckly arm brushed against his cheek. He wondered if he smelt of sex.

'Watch,' she instructed.

She had found the YouTube clip of his chase down the dual carriageway taken from the perspective of the dash cam. The scene played out in the same way Rowlinson had showed him with the traffic proceeding in an ordinary manner until Georgie took control of the slide bar at the bottom of the screen.

So far, the video had been viewed over a thousand times and received nearly two hundred 'likes'.

'If we stop it fifty-three seconds in . . .' she explained, clicking the mouse at exactly the right point. Priest didn't see anything particularly out of place to begin with until she drew his attention to the top right of the screen.

'That's the person I was chasing!' Priest exclaimed.

There was a blurry image of a figure wearing a dark hoodie climbing the verge on the other side of the road. The frame was paused at a fraction of a second before the pile-up.

'I've isolated the image,' Georgie explained, minimising the internet browser and bringing up another screen. Priest didn't recognise the programme but it showed the pixelated version of the hoodie thief. 'This software improves image quality. Its freeware so it's not great but—' She clicked a red button at the top of the screen marked APPLY, the computer whirred for a few seconds and the image of the hoodie thief returned with more clarity.

Priest sighed audibly with satisfaction. 'Well I'll be damned.'

In truth, the picture was only marginally improved but it was enough to enable him to make out that the thief's hood had fallen back at some stage during the climb to the top of the embankment revealing a shock of blue hair.

'It's the girl from the gym,' Georgie said triumphantly.

Priest sat back in his chair; his initial excitement had waned quickly. *The blue hair I found on my sofa came from Fox's coat. That can only mean one thing: she got there first.*

'Come on, Georgie,' he urged, getting to his feet. 'Time to get some answers.'

*

Georgie had established that the Budget Gym closed at 11 p.m. and with a quarter of an hour to go it looked as though nobody was taking advantage of the late closing time. The Italian restaurant next door was doing better trade, which was hardly surprising – the warm glow of the red and purple decor looked infinitely more appealing than the gym's harsh artificial lighting.

There was some movement at the restaurant's door – two in and two out – and a few people ambling towards a pub on the corner; a lone man stood puffing on a cigarette outside the late-night newsagent's further down. Other than that, Grace Street was uncannily quiet.

Georgie had been huddled in a small alcove on the opposite side of the road to the gym for almost half an hour now. They had decided to wait till just before closing time when there were fewer people around, but her propensity to over-plan had brought her into position far too early. Now she was cold, and the alcove stank of urine. She watched the comings and goings at the gym carefully, such as they were. Other than a woman with dreadlocks loping out ten minutes ago carrying a large holdall, nothing had happened, although she had occasionally spotted the blue-haired girl called Mims drifting past the window.

I hope you're on your own.

She pulled her coat tightly around her. It had dropped five degrees at least since she had pitched up for her stakeout as Priest had instructed and the fur lining on her anorak wasn't sufficient to keep the cold out. As she struggled for warmth, watching her breath swirl into wisps of vapour in front of her, she started to realise that going into the gym on her own wasn't a particularly clever plan.

'You need to go on your own,' Charlie had told her.

'Really? You don't think . . . ?'

'She'll run a mile as soon as she sees me. You're less of a threat.'

The three patrons they had encountered last time might well still be there, just out of view, and they would surely recognise her. And without Charlie, where would she be then? At the bottom of the Thames, presumably.

Georgie shuddered.

She tried to get her feet to move but they seemed to be stuck to the ground. Georgie suspected that her observation hideout served as a homeless man's place of residence for part of the week, which would explain the smell, but not her inability to move.

She was bloody scared.

'Oh, this is ridiculous,' she said out loud, forcing herself to move. *It's just a gym.*

She half stumbled across the road inwardly shouting at herself to get a grip. *There are very few monsters who warrant the fear we have in them.* She repeated the phrase over and over but, as she approached the blinding fluorescent radiance of the gym facade, even André Gide's comforting words weren't enough to shrink the knot in her stomach.

Georgie opened the door, which triggered a tone at the back of the gym. She quickly scanned the interior but couldn't see anyone. Maybe everyone had gone home? And left the door unlocked?

'We're about to close up,' shouted an unimpressed voice, which made Georgie jump.

She whirled around and saw that Mims was collecting dumbbells and piling them in a box in the corner of the room. The girl looked up, her blue hair ruffled and straw-like, and at first she regarded Georgie with disinterest, until recognition slowly overcame her.

'Wait a minute,' said Mims, squaring up. 'You were here with that guy who beat up Benny.'

'Charlie hardly beat him up,' Georgie pointed out.

Mims snarled and, for a moment, Georgie thought she might attack her, until she swore loudly, turned and bolted towards the back door. Georgie followed her but without conviction – *she* wasn't going to chase anyone the wrong way down a motorway. And besides, she didn't need to.

As Mims reached the back of the gym the rear door burst open and she rebounded off Charlie's heavy torso.

'Now then,' he said, picking the protesting Mims up off the floor and guiding her to her office and into the chair behind the desk, 'I think you have something that belongs to a friend of mine.'

Chapter 42

Twice, the blue-haired girl tried to break for it and twice Priest had to haul her back and deposit her in the desk chair, the latter time with enough force to let her know that fighting him wasn't an option.

Georgie looked pale under the gym's lights and Priest noticed a slight tremble in her voice as she pleaded with Mims not to run again. He shouldn't have sent her in alone but he had to have the back covered – he knew how fast Mims could run. Breaking through the back door had been pretty simple; the lock hadn't been updated in decades and was warped around the edges.

'All right!' Mims spat in the end, holding up her hands, her chest heaving. 'What the fuck do you want?'

'I want my friend's phone back,' Priest explained calmly.

'*Your* friend? That was Simeon's phone!'

Priest exchanged a quizzical look with Georgie. 'You knew Simeon?'

'Of course I fucking do,' she growled. 'Wait. What do you mean *knew*?'

Priest hesitated – he could see she didn't know. Her face changed from one of utter contempt to anxiousness in a beat, her eyes were no longer ablaze but searching his face for an answer. She cared, that was clear. But she didn't know. She was intelligent, too. The blue hair and nose and ear studs were a facade for something else. Had Priest misjudged her?

'I'm very sorry,' he told her. 'Simeon Ali is dead.'

Mims looked at the floor, her mouth agape. Her eyelids fluttered and Priest thought that she might cry until she wiped her face with the back of her hand. It seemed to be a display of defiance rather than grief, but that was perhaps her way of dealing with it.

'How did you know Simeon had a phone here?' she asked quietly.

Priest evaded the question. 'It doesn't matter. They call you Mims, right?'

Mims nodded her head and tucked her legs underneath her on the chair before leaning her elbow on the desk. Georgie indicated that she would find Mims a glass of water and disappeared while Priest took a chair from the corner of the room and sat opposite her.

'You're that lawyer, aren't you?' said Mims. 'The one that's representing the magazine.'

'That's right. My name is Priest.'

'Where'd you learn to fight like that?'

'I used to be in the police force.'

'They kick you out?'

Priest smiled weakly. Mims's hostility had evaporated; she sat crumpled up on the chair staring glumly ahead. She didn't acknowledge the water Georgie placed on the desk in front of her.

'I kicked myself out,' said Priest. 'Sorry about making your friends look like idiots.'

Mims scoffed but there was a hint of genuine amusement in her tone. 'They're not my friends. Benny and his fuckwit buddies come here because it's cheap. To be honest, seeing someone take them down a peg or two was worth the mile-long sprint afterwards.'

'You knew I'd taken Simeon's phone?'

'I knew you'd been in his locker and that you must have stolen the key. I followed you outside and you were waving this phone around and it clearly wasn't yours – you'd have some smartphone shit, not Simeon's old crap.'

'How did you know we'd stolen the key? We didn't, by the way.'

'Whatever. I thought you'd stolen it because I thought there was no way Simeon would have ever given it away. He kept stuff in that locker that wasn't anything to do with going to the gym.'

'Like what?'

Mims shrugged. 'I dunno. I kind of . . . we kind of . . .' She drifted into a sort of trance, her eyes stared behind Priest, unfocused. He guessed the realisation that Simeon was dead was starting to hit home.

'You and Simeon were – what? Friends? Lovers?'

'Fuck buddies,' Mims insisted. Then her tone softened and Priest saw a little more of the blue hair facade fade away. 'Lovers, then. Whatever. We had feelings for each other but that was a while ago. I hadn't seen him in a few months.'

'I'm sorry you had to find out this way,' said Priest. 'How long were you seeing each other?'

'A year. Maybe longer.'

Priest nodded as the first crystal-like tear formed at the edge of Mims's eye. Georgie shifted her weight. They had to get on, but Mims had to be given time. Priest bit his lip.

'Where's the phone, now, Mims?' Georgie asked, softly, sensing the same dilemma.

'It's at my house,' Mims replied without looking back at her. 'How did he die? Simeon, I mean.'

Priest took a deep breath. 'He was murdered, Mims.' This time she looked up, startled. 'He was asphyxiated and dumped in the boot of a car.'

Mims had her hand to her mouth, her eyes were now welling with tears. 'Jesus, no!'

'I'm sorry.'

'When?'

'He was killed on Thursday, his body was discovered on Friday, by us. We're trying to find out why and who is responsible.'

Mims shook her head with what seemed like disbelief. 'The police . . . ?'

'Are doing their best. As are we.'

There was a moment's silence as Mims fought back the tears – she seemed determined not to cry, or show any weakness. In return, Priest did not offer the indignity of comfort but kept on the other side of the desk as she slowly stood and turned to face them.

'You can come back to mine,' she said. 'I'll need to lock up here first.'

'Thank you. We'll meet you out the front . . .'

'No,' said Mims, sharply, turning to Georgie. 'Not her. I don't like her. Just me and you, lawyer-man.'

*

With great care, the owner replaced the blowtorch back in its box and picked up the iPhone from the nearby table. There were several pictures of Alexia's mutilated face taken from different angles and the owner was pleased with the overall effect. There was something very abstract about the result. Perhaps one day they would recognise the beauty of what had been achieved and hang pictures of it in the Tate for the public to drool over.

The owner downloaded the pictures onto a MacBook and zipped up the best three in a separate folder before taking a plain, battered-looking Ford Mondeo to an internet cafe in Soho. There, the photographs were attached to an email and sent to their intended recipient along with a mobile phone number and nothing else.

The owner sat back, arms folded, and watched as the status bar above the email changed from SENDING to SENT.

The first conversation with Dominique Elias had been a disappointment in many respects. The owner had lost control and veered off script, angered by the old man's arrogance, his blasphemous attempts at deception. But despite this lack of control, the owner had been fair. Elias had been warned. The consequences had been spelt out, but he had not listened.

He had not listened and that is why I had to act.

The owner looked around. The cafe was tatty, with Rastafarian artwork plastered on the walls and an array of shrunken heads hanging from the ceiling. They were plastic, of course, but still enough to draw the owner's disgust. There was one other patron, a black man in his thirties captivated by his computer screen, sitting at the table opposite and a woman behind the counter paying little attention to anything other than her nails. There was a smell in the air that disagreed with the owner, who detested the cafe. It was nothing more than a sad microcosm of the lonely existence of man on a dying planet. Just one that was painted with orange and yellow walls. But it was one of the few internet cafes in London with no CCTV inside or out, so even if they managed to trace his messages back to the computer's IP address, no one would connect the owner to the message. Or by the time they did, it would be too late. The owner was a specialist at merging into the crowd. The owner had always been part of life's backdrop. Soon all that would be changed.

Somewhere, a phone was ringing. The owner looked down and saw the phone buzzing by the computer and eventually answered it.

'Yes?'

No words were uttered at the other end of the line. There was just the sound of a man crippled with unimaginable pain.

'Ah, Dominique,' the owner said, smiling. 'Are you listening now?'

Chapter 43

It turned out that Mims lived in a flat just round the corner from Grace Street, more or less opposite the Bag of Nails, the pub where she had robbed Priest of the phone they were now heading to retrieve. The sound of thumping music was bleeding through the pub walls as they passed. A huddle of men passing round a roll-up outside eyed them wearily as Mims led Priest across the street to a row of terraces.

Georgie had expressed her displeasure when Priest had invited her to wait in the car.

'I'll be a few minutes, tops,' he had said.

'Can I at least have the keys so I can put the heating on?'

'The battery is almost as old as you so don't give it more than five or ten minutes.'

Mims's home was a one-bed flat above a kebab house with a 1970s kitchen that smelt of joss sticks. It was homely enough – warm and clean, simply furnished. The living room was the size of Priest's smaller bathroom, with a two-seater sofa covered by a knitted rug, an Ikea coffee table and a miniature flat screen TV on the sideboard.

A grey cat opened a languid eye from its basket in the corner as Priest took one end of the sofa, but otherwise the creature seemed disinterested in the new visitor.

'This must all be a bit of a shock,' Priest began, although he realised it sounded lame and predictable. Fortunately, Mims had put her animosity aside for now and collapsed on the sofa next to him.

'I suppose so.'

'You're too clever a girl to be working at that gym.'

'How do you know I'm clever?'

Priest nodded at the picture tucked behind the TV. It wasn't in a frame, just a four-by-six portrait photograph of Mims, with natural mousy brown hair, holding her degree jubilantly for the camera.

'Oh,' she sighed. 'Of course. A first in physics with astrophysics from Glasgow.' She glanced over at the photograph and Priest detected an unsubtle pang of disappointment from her look.

'What happened?' he asked.

She exhaled heavily, thought for a moment. Perhaps wondered whether to tell him anything, before saying, 'I'd like to say that I produced the most brilliant thesis which proved unequivocally the existence of dark matter and burnt out from the sheer enormity of it . . . but in truth I had an affair with one of my tutors and . . . well, my career options were suddenly narrowed.'

'I don't see how having an affair with a tutor would damage your employment prosp—'

'Then you don't know physics,' Mims interrupted. 'But, being kind to you, it has to do with the fact that I had an affair with one of the greatest living physicists of the last two centuries, and that's what makes entering the profession trickier for me. Everyone thinks I'm just there because of nepotism.'

'So, you coloured your hair blue and moved down here.'

'Moved *back* down here,' she corrected. 'My parents are from Barking.'

'They must be mad to live there,' Priest remarked, and despite it being an embarrassing attempt at humour she smiled.

'That's fucking awful. I'm sorry, by the way, about knocking you over. I used to run at uni and I still train in the gym. Quite a race, wasn't it?'

Priest grinned. 'It's on YouTube, if you want to relive it. Two hundred "likes".'

'That's cool.'

Mims got up without warning and went to the sideboard. She rummaged around in the drawer then produced the phone. Handed it to Priest.

'I'm sorry, the battery's dead,' she told him. 'I was just looking through it – only for a moment. I don't have the charger. I haven't seen Simeon, like I said, but that doesn't mean . . . you know.'

'Doesn't mean you don't care,' Priest suggested. Mims nodded, sadness in her eyes. 'Want to tell me what happened?'

She sat down again next to him and curled her legs under her, like she sat on the office chair in the gym. He noticed that she never seemed to sit or stand completely straight, she was always at an angle.

'I know that Simeon was helping you,' she began, turning to face him. 'He spoke very highly of you, by the way. Thought you were a champion of the underdog, like he was. Or at least like he wanted to be. He worked for the Elias Foundation, directly for Alexia at one point, and of course he knew what sort of person she was. But you should know that . . .'

'That she didn't take bribes from the Free People's Army,' Priest finished for her.

Mims looked at him, aghast. 'You knew?'

'I suspected.'

'But you were running the magazine's defence.'

'I was,' Priest confirmed, unapologetic. 'But there's a difference between knowing your client is lying and having a suspicion that part of the evidence might be a fabrication. Courts aren't about truth; they're about who can prove what.'

'Perhaps I was naive to think otherwise.'

'Not naive.' Priest shook his head. 'Just optimistic. And it doesn't make Alexia Elias a nice person, either. She was into all sorts of mischief, just not the actual mischief of which she was accused. I guess Simeon was trying to take her down because he knew that she was corrupt but he couldn't prove it. Then someone came along and convinced him that he didn't have to. He just had to make something up, convincingly, and produce some papers to back it up. Someone would print it and her reputation would be in ruins, irrespective of the truth.'

As he finished speaking, he could see that Mims had finally let go – tears streaked down her face, like the last of her blue-haired facade had melted away, leaving a vulnerable woman underneath. She was nodding too, wiping away the tears with the back of her sleeve. Priest got up and fetched her some toilet roll and she took a few moments to compose herself.

'That's right,' she said, drying her eyes. 'He thought it was easy at first. Just contact *The Real Byte* and give them the story. He knew it was wrong, but she had to be stopped. The corruption ran deep. Charity money was being laundered through the Foundation to benefit Alexia and the people close to her. Simeon couldn't prove that, so when *The Real Byte* opportunity came up, he saw another way of getting to her. That was Simeon – the one to touch the untouchable. But it went wrong . . .'

'The story wasn't enough. The Elias Foundation's PR agents did a good job covering it up, Alexia's friends rallied round her, some more people got paid off and she sued the magazine. So Simeon had to come out of hiding.'

'And now he's dead,' sobbed Mims. 'Why? For what?'

'Mims, did Simeon ever talk about telling the truth at any point while the trial was going on?'

She stopped dabbing her face and looked up, her cheeks were flushed and tear-stained, but Priest looked beyond that, to the look of realisation that was forming in her eyes.

'You think that whoever put Simeon up to this killed him because he had decided to tell the truth about Alexia?' she asked. The quiver in her hand and in her voice was unmistakable.

'I think that's a very distinct possibility,' said Priest gravely. 'A very distinct possibility.'

Chapter 44

It was closing in on midnight and small groups of men were tumbling out of the Bag of Nails across the road from Mims's flat, their raucous laughter cutting through the night air: an intimidating, wretched sound that was as nauseating as it was primitive. Mims had fixed Priest and herself a mug of murky-looking coffee – about the last thing that Priest wanted but he took the cup gratefully despite the fatigue that had washed over him and the thumping ache developing at the base of his skull.

He took a sip of the coffee. It tasted awful, bitter and acrid. A train rumbled underneath them and the old single-glazed windows rattled in their peeling frames. Must be the Victoria Line where the tunnels are less deep.

'Was there a reporter?' Priest asked. 'Someone else asking about Simeon.'

Mims raised an eyebrow. 'The blonde girl?' Priest nodded. 'Isn't *she* a charmer.'

'She give you any trouble?'

Mims hesitated. 'No. She came to the gym a couple of times, caught me outside. At first she tried to say she was a friend of Simeon's but I knew that was bullshit. Then she said she was trying to find out the truth about Alexia. I told her to fuck off.'

'Did she touch you?'

'Touch me?' Mims looked perplexed. 'I pushed past her at one point. Why? Do you know her?'

Priest ignored the question and changed the subject. 'Do you know who put Simeon up to all of this?' *Find him, find Simeon's killer, perhaps. She must know that, but she hasn't volunteered the information.*

'I don't know,' she sighed. 'I wish I did.'

'You had a look at Simeon's phone, though?'

'Yes,' she agreed, and with a visible flush of guilt. 'There were text messages between Simeon and someone else.'

'Someone calling themselves USER3412.'

'Yes. But that doesn't mean anything to me. I know we were only together for a year but I knew all those details about Simeon.' She tapped her head. 'Photographic memory. I know all his pin numbers, passwords, secret names and security answers. He couldn't hide anything from me, poor bastard. The number three, four, one, two is meaningless, in any order.'

'How did he refer to the person who started this? Did he have a pet name or something? He must have mentioned it.'

Mims sighed. 'I know that he was in deep. We argued about it a lot. I got fed up with the constant internal conflict he was having about it. He couldn't work out which side he was on. But I don't know anything about who the instigator is. I think he thought he was protecting me, in some way. Shielding me from the flak. I guess he didn't know me as well as I knew him.'

'Such is the ineptitude of men generally,' said Priest.

'To which you seem an exception.' She looked at him with tired eyes, her arm draped over the back of the sofa.

'No,' said Priest after a beat. 'I'm afraid I'm even more flawed than the vast majority of the species.'

*

Priest left Mims's flat with the dead phone and a heavy heart. Behind the belligerent front and the blue hair lurked a young girl who had lost a friend and a lover. Priest thought about what happened to people like Mims, whose enthusiasm and intellect had been drained and who had stopped believing. How many other suppressed geniuses were out there; with talents that could have changed the world, but which were now wasted and abandoned?

He trudged over to the Volvo, got in the driver's side. Georgie was fast asleep, slumped against the window, snoring gently. He thought about waking her but she didn't even stir when he struck up the engine. *Out for the count.*

He drove her home, pulled over outside of her house and killed the engine.

'Georgie,' he whispered, touching her arm.

She stirred. 'Is it PE today? Can you do me a note?'

'You're home. Everything's fine.'

Georgie came to and seemed surprised to find herself in Priest's car. 'Oh. Sorry, did I fall asleep?'

'Only for a bit. Thanks for waiting, though.'

'Did I dribble in your car?'

Priest smiled. 'It wouldn't have mattered if you had.'

He gave her a brief rundown of his chat with Mims, showed her the phone and explained his theory that if they could establish who had got Simeon involved with *The Real Byte* fiasco in the first place then they might find his killer; and at the same time they would find Alexia's killer, assuming Rowlinson's pathologist was right about the murderers being the same.

'Where do the three monkeys fit into all of this then?' she asked through a yawn.

'No idea, but there might be some answers on this phone as soon as I can find a charger for it. I'd try and source one now, but I have to eat something fat and unhealthy.'

She agreed and, whether it was the fatigued state she was in clouding her judgement or a genuine attempt at sporadic affection, she leant across and kissed him on the cheek before climbing out of the car and stumbling into her block of flats.

*

Elinor Fox had always had problems with her memory, which is why she carried an iPad with her everywhere and wrote everything down. Dates were a particular issue, as was anything involving numbers. She suspected she was a little dyslexic but she had never bothered to get tested. She hated labelling.

One thing she was good at, though, was tailing people. She had practised religiously, picking out a stranger at random, following them to their car and seeing if she could follow them all the way home without detection. She had a database of the addresses of everyone she had tailed along with notes, especially where the target had shown signs of suspicion: speeding up, stopping, constantly looking over their shoulder, that sort of thing. It wasn't easy. According to the FBI procedure, which she had researched, you could really only successfully execute mobile vehicle surveillance if you had a team of at least four cars to box in the target car. But, if you got lucky, and maintained the right distance between you and target vehicle, you could get away with tailing for a short distance in an urban environment, provided there are plenty of other cars on the road.

Fox's current target, however, had spent most of the time sitting in the car, doing nothing. It had turned out to be more of a stake-out, during which Fox had managed to get through two whole packets of Doritos. After what seemed like an age, Priest had appeared, having been into Mims's flat. He got into the car and they had driven off together. Fifteen minutes later they had pulled up and Georgie had got out. This was presumably where she lived.

Fox had pulled up on the other side of the road and killed the lights. Luckily, there had been enough traffic to merge into, and she guessed that the dazzle of her lights prevented Priest from recognising the car. Most cars look the same square on at night.

She had quickly made a note of the address, or at least the street and building name. But when Georgie had opened the door, the Volvo's internal light had flickered on, giving Fox a perfect view of the kiss they had shared before she had staggered home.

And so it became clear. Fox had suspected Georgie all along. The woman who had burst in on them at Priest's flat was irrelevant. She certainly hadn't acted like a scorned lover, just stood there with her arms folded. Unimpressed, yes, but not cheated. Priest's sister maybe?

No. The girl in the way was the ginger one. *Three's a crowd, little missie,* Fox had thought. She had thought about following Georgie to her flat, see exactly where she lived, but decided against it when Priest drove off. *Not yet. First it's time to mark my territory,* she had thought while striking up the ignition.

*

When Priest finally opened his front door it was close to two in the morning. He'd managed to swing by the Bodrum and pick up a kebab filled with week-old salad. It was sitting at the top of his stomach, refusing to digest. He would have given his right arm to fall into bed with Jessica and feel the warmth of her body next to his. They had made love twice, but never slept together. He wanted more, he realised. Even at two in the morning with a thumping headache and exhaustion overcoming him, he wanted more.

He was disappointed. More than that, infuriated, because what he got was not Jessica but, judging by the coat slung on his kitchen chair, Elinor. It took him a moment to react. *How did she get in?* Realising the answer, he checked the inside cupboard where he kept the mugs and glasses. There was a key rack nailed to the cupboard door. He sifted through the keys but already knew the spare front door key would be missing.

He would call a locksmith first thing in the morning. And apply for a restraining order.

He crept through from the kitchen and pushed the door of his bedroom open. The shape of a woman filled his bed, covers pulled tightly over her, looking for all the world like she had slept there her whole life.

Fuck off, Goldilocks.

Priest closed the door, careful to not make any sound, and padded off to the spare room.

Chapter 45

Priest woke to the sensation of someone sitting on him.

He was in the spare bed, the duvet barely covering him and the pillows were bare and cold. He was on his back, with a weight across his midriff. He opened his eyes, knowing with dread what was coming.

Elinor Fox smiled at him and he had to admit to himself that she was attractive, with elfin features and silky hair. An old man's dream. She was wearing one of his shirts again, the top three buttons were undone. No bra, her bare chest was tanned, her neck was long, and swan-like.

'Oh, Christ,' Priest complained.

'Nearly,' she said with a wink. 'Like a female version, I guess. Sleep well? You didn't come to bed last night.'

'I found it occupied.'

Elinor's smile faltered, her eyes fluttered. She ran a finger over Priest's chest while biting her lip. It was all a big act – a big, pathetic act. Priest suppressed the urge to throw her off and swallowed back the anger.

Christ, how old was she? Late twenties, if that?

'I don't get you,' she said, watching her finger swirl over the duvet. 'You give yourself to me, quite willingly, and now it's like we never did it at all. I'm beginning to think I imagined the whole thing.'

Funny, that's what I was beginning to think, too.

'It's complicated,' he breathed. He concentrated on the ceiling above her. He wasn't going to give her the satisfaction of throwing her off, or the satisfaction of succumbing to her. She wanted one or the other, it probably didn't matter which.

'How are you getting on with our little puzzle?' she asked. 'I take it you weren't out late last night for social reasons.'

'Tell me about Mims.'

'Who? Oh, the girl with the blue hair. She was Simeon Ali's lover. Sad really: she was all he had. Simeon had no family here, not even any real friends. He's an only child. His mother is dead, his father is back in Turkey, and they were estranged. Mims will be the only one to mourn him.'

'How do you know all that?'

She smirked, ran her tongue over her top lip. For a moment, she didn't look all that attractive anymore. Nevertheless, Priest felt a burning in his groin.

'If you must know,' she said, leaning across him and putting her hands on his shoulders for support. Her hair dangled in his face. 'I was following Simeon for months.'

'Why?'

'Because I was interested in the Elias case and I worked out who the whistle-blower was ages ago so I thought it would be useful to, you know, get a bit of background.'

Priest had had enough of her teasing, the smell of her cheap perfume, the overdramatic flirtation. That annoying flick of her hair. *She knows more.*

'Did you find out how Simeon got roped into this mess?' he asked, making sure she knew it wasn't a casual question.

She sat up, put her finger to her lip. 'Let me see now . . .'

'Someone knew that Simeon had worked for the Elias Foundation and that he knew a lot about Alexia. That person persuaded him to come forward. Now this is important, Elinor: *who was it?*'

After he said it, a thought popped into his head. Was it Elinor? Had she been the one to persuade Simeon to come forward?

She laughed, but avoided his eyes. It was a curious noise, her laugh. She had such a neat, pretty face, making the hollow bark she emitted a complete juxtaposition. The noise grated on him, but as her lithe figure writhed over him, he could feel his own body respond.

'Elinor,' he prompted, trying to stay focused.

'Did you know she has a degree in astrophysics? Mims, I mean.'

'Was it you?' he demanded.

'Where's your little friend today, by the way? The ginger one?'

Priest shook his head in disbelief. 'Why do you care?'

'Just wondered.'

'Was it you, Elinor? Did you get Simeon into this case?'

Elinor laughed again. 'No, darling, *you* did that, didn't you?'

'OK, fine. You said your mother thought Alexia was a bad person, that's why you're so interested in the case. Who is your mother? How is she connected to the Elias Foundation?'

Elinor exhaled, her smile dark and cruel. 'Oh, Charlie, why do you have to make everything so complicated? This cross-examination is really tiresome.'

She leant over again and kissed him full on the lips, as she ran her hand over his face. Priest didn't resist, although he had expected it. Her mouth tasted alien, and yet there was something familiar too. He closed his eyes, let her fondle his hair while she gently moved her hand down, pulling the covers away. His heart rate quickened and he slid his fingers across her bare leg. She inhaled deeply in response, undid another button on the shirt with her free hand and pulled it off her shoulder. She pulled her mouth away from his and took hold of his hand, guiding him towards her breast. When he had reached as far as her midriff, he stopped her.

'Wait.'

He reached across to the bedside table and opened the top drawer. She watched him curiously as he produced a set of handcuffs, which he pressed into her hands.

'Oh, Charlie.' She licked her lips and laughed again. 'You dirty old man.' She fell across him, kissed his neck, moved the cuffs over his head to the iron bedhead; he reached behind him while she moved further up his body, kicking the covers back with her foot, the handcuffs clicked and she moaned, frustrated, tried to manoeuvre herself down so he could enter her but she wasn't able to with her hand bound to the bedhead.

'Let me—' she grunted, looking up where her hand was cuffed to the bed. Both hands. 'Wait!'

Priest cupped his hand under her thigh and lifted her off him with ease. She cried out with surprise and irritation but, with both hands out of use, all she could do was tip over as he neatly slid from underneath her, half falling, half jumping out of the bed. Her arm must have twisted as she went because the next noise out of her was a yelp of pain.

'*What the fuck!*' she shouted, staring at her restrained hands, then back at Priest, fury and confusion in her eyes.

'Hiatt standard steel chain cuffs,' Priest explained. 'Best in the business. They're using Speedcuffs nowadays of course but back in the nineties when I was on the beat these were all the rage.'

'You fucking bastard!' she spat. 'What do you think you're doing?'

She pulled hard on the cuffs and although the bed juddered a little she looked secure enough. The bedhead was solid iron. There was a way out, but she was too enraged to see it.

'Careful,' he advised. 'If you rattle that too much you could trap the radial nerve and get handcuff neuropathy. It's really painful, so I'd just sit tight.'

She shook the bedhead for a few more moments, realised he was right and slumped up on the pillow like a feral dog, snarling at him.

'You cunt,' she seethed.

'That's the spirit. Now you just sit there and I'll be back later and maybe you can be a bit more helpful, how about that?'

'Fuck off.'

'I certainly will,' Priest said brightly, winking at her as he left the room.

Chapter 46

Priest skipped up the steps to the office two at a time clutching the papers and the phone Mims had given him. It was half past seven and the Nook was quiet, although the traffic on the Strand was already starting to back up as people made their way to work. It wouldn't be long before the thoroughfare on which Priest & Co.'s office stood was filled with bankers and office workers carrying paper coffee cups and briefcases. Dark clouds rolled overhead threatening rain, the wind whipped up leaves and sent them pirouetting across the street. The temperature had dropped again and in the dull light of morning Priest reached an inescapable conclusion: winter was approaching.

Covent Garden's East Colonnade Market was usually a riot of colour and charm, from the lush aroma of its handmade soaps to the troves of unusual jewellery and homeware. Priest often thought that the cacophony of street performers, shoppers and musicians had a poetry of its own. The market had still been getting ready to open when Priest had ventured through, like an orchestra tuning up, but fortunately the Middle Eastern man who ran the phone stall was already vending and, although he cast Priest a doubtful look, he had amongst his stash of old wires and cables a charger for a 2003 Nokia 5100.

The office was empty but that was just as well; Priest hadn't had a shower in two days or shaved in three. He probably looked and smelt like a career vagrant. He was blessed with thick, silken, mousy brown hair that was still without a single streak of grey, but even this was starting to feel oily as he ran his hands through it and across his face in an attempt to wipe away the lassitude. He'd give it a few hours and then slump back home, once he was sure that Elinor would have worked out that all she needed to do was run the cuffs through the circular iron bars of the bedhead like a buzz wire until she was at the far end. Then she could just reach in to the bedside drawer and find the key.

He wondered how long it would take her to work it out. Ten minutes? Less? She'd probably then proceed to trash his house but that was fine. She'd make a mistake sooner or later, he was sure of it, and her temper was the most likely trigger.

In his office, Priest plugged the phone in and left while it charged. He found the Piccolo Cafe across the road open but devoid of other customers. He bought a large plastic cup of tea, bid the proprietor a hearty good morning and returned to the office.

The phone had turned itself on – the battery was at eight per cent. Priest spent the next two hours engrossed in its contents.

*

Georgie's alarm had buzzed at half past six exactly. She had stretched out in an uncoordinated attempt to stop it and ended up knocking the unit on to the floor.

Georgie had a rule – it didn't matter what time she went to bed, she always got up at six thirty on the dot. *Successful people don't need much sleep,* her late father used to say. Thomas Edison only slept for three hours a night. When Georgie was in her early teens, she had developed a routine around this doctrine and, although she now realised that she was not of the Edison-sleepless ilk, the habit had stuck.

She had been showered and dressed with her hair dried in half an hour. Li would be up at some point mid-morning and would be ready to leave the house by lunchtime. Clients never slept over. Li had limits to her services.

Now, she felt groggy, but the promise of a ten-minute power nap after breakfast kept her going. It wouldn't work of course – only superhumans could power nap – but Georgie liked the idea.

It had been a strange evening: first the trauma of going into the gym alone, which had rattled her nerves, then the disappointment at having to wait in the car while Charlie spoke to Mims. At least Charlie had the phone back. Now maybe they could find some answers.

She spent the next half an hour catching up on paperwork. Then, she packed the pockets of her Dora the Explorer body warmer with a pair of gloves, her purse, phone, reading glasses, tissues and a selection of hair bobbles. For some reason, Elinor Fox popped into her mind. Elinor with her flirtatious smile and playful lips, and her curvy body and small breasts, much like hers; no different in fact, yet somehow she was so much more womanly than Georgie was. *Why can't Charlie see through her like I can?* Fox's reaction to finding Simeon's body in the back of her car had raised an alarm bell with Georgie. Something about the way she'd exploded into overdone distress – shouldn't there have been a pre-stage of shock, numbness, or something?

But then again Georgie had never experienced anyone finding a dead body in their car before. *Who knows how you might react?*

She slipped on a pair of Converse, intending to take the Tube to the office this morning to save time. No doubt Charlie was already there with Simeon's phone and she was desperate to know what was on it. Georgie took a moment to check what the weather was like through the window. She could see over the Victorian terraces in the next street and to the river beyond. The sunlight was dancing off the grey water until it was disturbed by a rowing team, hauling their way through the early morning air. Her eye line was drawn back to the foreground, to the road running past her flat and the cars parked illegally along it – still, they had no choice because it was either that or park . . .

Georgie wavered – stared out of the window, to the street below. A feeling of panic seized her. *Could it really be . . . ?* She moved to get a better look, and there it was. Below her. A figure in a hooded coat – looking up at her window. She couldn't see the figure's face in the poor light but it was familiar. She knew that was . . . could it be?

Martin.

She had an urge to retreat further into the bedroom, climb under the desk, hide; but she couldn't move. He stood on the pavement on the other side of the road, hands thrust in his pockets, just looking up at her window. How long had he been there? Was he waiting for her to look out?

How did he even know where she lived?

She tore herself away from the window, staggered back and fell onto her bed. As she lay there staring at the ceiling, the memory of his hand on her throat as he had pushed her into this very position and prised her legs apart with his knee came flooding back.

It isn't fair!

In a rage, Georgie jumped off the bed and ran out of the room. She leapt down the stairs, towards the front door, her hands balled into fists and her heart pounding. *How dare he come here!* She hit the exit button, heard a click and thrust the door open, spilling out into the fresh air, feeling the biting cold on her face. She ran around the corner of the building to the stretch of road outside her window where she knew he would be standing, looking up, goading her.

Except when she rounded the corner, all she saw were parked cars and street lights. She whirled around. A woman coming towards her walking a dog eyed her suspiciously, the dog barked. A lorry was reversing into a driveway.

She spotted him about to round the corner, head down, hands thrust into his pockets, hood up. Fury overcame her. *How dare you.* She ran, the lorry slammed on its brakes. Someone shouted a profanity at her. She didn't care. Nothing mattered to her in that moment other than catching up with Martin. She almost lost her footing on the kerb. The forward momentum carried her into the man in the coat and they fell forward, Georgie's hand on his shoulder. He reacted, defensive, shouted.

'Hey!'

'You!'

He turned, crashed into the hedge, fear splashed across his face. *Her* face.

Georgie recoiled. It didn't make sense. It wasn't Martin.

'What are you doing?' she said, brushing herself down irritably.

Elinor Fox was wearing a heavy, oversized coat buttoned up. The hood had fallen down, her long hair was tied back. Georgie felt her stomach clench. She had been so sure, but so wrong. *How?*

'Oh, Georgie,' Fox said, suddenly relaxing. 'It's you. You gave me quite a scare.'

'What are you doing here, Elinor?'

'Getting pushed into a bush by an angry lawyer, for some reason.' Georgie folded her arms. Fox relented. 'OK, fine, I was just hoping to have a word with you about the trial.'

Georgie pushed past her. 'I can't help you.'

'*Wait!*'

The urgency in Fox's plea forced Georgie to a standstill. She turned. The reporter was shuffling her feet, trying to look innocent, but she wasn't wearing any make-up and her cheeks were flushed. *Did she run here?*

'Wait,' Fox repeated. 'I want the Eliases taken down as much as you do.'

'Why?'

'I've always hated them. My mum told me about them a long time ago, so I started looking into it but no one was prepared to talk, except Simeon.'

'So this is like your personal little quest?'

Fox let out a frustrated snort. 'Oh, for fuck's sake, Georgie, we're on the same side.'

'It just doesn't seem like a very good explanation.' George folded her arms. 'Your mum said they were worth looking into, and now it's like a crusade.' She started to walk off again but Fox called her back. Her tone had changed again, an attempt at *nice*.

'Georgie, wait. OK. I'm sorry. I came here looking for Charlie, but you just happened to walk out when I arrived. That's all. Will you talk to me?'

Georgie hesitated, the rebuttal was on the tip of her tongue. She sensed Fox was lying but there was something about the way she was looking at her that made Georgie swallow it. All of a sudden, she looked like any other girl, friendly even. She wasn't fooled, though – Fox could turn it off as quickly as she could turn it on but there was something else. She would have to be careful, watch what she said. It would all be on record. But if she could find out what was really driving Elinor Fox, that might be helpful, because it sure as hell wasn't just because her mum mentioned that the Eliases were crooked.

'All right,' she said, mustering a smile, of sorts. 'Ten minutes. That's all.'

*

The nearest cafe was on Kensington High Street and was as good a place as any to talk. At this time of day there were hardly any other patrons. Just a woman on her own buried in the latest Dan Brown book and an older couple making their way through a plate of scrambled eggs.

Fox had opted for a can of Coke, Georgie had a bottle of still water. Fox had paid. Georgie hadn't objected. She needed Fox to feel relaxed, although she knew that she was probably thinking exactly the same thing. The mind games had already begun. The reporter had slung her oversized coat on the back of the chair. It reminded Georgie of one she had once seen Charlie in.

Fox cleared her throat, leant across the table a little, giving off an air of confidentiality. 'I believe that Alexia Elias has been siphoning money out of the charity for years, decades even, but no one can prove it.'

'How do you know that?'

'It's conjecture,' Fox admitted. 'But I have sources.'

'Have you always been freelance?' Georgie hoped that the quick change of subject might keep the upper hand with her and judging by Fox's tiny grimace she was right.

Fox took a swig of the Coke. 'I worked for a few local papers where I grew up. Nothing special, but it was a start. It's a difficult profession to get into, especially when you don't have anyone to help you up the ladder.'

'You haven't always lived in London then?'

Fox smiled, and for a moment Georgie could almost believe it was genuine. 'No, I grew up by the sea. Proper little country girl. We moved here when I was eighteen; my mum got a job as a head teacher near here. It was what she always wanted and there weren't any opportunities in Norfolk.'

Georgie registered her words. *Norfolk*. 'Dominique and Alexia Elias lived in Norfolk.'

Fox nodded, like it wasn't a big deal, then mirrored Georgie's trick to twist the conversation around. 'You've worked for Charlie for long?'

'A while.'

'What's he like to work for?'

'He's a good boss, and a good lawyer.'

'A good boss.' Fox repeated the words, for no apparent reason. For a moment, neither one said anything. Georgie sensed that they had reached an impasse. *Nice* Fox was fading away.

'You seem very friendly,' Fox said, turning her head partially away.

'We work together.'

'Hmm. I'll bet.'

Georgie didn't like the sudden change of direction, or Fox's intonation.

'To be honest, it's really none of your business.'

'Of course not,' said Fox, without an ounce of sincerity. 'None of my business.'

'It's been nice talking to you,' she said, getting up. 'Thanks for the drink.'

'No comment for me, then?'

'Not today.'

Georgie turned to go but the way Fox had turned the conversation onto her relationship with Charlie had made her feel uneasy. Like there was something she was missing. Rattled, Georgie headed for the stairs. Behind her, she heard Fox call out.

'Bye, Georgie. Oh, and watch out for those bees!'

Chapter 47

Gail Woodbead lay in bed. She hadn't slept all night. She had tried to, but whichever way she lay, she couldn't get comfortable. She had remained there for hours, eyes wide open, feeling the sheets get stickier and stickier with sweat.

She leant across and checked her phone. One message from Andros: WHEN ARE YOU COMING HOME?

Gail put the phone down, stared at the ceiling. She had told him she would be home last night, but she had no intention of going anywhere just yet.

Her mind was made up. She would see the trial through, then leave. Everything. Andros, *The Real Byte*, Tomas Jansen, London. Maybe even England. Hell, there was a whole world out there.

She climbed out of bed. She could hear music from the room next door – Tomas was up and about. Maybe he hadn't even gone to sleep. She showered, letting the hot water scald her until it ran out and she had to wash of the last of the shampoo off in cold water. All the time, she kept coming back to Tomas and his grand vision, his desperation to destroy Alexia Elias. And Bella.

Bella had been twenty when she had first started working as a temp at *The Real Byte*. She was attractive, with a vulpine face and raven-black hair. Young, pretty and naive. Just Tomas's type, and it didn't take him long before they were sharing a bed. At first it was nothing out of the ordinary, and Bella came into work bursting with joy, beaming from ear to ear when he winked at her across the room, the redness flushing her face.

It probably hadn't changed overnight but, over the years, Gail's recollection had crystallised into a single image of Bella, the colour in her face extinguished, and a bruise across her cheek the size of a man's fist.

'What happened?' Gail had asked.

'It's nothing.' The girl had turned away, angry and ashamed. She hadn't come in to work the following day, or ever again.

Gail turned off the shower, wrapped a towel around her. Stared at the image in the mirror. A middle-aged woman stared back at her, with crow's feet and sagging breasts.

This is fucking ridiculous.

She stopped. There was movement outside the door, she heard the floorboards creak. The en-suite door was paper thin: the lock looked like it was from a doll's house.

In one of his many ramblings, Karl had said that the police were assuming that Simeon's killer was the same as Alexia's, although goodness knows where he got that information from. Snapchat, or something equally juvenile probably. Whatever the source of his amateur musings, it seemed to Gail entirely possible that the killers were different. Entirely possible.

And given that Simeon's death spelt virtual ruin for *The Real Byte*'s case, did the finger of suspicion in Alexia's case not plainly point to Tomas? He had the most to lose. They all had an alibi for Simeon's murder. But they hadn't been questioned about Alexia's. Not yet.

But Bella had been hit in the face, and she didn't even know it was Tomas that had been her attacker. *Alexia Elias had been mutilated.*

The more Gail twisted the idea around in her head, the more it started to take a recognisable shape. *Tomas – after finding out that Simeon had been murdered, takes matters into his own hands – murders Alexia.*

But what to do? Tell the police? She had not one scrap of evidence. Tell Charlie Priest? No, she still didn't fully trust the lawyer not to be on Tomas's side.

She listened at the door, the movement had stopped. Was he in the bedroom? She held her breath, the light seeping under the door had been broken by two shadows.

She put her hand on the door, ready to push against it if need be, but after a minute or so, the shadow disappeared and Gail breathed out again.

*

Priest emerged from the phone like a free diver finally coming up for air, sucking in the sweet-tasting oxygen and being thankful for it, but also knowing that the sight of the coral on the seabed would never be surpassed.

He had given the phone to Solly with instructions to see if he could unearth anything other than the instant message exchange. There seemed to be some other files, but he was unfamiliar with the phone's software and couldn't get into them.

He had written out the message dialogues by hand to fix them into his long-term memory. There were two correspondents. The first was a six-digit SMS short code. The code wasn't traceable, and didn't appear in the US or UK Short Code Directory. The messages were all outgoing. They were the same word each time, sent from Simeon's phone.

OK.

One a day, always roughly at eleven o'clock. Forty-two messages in all.

The other messages were all with someone whom Priest suspected to be the instigator. USER3412.

Mims had been right. Simeon despised Alexia Elias but he hadn't found any actual evidence of corruption, although it was the elephant in the room amongst Simeon and his other co-workers, all of whom had subsequently 'moved on', in Simeon's language. Paid off, probably. USER3412 had persuaded Simeon to engineer something based on rumours circulating after the Free People's Army scandal. The messages dated back two years and weaved a story of a vulnerable man trying to do what he thought was the right thing and who might have done it, had his conscience not choked him at the very last minute. The messages were a sad epitaph for a would-be hero, a dead one, right up to their chilling conclusion—

SIMEON: I'M SORRY
SIMEON: ***SIMEON HAS LOGGED OFF***
USER3412:   FINE. BUT DON'T SAY YOU WEREN'T WARNED.
USER3412:   ***USER3412 HAS LOGGED OFF***

Priest scratched the back of his neck. William had concluded that Simeon's killer could have been male or female. Priest tended to agree. Elinor Fox was therefore in the frame, but why kill Simeon? She had motive to kill Alexia, but not the witness.

He had also made a careful note of USER3412's articulation. They had used syntax that was strategically untidy – mistakes that looked forced, peppered with sentences that were laid out faultlessly. Like a real writer.

Just like Simeon's flat; the scene had been staged.

It didn't make sense, unless a professional writer was deliberately writing poorly.

A professional writer like . . .

Elinor had been one step ahead at every moment. But that didn't make her a killer and, besides, what was her motive, really? Her mother believed that Alexia Elias was a bad person? That wasn't very compelling. And Rowlinson had let her go. He can't have found any forensic evidence to link Elinor to the body in her car, although she had openly admitted to having tailed Simeon for months.

Then again, maybe Rowlinson had been too hasty to release her. Priest's chest was vibrating. He had left her back at his flat, cuffed to the bed. *I should have seen this earlier.*

As he got up, there was a knock at his door, followed by Georgie.

She started off at quite a pace, 'I just want to say that I know you think Elinor Fox's reaction when we found Simeon's body in her car was genuine but I've been thinking it through and I'm really not very sure about her at all because every time I close my eyes and picture her face when she first looked in the boot I see this crocodile grin forming and then it disappears when you turn round and—'

'Georgie, please.' Priest held up his hands and she stopped short. 'If you don't inhale you'll pass out.'

'I'm sorry, I just think—'

'Yes, I agree.' Priest nodded, but she seemed not to notice his intonation.

'OK, maybe you're right but she does seem very suspicious.'

'I said I agree.'

Georgie let the door close behind her then bit her lip. 'Oh.'

'Come on,' said Priest, grabbing his jacket from the back of the chair and slinging it on. 'You can come with me.'

'Where are we going?' she said, her eyes wide. She opened the door and he led her downstairs to the front door, hurried through reception and outside; Georgie was a step behind all the way.

'My flat,' he called over his shoulder. 'I left Fox handcuffed to my spare bed.'

Georgie paused. 'You left her *how*?' She continued before Priest could explain. 'No, it doesn't matter. She isn't there anymore.'

'How do you know?'

'I just had coffee with her. I think she was wearing your coat.'

Now it was Priest's turn to pause, and to experience a moment of anxiety. *Did Fox kiss and tell? Christ, she must have left the flat straight after me.* 'I thought you didn't like her.'

'I don't. I just thought I could get some information.'

'Any luck?'

'Not really,' Georgie admitted, much to Priest's relief.

'We better check my flat anyway. She might have gone back there.'

'You just left her there? Why?'

'Because I'm a fuckwit. Now hurry up!'

Chapter 48

Priest meandered through the crowds past the Royal Opera House with Georgie half jogging behind him to keep up. Dark clouds had gathered overhead. The musicians and street artists were looking up anxiously. The wind was changing direction and the air smelt of rain.

'Goodness you walk fast,' Georgie wheezed.

'She obviously worked out how to get out of the cuffs pretty quickly. Where did you have coffee?'

'A cafe round the corner from mine. She was outside my house.'

'Shit. How does she know where you live?'

'I don't know. She's like a bad rash that won't go away.'

After a few minutes they arrived at Priest's building. He led Georgie through the front entrance, across the flagstone floor. Above them, a conical-shaped lead crystal chandelier was suspended over the open space, crowning the reception hall spectacularly.

Priest nodded at a security guard who returned the acknowledgement and opened another set of secure doors which led to three lifts and a plush staircase leading up.

'Jeez, what's the rent on this place?' Georgie muttered.

'Nothing,' Priest replied, calling the lift. 'I own it.'

'The penthouse?'

'The building.'

Less than a minute later Priest was unlocking his front door and stepping inside with Georgie; the burning in his head had intensified into a full-on inferno.

Priest held up his hand and Georgie stopped. He closed the door softly behind him. The short entrance hall led through to the kitchen – everything was still. A breeze drifted in from somewhere, probably an open window. The distant hum of shoppers floated in with it. Otherwise, it was eerily quiet.

'What about the security guard downstairs?' asked Georgie.

'Ted? She'd just need to flutter her eyelashes and say she knows me. He's lovely but probably the worst security guard in London. She's got a bloody key so once she was past him it was easy.'

He padded across the kitchen floor past the lounge and through to another narrow corridor. Sunlight filtered through the skylight onto the panelled walls where a series of high-resolution vintage film posters were grandly framed: *Nosferatu*, *Night of the Living Dead*, *Black Sunday*, *The Birds* and his favourite, *Freaks*. At the end of the corridor, the door to the spare room was ajar.

He turned back to look at Georgie who had been half distracted by the portly image of Alfred Hitchcock on the poster of *The Birds*. She looked back quizzically and he waved at her in a gesture intended to say that he would explain later. She looked behind Priest and pointed to the partially open door as if to ask, *in there?*

Priest nodded and she hung back, waiting for him to venture forward. This seemed prudent but was Elinor Fox's slight frame really capable of murdering two adults? Alexia maybe, but Simeon?

Priest wrestled with the idea as he crept forward. He reached the end of the corridor and pushed the door open a little more to see into the room, to the end of the bed, to the duvet slung on the floor and the bed sheets torn down the middle. He opened the door fully and took in the scene.

The room looked like a tornado had hit it. Both bedside tables had been upturned and the contents of the drawers scattered across the floor. The curtain had been yanked from its rail and ripped into several pieces and the bed slunk to one side over a crumpled leg.

Elinor Fox was nowhere to be seen.

'Oh my God!' Georgie exclaimed, entering the room and standing next to Priest surveying the damage. 'Was there a wild bear in here?'

'Not exactly,' Priest mumbled.

He inspected the bedhead. The cuffs had been discarded in the corner, the key next to them. Fox had managed to work out where the key was and had moved the cuffs through the rails as far as she could but not far enough. However, where Priest might have expected Fox to have given up, he found one of the middle railings, presumably the one she could reach closest to the drawer, bent inwards with the top having separated from the main frame so the rail jutted out at an angle.

'Wow,' said Georgie. 'She broke your bed.'

Priest took hold of the broken rail and tried to move it. It warped a little further but not much. Surely Fox couldn't have done this?

He had a sinking feeling that he had caught a killer, then let her go again.

'I'm not sure,' said Georgie, 'but I'd say she didn't appreciate you locking her to your bed.'

'No. It appears I may have misjudged the situation somewhat. I thought we were dealing with an obsessive fantasist. In fact, we're dealing with a madwoman.'

He left the spare room and Georgie followed. He found it hard to imagine that, after flying into such a rage, Fox had just wandered out of the front door but everything else appeared to be untouched. Georgie helped him search the flat but it all seemed in place.

'Where would she have gone?' Priest thought out loud.

'We should call Rowlinson,' Georgie suggested. 'The Met can find her.'

'Not yet. Not until we know more. Once the Met start buggering around with this we'll lose our advantage; they're experts at fucking things up, even under Rowlinson.'

'But she might have been responsible for a double murder!'

'She's a sociopath, probably, and she has very sharp nails but, as any brother of a serial killer will tell you, that doesn't necessarily make her a murderer.'

'I didn't say it d . . . ' Georgie's protest tailed off as she looked down. 'Wait. Why is the floor wet?'

He stopped and followed her gaze. They were standing in the kitchen and, although he hadn't noticed it before, Georgie was right: a distinctive trail of water followed a path from the lounge to the front door.

He looked again. There were splash patterns, as if someone had carried a full glass of water across the floor. *What the hell . . . wait.*

Priest bolted through to the lounge. After a moment he let out a cry of anguish and returned to the kitchen to find Georgie looking at him, baffled.

'She took Hemingway,' Priest raged. 'The bitch took one of my fish.'

Chapter 49

Georgie brought over the cup of tea and placed it in front of Charlie. He seemed to have taken the loss of his fish badly, or the fact that he had possibly let a potential double murderer slip through his fingers. Or both. Either way, he seemed upset.

He had skulked into the kitchen and sat at the breakfast bar, staring across at the oven. Not quite knowing what to do, Georgie had rummaged through the cupboards and found one with six boxes of black tea, mostly Earl Grey but others too, some of which she had never even heard of. She knew he sometimes had lemon instead of milk but she had no idea how to put a concoction like that together so she had gone with milk, which he seemed grateful for.

'What does she want with Hemingway?' he mumbled as she took a stool opposite him.

'I don't know.' She wanted to say something comforting, but a thought was pulling at her. A nagging idea. 'You know,' she said, slowly so she knew he was taking it in. 'It might not be her.'

'No. She knows I love those fish.'

'Not that. I mean the murders.'

Priest looked up. Tapped his finger against the side of the cup thoughtfully.

'She's been one step ahead of us all along,' he said. 'She knew it was Julian Greenwood in that photo, she knew that he is Dominique's illegitimate son, she knew about Mims and Simeon. I thought it was because she was a good, albeit nosy, reporter.'

'Maybe it was.'

'I don't know,' he said, exasperated. 'Nothing makes sense.'

Georgie got up and poured herself a glass of tap water. A strange feeling had crept over her, one that she didn't like. She wanted it to be Fox, but why? Because it was an explanation, something they could use to sort this mess out? Or because she just didn't like her? And what if it *was* Fox? Then her reaction to seeing Simeon's dead body had been callously feigned.

She stayed by the sink, thinking it through. But she kept coming back to the same conclusion. *Why would Fox have killed Simeon and then purposefully placed the body in her own car? She's not that dumb.*

'We have to find her,' Priest said at last.

'OK,' Georgie breathed.

'Of course she has a hostage so we have to be cautious.'

She didn't catch on immediately. 'Who . . . ? Oh, your fish.'

'Come on.' Charlie took his jacket from the back of the chair.

She hesitated. 'You think she took a blowtorch to a woman's eyes and burnt them out?'

'I don't know. But I intend to find out. And if she did, you know what that means?'

'What?'

Charlie finished pulling his jacket on and ushered her to the door. 'It means my fish is in mortal danger.'

*

Outside, Priest and Georgie had to battle their way through a congregation spilling out of a small gallery underneath Priest's apartment block. Mostly corporate sponsors in pinstriped suits, more men than women, clutching large fishbowl-sized glasses of red wine and laughing with each other in a forced, detached way. A few arty types too, in garish tweed sports jackets and absurdly cut beards.

'Some French artist's new exhibition,' Priest called back over his shoulder by way of explanation.

'Bit early for drinking,' Georgie remarked.

'Not in France.'

'I've been thinking about the Elias house in Norfolk,' Georgie said as they made their way back towards the office.

'Me too. No doubt we're thinking the same thing.'

'Why was the cellar flooded? The house is two miles from the coast, on high ground and built on clay.'

'Quite. Perhaps the flood wasn't the result of something natural. Solly pulled off the title deeds from the Land Registry; the house was transferred into Alexia's sole name in 1989, which incidentally is the same year they bought the house in Kent where they now live. That house is also in Alexia's name only.'

'Why would they flood the cellar?' asked Georgie.

'Possibly to make their quick exit look like it was because the property was defective, and also to explain why they didn't want to sell it.'

Georgie agreed. 'Something happened in 1989. Something that meant Alexia and Dominique had to leave their home but without arousing suspicion.'

'Maybe I can leave that bit with you. The local archives might be a good starting point?'

'I guess they're in Norwich but I'll check.'

'OK.' As they crossed the road, Priest's phone buzzed. He checked and found a message from Solly. He'd found something on Simeon's phone, something other than the exchange of messages with USER3412. 'I've got to check something out. Are you going to be OK?'

'Of course.' She seemed slightly perturbed that he asked the question but flashed him a smile before saying, 'I'll get a train.'

'They're on strike. Didn't you see the news?'

'Oh.' Georgie thought for a moment. It wasn't ideal to involve someone else but there seemed no choice. Charlie couldn't drive her; he had other things to attend to. 'Don't worry about me. I'll get a lift.'

'You sure?'

'Absolutely. Let's get back and I'll arrange to be picked up from the office."

Priest drove to the office and abandoned the Volvo outside the Piccolo Cafe, which would annoy the owner no end but he didn't have time to worry about that. When he got to Solly's office he knocked and waited for the accountant to clean the handle before opening the door at an angle predefined by the clear line marked across the carpet. Inside, everything was as it usually was and Priest was shown to a seat opposite Solly.

'Ah, now, Priest,' Solly began. 'You asked me to look at this mobile telephone to see if I could retrieve any data from it of significance other than the messages stored on the SIM card.'

'Yes,' replied Priest patiently. 'I did.'

'Well, you may or may not be pleased to know that I have managed to mine various fragments of deleted emails, more particularly the attachments thereto.'

'But not the emails themselves?'

'I'm afraid not. But I have managed to recover one document in its entirety, which you may find of interest, although I note you did not define what data you would consider to be *of significance* and therefore I feel it would be better if you judged for yourself whether the document has any relevance to Priest & Co.'s current case.'

He nodded. Half the time Priest had no idea what Solly was talking about but no doubt, as always, all would soon be revealed.

As it happened, Solly had printed the document he had referred to and handed it to Priest, who quickly scanned it.

'You've no idea where this came from?' asked Priest when he finished.

'I cannot say for certain, but I believe it came from the same individual that messages under the name USER3412,' Solly replied. 'Is it helpful?'

'I'm not sure,' Priest said, rubbing his head. 'I'll let you know.' He got up.

'Where are you going now?' Solly enquired, picking up a packet of baby wipes and a bottle of supermarket own brand antibacterial spray.

'To see my brother.'

'Oh, of course, the notorious serial killer. How nice. Now, if you don't mind I need to sanitise that chair you've been sitting on. Good day, Priest.'

*

Georgie skipped out of Priest & Co.'s office, waving cheerily to Maureen who winked at her from behind her desk. Outside, she took out her phone and rang Li.

'Hi, it's me,' she said when Li picked up at the other end.

'God, you've got good timing. I'm starving. Wanna grab something with me?'

'Can we drive past Norwich on the way?'

Li didn't respond at first, then said, 'What?'

'I know it's inconvenient, I know it's a long way, but you definitely said you weren't doing anything today, so . . .'

'Sure – it'll be fun. Girls' road trip. Actually, gives me an opportunity to meet an old acquaintance of mine that moved up there a few years ago.'

'You're a star, Li. I'll be home in fifteen minutes.'

*

Norwich.

Elinor Fox narrowed her eyes. It had been difficult catching the whole of Georgie's telephone conversation crouched in an alcove underneath the steps to the Priest & Co. office, but it had been enough.

I bet I know where you're going.

She didn't need to follow her anymore now. She knew where Georgie would end up. All she needed to do was retrieve the fish.

Fox pulled the hood over her head, waited for Georgie to pass, then merged into the crowd.

Chapter 50

The fragments of data Solly had recovered from Simeon's phone puzzled Priest. It was possible that the text was unrelated but the prospect that it was part of a document sent by the same person who had lured Simeon into this dark conspiracy was too intriguing to ignore. Sitting in the car park at the Fen Marsh institute, Priest read as much as he could, but there was pages and pages. All the same story about a girl locked in a basement.

What is *this?*

He had skipped a few sections in the middle and flipped to the end. The story ended with the girl escaping, clutching a wooden doll.

'Come on, Ash Doll,' she whispers. 'We can go together.'

Priest had been relieved. The girl's ordeal was torturous to read. Dolls were a recurring theme. The girl's abuser was sick. Even though it was only a story, Priest's hatred of him was real.

There were occasional respites, moments where the girl was ruminating about her confinement, or staring out of the window.

The girl closes her eyes and thinks of the church spire, just visible beyond the trees. On a clear day, the girl can stand on boxes piled on top of each other and reach the windowsill. From there she can see out across the valley and to the top of the church. She finds comfort in this simple image, just an upside-down ice cream cone above a tree. But it makes her calm. It gives her hope. In there, God is waiting for her.

Priest closed the papers, packed them into a bag. The story must have some relevance, but what?

The car park was full. He could just see the entrance to Fen Marsh over the car roofs. With its large peach-coloured bricks and teal fascia, Fen Marsh presented a benign exterior compared with the foreboding red bricks of Broadmoor. But that was a deception. It was a small facility, with fewer than eighty patients, but some of the country's most feared criminals were kept confined behind the shiny new walls. Priest hated it.

Inside the reception, Priest surrendered his phone and wallet and everything else he had in his pockets, before he was ushered through to a waiting area. After a few minutes, a nurse appeared.

'You're here to see Dr Priest?' she asked, anxious.

'Doctor? You still call him that? I'm pretty sure they revoked his doctorate.'

She shrugged. 'He insists.'

He stood up. 'Best not keep the good doctor waiting then.'

*

William Priest set the paper down on the table and turned sideways, crossing his legs and placing his hands behind his raised knee in what Priest had learnt to recognise as 'William's thinking pose'. The same two male nurses shuffled their feet behind them again. They exchanged nervous glances; no doubt they had also learnt to be on high alert when Dr Priest crossed one leg over the other. No time to worry about them now, though.

'This is just awful,' William rasped.

'That's some statement coming from a serial killer.'

William waved his hand, dismissive. 'No, no. Children aren't fair game at all. I once killed a man with a cheese grater. He may have been twenty-three. I don't know. But that's my limit, and it was never sexual.'

Priest resisted the temptation to contradict him. *It was never sexual in the conventional sense, you mean.*

'I'd say an account of quite awful childhood abuse,' said William. 'In the form of a pseudo-diary. But who is the author?'

'You think it's real?'

'That was always your problem, Charles. You could never tell what was real and what wasn't.'

He ignored the jibe. 'It sounds like she's being dressed up as a doll. You think that's part of the . . . fun?'

'As deplorable as it sounds, yes.' One of the nurses coughed – he may have been genuinely trying to clear his throat but William took it as a challenge. Turning in his seat only marginally, he spat at the nurse, 'And you needn't laugh, Anton! If you find the concept of me, a known mutilator of men, seeing deplorability in indecent acts committed against children then you need to read my file more closely. You'll see that most of my victims were paedophiles. I took my rage out, properly, on those that deserved it.' Then he turned back and said to Priest under his breath, 'And the occasional venture capitalist, wouldn't you say, Charles?'

'Concentrate, Wills.'

'My apologies. Where was I?'

'The doll,' Priest reminded him.

'Ah, yes.' William relaxed in his seat. 'I understand that there is a subculture of men who like to dress up as living dolls for various disturbing psychological reasons. I think they are called *maskers.* As for dressing a child as a doll for sexual pleasure, I dare say it is possible but I have never come across it.'

'A perversion you've never heard of is one worth noting.'

'Quite. But it is conceivable. A doll represents an unattainable attractiveness. They cannot find a real partner who is satisfactorily perfect so they dress up as a doll, which is. Here, the abuser creates something similarly perfect, so he can defile it. He's filth, Charles. Filth.'

'We're agreed on that,' said Priest, rubbing his temples. 'Who do you think wrote it?'

'Well it seems only a limited number of people could have. The abuser, the woman mentioned in the early passages, the victim, someone who knew the story or it's simply all made up, and this is a red herring in whatever quest you are currently undertaking.'

'If it was the victim . . .'

'Then somebody is observing themselves, as the story is written in the third person. A little close for comfort, brother, don't you think?'

Priest had immediately recognised the discomforting similarity between the account Solly had pulled off Simeon's phone and the condition he shared with William, which habitually catapulted him into a trance-like state in which he would observe himself from afar.

He felt a flush of shame. The condition that Jessica knew all about.

'I know you have a disliking of our common problem, Charles, but you are going to have to face up to it one day.'

'It's getting better,' said Priest, looking at the whitewashed walls and through the window to the garden where patients wandered around distractedly tending to overgrown weeds. *This is where seeing ghosts gets you.* Priest tried to swallow but found his throat was uncomfortably dry.

'You mustn't blame yourself, Charles.'

'I don't.'

'You're a poor liar. Most depersonalisation sufferers constantly rue the day the onslaught came. What did I do wrong? What if I had done things differently? I doubt you are any different to me. The simple matter is that you have a genetic susceptibility to it. You had a fifty-fifty chance of inheriting the gene. Our sister is the lucky one, but your ghosts, as you call them, would have come to haunt you, whatever.'

He looked away. William was right. He had spent the best part of two years self-scrutinising every aspect of his life, but without coming to any conclusion. It was part of the reason why he could never let go of William. As crazy, perverse and dangerous as he was, William was the only one who really understood his younger brother.

That is a fucked-up thought.

'Maybe you're right,' Priest admitted. He felt weary all of a sudden.

'Mm. Where did you get this, by the way? It's hardly your usual read is it? Could it be connected with our earlier discussion?'

'Perhaps.'

'Of course, and no doubt confidential. I shall treasure our chat as always. Oh, and brother –' William placed his hand gently on Priest's arm as he got up to leave '– if you find the pervert who dresses children up as dolls for the wrong reasons, then don't hesitate to send him my way.'

*

The New Playhouse Theatre had stood on a Soho street corner near the John Snow memorial since 1879. A circular building bookending a four-storey row of converted Victorian houses in shades of pink, white and grey, the theatre had closed its doors on 23 November 1961 and remained derelict ever since. A few revivals were attempted but a survey in the early nineties identified a number of major structural problems with the upper circle, making a restoration unviable. A consortium of investors made one final attempt at resurrection in 1992, but when that effort failed less than a year later, the building was forgotten, sold off and eventually became the property of local businessman Sir Eric Warner, albeit through inheritance rather than choice.

With the building effectively sterilised, Sir Eric had sought to salvage something and applied for a conversion into flats. The cost of the project was enormous and unlikely to yield much by way of profit but Sir Eric couldn't bear to see the old building completely go to waste. Thus, it was with considerable enthusiasm that he now opened the door to the owner of the white Ford Mondeo parked outside who strode in and looked around admiringly at the cluttered foyer with the intention of hiring the space for an art project of an unspecified nature.

And why not? If the theatre was to be abandoned completely, subject to the borough council's procrastinations over planning issues, then one last performance of any artistic merit would be worthwhile.

Sir Eric studied his visitor as they made their way through to the auditorium and concluded that the phone manner didn't fit the physical appearance but was otherwise unperturbed. And the stranger certainly seemed passionate about the project, asking plenty of appropriate questions, mostly about acoustics.

Of course, Sir Eric had few answers of any credibility but was happy to indulge in a deliberation over the position of microphones to record a monologue of some description.

A keen interest was shown in the control booth, although of course it was devoid of any equipment, and much excitement was exhibited at the little window pointing out to the stage.

'And the lighting?' Sir Eric enquired. 'It is extremely dull in the auditorium. Will that pose a problem for you?'

'Oh, I think not. Nothing that cannot be overcome, at any rate.'

Sir Eric felt the meeting was positive, albeit that his new renter had many strange mannerisms. A modest fee was agreed and Sir Eric shook hands and watched the Ford Mondeo drive off.

An art project. *How fascinating.*

Chapter 51

Li drove a custom-made bright yellow Mini Cooper S Roadster with black stripes on the bonnet and black and yellow leather seats to match the paintwork. It was the most ridiculous and fun car Georgie had ever seen and if it wasn't for the fact that she knew Li had paid for it from prostitution, she might have even enjoyed the roar of the two-litre engine as the little mechanical bumble bee surged into the fast lane of the M11.

They had, mistakenly in Georgie's view, put the soft top down and she had to shout to be heard above the howl of the wind, her hair flapping around her face. Somehow Li didn't seem affected and looked perfectly at home in her Gucci leather jacket and skinny jeans as the car advanced beyond ninety-five miles an hour.

'This is a long way to drive to go to a library,' Li shouted.

'The Norfolk Record Office, not a library,' Georgie called back. 'It's the county archives.'

'An archaic building with lots of archaic books, Georgie. Ergo, a library.'

Georgie shrugged – Li was probably right.

'What are we looking for, anyway?' Li asked.

'Newspaper articles from 1989.'

'And this is work?' Li sounded genuinely surprised.

'I appreciate it's a bit different from what you do,' Georgie shouted back. Li laughed, although Georgie wasn't sure she had intended it to be funny. 'Anyway, I'm really grateful for you driving me but you don't have to stay, you know. Just drop me off and pick me up again in a couple of hours. You can look up your friend.'

'I'll help you, you silly cow. My friend can wait. Anyway, if it's for that hunky boss of yours then maybe in return you can introduce me, properly.'

'Sure.'

Georgie knew it didn't sound convincing, although she wasn't sure why the thought of Charlie meeting Li bothered her. Was it because she was slightly ashamed of Li's profession, or the fact that Li was extraordinarily attractive?

Maybe a bit of both.

*

As they turned off the motorway, Georgie was thankful that Li was forced to slow down, although she found herself gripping the door handle a few times as Li hauled the Mini round an S-bend.

'Did you know the chevrons warn you about the angle of corners?' Georgie shouted, pulling her hair out of her eyes for the umpteenth time.

'You worry too much, Georgie. Anyway, have you had any more thoughts about our chat the other night?'

Georgie looked down at her lap. She knew that Li was going to raise the matter of Martin with her again. It wasn't that she was uncomfortable talking to Li – her flatmate was too easy-going for that – but with Li there came a certain unpredictability; she had meant it when she remarked that *something* should be done. What did that mean? Whatever it was, Georgie was sure that what *she* regarded as *doing something* differed from what *Li* regarded as *doing something*. Li hadn't been explicit but the elephant in the room was clear enough: Li could make things happen. Her mysterious pimp, Mrs White, was a very powerful lady and Li made her a lot of money. If Li wanted something done, it would be done.

Georgie shivered. A part of her wanted retribution. But that was different from revenge.

'Sorry,' said Georgie. 'I've had a lot on with work. People keep dying in terrifying circumstances and I've had to do a lot of overtime.'

Li laughed again, assuming Georgie had made the comment in jest.

'It's fine,' she said. 'When you're ready. I've got some ideas.'

I'll bet. 'Thanks, Li. I think I've managed to get over a lot of it, though.'

'Right.' Li nodded like she didn't believe a word of it, bringing another flush of red to Georgie's cheeks. 'That's why you still sleep with the light on.'

She was about to protest when she realised that Li was right. *Don't be afraid of the dark.* But how could she not? In the dark, things happen. Bad things. Georgie pulled her coat closely around her shoulders and huddled up against the side of the car. She hated the dark. It was ridiculous. But then sometime*s the dark can come alive and eat you.*

*

The Norfolk Records Office was, as Li had predicted, a dimly lit library with a central area comprising four desks squashed together, from which back-to-back bookshelves stretched out in a pentagon shape interspersed with various smaller cabinets and units. The curator, who identified himself only as Vern, was an elderly chap with a hefty frame and red, blotchy skin. He seemed annoyed to have to plod through the otherwise empty hall with Georgie and Li to show them the records from 1989.

'Here you are,' he said in an unenthusiastic Norfolk accent. 'For all the good it'll do you. School project is it?'

Li cocked her head to one side and looked as if she was about to give him an earful so Georgie jumped in. 'We're students,' she said pleasantly. 'It's just research.'

'Aye. Keeps you off the streets, I suppose.'

With no further words of encouragement, Vern turned and hobbled off.

'Well, how rude,' Li remarked when he was still in earshot.

Georgie ignored her and started opening drawers. They were poorly marked and most of the labels had peeled away but generally they were full of scrapbooks containing news articles from the right era. Mostly the local papers, the *North Norfolk News* and the *Eastern Daily Press*, but occasionally a national was squeezed in with dog-eared corners and faded type, presumably because it was running with a main story from the area.

'What are we looking for exactly?' asked Li, taking one of the books out and blowing the dust away.

'There's a little village called Tome near the coast,' Georgie explained. 'You're looking for anything of significance that happened in or near there in 1989.'

'Significance being . . . ?'

'Anything. Here's a map.' Georgie pulled out a yellowing document from one of the drawers, which she spread out on the table. It showed Norfolk and Georgie was able to point to Tome. 'Here. Anything near here, maybe these villages here and right up to the coast to this—' Georgie peered over. The edge of the land was marked, although it didn't seem part of any settlement or other point of interest. 'Devil's Point.'

Li nodded and started flipping through a book. 'Got it.'

An hour passed. Then two. It seemed that 1989 was a particularly quiet year for newsworthy stories in the county of Norfolk, although there had been a minor earthquake near Ipswich which caused an old man in Sheringham to fall out of bed. In a series of unrelated incidents, a number of missing dogs featured. A drowning at some local beach was about the only thing of interest and by the time the third hour ticked away, Georgie was beginning to feel disheartened.

'I'll see if I can get us some coffee,' Georgie announced, standing up. 'Maybe give it another half an hour and, after that, give it up as a bad job.'

'Are you sure?' said Li. 'I was just getting into this. Did you know how many duck-related accidents happened in July 1989?'

Georgie smiled and started to make her way across to where she thought she might have seen a vending machine. She had got halfway when Li shouted over.

'Wait! Come and look at this.'

She rushed across and peered over Li's shoulder. She was looking at a double page spread of a story about a woman who had gone on holiday to Thailand and been mauled by a tiger. It didn't seem immediately relevant.

'Thailand isn't in Norfolk,' Georgie pointed out.

'No,' Li said, excitedly pointing to a smaller article in the corner of the page. 'Here.'

Georgie read aloud: 'Police are looking for the body of a young girl who may have jumped off the edge of Devil's Point last week. The incident occurred on the afternoon of the first of November 1989. Police were called by local residents who had found the young girl – whose name is not yet known – standing on the edge of the cliff. Reports indicate that the girl then jumped onto the rocks below but her body was never discovered. Police are asking anyone with information to come forward.'

She drew several circles round the article and a question mark.

'Devil's Point,' said Li. 'That's . . .'

'Less than two miles from Tome,' Georgie finished.

'There must be more on this.'

Georgie pulled out all of the papers that followed the edition in which the tiny article was found for the next two months; they started to trawl through them. Li had started bashing key-words into Google through her phone. Half an hour later they had found nothing.

'It doesn't get another mention,' said Georgie, baffled. 'It's like it never happened.'

'Just this. It's a website called *Conspiracies, Myths and Urban Legends Revealed*. The vanishing girl of Devil's Point. There's reference to the original article . . . then it talks about the fact that there was never any further media coverage . . . then . . . oh, right. The girl's an alien. Obviously.'

'She's no alien,' barked a voice from behind them. Georgie jumped and sent a ring binder clattering onto the wooden floor.

'You shouldn't creep up on people,' said Li in an annoyed tone.

'The girl of Devil's Point,' said Vern. 'If that's what you're interested in.'

'You know something?' asked Georgie, lifting up the ring binder and depositing it back on the table. The rings had snapped and the papers had scattered everywhere. She started sorting through them.

'I was there,' he declared.

Georgie stopped messing around with the papers and looked up at the curator, noticing him properly for the first time. His beard spread outwards, silver and wiry and gave him a feline look, but the heavy white eyebrows topped a set of watery grey eyes that gave off an air of authority she hadn't previously detected. Maybe there was more to Vern than a grumpy old man.

'You were at Devil's Point on the first of November 1989?' Li asked, evidently wanting to be precise. Li rarely had time for time wasters.

'Aye. And I saw the girl, too. She was real enough. Barely ten, maybe less. Beautiful long blonde hair, she had, I remember that. And sad eyes. Very sad eyes.'

'What happened?' asked Georgie, putting the broken binder aside and sitting up, her heart racing with excitement.

'We were with the Tome History Group and I was leading a talk; suppose it was more of what you might call a ghost walk. Devil's Point is supposed to be haunted by the ghost of a Celtic sailor who jumped off the edge because he saw the sun eaten by the sea and thought he could capture its essence. Stupid story, probably made up, but people were interested. Anyway, when we got to the cliff edge, she was standing there, in a white dress, with her back to us. We called to her, panicked we were, she was so close to the edge. We crept forward, careful not to scare her but she turned and looked at us and, oh God, I remember that look and I'll remember it till I die. It said, *you come any closer and I'll jump*. So, we called the police and Rose came as quickly as she could, probably thinking how dumb we all were and, well . . .'

The old man trailed off and looked mournfully at the floor. The memory clearly gave him great pain, Georgie's feelings for Vern softened.

'She just jumped off?' said Li sceptically. 'Just like that.'

'Like a little bird,' whispered Vern. 'Just one that hadn't learnt to fly yet. Rose tried to coax her back but . . . she just jumped.'

'The paper says they couldn't find a body,' Georgie prompted.

'That's right,' said Vern, looking up and apparently composing himself. 'We looked, obviously. Paper don't say that but Rose scrambled down the cliff side as far as she could go but the girl must have hit a rock and . . . I guess the sea took her. I would have gone, too, but . . .' Vern nodded at his knee. 'Old football injury. I'd never have made it.'

There was silence for a while. Georgie fiddled with the zip of her jacket, not really sure what to say next. If it was true that the sea had claimed this little girl's life then that was awful, made worse by the fact that nobody knew who she was, where she had come from. She had just been erased from the world. It occurred to her: *the sea is like the dark. It can eat you up.*

'You mentioned someone called Rose,' said Li.

'Aye. Rose. She was the police at the time, just moved to the village. I still keep in touch with her, as it happens.'

'Do you think you could contact Rose for us?' Georgie asked. 'We'd really like to talk to her.'

'Aye, I suppose,' said Vern, taking out a large phone. 'I'm friends with her on Facebook. I'll message her now.'

'*Facebook?*' asked Li, amazed.

'That's right,' said Vern, apparently not detecting Li's astonishment. 'I love to poke people. Now then, Rose ... Rose ... Here we are. You've a bit of a way to travel, mind. She lives down south now, although I'm not exactly sure where. Head teacher of a little primary school down there. Guess the police life didn't suit. I'll put you in touch.'

'Thank you,' said Georgie; the idea of the bearded curator poking people on Facebook had brought a smile to her face.

'Right, I've messaged her. Now, anyway, what's this all about?' asked Vern. 'Why all the interest in the girl of Devil's Point?'

Georgie stared vacantly out across the room, past the corridors of bookshelves to the far wall. She had performed some age calculations and the dates fitted the profile she was beginning to build. They were getting closer to the truth; she could feel it. 'We're interested because I don't think the sea took the girl of Devil's Point. I think she's still alive.'

Chapter 52

On the phone, Priest listened to Georgie's account of what she had unearthed at the Records Office with a mixture of trepidation and intrigue. The incident was reported at roughly the same time as the Eliases' abandonment of their Norfolk home.

'When we went for coffee, Elinor Fox told me that she used to live in Norfolk, by the sea,' Georgie explained excitedly. 'If the girl at Devil's Point were still alive, she'd be Fox's age, and they have the same hair colour.'

'If she's even real,' Priest pointed out. It was a possibility, he had to admit, but it wasn't clear how it all fitted together.

'I think we should check out the Elias house again,' Georgie said. 'We never really looked at it properly the last time around. Things were kind of overtaken by finding Alexia. Do you think the police will still be there?'

'Doubtful. They might have put a PC on the door for twenty-four hours, but budget constraints and the remoteness of the site make it unlikely they'll keep a presence there for much longer. They might have set up cameras instead. I suggest you come back here.'

'OK.' Georgie sounded uncertain and Priest suspected she was searching for an excuse. She was going to the Elias house whether he told her not to or otherwise. 'We might just pick up a bite to eat on the way—'

'Georgie,' he cut her off. 'Listen, the cameras will be set up facing the house and in the front entrance. There'll be three and no more: they won't have the whole place covered, it's not practical. Go in the back and stay out of the front hallway.'

'Thanks, Charlie. I'll phone you as soon as we're done.'

'Who's *we*?' Priest asked warily.

'Li, my flatmate. She drove me here.'

'Is she the half-Japanese one?'

'Yes,' Georgie stammered. It probably hadn't occurred to her that Priest would recall a detail like that. He had only seen Li once but he never forgot a face.

'Just be careful,' were his final words before hanging up.

*

Jessica sat on the other side of his desk, waiting patiently for the call to finish. She looked fantastic, in a black and white striped top and pencil skirt, reducing Priest to his default position of ineptitude when she was around. He was wearing jeans that were sporting an ink stain near the pocket.

'What on earth have you got yourself in to this time, Charlie?' Her eyes were narrowed, suspicious.

'Oh, nothing. Just a libel action.'

'If I didn't know any better I'd say you were just sending Georgie off to investigate a crime scene. How does that fit into a libel action?'

Priest decided to change the subject. 'Tea?' Jessica rolled her eyes.

'And let me guess,' she said drily. 'The girl you were with the other night was also part of this libel action?'

Priest put his hands down, the game was up. He really didn't have any comeback prepared. 'If I said *yes*, would you believe me?'

'It's none of my business, Charlie. We're not together, are we? You can do whatever you want. So can I.'

Priest felt a twang of guilt, and a thud of jealousy. *So can I.*

'It's not what it looked like,' he said, trying to be delicate.

Her eyes were fierce – she had come here for an explanation and he didn't have one. She never just dropped by the office. This was important, and he was making a hash of it.

'I'm sorry,' he said. 'I'm not good with things like this.'

'If I knew what *this* was, I might be able to agree with you.'

If he could just say it. It seemed so simple, and yet so impossible. He just needed to be clear on what he wanted, what he felt. But all he could think about was his marriage to Dee, what a horrendous failure it had been, how catastrophically he had been emotionally wounded. The scar was deep, and scabbed. It wasn't the trauma of divorce – plenty of less durable people had been through that and survived. It was the terrifying thought that, in a world where nothing seemed totally real, his feelings for Jessica were nothing more than a simulation, like his feelings for Dee had been.

So he pushed people away. It was what he did, how he coped. If he never got close to anyone, he'd never confirm the truth.

But there something else this time. Jessica Ellinder was different.

'I don't work very well,' he said slowly, watching her face for a reaction. 'I'm damaged.'

Jessica got up, and his heart leapt. *I've said the wrong thing again.* But to his surprise, she didn't seem annoyed. 'OK. Let's do what you suggested a while back.'

'Which was what?'

'Start again.'

She waited. He let the words swirl around in his head. A feeling of relief washed over him. She smiled, and it reached her eyes. He was about to respond when there was a knock at the door and Maureen came through.

'This just came for you, Charlie. Courier said it was urgent.'

She handed him an envelope and bustled out. Priest was about to open it when he realised Jessica was on her way out.

'Dinner later,' she told him. 'I'll text you. So you can get back to your libel action.'

She nodded at the envelope, smiled and walked out.

Priest watched her go before tearing open the note and seeing another time and date printed on a card. *What does Jack want now? We only met yesterday.*

Whatever it was, it was pressing. He had less than an hour before the meeting.

*

Li pulled up outside the hedge running adjacent to the Elias house near Tome and craned to see through to the other side.

'Is this it?' she asked doubtfully.

'This is it,' Georgie confirmed, unclipping her belt.

'Are you sure you're going to be all right on your own?'

'I'll be fine. Honestly. Go and see your friend and meet me here in an hour. I just want to take a look around.'

'How do you get to the house?'

Georgie thought about it, scanning the hedge for the gap. 'I kind of just fall through the hedge.'

'OK. Be careful.'

She got out and waved her off before squeezing through the gap in the hedge and trudging up the incline to where the Elias house loomed over her. A breeze whistled through the trees and birds circled overhead – from here they could just as easily have been vultures.

South American police officers say that vultures don't circle around roadkill. They circle around where roadkill will soon be.

Georgie shivered, and hurried up the hill and round to the back entrance like Charlie had suggested. The back door was locked and the windows were boarded up. All except one. On one small window near the edge of the house, the boarding had been partially removed. Perhaps some kids had broken it off to get inside. Whatever the reason, the glass had been smashed out and, although the opening wasn't big and Georgie had to be careful not to cut herself on the shards studding the frame, she managed to squeeze through.

Inside, past the police tape and the warning signs, the house was still, the smell of mould she remembered from last time lingered in the air but now it was more potent. The floorboards creaked underneath her steps. She thought about the pool of water in the cellar and Alexia's body half submerged in it. The death pool.

'Hello?' she called out, her voice reverberating around the empty hallway. She knew there was no one there but it made her feel better to hear a voice. She stepped forward and jumped, the door had slammed shut behind her.

She whipped round in horror.

It was just the wind.

The door slamming had put her on edge and she crept forward, no longer confident she had made the right decision. The back of the house was dark, and ahead the doors were shut, their secrets contained, save for the door leading to the basement where Alexia's body had been left.

They will have moved it by now, surely. They wouldn't leave it here.

Georgie made her way through the corridor so she could see the front door at the other end of the hallway. There were no cameras around that she could see but this was still a silly idea, she realised. She should go back. There was nothing but death in this house. Death, rot and mould. And darkness.

She was about to turn back when she heard something in the distance. At first, she thought it might have been a tap dripping, but as she moved cautiously further into the hallway, her chest fluttering, she realised it was something else. *Ting . . . ting . . . ting.* The soft tone of music, coming from the open stairwell leading to the basement.

Chapter 53

Georgie stared down the stairwell into the gloom and shivered. The darkness was waiting for her, like in her dreams. She could sense its moist hands rising from the bottom of the stairs and edging towards her.

She jumped back. It was ridiculous, of course. Darkness doesn't move. *There'll be nothing down there*, she told herself.

She walked back towards the stairs leading to the first floor; beyond that was the front door. The music became quieter with every step she took. Six steps back and it was almost imperceptible. The same phenomenon took place when she walked the other way past the stairwell and stood in the kitchen doorway. No music. *It's definitely coming from the basement.*

She tiptoed forward so she stood on the top step, just inside the stairwell. The bottom step was invisible, engulfed in blackness. She fumbled around for her phone. It took her three attempts to unlock the screen, her fingers unable to input the right passkey. When she did, the light from the screen was lamentably weak. *Useless pay-as-you-go phone!* With all her emails going to her iPad, Georgie's phone reeked of old technology and a cheap LED display. There was certainly no torch, not even a camera.

Georgie held her breath and listened again. The tune was simple, lots of little arpeggios tapped out on a xylophone, like a children's nursery rhyme, only one she didn't recognise. Every so often, the tune would stumble over a flat note, giving the symphony an eerie, lopsided effect. *Ting, ting, ting* . . .

She looked around her again but the house was empty; she had checked it herself, from top to bottom. Well, almost bottom. The only room she hadn't been in was the basement.

She turned her head slowly and stared again into the darkness, knowing, with dread, that she was going to have to put aside her fear and walk down those stairs, with her feeble phone light and her quivering legs. She closed her eyes but the melody kept on playing, over and over, the same bum note grating on her to the rhythmic thumping of her heart.

There are very few monsters who warrant the fear we have in them. Georgie straightened up, determined and ready. *Ting, ting, ting* . . . The music played on as she took the first few steps down.

When she reached the bottom, the tune had slowed and the notes had become disjointed, as if they were no longer part of the same melody but a series of isolated sounds, randomly following each other. *Ting. Ting. Ting.* Georgie felt for the light switch at the bottom of the stairs, her hand creeping along the damp brickwork until she eventually found it, praying that the power had been restored. She pressed and, to her relief, the basement was suddenly illuminated by a single, naked bulb swinging above her, the dim light dancing off the water stretched out in front of her, so still that it appeared to be a giant mirror.

The rigging was still in place behind her from where SOCO had flooded the basement with powerful lights, but the equipment was gone, the police having hauled Alexia Elias's corpse away and abandoned the scene. But not everything from their investigation had gone: the putrid stench of death remained resident in the underground space.

Georgie swallowed. Whatever type of person Alexia had been, this oppressive brick prison was the last place she had been alive.

Now that the lights were on, Georgie could see that the first twenty yards of basement was raised above the remainder of the room. A set of steps led down to the lower section but the water was only a few inches from the top and spanned the breadth of the depressed area, wall to wall. *It can't be* that *deep, surely.* The water was completely still, like a dark, opaque glass surface. It reminded Georgie of the black water pools in the Waitomo Caves in New Zealand, which had been a short, terrifying part of a three-month backpacking expedition after university.

She felt her chest quiver. As the final musical note died out, Georgie could just about make out what she supposed was the source of the music.

It sat in an alcove cut in the middle of the brickwork across the water like a shrine.

Her throat constricted – someone was playing games.

She paced for several minutes, her mind whirring with possibilities. Above her, the bulb cast weak light, creating shadows along the front wall. Georgie hated shadows – shadows were threats, agents of the darkness that haunted her. She had to make a decision. She could phone Charlie but what good would that do? How ridiculous would he think she was? Charlie would say that somebody had put the object there for a reason – just like the photograph in Simeon's secret room – and the reason was because they wanted it to be found. It was another breadcrumb.

She checked her phone. No signal down here anyway.

So, go on then, just wade through the water and get it, then we can be out of here.

'OK,' Georgie said aloud, her chest heaving. 'Shoes on or shoes off?'

She looked down at her white Converse – they would be ruined and she would have to ride all the way back to London with cold, wet feet, assuming Li remembered to pick her up.

'Shoes off then.'

Georgie kicked her shoes off and rolled her trousers up to her knees. *Great, I look like a Victorian woman going for a swim. See? This is fun.*

She paced up and down a few more times, summoning up enough courage before dipping a toe in to the water. 'Shit, that's cold!' *Steady, Georgie. Just take it steady.*

She gritted her teeth, braced herself, and stepped into the water. Her foot disappeared alarmingly quickly, followed by her ankle and most of her calf.

'Shit!'

She nudged her foot forward, there was another step down, and another one beyond that. *So much for pulling your trousers up.* The water was now lapping at her buttocks. She closed her eyes, wondered about giving up. *There were eels the size of her leg in the Waitomo Caves.* In the distance, the object in the alcove glimmered. Georgie was breathing heavily, a combination of the freezing water and fear gripping her chest.

She swore that the object had eyes. *It's watching me.*

She looked back, safety was only a few feet away. But what would it do to her if she turned back now? She was, after all, already soaked in rank basement water. She would have failed.

Oh no you don't, Someday.

Georgie strode through the water, not caring now about how wet she was getting, just trying to get to the other side as quickly as possible. There was one more step; the water was at her midriff but the floor now seemed to have levelled off, albeit unevenly: she kept faltering over sharp edges and whatever else was hidden by the murky brown liquid. She seemed to be getting wetter and colder with every stride until at last she reached the far side of the pool, breathless and saturated.

See? That wasn't so bad.

She reached up to the alcove, which turned out to be nothing more than a few dislodged bricks, and took the object down. Held it up to the light. A wooden doll, worn and aged, its red dress torn, face faded except for two black eyes. There was a key in its back, which turned once. The tune struck up again, slower and laboured. The doll's hair, once yellow, was filthy, matted and peeling off.

Georgie froze, her hands clasped around the doll. The tune died again and a fresh surge of dread washed over her. There was movement in her peripheral vision on the raised section.

She turned her head, slowly, willing it to have been a trick of the light but knowing it was not. *Don't be afraid of the dark, Georgie.* Her lip quivered, fear and anger collided internally, sending waves of icy pulses through her arms and legs.

Elinor Fox knelt at the water's edge next to a bucket watching her curiously, her long blonde hair resembling the painted doll's, her eyes transfixed on the water.

'Hello, Georgie. Fancy seeing you here.'

Georgie screwed up her face, tried to think of a response but nothing came, just the sound of air escaping her lungs and her heart pounding in her chest.

'I know our little meeting in the cafe didn't go well,' said Fox, her voice echoing off the brick walls like it was coming from all angles. 'But I want to be friends.'

She turned to look at Fox. She tried to read her face, to work out what chance she stood of just running through the water at her, but the light was too dull and Fox was too far away. She was just kneeling and staring straight ahead. *What does she want?*

'Would you like to be friends, Georgie?' Fox looked across but her gaze seemed distant.

Georgie nodded, not knowing what else to do. *Just let me go. Please, just let me go.*

'Speak up!' Fox shouted.

'Yes!'

Fox nodded. 'That's good.' She stood up quickly, Georgie held her breath. 'I see you've found my doll.' Georgie looked down at the ravaged object in her hands. *Your doll?* 'You needn't have got so wet, though. There's a ledge that runs around the wall. The water's only an inch deep. You just need to know what you're looking for.'

Her teeth were chattering but she fought through the discomfort, determined not to look weak. 'How did you know that?'

Fox shrugged, like it hadn't occurred to her. 'I don't know. Sometimes I have trouble remembering things.'

With that, Fox kicked the bucket over and water poured into the pool, as did a grey object. Georgie looked again but the water was too murky. *What the hell was that?* Fox had put something in the water – something that had instantly been consumed by the pool and disappeared.

Wait. Was that . . . ?

'Have you any idea how hard it is to transport a lionfish from London to Norfolk in a rented car?' asked Fox. 'Let me tell you – it's close to impossible. I totally thought it would die but I kept topping the water up with Evian and the little fella is as bright as when he was swimming around merrily in your boyfriend's tank!'

Georgie tried to swallow but she couldn't, her throat was bone dry. She searched the water desperately, but the fish had vanished.

'I thought they were just pretty fish,' Fox was saying. 'But it turns out they're really interesting. Did you know that? I read all about them on Wikipedia before I came up here. Their fin rays are highly venomous. Listen to this.' Fox produced her phone and proceeded to read from the screen. '"*In humans,* Pterois *venom can cause systemic effects such as extreme pain, nausea, vomiting, fever, breathing difficulties, convulsions, dizziness, redness on the affected area, headache, numbness, paresthesia, which means pins and needles, heartburn, diarrhoea, and sweating. Rarely, such stings can cause temporary paralysis of the limbs, heart failure, and even death.*" How amazing is that?'

'I . . .' Georgie couldn't raise her voice. Her throat was swelling up, she felt short of breath. 'I have . . .'

Fox smiled. 'Yes, I know.' Georgie froze. *She knew. Watch out for those bees,* she had said as her parting words. 'You've got anaphylaxis. So all that stuff I just read out probably isn't applicable. You're more likely to go into anaphylactic shock and then . . . well, we'll have to wait and see. Maybe you'll drown, I don't know.'

Georgie stood stock-still, scanning the water. She was taking short, sharp breaths but she could already feel her blood pressure dropping, her vision blurring. Her legs no longer felt strong enough to hold her up. In the far corner, she thought she detected a small splash as the lionfish breached the surface for a moment, but she wasn't sure. It could be anywhere; she couldn't even see her own feet.

She looked up, willing herself to say something, anything, but Fox had already walked to the stairs and was looking back over her shoulder, menacingly.

'I don't deal with rivals very well, Georgie,' said Fox. 'And for someone who's supposed to be pretty clever, you are fucking dumb.'

Fox hit the light switch and Georgie was plunged into darkness.

Chapter 54

Don't be afraid of the dark.

Georgie couldn't move. The water lapped around her waist and she had lost all feeling in her feet and legs. She concentrated on breathing, in through her nose and out through her mouth, every muscle in her body was tensed as she fought to suppress the urge to panic. *You must stay calm. If you panic, you'll hyperventilate.*

The light from her phone display was unable to penetrate the complete blackness that surrounded her, the shroud that had appeared when Fox had turned off the light and left, *left her here alone.* In the dark . . .

In the dark!

Another thought occurred to her: Fox had been there all along, in the shadows, watching her toss off her shoes and wade through the water. Georgie felt as though she might be sick.

Somewhere circling in front of her, the lionfish was no doubt also panicking, in this alien environment, in water that wasn't properly oxygenated and too cold. Maybe it would die from shock. Georgie bit back her tears. It was the only anchor that she could grab on to – the fish might die and she might be able to make it to the other side of the water.

She screamed internally. *Think logically!* She closed her eyes, forced away the images of Martin's greedy smile just before he turned off the light, and thought about home. *If you've lost someone in a supermarket, will you find them quicker if both of you are moving or just one of you?*

It was quicker if both people were moving but she had no choice. The other side of the water was twenty yards away, maybe less. She rolled her trousers down, her hands shuddering in the water, but the material was painfully thin. *Why didn't I wear jeans?* The lionfish's fins were stiff, needle-sharp spears. If threatened, or distressed, which it surely was, Hemingway would shudder violently near any perceived danger, making sure its spines disabled the potential predator. Georgie's body would react instantly to the neuromuscular toxins in the venom. Her immune system would go into overdrive, flooding her body with histamine. Her lungs would swell, breathing would become almost impossible and she might even have a seizure.

Fox was right: if she toppled over, paralysed, she would drown in less than a minute.

'Come on, move!' she commanded herself.

A small splash nearby stopped her and almost sent her into meltdown. It had been a few feet away, no more. A fin breaking the surface of the water, heading towards her? *Oh my God, oh my God!* Trembling, she thrust the pitiful phone light in the direction of the noise but she couldn't see the water round her legs let alone any further.

She thought about running, kicking her way through the water. It was surely her best hope.

Then another noise aroused her attention. The sound of the door at the top of the stairwell opening and a light splashing off the brick wall.

'Georgie?' called a voice.

Her heart skipped several beats. *Could it be?*

'Li!' she called out.

There was a scraping sound as Li negotiated the stairs. 'What the fuck are you doing down here?' Her flatmate was half laughing, oblivious to the danger she was in.

'There's a light switch at the bottom of the stairs, on the left!' Georgie shouted.

A few excruciating moments passed before the bulb spluttered into life and Georgie saw Li looking around the basement in awe, then seeing Georgie at the far end, the water up to her waist. Her expression changed from amazed to confused.

'Is this a public pool?' Li asked. 'Only I forgot my bikini.'

'There's a lionfish in the water!' Georgie blurted out. 'It's a bit bigger than the size of a small football and white with black stripes and lots of fins. I need to know where it is so I can get out!'

Li hesitated, blinking as she processed the information and for a second Georgie thought she might burst out laughing, assuming it was a joke.

'My anaphylaxis!' Georgie screamed, desperate. 'Bee stings, remember? It's the same if I get stung by a lionfish!'

Realisation crossed Li's face. She dived to the edge, shining her phone's torch light across the surface of the water.

'Take a few steps forward,' Li instructed. 'Move the water around where you are.'

'But I think—'

'Just do it!'

Georgie did as she was told, although it felt as though her legs might buckle at any moment. They looked pathetic, ill equipped to support her body.

'Just concentrate on my voice,' Li told her. There was something reassuring about the way she was speaking; a calmness Georgie hadn't heard before. Whatever it was, she was grateful for it. It might keep her alive.

'Another few steps,' Li said, moving to the other side to check the pool. Georgie shuffled forward, it was agonising progress but every small step was a step closer to safety and with Li surveying the water she might be able to react if . . .

'There!' Li was pointing to something in the far corner, behind her. The lionfish must have surfaced, although Georgie couldn't see it but there was no time to think about it: if the fish was behind her then she could . . .

'Run!' Li shouted.

Georgie ran, thrusting herself through the water, sending spray everywhere, the stone floor cutting into her feet and sending shock waves of pain up her legs but she didn't care – she was almost at the end, almost within reach of Li's outstretched hand – when she stepped on something. Trying to avoid penetration, her leg collapsed underneath her. *Was that it?* Georgie felt herself falling forward into the water, head first, her arms flailing uselessly in all directions. She wasn't going to make it. She was going to die in this basement like Alexia Elias. Fox was going to win.

She tasted the vile water in her mouth, grit and mud filled her stomach as her hands felt the pool bed and jagged edges of the stonework. She couldn't breathe, couldn't inhale. Panic seized her. Her mind went blank.

Just as she thought she might pass out something else happened. There were hands under her arms, pulling at her. There was a commotion in the water, someone shouting and then the sensation of air as her head lifted free. Li was in the water and had her round the torso. She hauled Georgie up the steps, throwing her like a bale of hay onto the side before collapsing next to her.

Starved of oxygen, Georgie heaved and spewed muddy water and vomit out in front of her. Every inch of her body hurt – her lungs felt like they were on fire.

But the relief was intoxicating. She was alive.

Dripping wet, Li sat up, rolled over and slung a hand over Georgie, laughing. 'Fucking hell,' she gasped. 'I thought you were supposed to be just having a look around.'

'Sorry,' Georgie said breathlessly, although it hurt to talk. 'I don't know what happened at the end.'

'Think you blacked out.'

'Thought I'd stepped on it. Felt like everything had caved in on me. Must have been a blasted rock or something.'

'You panicked. No shame in that.'

'Thank you. Thank God you saw the fish behind me.'

'I didn't.' Li smiled. 'I have no idea where the damn thing is.'

Chapter 55

Priest stood back and looked at the building in front of him before checking the address on the letter. It matched, but why did Jack Oldham want to meet in an abandoned theatre?

The New Playhouse was deceptively named since it was neither new nor could reasonably be described as a playhouse. Not any more at least. A set of cracked steps led up to four doors plastered in old production posters; presumably someone had gone to the trouble of creating a shrine for this relic of the arts, but a revival seemed unlikely if the planning notice attached to the wall was anything to go by. This time next year it would be flats.

He considered the situation. Every other meeting he had had with Jack had been in public, but things were dire for the Elias Foundation, and in a game of murder and corruption, twenty-four hours was a long time. Maybe things had changed again and Jack was being more cautious. Although a quiet bar somewhere was surely still a better option.

He pushed at the doors and found the far right one open. The hinges groaned but he could see tears in the posters between the door and its frame, meaning that someone had been in here before. In the entranceway, he found two dusty ticket booths and a lot of cobwebs. The carpet had been ripped up and the concrete floor was covered in rubbish: polystyrene cups, tickets, crisp packets, paper and flyers were strewn everywhere.

A shop mannequin, naked except for the theatre staff hat he wore, stared at Priest from behind one of the counters.

The letter had been quite specific, down to the row and seat number, and Priest was beginning to feel uneasy. If Jack had set up this meeting, he'd have met him in the foyer – he wasn't a dramatist, he was a busy man. Someone was playing games and it wasn't Jack Oldham.

Priest wiped his brow, irritated. There had been a time when he'd have radioed for backup. There had been procedures to follow, and help at hand. Now he was on his own. Priest glanced behind him. There were dangers ahead, but he had to risk it. For Simeon. *No going back now.*

He moved forward cautiously. A set of stairs to the right that looked like they ought to be condemned led, according to the faded signage, to the circle. The stalls were ahead, apparently, past a bar area.

He opened the door to the bar and ducked at the sudden movement ahead of him. He wheeled away, raising his arms up to protect his face – the door slammed shut in front of him, the noise ricocheting around the building. He recovered – it had only been a pigeon. The stupid bird had charged through the door the second it was opened and out into the foyer where it disappeared into a hole in the roof.

I'm getting too old for this.

Priest tried the door again and ventured into the bar area. The chandelier overhead was on, albeit only half of the bulbs were working and several of those were flickering uncertainly and giving the room a gloomy, ghost-like atmosphere. The bar had been raided; just a few dust-covered bottles of wine sat on a shelf, a few with drops of liquid still in them. There were tools in the corner, and a ladder covered in sheets. It looked like somebody had had the idea of trying to repair the building at one point but had abandoned it, possibly realising what a mammoth task it was.

He looked around: no signs of life and he was dead on the meeting time. He clicked his tongue and thought about the state of his spare bedroom after Elinor had torn it apart in a rage. He wished he could make up his mind about her, but the messages were too confusing. Was Georgie right? Was she the girl of Devil's Point? Did that make her the killer? If so, why?

The door to the stalls wouldn't budge at first until he put his shoulder against it. With a horrible screech, the door gave way and he stumbled in to the main theatre. It was even more dimly lit than the bar, just a few dozen fake candle lights glowing orange around the walls casting weak light around the edges and making the centre of the stalls look like a gaping black hole. The curtain was down and he got a sense of just how small the theatre was: a few hundred seats at most, and the circle above them had less.

Priest walked down the aisle, every step sunk a little into the loose floorboards, which creaked under his tread. A stale smell hung in the air – the smell of must and rot. When he reached row H, he looked along to where a figure sat perfectly still, dead centre, looking straight ahead, hands on lap and shoulders square. It was too dark to see who it was, but it was immediately obvious that the shape was too large to be Elinor Fox.

He checked around him but, other than the figure on the seat, which could easily have been nothing more than another mannequin in this light, he was the only occupant of the theatre.

Enter stage right . . .

He edged across the row. The figure did not move until he took the seat next to him whereupon he turned his head slowly and looked at Priest with bloodshot, sunken eyes.

'You received my message,' croaked the figure.

'I did. Prudent of you to exercise discretion,' Priest remarked. 'We cannot of course meet in these circumstances.'

'No,' the figure agreed. 'You being the lawyer on the other side and all that.'

Priest turned again and met Dominique Elias's gaze. He seemed to have aged ten years since they had exchanged words outside the High Court. His face was drawn tight, with pinched cheeks and an etiolated yellow tinge to his skin.

'So, what now?'

Dominique swallowed. Didn't respond at first. Instead, he turned his head back to the stage and seemed at peace staring at the curtain. Perhaps, in his mind, a performance of great merit was playing out in front of him; he was nodding rhythmically to some inaudible tune.

'I remember this theatre from my childhood,' he said distantly. 'Such a wonderful place, full of colour and culture. Now look at it. A ruin. All the players dead and all the audience with them.'

'I'm sorry about what happened to Alexia,' said Priest, trying to get him to focus. 'It was undoubtedly a shock.'

Dominique nodded, but it didn't seem as though he had taken in what Priest had said. Instead he crossed one leg over the other and turned; regarded Priest thoughtfully.

'I had no real choice in coming here, Mr Priest.'

'There's always a choice, Dominique.'

Dominque laughed. 'We both know that is a fallacy. For creatures that consider ourselves free, we rarely actually are.'

'You invited me here.'

'Me? No, no. I sent you the message, but you're not here at *my* invitation.'

Priest glanced over his shoulder. *If not you, then who?* There was a breeze coming from somewhere undetectable and every so often the dull lighting flickered wildly. He leant forward, suddenly conscious of the semi-darkness, the tense stillness of the room.

'I spoke to him, you know,' Elias murmured.

'Who?'

'The puppet master. The one who is controlling us all.'

Priest hesitated. *He?* 'What did he say?'

'He told me what would happen if I ignored the tug on the strings.'

Dominique had drifted off into himself and was leaning over, almost hunched double in the seat, his breathing heavy and laboured.

He waited for an explanation, afraid to break the silence, as if Elias might shatter if he did. Without warning, Elias sat up and looked at him, his hollow eyes barely visible.

'Do you mind if you wait here while I try and get the curtain up? It would give me great pleasure to see the stage once more, even in this appalling light.'

'I'm not going to stop you.'

He watched as Dominique moved out of the seat; he seemed to have trouble getting up at first, something was causing him pain. He hobbled over to the stage and disappeared behind a door. Moments later, the curtain was raised with agonising slowness before Dominique reappeared under it, panting but evidently pleased with his work.

'Magnificent,' he remarked, looking around him in awe. Priest shuffled in his seat. A feeling of uneasiness had settled in the pit of his stomach. *Something's wrong. Very wrong, with all of this.* 'I used to love the puppet shows the best, Mr Priest,' Dominque announced from centre-stage. 'I loved the way they seemed alive, even though they were just parasites, feeding off the host that was the puppet master. We've very much like puppets, you and I, Mr Priest.'

Priest sat back with his arms behind his head and watched the old man cavort around on stage. It was a sad spectacle, seeing him examine every part of the stage with childlike curiosity. *He's lost the plot.* 'I don't feel like a puppet, Dominique,' Priest called back. 'I feel in control.'

'Ah, and no doubt you are right. You *feel* in control, as does the puppet. But are you *actually* in control? I doubt it. No more than I am, anyway.'

'Tell me about Julian, Dominique. Who's in control of *him*?'

Dominique sighed and spread his arms out, looking up at the ceiling in despair. 'My boy. I love him, Mr Priest, although it may surprise you to hear that. I feed his mother so much money and I make a careful note of his progress. He is my blood, after all. Do not make the mistake of thinking that I do not care.'

'We found a picture of him, Dominique, at Simeon's place. It showed Julian standing on a hillside outside your old house in Norfolk, the one you and Alexia left in 1989. Somebody put that picture together and left it for us to find. Was that you?'

Dominique had retaken his position at centre-stage and was staring up to the circle above him and looking for all the world like he might break out into song at any moment. Priest sat up, his heart racing.

'Who is it, Dominique? Who's your puppet master?'

*

The owner lugged the bag out of the back of the car before stopping to wipe his brow and admire the entrance to the New Playhouse. The last door on the right was already ajar, which was good. Things were in place.

The owner hauled the bag over the right shoulder and crept in, careful not to make too much noise. The arrival should be five minutes after Priest and Elias but one or both of them might not yet have taken their seats so, for now, a certain amount of discretion was required.

The foyer was apparently vacant, save for the weird mannequin. The owner took the stairs to the circle but stopped short of the public area, instead unlocking a small door which would have been easy to miss if one didn't know it was there. It had taken a long time to find out who still owned the theatre and negotiate a key, all in the name of a fake art project.

Inside the small room, the owner seated himself behind the control panel, or where the control panel would have been had all the equipment not been ransacked when the place went bust decades ago. The owner was looking through an opaque window to the theatre below where Priest and Elias should be sitting. The lawyer was very obediently in his seat, but Elias was on stage, just standing there, curtain up like he was in a starring role.

'Oh, how perfect,' the owner muttered. 'How fucking perfect.'

He reached across and undid the top of the bag and then slid the window across a few inches to hear what was going on below, placing an iPhone on the control desk so the camera looked through the gap that had been created in the window. Started recording. The sound would be muffled, possibly even non-existent unless Elias shouted but the owner had set up recording apparatus all around the theatre because it couldn't be guaranteed that Priest and Elias would sit where they had been told. The microphones were already running.

When Elias made his confession, the world would know.

Chapter 56

Priest got the feeling that Dominique's act was staged, quite literally. He seemed unhinged, constantly fidgeting with his hands, not really knowing how to stand. He was waiting for something, but what?

Then he started talking, quietly at first, so Priest had to lean forward to hear but then louder, until his voice filled the theatre and the strangeness of what he said was amplified a hundred times as it reverberated around the peeling walls.

'I first interfered with my daughter when she was five years old,' he rasped in a quivering voice. 'She did not belong to Alexia, but another woman. She was delivered to me to raise, but I abused that privilege. I took her into the basement and made her dress up as a doll and we played for a while before I . . .' Elias's voice gave out, tears welling in his eyes. He cleared his throat, almost retched. He was trembling all over. Priest's eyes widened in alarm as Elias tried to continue. 'I am a paedophile, a child-abuser. I am amoral. I am sick. But I am not totally without humanity. I am capable of love, as I loved my daughter and as indeed I still love my son, but I cannot control my desires and I am disgusted with myself. My daughter, Elinor, was perfect in every way,' Dominique continued, decades of guilt tumbling out of his mouth.

Priest increased his grip on the seat and stared, mesmerised by the monologue unfolding in front of him. *Fucking hell – Georgie was right. Elinor is the girl of Devil's Point. That's why she is so messed up.*

'One day, Elinor escaped us. Escaped me.' Tears were streaming down the old man's face but he fought on, apparently determined to exorcise the demons that festered within him. *For all the good it'll do you, Dominique.* 'My wife, Alexia, knew what I was doing, what I was capable of. But she did nothing to stop me. She even . . . she even helped sometimes. We . . . shared the same . . . *needs*, you see. These needs were satisfied in different ways, but they were spawned from the same root. But we took good care of Elinor. She was bathed, fed well, given toys and access to television. We read to her, played with her and she was happy being a child. All that we asked in return was that, when we dressed her as a doll, she did what she was told.'

Priest had had enough, fuelled with anger and disbelief, he got up. Headed to the stage.

'That's enough, Dominique!'

Dominique looked panicked. He began speaking at ever increasing speed, as if he had to cram in everything before Priest got to him.

'I used to look out across the water to the sunset in Tome. It was the only place where I could find some form of peace. I can still hear her voice, her cry, ringing in my ears. It haunts me. That's where I want to go – to where the sun sets behind the water. Take me there. To where the sun . . .'

Priest cut across him, almost at the stage. 'Dominque!'

It all fitted together – this whole affair had been about revenge. Revenge for what Dominique had done to his daughter, with

Alexia's help. Simeon was going to be the undoing of Alexia but he bottled it and was murdered for it. Then the plan had expanded. The instigator didn't just want the Eliases ruined, they wanted them exposed.

See no evil, hear no evil, speak no evil.

And now the confession was being delivered, judgement was imminent.

Wait! Dominique didn't invite me to this theatre to hear this. Someone else did. Priest lost his footing and stumbled over the row in front, shouting with anger and pain as he trapped his leg in between the seats.

Then there was a crack and Priest fell to the ground.

*

The owner was listening to the recoding through earphones plugged into the MacBook that had been rigged up the day before. There was a microphone under a seat on the front row and Elias's confession was coming through loud and clear, just as the owner had told him to do it.

From out of the bag, the rifle was produced. Elias was further away than the owner had anticipated but still within an acceptable range. Nonetheless, the task was made more difficult by Elias's jagged movements on stage.

The owner fed the rifle through the gap in the window and looked through the sight at the back of the lawyer's head. Adjusted the range and let his aim relax. How he would love to blow Charlie Priest's head off as well, but although he had seen Elinor go to Priest's flat more than once, that wasn't the plan.

The owner moved the gun upwards towards the stage where Elias was staring into the distance, staring straight up at the control box. He couldn't possibly see him from there, could he?

The owner was irritated. Priest had got to his feet and was shouting across the theatre, cutting through the confession. Couldn't that interfering bastard contain himself for just a few minutes?

The owner took aim, this had to be ended sooner than planned but there was enough on tape to run past every social media channel invented and watch Elias's fate go viral in a matter of hours.

Priest was waving his arms around and heading for the stage. It was now or never.

This is for Elinor!

The rifle kicked back as the bullet exploded from the muzzle and thundered through the air until it met its target. Priest was already on the floor, but Elias was getting up! The bullet had hit his shoulder and sent him sprawling backwards but it wasn't a kill shot.

Panicked, the owner took aim again.

*

Priest watched with astonishment as Dominique flew backwards. He knew straightaway what had happened. After six months training with the National Police Firearms Training Centre in Kent as a young police officer, he knew what a gunshot sounded like.

He ducked behind the seat and looked out to where the shot had been fired from. The control box, below the circle. *Shit!* He could see the gun jutting out and the shooter was leaning forward to get a better view.

Behind him, he heard Dominique slump to the floor.

Then a further shot ricocheted off a seat near him and he ducked down low to the floor. He had nothing to return fire with

but *if the shooter wanted to hit me he would have done it by now.*
A fourth shot rang out, further away this time. Priest tried to see
through the gap in the seats but it was impossible.

He started to crawl under them towards the aisle where a
dull EXIT sign hung on the wall but he knew it was too late. The
shooter would be long gone by the time he reached the door.

Chapter 57

By the time Priest had made his way to the control box, the shooter had gone, as he'd expected, leaving behind the empty gun and the holdall bag.

Fuck it!

He looked back at the stage. Dominique's body was slouched against the back wall, a trail of blood across the stage floor. Priest had walked right into the middle of a set-up. Dominique had confessed his crimes and Priest had played the part of the witness. The paedophile had been right: they were both puppets.

But who's the puppet master?

His phone was ringing. He answered to find Rowlinson at the other end.

'Priest?' Rowlinson sounded anxious. 'Simeon's toxicology report's back from the lab.'

'And?'

'Simeon didn't die of asphyxia. He died from CO_2 retention. He suffocated but not because someone wrapped his head with cling film; the bit we found in his mouth must have been planted there to throw us off.'

'CO_2 retention,' Priest repeated, his mind racing. 'You mean he was poisoned by his own breath. In an airtight room or something?'

'Meaning that the point of death could have been hours or even days after the killer got hold of him.'

'Oh, shit.' The significance suddenly dawned on Priest as he stared down at the holdall bag lying in a heap on the floor. *I've seen that somewhere before.*

Rowlinson continued to talk urgently in his ear. 'It means that all the alibis *The Real Byte* staff had have all gone out of the window!'

'Tiff, Dominique Elias was just shot in front of me.'

'*What?* Who the fuck shot him?'

Suddenly it occurred to Priest where he had seen that bag, and everything fell into place. *It was in court on the first day.* 'The same guy that murdered Simeon and Alexia. Karl Jones, the tech guy.'

'How do you know that?'

'Because he left his bag here.'

*

Karl Jones was sweating profusely from pores he didn't even know he had. Abandoning the gun and the bag hadn't been in the plan but the fucking lawyer had been far more animated than he'd expected. He assumed he would have been rooted to the spot at the sound of the gun, but the irritating bastard had actually tried to make it up to the control box.

At least he had recovered the phone and the MacBook. He had the evidence, all he needed to bring back true balance was the boy.

By now the delivery guy would be well on his way, transporting the safe.

He had left Julian drugged in the back of a Ford Mondeo estate, parked round the corner from the theatre.

Picking him up had been easy. Karl had just said he was his uncle and handed over a faked letter from the boy's mother. They didn't even read it! Fortunately, the boy was as dim-witted as his nefarious father.

'Julian, I work with your mother at the post office. My name is Karl. I'm afraid that your mother has been taken ill and she's asked me to pick you up and take you to the hospital. Have you got all your things?'

Karl collapsed in the driver's seat and slung the MacBook next to him, then pocketed the phone; fumbled with the keys to start the engine. There was a muffled noise from the boot where Julian was: his hands, legs and mouth bound with duct tape. When Karl had thrown him in, his face had been red from crying and his nose had been streaming.

'It's nothing personal,' Karl had snapped, before closing the boot. 'Your father didn't love my Elinor – he said he did, but it was a lie. He was a rapist. A filthy rapist. That is why I was denied her. But he also loved you, too, and that binds you to the cause.'

He fired up the car engine and swung out into the road, U-turned and hit the accelerator hard. Muttered, 'But you have to learn first what it is like to die before you can learn what it is like to be reborn.'

*

Priest jumped in the passenger seat of Rowlinson's BMW 5 Series. The DCI drove, tailed by a marked car with three uniformed officers in, sirens blaring as they tore across London.

Someone at Rowlinson's end had established that Karl Jones lived in a semi-detached house within the suburbs. The kind of place where kids hung around on the corner smoking spliffs on school days and it seemed like most people had dumped an old sofa or, occasionally, a washing machine in the front garden.

Rowlinson's men made short work of the door, battering it down and filing into the house efficiently. The call came back through within a few minutes: the house was empty and Jones wasn't to be found.

He followed Rowlinson in through the front door; the first thing to hit him was the heat. He studied a thermostat on the wall, which was set at thirty, the highest setting. Priest turned it off.

'He liked it hot,' Rowlinson called over his shoulder, as he examined the flyers and leaflets cluttering up a Welsh dresser in the hallway.

'Unnaturally hot,' Priest remarked, remembered how he had found Simeon's flat with the heating turned right up. *Had Jones been there before or was Simeon trying to tell us something?*

Apart from the Welsh dresser, the hallway was bare. A wooden floor covered in dirt led through to a small kitchen. There was a lounge to the left and a staircase to the right. There wasn't anything particularly out of order on the ground floor, although it was sparsely furnished. Just a double sofa in the lounge, the sort of cotton-covered beige unit that looked like it belonged in an old care home. A wide screen TV sat in one corner and a wooden cabinet in the other. The whole place stank of body odour.

Upstairs, however, yielded much more harvest.

Karl's bedroom was a mess – clothes thrown all over the floor, drawers open, as was the wardrobe. It looked like the place had been ransacked but Priest suspected otherwise.

'Looks like he was planning to leave in a hurry,' he said, looking around.

'You think he had time to come back here after he shot Dominque?' asked Rowlinson.

Priest looked at the drawers closely. 'No. I think he did this earlier in the day. He knows the game's up. He's just going to bring the final act to a swifter conclusion.'

'What's the final act?'

'I don't know yet,' said Priest, pulling a chair across and using it to climb up so he could inspect the top of the wardrobe. 'There's a thin layer of dust that looks awfully like the shape of a missing suitcase up here, though. So, I suspect it involves travel of some description.'

'Put Jones's face out to every force in the country,' Rowlinson barked at a sergeant hovering by the door. 'Notify border control, too.'

The sergeant grunted an acknowledgement and scurried off.

'Sir?' shouted a voice from another room. 'You'd better take a look at this.'

Priest followed Rowlinson through to what was presumably the spare bedroom, which had been converted into an office of sorts, or more like a control centre. The whole of one side was taken up by a long, custom-made desk built into the wall itself. There were three computer monitors and a server unit in the corner spewing out leads of different colours that ran across the room and behind the desk into various smaller units. Two fans positioned either side were aimed at the server to cool it down. One of the monitors was on a lock screen, the other two were blank.

'Get a tech team up here ASAP,' Rowlinson told the officer. He also disappeared, speaking urgently into his radio, leaving Priest and Rowlinson alone to assess the room.

The back wall was covered with photographs of varying sizes and quality; all with one common subject matter.

'This is Elinor Fox,' said Rowlinson, concerned. He was examining a four-by-six picture of Elinor at a party wearing a long red dress and holding a glass of wine, laughing with other people at the bar, oblivious that she was the subject of the photograph.

'Same here,' said Priest. This time Elinor was in a crowd, pointing a Dictaphone at an unseen panel of people. And again, walking down Oxford Street carrying a shopping bag, going into her Blackheath home, coming out again, shopping at a super-market, cleaning her car, meeting a man at a bar. Some of them showed a much younger Elinor, with shorter hair and skinnier arms, at university maybe. With friends on a grassy hillside. All the time never realising she was being photographed.

'Oh, shit,' muttered Priest. 'A little obsessive, don't you think?'

'Look at this one,' said Rowlinson, handing Priest a photo-graph with torn edges apparently taken with a Polaroid. The quality was poor, wrong exposure and, with the sun hovering in the background, the people weren't easy to make out at first but, after some scrutiny, it was clearly a young Elinor Fox at a ball, this time wearing a short black dress, smiling with braces around her teeth. *Is that?* Priest looked closer at the tall, thin, bespectacled man next to her. He had a beard and long hair, and an arm awkwardly hooked around her waist. She didn't seem impressed.

'I think that's a younger Karl Jones,' Priest concluded. It was difficult to tell – the Karl Jones that Priest knew looked so different but there was something familiar about the way he stood, his pose.

'I'm not so sure. I only met the guy once but this doesn't look like him.'

'Something's amiss, but it's him with Elinor. I'm sure.'

Rowlinson looked closer. 'Really? You think they were an item?'

'She's doesn't look very comfortable with him and it's the only one I can see where they're together. Except here—' Priest took down another photograph, apparently taken on the same night, at least Elinor was wearing the same dress but this time she was in a group, squeezed between two other men. Karl was at the back, posing like the rest of them, but his eyes were clearly lingering over the girl in the black dress at the front.

'I don't like the way he's looking in this one.'

'Elinor told me she had a stalker at university,' groaned Priest. 'It just didn't seem significant at the time.'

'Ah, double shit, Priest, look at this.' Rowlinson handed across the photograph he had been studying and directing him to the back of it.

Priest read aloud the pencil scrawl on the reverse of the photograph – 'The Three Monkeys' Ball. Fifteenth of May, 2001'.

'The three monkeys. See no evil, hear no evil and speak no evil.'

'Jesus,' murmured Priest. 'It was Karl Jones all along. He engineered the whole thing, right down to soliciting Simeon into *The Real Byte*'s case.' *And those initials were in the messages between Jones and Simeon on the burner, SNE, HNE, SNE. See no evil, hear no evil, speak no evil. I should have seen that at the time.*

'What the fuck is this all about, Priest?' Rowlinson demanded, turning to him.

'Revenge. The whole thing's about revenge. Dominique is Elinor's real father, but Alexia wasn't her mother. Dominique said her real mother had delivered her to them. I think he meant she just turned up one day. I guess that's how they managed to hide her; no one knew they even had a kid. Dominique confessed to abusing her. He made her dress up as a doll. Alexia helped, although Dominique was the primary abuser. They were both sick perverts. Nobody even knew Elinor existed; she was locked in the cellar that's now flooded at the house in Tome. But she escaped. When Karl met her, he became infatuated with her, stalked her. Somehow he must have found out about what happened to her as a child and he's taking revenge on her behalf.'

Rowlinson rubbed his face with his hand. 'Jesus wept.'

Priest continued to search the room, looking for anything that might give them a clue as to Karl's next move. Under the desk, he found a dog-eared red folder. Flipping through it, he saw it contained more diary entries, written in the same strange detached way as the one Solly had extracted from Simeon's phone. There were other documents, too. Medical records, letters from psychiatrists. He didn't recognise the names of the addressee but Elinor was the subject. A few words leapt out at him: *suppressed memories. Reaction to extreme trauma. Amnesia.*

So, that's how he knew.

'But, if you're right,' urged Rowlinson, 'then everyone's dead. Simeon, Alexia, Dominique. The job's done, isn't it? Who else is there to take revenge out on?'

Priest stopped and stared at the wall of photographs. *Who indeed? They had all been disposed of. The man who betrayed Karl in his quest to expose Alexia as a fraud. Alexia herself, who endorsed her husband's abuse and of course Dominique himself. Unless . . .*

He picked out another photograph. It was the same one they had salvaged from Simeon's secret room, of Julian Greenwood plastered into the foreground of a picture of the Elias house in Tome, near Devil's Point, where Elinor had supposedly jumped.

'Oh, no.' Alarm overcame him as the realisation hit home. 'Tiff, call Missing Persons. Find out if anyone has reported Julian missing.'

Chapter 58

Helena Greenwood's world had collapsed around her.

Less than a few hours ago, she had finished her cigarette and tossed the butt out of the car window while waiting for the end-of-school bell. None of the other parents would have been caught dead smoking in the car park and, ordinarily, Helena was of the same disposition, but today she had needed a nicotine fix. Bollocks to the PTA's disapproval. They could write to her if they wanted.

Julian had missed three out of five days of school last week and she had received another letter from the head teacher, a rat-like woman in her late sixties who should have retired years ago, complaining that Ofsted now required a ninety per cent attendance record and Julian's absenteeism was threatening the school's outstanding rating.

Bollocks to the rat-woman, too, Helena had thought. She should try being a single parent. It was bloody hard.

And another thing had crossed her mind: bollocks to Dominique, too. His money was welcome but his condescending message to her last night hadn't been. *Just checking everything is OK? Is Julian OK?* Funny how over the last ten years he had hardly been interested and then, all of a sudden, he had messaged her four times in one evening.

Now she knew why.

Just as she had been about to light another cigarette, the bell had sounded and car doors had started opening around her. She had replaced the unlit cigarette, straightened her hair in the visor mirror and got out of the Fiat, slamming the door shut behind her with just as much venom as everyone else in their Mercs and BMWs. It didn't matter how expensive your car was, the doors always slammed the fucking same.

Helena had marched across the playground, ignoring the stares she was attracting from the other parents. By the time she had reached the front doors, happy-looking children were already piling out of the school.

How naive she had been to believe that a man ten years older than her and married to a successful CEO would leave his wife *for her*. Helena. A Post Office Customer Services Adviser. Dominique had come in to the store at the same time every day. Same stupid grin. Sometimes he had packages to post, sometimes he'd buy stamps. Then he started just . . . being there, and she had noticed there was something suave about him. And that Bentley he drove, with the beige leather seats that massaged you. She could have got used to that. A whole different life.

Stupid cow. Still, the product of their brief affair, Julian, had changed her life, generally for the better. Until now, when everything had come crashing down around her.

She had hung around by the gate, arms folded, conscious that she smelt of fags and regretting the bitter taste of the tar in her mouth. It hadn't even been satisfying. Small groups of families passed her, wrapping their kids up with hugs and praise, occasionally one of them had cast her a sympathetic look and given a half-wave. She hadn't return the gesture.

Then they had gone and the playground had been empty.

Annoyed, Helena had walked over to the front doors, but as she had been about to go in, they had opened and a dumpy woman half Helena's height with wild, animal-like hair appeared. Helena had recognised her as the deputy head but the name had escaped her. She had been dressed horribly in purple and brown, a combination that had made her look as though she had put her clothes together from a jumble sale in the 1980s.

'Oh, Miss Greenwood,' the woman had said, seemingly surprised to see her. 'You're here?'

'I'm here to pick up Julian. Like always.'

'But,' the dumpy woman had faltered. 'But Julian went home at lunchtime today. I thought you knew.'

Helena's body had seized up, and what happened next was a blur. Julian had gone home at lunchtime but no one in this fucking useless school could tell her who with, only that the man had said he was Julian's uncle. The deputy head had descended into panic and went about frantically phoning God knows who. The head was on a golfing holiday in Portugal during bloody term time!

The worst of it was that none of them had been really worried about Julian – *Oh, kids go missing all the time, he'll turn up* – they had been worried about their stupid Ofsted rating.

She had pounded her fists on the car door until she had managed to crumple the metal underneath the handle. The dumpy woman had told her to go and cool off while she made tea and phoned the police. *In that fucking order!*

'Julian!' she had shouted aloud. 'Where the *hell* have you gone now?'

Now, Helena Greenwood was sitting with her hands pressed together, staring at the phone. The curtains were drawn and the door was bolted. How on earth half of the estate had found out about Julian going missing was a complete mystery, but people who wouldn't normally have stopped to even wave at her in the street were now, all of a sudden, flooding her mobile with supportive texts and well wishes. A few had even turned up at the door.

'Can we do anything to help, Helena?'

Yes. You can find my fucking son and bring him back to me!

Helena had smiled, feigned appreciation, and closed the door.

Come on, ring.

'Julian doesn't have an uncle,' she had told the deputy head.

'Well, he had a letter.'

Stupid fucking woman!

Then there had been the phone call from Dominque.

His voice was as thick as tar. 'Hello, Helena. I was just wondering if Julian was fine?'

'No,' she had screamed at him. 'Julian is *not* fine. He was picked up from school earlier by someone claiming to be his uncle. Was that you?'

There had been silence on the other end of the line. Infuriating silence.

'*Well?*'

'No.' The reply had been quiet, but there had been unmistakable quiver in Dominique's voice. Helena had felt her head spinning into oblivion. 'No, that wasn't me.'

'You know something, Dominique. You've ignored me for almost a decade, then you start hounding me about Julian. Now he goes missing. What's going on?'

'I . . . I don't know, but . . .'

'*Dominique*! Don't bullshit me!'

There had been more swearing, more questions and more denials. Then Helena had hung up. Of course, she had told the policewoman everything. They would check it out, straightaway. That had been an hour ago.

It broke her heart: Julian was nothing more than a piece of paper on somebody's desk, along with hundreds of other pieces of paper, each with their own miserable story to tell.

'Oh, Julian,' she whispered. 'Come back to me.'

Chapter 59

Rowlinson's BWM had built-in blue lights and a siren and both were blaring as they hit the motorway and accelerated hard into the fast lane. There hadn't been time to organise any proper backup; the others had been ordered to stay behind in case they were wrong and Karl Jones returned home.

Rowlinson finished his conversation with Missing Persons and reported it back to Priest grimly.

'Julian was reported as missing late this afternoon when his mother attended school to pick him up and found he'd already gone. The school say a man came to collect him at lunchtime fitting Jones's description. The school were pretty lax about it. Jones said he was the kid's uncle and he had a letter from the mother. No doubt a few jobs will be lost on that one.'

He nodded and returned to the red folder. He had taken the diary from Karl's house and had skimmed most of it while they negotiated their way out of Greater London, hoping it would give them something to work on.

The girl closes her eyes and thinks of the church spire, just visible beyond the trees. On a clear day, the girl can stand on boxes piled on top of each other and reach the windowsill. From there she can see out across the valley and to the top of the church. She finds comfort in this simple image, just an

upside-down ice cream cone above a tree. But it makes her
calm. It gives her hope. In there, God is waiting for her.

'Where are we going?' asked Rowlinson.

'To a place called Devil's Point.'

'Why there?'

'I think Dominique was trying to tell me something before
he was shot. He kept talking about a place where the sun sets
behind the water.'

'But Norfolk is the east coast.'

'Yes, but Devil's Point faces west, across the Wash. It's one
of the few places you can see the sun set behind the water on
the east coast.'

*

The closest they could get to Devil's Point was a small grav-
elled car park a quarter of a mile below the cliff face. There was
a viewpoint looking out over the sea and a couple of picnic
tables next to the car park – the stop was probably popular in
the summer for coastal drives. The road ended at the car park
but there was a track beaten into the heath by ramblers that
wound its way up to the top of the cliff. There was also evidence
of a possible track up to the top which might be passable in a
vehicle but it wasn't clear. Priest wanted to approach the Point
discreetly, which would have been difficult to achieve in a four-
hundred-horsepower car.

They got out and Priest looked around. No one in sight, just
the gulls circling overhead and squawking angrily. He felt light-
headed, it had taken them just over an hour and a half with the
BMW's twin turbo engine screaming to get them here and all

the way one thought had harassed Priest: what if he was wrong? What if Karl was elsewhere and Julian was already dead?

'We did some checks on Dominque Elias,' Rowlinson said, as they made their way towards the pathway.

'Does he have previous?'

'No. He lived a fairly uneventful life, by the sounds of things. He did twenty years in banking but for most of his life he's just been Alexia Elias's husband – I guess he made enough to enable him to do whatever he wanted.'

'I'll bet.'

'What's the truth of it, Priest?'

'She was taking charity money all the time, leaking it through various offshore companies, but Jack Oldham, the charity board's chairman, could never prove it and there was a network of well-paid partisans to create enough of a distraction to keep us off the scent.'

'You should have handed it over to us.'

'We did. You weren't interested. Something about budget cuts and not enough evidence.' Rowlinson at least had the decency to look ashamed, although it obviously wasn't him who had made that call. 'You were saying about Dominique?'

'Yeah. One interesting thing.'

'Let me guess. An allegation.'

'Two. One in 1998 and one in 2001. Never went anywhere but he was interviewed, voluntarily.'

'Where?' Priest felt his throat constrict, his fists ball. Shooting Dominique had been too good for him.

'An Elias Foundation-sponsored children's home in Sussex.'

'Jesus fuck. How old?'

'Nine and ten.'

Priest looked away, sickened.

'They're raiding Elias's house in London now,' said Rowlinson, but it did little to pacify Priest.

They reached the pathway, but it wound up too slowly so Priest scrambled up the rock face, Rowlinson behind him. The incline was sharp but manageable. Every so often they crossed the track, trampling over ferns and moss, occasionally losing footing but climbing all the time.

'I don't get it!' Rowlinson shouted up. 'What's Julian done to upset Jones so much?'

'Nothing. That's not the point. Julian is the boy that was allowed to live a normal life, it's Karl's way of punishing Alexia and Dominique for what they did to Elinor, who he's been obsessed with for years. He wants to punish Julian, too, for taking her place. Karl found out about what had happened to Elinor and he's trying to balance everything out – it's his own warped karma.'

'But Alexia and Dominique are dead!' Rowlinson panted. He was falling behind but Priest didn't wait for him to catch up. The peak was in sight, one more cross of the track and he would be there. 'They're not here to be punished.'

'He's doing this for Elinor, not the Eliases,' Priest shouted back.

He leapt over a rock on the edge of the cliff and found himself on a flat space overgrown with prickly bushes and small trees, with the track descending into the distance either side of the rock face jutting out in front.

He stopped, his face fell.

What in the name of God is that?

Rowlinson heaved himself up next to Priest, wheezing and wiping his mouth with his sleeve. At first he didn't see what was at the end of the cliff, looking instead to where the track wound back down the bank. In the distance, the North Sea lapped at the scree below. The sun had almost disappeared behind the horizon but cast a brilliant blaze of purple and red across the sky.

'Tiff,' breathed Priest. 'Look.'

At the edge of the cliff stood a freestanding steel safe, a large cuboid with a circular dial in the centre easily big enough to store a young boy. On top of the safe was a box. As Priest made his way over he saw that this was actually a crude panel spliced together from different components comprising two analogue circular buttons, one above the other, and a simple digital display, which seemed to be off. To the left of the box, a piece of card had been taped to the safe lid, a corner raised slightly. On the card were printed words: PEEL ME.

Priest raised his hand, but Rowlinson had already taken hold of the card and pulled it.

'I'm tired of this game,' he fumed.

'No, wait!'

Rowlinson discarded the card, which turned out to be concealing another set of words. This time, the words had been crudely etched onto the metal safe by something sharp.

They examined it further.

Priest read and exhaled loudly.

RULES:

DO NOT OPEN THE SAFE.

DO NOT MOVE THE SAFE.

CHOOSE ONLY ONE BUTTON.

'Ah, Christ,' Rowlinson breathed.

Without warning, the digital display lit up with a reading. 0.59.

'Jesus. It must have been triggered when I pulled the card off.'

Priest inspected the back of the box. Two black wires trailed off down the back, splitting at the base and going in separate directions. He traced them back around to the front of the safe, lifting them upwards off the ground and moving them to a clump of grass a few metres behind them.

Rowlinson peered over his shoulder. 'Holy God. There's enough explosives here to send us to Hell and back.'

The charges were set in a semicircle where the cliff jutted out above the waves crashing on the rocks below. The intention was clear. If the explosion didn't kill them instantly, then the whole of the cliff face would break off and be washed away, along with whatever was on it.

Priest turned back to the safe and as the last sliver of light from the sun vanished into the sea, the countdown continued.

0.58

0.57

0.56

'Which button?' Rowlinson said urgently. 'It says choose one. Up or down?'

Priest looked at the box again. Karl had put the contraption together himself, wired it pretty well. The box was bolted onto the safe, so no prospect of lifting it off. Pulling the wires out was possible but likely to result in the charge going off.

A breeze had whipped up in the absence of the sun and he felt his brow starting to melt. Rowlinson shuffled around behind him, panicking.

'Come on, Priest! You know this bastard. Which button?'

0.44

0.43

Priest closed his eyes and saw Karl's face. He was big, awkward to talk to, obsessive, a computer geek. *Come on, think!* He thought about the diary. *Could Karl have written it? Was that why it's written in the third person? But where did he get the detail from?*

He dismissed the idea – *which means if Karl didn't write it, then who? Elinor?*

'This is his grand finale,' he muttered.

'Yes! I know – like you said. Up or down?'

0.35

0.34

'Down means we all get blown into the water. I say we pick up,' cried Rowlinson.

'Up as in blow us all sky-high?'

Rowlinson was hovering around the box, his hands flapping dangerously close to the buttons. Priest positioned himself between the detective and the safe, lest he make a rash decision.

No need to be rash. Just need to be logical.

'How did Elinor survive?' he asked, although more to himself than Rowlinson.

'I don't know!' shouted Rowlinson, exasperated. 'Must have been a fluke. Maybe she missed the rocks and was washed up on the beach.'

0.28

0.27

'He wants us to survive, Tiff, well, maybe not *us*, but Julian. He won't want Julian to die, just like Elinor.'

'Then we need to pick a *fucking button*!'

0.24

'Wait!' Priest snapped. '*Who's* in the safe?'

'What? Julian? I don't know! Hell, does it matter? We're going down as well, whoever's in it.'

'Karl wants us to get out of this, just like Elinor did. This isn't the finale, Tiff. It's a distraction. But why?'

'None of this is saving our arses, Priest. Up or down?'

0.20

0.19

'I don't know. There's no symbolism for Karl in that choice.' *Up or down? Why is that important? Not up or down, but something else, maybe? North or south? Top or bottom?*

0.17

0.16

'Up!' cried Rowlinson. 'Towards Heaven. Towards God.'

'No. Karl doesn't care about that. Elinor is his God.'

The sound of the ocean roared in his ears, louder and louder. An approaching doom, smashing into the cliff below. He closed his eyes, forced out the images that cluttered his thoughts – Jessica, Sarah, Tilly. Then Elinor. *What have I done?*

'Need to be doing something constructive, Priest!' Rowlinson urged.

'I'm trying! But it's not straightforward with you whittling in my ear!'

0.13

0.12

Priest saw Alexia's blowtorched face in his mind's eye, Karl Jones in the theatre control box behind a sniper rifle, the photograph of Julian outside the Elias house. *See no evil, hear no evil, speak no evil.*

'What do you want, Karl?'

Then Jessica was back in his thoughts. Would he ever see her again? Was this his curtain call?

0.11

0.10

0.09

'Priest, *do something*!'

Rowlinson had lost it. He charged forward, knocking past him in an effort to get to the box. It was only because he was stronger and heavier that Priest was able to repel Rowlinson's desperate lunge, seizing his hands inches away from the bottom button and spinning him back around before pushing hard against his chest. The detective fell backwards and sprawled across the grass, cursing and swearing, surprise registering on his face as he looked back him.

'What have you done, you bloody madman!'

0.04

0.03

Priest turned back to the box, the image of the cliff exploding and everything with it falling into the sea flashed across his mind.

0.02

He heard Rowlinson scream something else but it was incomprehensible. He felt he should shout something as well. Something fitting for what might be his final moment. Something poetic.

0.01

Suddenly, Priest realised what he was supposed to do.

Chapter 60

The display had registered at zero for a few seconds, then a few seconds more. Priest turned to look over his shoulder. Rowlinson was sitting on the grass with his arms covering his face, for all the good it would have done him if the bomb had gone off. Slowly, he lowered his defence and looked around.

'What happened?' he asked.

'Nothing.'

'Which button did you press?'

Priest hesitated, making sure that there were no more surprises, but the display had switched itself off. He stepped back to examine the safe.

'None of them. Karl didn't want anyone to intervene. That was the point. My guess is that both buttons blow the charges. The choice was between intervention and nature, not up or down.'

Rowlinson got up and brushed himself down. 'You could have fucking said that earlier.'

'Mm,' Priest mumbled, distracted. 'Yes, of course, sorry old man.'

Rowlinson joined him, out of breath, his face flushed. 'I thought we were actually going to die.'

Priest examined the dial. 'Yes, until we had about a second left, I thought so too.'

The safe door clicked automatically and the door moved. Priest hauled it open the rest of the way and bent over to peer inside. He looked away, wiped his eyes and turned back but the image was the same. *Bastard!*

'It's empty,' he announced to Rowlinson, standing up.

The detective's lip quivered but he didn't say anything. Just pushed Priest out of the way and looked for himself, then turned to roar at the sea.

'*What the fuck?* We just risked our lives to save some stale air!'

'This was just a distraction,' Priest reasoned. 'Karl has something else in mind.'

'*What?* What does he want?'

Priest stood with his back to the safe looking inland. There was a track running through the marshes from the car park below them, stretching out to where the terrain dipped. In the distance, he could just make out a cluster of small houses, which he assumed was Tome. Street lights were on, pinprick spots of light at irregular intervals and the church spire rising above them at the far end of the miniature village. *Devil's Point had been a decoy; Karl had known that they would find it irresistible.* Priest cursed his stupidity. He had been royally outwitted, and the mistake might prove fatal.

'Priest?'

'He wants Elinor. He wants her to be united with her half-brother.'

'Why would he want that?'

'It's the only way he knows how to restore the balance.'

Rowlinson had calmed down, or at least he had caught his breath. He stood beside Priest looking out into the hazy expanse below them, and to Tome. Somewhere beyond that, Alexia and Dominique's house sat on a hillside, rotting.

A long way for a little girl to run all those years ago.

Something that had puzzled Priest since he had read the diary in Rowlinson's car had now been resolved though. There was a passage about Elinor looking out of a horizontal window slit to where she could just see the top of the church spire against the skyline on clear days. It gave her comfort and she thought of the church as somewhere where there might be sanctuary. But when she had escaped, she hadn't gone there, but to Devil's Point.

It now seemed obvious, looking at the topography of the vale; the natural dip that Tome sat in would easily have been missed by a little girl with no real sense of the outside world who was running blindly from a place of horror.

Something else was obvious, too. Elinor hadn't murdered Alexia and Dominique. She was the victim, but not the redeemer.

'I still don't understand,' Rowlinson was saying. 'How does reuniting Elinor and Julian restore any balance?'

'It isn't reunification in itself that achieves that,' Priest replied, looking out to the church.

'Then what?'

'How do you balance out a set of scales with too much weight on one side?' Priest turned to Rowlinson, who grimaced, clearly frustrated.

'Put more weight on the other side, of course.'

'Quite. Alternatively, remove all of the weight from both sides.'

Rowlinson looked back at the safe, a mixture of fear and anger registered on his face. 'He meant for us to be blown into the water, didn't he?'

'You and me, you mean? No, I think he wanted us to pass the test, but if we hadn't I doubt he would have been too upset.'

'Huh.' Rowlinson nodded. He was clearly feeling philosophical about this brush with death. 'Then how do we stop him? Has he even got Elinor?'

'Oh, he's got her. He's a master at getting his pawns in the right place at the right time, don't forget. Including us.'

Rowlinson rubbed his face in despair. 'Then where is he?'

Priest nodded out towards the church. 'The place where he knows Elinor will feel safe.'

*

Karl Jones pulled the white Mondeo up outside St Martin's Church in Tome and killed the engine. The church sat on a raised mound on the edge of the village. The yellowing plaque outside announced its name in black, archaic letters. Underneath there was a notice saying that services were shared with three other parishes and worship would only take place on the last Sunday of every month.

He lifted the boot up slowly, just enough to peek inside. Julian was sleeping. He had become rowdy in the journey north, shouting when the car came to a stop at traffic lights and pleading with Karl to let him go. He had pulled over and administered a modest dose of ketamine and the noise had blissfully stopped. The effects would last for another hour or so, which was convenient because it allowed Karl to leave him in the car while he visited the church and return for him later.

The street light outside the churchyard gates was broken but there was a light on in the church itself. Karl trudged up the path past the bowing headstones, and as he got closer, he heard the soft whine of the organ from within. His heart rate quickened as he approached the front door because he knew who was on the other side of the door. Whose fingers were gently caressing the keys, playing a sad melody. Just for him.

He nudged the door open and peered through.

The church was small. Seven or eight rows of seats divided by a central aisle leading to a raised area and eventually the altar. An impressive-looking cross, ten feet high, dominated the rear wall in front of a circular stained-glass window, although the scene portrayed was not one that Karl recognised.

There she was. Like an angel. Two fingers moving absent-mindedly along the organ keyboard. Her hair was tied back in a ponytail and how he wished she had worn something more feminine, a black dress like the one he remembered from the Three Monkeys' Ball, but even in black jeans and a beige jacket she looked as perfect as he had imagined, hardly different from the young girl who had danced with him all those years ago.

Karl stood in the doorway, mesmerised, until she sensed the door had opened and turned, flashing him a hypnotic smile.

Her smile faded, of course, on seeing him, but he had expected that. He had deceived her, no doubt. Saying that the lawyer had wanted to meet her at the church tonight had not been the truth, but it had guaranteed that she would be here. Priest had been the one to deceive her, not him, with his money and muscles. *He doesn't know you like I know you, Elinor.*

'Elinor?' he said, with the hope and wonder of a child.

She frowned, her reply faltered and she turned back to the organ. 'Sorry,' she mumbled. 'I was expecting someone else.'

He shuffled forward, ducking his head under the church door. 'No, you weren't. Elinor, it's me.'

She looked back, startled. Perhaps she hadn't heard him call her name before. 'Who are you?' She slipped off the organ seat and approached the lectern to get a better view.

'It's me,' Karl repeated. 'I . . . I know it's been a long time.' He found it difficult to talk, something was impeding his mind from articulating what he wanted to say. *I sound like an idiot!* She was just so beautiful. And how she stood, with her hips slightly lopsided, how playful she looked. Like the little girl she had been before she jumped off the edge of Devil's Point.

She was staring at him, recognition dawning on her. *She knows me!*

'My name is Karl Jones, but at uni everyone knew me by my middle name – Michael. You remember me, don't you, Elinor?'

Her lips parted– *oh what a glorious sight.* She took a step to the side cautiously, but a definite step towards him.

'Michael Jones?' she repeated, softly. 'Oh my God.'

'Yes!' Karl laughed and advanced up the aisle, elation flowing through him – the euphoria was overwhelming and just the sight of her body, her hips, her arms and, underneath her jacket, her breasts heaving as her chest rose and fell, filled him with a surge of energy, an intoxicant he had never felt before. *My God, at last!*

'No,' she said in a small voice, shrinking back towards the altar. 'Stay away.'

'I'm not . . . going to hurt you,' he stuttered. 'Please! I would never hurt you, *Elinor!*'

'You . . . You look so . . . different.'

Karl laughed. 'Yes! I've changed. So have you. You've blossomed into a beautiful woman, Elinor.' He supposed that she was right, although it hadn't occurred to him as important. He had left the hippy-looking Michael Jones behind a long time ago.

'I . . . What are you doing here? What do you want?'

He broke out into a run. At last, the work was almost complete and just like in his dreams, only this time he could join her, and Julian. They would be a family.

Elinor had started to back away but his sudden movement towards her had caught her by surprise and she had slipped on the flagstone floor. She screamed before they collided. Karl clattered into her, his weight bringing her crashing to the floor. He felt her little body in his hands, the warmth of her flesh, the smell of her hair. It was exhilarating, enough to drive him to madness.

'No!' she wailed, struggling uselessly underneath him, crying and struggling like a trapped animal.

'It's OK.' His breath was short; he could hardly talk but he must comfort her. He must subdue her. She was panicking, gasping for air. He took out the needle from his pocket and flipped off the top. Her face was twisted upwards and her eyes widened when she saw it.

'Wait—' she pleaded. 'Wait!'

'It's just a dream, my love. Like the ones you wrote to me about. Just one more little dream.'

He slipped the needle into her neck and squeezed in the ketamine, watching the liquid disappear into her body.

Within minutes, she had stopped thrashing.

Chapter 61

Priest threw the churchyard gate open and ran up the grass incline, keeping to the shadows and avoiding the pathway. Rowlinson was a few paces behind him, hissing urgently into his phone.

When they reached the front door, Priest stopped. Listened carefully. They had passed the white Mondeo parked on the roadside but it appeared to be empty. There were lights on and a sound of movement from within the church, low murmurings and the faint sound of footsteps. The door was ajar but Priest couldn't see any further than the porch.

'Go round the back, Tiff,' Priest instructed.

'Backup's ten minutes away. We need to wait for it.'

'It'll be too late by then. We've already lost enough time. Go round the back.'

Rowlinson might have been about to protest but Priest shot him a look. He grunted with annoyance before dashing round the side of the church.

Priest pushed the front door open and crept in to the church.

The first thing that hit him was the smell – it was enough to make his stomach churn.

Karl Jones was standing at the end of the church. He stood with his back to Priest on top of the altar, facing a giant cross looming above him, silhouetted against a dark, circular window. He was looking up at it, in a kind of penitence. Waiting. Watching.

At Karl's feet, Elinor and Julian had been draped across the altar, their bodies hanging limply over the edge, Elinor's longer arms brushing against the floor. Priest held his breath, focusing on Elinor, watching her body for signs of movement. The boy, too. He was also frighteningly still.

A horrible realisation dawned on him. *I'm too late.*

Karl was clasping something in his hands. Priest couldn't see what it was until he lifted the object high above his head and the spotlight above him caught the smooth metal, producing a glint of light. Priest watched in horror as he poured a clear liquid over himself, drenching his shirt and most of Elinor and Julian in the process before casting the petrol can aside, waiting for it to clatter into the corner of the aisle.

'Karl,' Priest called out evenly.

Karl stopped and turned his head to one side, although he could only possibly see Priest in his peripheral vision from that angle.

'You made it then,' he said, turning back. 'I'm impressed, and also rather pleased. I wanted you to see this, but if you hadn't shown up in time then I knew you'd be dead. That would have been fine too.'

Priest took a few paces forward but didn't go too far. Petrol was running down the cracks between the flagstones, down the back of the pews. Knitted hassocks bearing ancient family crests were soaked. Even the walls were covered with dark shadows, which Priest realised were splashes of fuel. There must have been gallons of the stuff.

One small spark and this whole place will light up like it's New Year in Shanghai.

'Better that I'm here, though, right, Karl?' Priest suggested. 'Otherwise I'd have missed the final moment when you restore the balance. That's what this is about, right?'

His heart lurched as Karl produced a box of matches from his pocket, played with it in his hand, showing him just enough of what he was doing to let him know who was in control. *You're not hanging around, are you?*

'I'm right in saying that either button would have blown Devil's Point apart, aren't I, Karl?' he said with more urgency.

Karl didn't reply, but Priest heard him sneer. He took another few steps forward but panic was starting to set in – he didn't stand a chance of getting to him in time before the fires of Hell were unleashed on the altar; and Karl wasn't apparently in the mood for conversation. *Must do better. Think!*

'You gave me a choice between intervention and nature, didn't you? I either had to press a button and intervene or let things take their course. And that's what you wanted. To prove myself to you, to get to see all this, all I had to do was nothing.'

Karl took out a match.

'Witness the final act, Mr Priest. That's what I want you to do. If you were pure enough to understand the test on Devil's Point then I have chosen you well. Witness what happens here and then tell them everything you've seen. Then my work will be complete.'

'Who's *they*, Karl?'

'The world! Everyone! Then when Dominique's confession is out there, they will know that he had *three* victims, not one!'

'That's what this is all about?' said Priest, horrified. 'You want to be one of Dominque's victims, along with Elinor and Julian? You tried to ruin Alexia Elias first through *The Real Byte*. You solicited Simeon to help but you told him too much, you went too far. Simeon got cold feet and bailed on you.'

'He was going to go to the police!' Karl roared, turning his head to profile again.

'If he had, he'd have ruined everything,' Priest supposed. 'So you killed him. You somehow got Simeon into the safe the day before the pre-trial conference and he died at some point during the day. You had a perfect alibi, at least for a short while. It's genius. I guess you must have realised that the police would work it out at some point but you were just buying yourself a few days to get everything together.'

'Simeon had outlived his purpose, but killing him gave me no pleasure.'

'You placed him in the back of Elinor's car so she would get the story. That's right, isn't it? You've always been looking out for her like that.'

'You've no idea how I feel.'

Karl looked across to where the petrol can was tipped on its side. There was something desperate about the way he said that. The power of it arrested Priest, stopped his progress across the church and left him short of breath.

'Have you ever known so much desire, Mr Priest, that you would kill just to have a minute of satisfaction?'

Priest was paralysed, unable to respond. Had he? He thought about Jessica and his depth of his attachment to her, a woman he hardly knew in reality. Would he kill for her?

'I understand why Alexia and Dominique had to die,' he said, recovering his self-control. 'But not the boy. Why kill him, too?'

'You put too much emphasis on death as a punishment, or an ending. Death is the first stage of rebirth. We three are the victims of a great crime and together we must take back what we have been deprived of.'

'What have you been deprived of, Karl?'

'*Everything!*' He turned around to face Priest. The petrol was dripping from his black hair and beard and his eyes appeared as nothing but two dark, impenetrable voids. Standing on the altar with his shoulders square and legs apart, he was an imposing sight.

'She was taken from us all, don't you see?' Karl glared at him manically. 'She was corrupted and in that corruption I was denied her, so like any fault, I am reprogramming. I cannot undo what has been done to her, but I can be part of it, so she is not alone.'

'And Julian?' Priest said calmly. 'Why does he need to be reprogrammed?'

'Because it will end his bloodline, and the balance will be restored. All traces of that evil man, his evil wife, and their victims will have been carved out of this earth.'

'Julian wasn't abused, though, Karl, was he? *You're* the one making him the victim.'

'In what way is abandonment not a form of abuse?'

Karl brought the match up again. He seemed to be in a trance-like state, fixing his gaze on the wall above Priest's head. In his other hand, he held the matchbox ready.

One spark, that's all it'll take.

Priest didn't think it through any further. His stomach felt like it was already on fire, the fumes from the petrol were overpowering. He bolted towards Karl, head down, waiting for the feeling of flames to consume him, screaming incomprehensively as he surged forward.

He reached the altar quicker than he had imagined but Karl had already reacted and struck the match. Priest saw the flame take hold of the timber, waiver in the breeze, then settle down. Karl lifted his head to the ceiling and held out his hand before Priest charged into him.

Priest had surprised even himself at the distance he had covered across the chancel. He connected with Karl with enough force to bring him crashing down on the other side of the altar.

The flames danced across the vast pool of fuel, burning lustfully higher and higher, spreading out in all directions, quickly catching Karl's saturated clothes and taking hold instantly.

Priest scrambled backwards, slipping on the wet floor but escaping, albeit temporarily, as the fire started to take hold.

Karl stood up, his arm ablaze, then his shoulder, as the flames started to envelop him, burning his flesh and drawing from him agonising howls of pain as he thrashed around on the fuel-soaked floor. Priest lifted Julian and hauled him off the altar just as the fire caught the end of the cloth.

'No!' screamed Karl, lurching forward. 'Let them go!'

Priest kicked out and caught him in the chest, sending him sprawling backwards and skidding across the pool of fire. The flames danced around him. He was soon swathed by the heart of the blaze, his shrieks of pain and anger echoing around the stone walls.

Slinging Julian over his shoulder he made to grab Elinor but, with Julian's dead weight getting in the way, he couldn't lift her so easily. The best he could do was fall backwards, dragging the bodies with him and only just in time as the fire ravaged the altar, growing stronger and more intense with every moment that passed.

He dragged Elinor and Julian to the far corner. The fire seemed to spread faster down the northern side of the church, ripping into the velvet curtain across the vestry door – the flames now as high as the windows. The heat was excruciating and Priest sank back against the wall as far as he could get but already he could feel the skin around his face burning.

He held up his arm to protect himself but there was nothing he could do. He was trapped. The fire had already reached the back of the church. He was hunched against the wall in the only area that hadn't been touched by the inferno, desperately clinging to Elinor and Julian, but whether they were alive or dead he had no idea.

This is it. The day of reckoning. My own personal rapture.

He gasped for air. If the flames weren't going to kill him then the smoke would surely choke him. Great waves of thick, black fumes rolled over him and as his brain started to shut down it appeared as though a flock of ravens were shrieking in anger as they circled overhead.

For a second he lost his vision. The church was black. Karl's screams had morphed into a blood-curdling howl, until eventually he was silent and the only sound was the roar of the fire and the crackle of burning flesh.

He closed his eyes. He saw Jessica's face and she was mouthing something at him.

His name?

'Priest!'

The sound of the fire was deafening, but there it was again.

'Priest!'

He opened his eyes. Rowlinson looked as though, somehow, he was embedded in the wall, his body extended towards him, hand outstretched, calling his name.

How is he doing that?

He lifted his arm, it felt like it weighed a tonne. Couldn't do it. And the image of Rowlinson wasn't real. It was nothing but a mirage.

Then Rowlinson's hand gripped his and there were more hands helping. He had the sensation of movement, of being dragged along the floor, Elinor and Julian with him.

The last thing he saw before he passed out was the pale moon peering behind the church spire as it collapsed with an ear-splitting noise.

Chapter 62

Priest pulled the tray out of the grill and examined the two burgers with a spatula. Satisfied that they looked sufficiently chargrilled he pulled them out and deposited each in a bun before piling on a selection of salad, radish, gherkin, ketchup, mayonnaise and cheese into each and offering one across his kitchen breakfast bar to Georgie.

'It's a Priest Burger,' he explained.

She took it with clear trepidation and prodded the top of the bun. 'Why a *Priest Burger*?' she asked, suspiciously. 'Why not just a normal burger in a bun with what appears to be salad?'

'You forgot the special ingredient,' Priest said, taking a bite.

'Which is?'

'Mainly carbon.'

Georgie nodded and then took a tentative bite. 'Not too bad,' she concluded.

So far Georgie had spent a lot of time explaining to Priest how Hemingway had come to an unfortunate end, the news of which he had received with dignity. In return, he had recounted the story of meeting Dominique in an abandoned theatre and watching Karl Jones shoot him. He then recounted the story of what happened at Devil's Point. She had sat, wide-eyed, riveted to her seat, and listened.

'You mean Karl Jones, the big nerdy one?'

'Yes, the big nerdy one.'

Georgie nodded.

'You don't sound surprised,' Priest pointed out.

Georgie shrugged. 'Once you explained about the safe it was always going to be one of *The Real Byte* staff. Or you, I guess.' She said it so matter-of-factly. The suggestion caught Priest off guard.

He retorted, 'Equally, it could have been *you*, if you think about it.'

Georgie looked puzzled. 'But I know it wasn't me.'

'That's logical, I suppose.'

'Were the charges on the cliff actually set?'

'Bomb squad say they were primed and, by all accounts, both buttons would have set them off.'

Georgie whistled. 'He wanted to kill you then?'

'I actually think he wanted me to witness the last scene but if I'd have died then, in his mind, I wouldn't have been a worthy witness anyway. He deliberately left that part to fate.'

'All this for a schoolboy crush. You think Karl was mentally ill?'

'I think they both were. But let's not dwell on that too much.'

Priest finished his burger and put the plate aside.

'So let me get this straight,' said Georgie, picking the gherkin out of her burger. 'Elinor Fox was abused by her father. She can't recall any of it, but, at the same time, she recalls everything, in a diary, without realising it's actually her she's writing about. And Karl realised this.'

'Karl had access to her medical notes, although I'm not sure how yet. I saw a letter from a psychiatrist at his house about Elinor's fragile mental state. She's done a lot of time in a psychiatric hospital but she's now deemed capable of independent living.'

'What's wrong with her?'

'She suffers from a complex personality disorder, but it's what's happened to her memory that's interesting. You see there are two sorts of memory: *implicit* memory and *explicit* memory. These are dealt with by two very different subcortical structures in the brain: the amygdala, which processes *implicit* memories – these are emotional responses – and the hippocampus, which processes *explicit* memories; these are your traditional memories, the things you can actually recall.'

'I assume then that her *implicit* memories are intact, but her *explicit* memories are decayed?'

'That's right. So, Elinor knows, somehow, that she hates the Eliases, but she's not sure why. Equally, she knew the plight of a girl trapped in a basement for five years of her life, but doesn't realise that it was her. As a defence mechanism, her mind has detached that part of the recall for her. She interpreted this as a fiction, something she made up. A good story.'

Georgie took another bite. 'Still, she tried to kill me with one of your fish.'

'I think she wanted to scare you.'

'No. She knows I have anaphylaxis.'

'Did you tell the police that?'

Georgie thought for a moment. Swallowed more burger. 'She's going to spend a lot more time in hospital whatever I say, right?'

'Maybe. But none of this will bring Hemingway back.'

She managed a smile. Then something seemed to occur to her.

'You remember when we left the RCJ together on day one of the trial, and we bumped into Dominique?'

'Yeah.'

'He saw her. Elinor. You were talking to him and he saw her, on the steps – I've only just remembered what happened. He went quiet, distracted. I don't think he knew who she was at the time – she must have been almost unrecognisable after all these years, but something about him changed all of a sudden.'

Priest thought back – she was right. He hadn't known Elinor at that stage but Georgie had said she was there, mingling with the other journalists.

He didn't have time to think it through. Georgie was on to the next question. 'But if Karl killed Simeon because he said he was going to tell the truth, why did he dump the body in Elinor's car?'

'He wanted to make sure Elinor had the exclusive and what better way to do that? He knew she was never in any danger of being arrested, forensics would see to that. And he was right, she got the exclusive. It was his warped idea of a gift to her.'

Georgie grunted. 'I'd prefer a box of chocolates and some petrol station flowers.'

'You're easily pleased.' Priest smiled, and she smiled back. 'Oh, I almost forgot.' He produced a piece of paper and laid it out in front of her. She took the paper and unfolded it.

'What's this?'

'It's a letter, from Simeon to Mims. She contacted me earlier and gave me a copy.'

'But Simeon's . . .'

'Dead, yes. No change there. He sent this long before he died.'

'Why has it only just arrived?'

'It was airmailed to a courier in California. They're a firm that specialise in unusual situations. Their instructions were simple. Every day at eleven o'clock, Simeon would check in with them by text. If he didn't check in by the end of the day, they were instructed to send the letter to Mims.'

Georgie looked down. The letter was handwritten, with care. 'So the letter would only get released if something happened to Simeon that prevented him from checking in.'

'That's right. Although, judging from the first line, I guess he'd envisaged fleeing rather than being murdered.'

Dear Mims

If you have received this letter, then I am in exile. Do not try and find me. Do not tell anyone about this letter, or its contents, except for Charlie Priest. I trust him. You need to trust him too, and me.

Dominique and Alexia Elias are going to be exposed, I am sure of it. But I'm no longer sure whose side I'm on. Everything is so confused. I can't tell who's bad and who's good anymore.

A long time ago I met a man who wrapped me up in his crusade so completely that I was swept away with it. This man's name is Karl Jones. I also call him USER3412. I was sure when I first started out that all this man wanted to do was to expose Alexia Elias as a woman who took bribes from a terrorist organisation.

He contacted me just after I had stopped working for the Elias Foundation. He said he was a reporter, looking into the Turkey scandal. He said I could talk to him and they wouldn't name me as a source. I agreed and we met at a cafe in Soho, several times. We became friends. We both clearly had a deep dislike of Alexia Elias. We both knew she was corrupt but had no real proof. Then one day he just suggested to me that perhaps we didn't need proof, we needed evidence.

I agreed to make something up, based on what I knew and some other documents. In doing so, I know I was extremely foolish, but we had to take her down, somehow.

Now, I am beginning to think that either the plan has changed, or the plan was never just about that in the first place.

When I met Karl recently at his house, in his kitchen, I saw a photograph on his side table. I took this photograph; I needed to know what it was. I recognised the boy from my own research. It was Dominique Elias's son. But later I realised that the photo was a fake.

I have no idea what it means, but I am sure it is significant. The photograph is hidden, but Priest will find it, maybe with your help.

I don't know what will happen now, but if I have been a part of something wrong then I will take whatever punishment awaits me.

So I have left a trail for Charlie Priest to follow, in case anything should happen to me. Find Priest and make sure he follows the trail. My phone is in the usual place. Give it to him.

I know that you disagreed with everything I've done but I thought I was doing the right thing, however misguided that seems to you now. I know you owe me nothing, but please, I need your help. I hope you judge me as the man you knew, not the man I have become.

For what it's worth, I'm sorry.

All my love,

Simeon

Georgie looked up, aghast. 'We were right. We were meant to find the secret room at Bristol Road and the picture of Julian. Simeon was trying to tell us what he knew.'

'He planted the clues first. The house was made to look odd. He knew I'd see something strange, like it had been staged. The heating was right up, like he had experienced at Karl's house. It was just to make us start thinking. The letter was further security. If we hadn't have worked it all out, Mims would have come up with the phone.'

'The keys at the estate agents.'

'Another plant, to help us find the phone.'

Georgie shook her head in disbelief. 'Why didn't he just ring you, or find some other way to send you a message?'

'I think it's clear from the letter,' said Priest, exhaling. 'Mims said the postmark indicates that this was sent from the US over a month ago. Simeon didn't have anything to tell me, other than he was lying about the bribes, which would have been the end of the case. He didn't have evidence of any other wrongdoing. Not at that time. All he had were conjectures and suspicions, which he didn't want to resort to if it meant losing the libel trial.'

'But he knew there was more to it, something to do with Julian. He just didn't know what, so he left you all those clues in the hope you'd work it out. And you did.'

'I had a bit of help.' Priest winked at her and Georgie blushed. 'You ready?' he said, getting up and putting on his jacket.

She took one last pained bite and followed him out.

Chapter 63

Rose set about making tea while Priest and Georgie sat at her kitchen table looking out through the patio doors to the yellow fields that disappeared into the horizon. Her farmhouse was surrounded by acres of rolling hills and golden meadows and, so she had told them when they had first arrived, on a clear day she could see the sea from her bedroom window.

Rose's husband, Dennis, a square-shaped man in his sixties hidden inside a black turtle-neck jumper, munched loudly on a piece of toast next to them.

When the tea was ready, Rose placed cups and saucers in front of her guests and took a seat next to her husband. She busied herself pouring the tea, all the while humming softly. When she had finished, she looked up at Priest. She had a nest of silver hair and a petite face with a confident smile – Priest would have had her down as a school head teacher, even if he hadn't known that was the case anyway.

'I suppose you want the truth, Mr Priest,' Rose sighed, pushing the cup towards him with a smile.

'Oh, Rose, don't put it like it's a chore,' grumbled Dennis. 'The man told you *his* story, now you tell him ours.'

'If it's not too much trouble,' piped up Georgie.

Priest had established before they came that the people who Elinor had called Mum and Dad – Rose and Dennis – were not her biological parents, but had adopted her. For all intents and purposes, though, they were a family.

Rose nodded, again with a smile, and took a sip of her tea. Priest watched as she placed the cup down and examined the back of her hand before she spoke.

'It's true that I was there the night we found Elinor on the edge of Devil's Point, as was Dennis, although I didn't know he would later become my husband. He was just a local busybody whom I found thoroughly irritating. How little has changed! I was a WPC at the time – God knows why. I don't know whether you know anything about the police, Mr Priest, but it's not easy being a woman in that environment.'

'I can well imagine,' Priest agreed. His ex-wife had never had that difficulty, but there was an air of masculinity about her that had seen her through a few difficult early years.

'What happened is much simpler than you imagine. You've been told the truth: Elinor *did* jump off the edge, although I don't think she meant to. She was lost and confused and I think she may have just lost her footing: I don't think she was trying to kill herself. But either way, she didn't die. I scrambled down the rocks on the side with Dennis and we looked but there was nothing. In the end, I shouted back up and the crowd dispersed. I guess because I was the authority around there everybody assumed I would file some report somewhere and that would be that.'

'You wouldn't believe how them folks just went away minding their own business as if nothing ever happened,' Dennis cut in. 'Scandalous behaviour.'

'Yes, thank you, Dennis,' Rose sighed. 'Anyway, we found her in the end. By some miracle, she'd missed the rocks and plunged into the water but got herself trapped in the scree. Over time, the water had cut into the rock face and there was a sort of cave underneath; I was about to give up when the ocean just deposited her there. Like Poseidon just coughed her up.'

'It was Fate, not Poseidon,' Dennis growled.

'Well, perhaps. To this day, I don't know how she survived. She was so little, so fragile. Like I said: a miracle.'

'A relaxed body sustains less injury in a car crash,' Priest offered. 'The same principle applies to falling. Maybe it was because she was so confused, she didn't even react.'

Rose nodded. 'That's very true.'

'So, what happened next?'

'Dennis and I took her to the hospital. I tried to radio for help but couldn't get through to anybody. We sat with her for hours. She never said a word. So what were we supposed to do? I couldn't very well just give her up to social services – the system would have eaten her alive. Dennis was equally torn. So, we agreed that I would take her. It was meant to be temporary at first – until we could find out what to do next but . . . well, one thing led to another. Dennis and I became close and . . . it didn't seem right, dumping her again. After a while, we moved away from Tome and settled here. To start a new life, as best we could.'

'Eventually, we formally adopted Elinor,' Dennis explained. 'The process took two years. We had to remain a little unclear about how we ended up with Elinor but . . . well, the important thing is . . .'

Priest held up his hand. 'Far be it for me to pass comment. What you did was what you thought was right, and that's what you ought to be judged on.'

'Well, that's kind of you to say. She had nothing, that girl, just the clothes on her back and the doll. We gave her something to live for.'

'Doll?' Georgie said, interested.

'Yes,' said Dennis. 'A little wooden doll with a wind-up key. She had it wrapped up in her dress. Lovely thing, made of real ash.'

Georgie nodded and smiled.

'So, you gave her your surname but she kept her first name?' Priest said, moving the conversation forward.

'I couldn't let her give that up,' replied Rose. 'It was the only word she spoke for weeks – just her name.'

'Handful she was growing up,' muttered Dennis.

'Hardly surprising,' Rose snapped. 'Given what she had been through.'

'And the diary . . .' Priest prompted.

'We were very worried about it,' said Dennis, shaking his head. 'The doctor said her subconscious was reliving the story, looking for an outlet. But Ellie had no idea that she was actually writing about herself. It's called dissociative amnesia, or something. You've probably never heard of it.'

Priest smiled. 'It rings a bell.'

Dennis continued. 'It was horrifying. To think that what she was writing wasn't her imagination but actually a suppressed memory, rising to the surface. The only godsend was that she didn't recognise it as such – she thought it was her own imagination telling her a story.'

'Anyway, they're dead now, I hear, those horrible people. Good riddance,' Rose added.

'How did you know that Alexia and Dominique Elias were involved?' asked Georgie.

'We were never sure,' said Rose, defensive. 'We knew that Ellie had developed a sort of morbid fascination with the Eliases and we knew they used to live in Tome . . . but we had no way of proving anything. She kept asking and I just kept saying to stay away from them.'

All the time, you were fuelling her interest, rather than dampening it down, thought Priest. *Although you weren't to know.* 'Tell me about Karl Jones. Where does he fit into all this?'

'Oh, dear me,' breathed Rose, hanging her head. Dennis got up and started searching through a bread bin on the kitchen worktop. 'Yes, of course. Well, for a start, we all knew him as Michael. He went by his middle name. There were, as I recall, two Karls in his class so people just started using his middle name.'

'He was funny-looking, too,' Dennis chimed in. 'Didn't look a bit like the photographs the news showed. I heard he was in a car crash a few years back. Buggered up his face: he had to have surgery.'

'Is that why Elinor never recognised him?' Georgie asked.

Rose nodded. 'I suppose so. The Michael we knew had long hair, down over his shoulders, spectacles and he was so much thinner. She probably never studied pictures of him when she was looking into *The Real Byte*, so no wonder she didn't spot him.'

Priest could see what had happened; it was only because he was thinking about Karl that he had recognised him from the photograph in his house, but even then he had known something was wrong. It was hardly surprising that Elinor, who had problems with her memory anyway, hadn't made the connection.

'What happened?' said Priest.

'They met at university. They were both doing media studies and Michael – Karl – was clearly infatuated with her. We used to get flowers, cards and chocolates here all the time. And letters too. They were all addressed to Elinor. She knew about some of them but we binned a lot before she even saw them – I didn't want her upset. Poor child had been through enough, even if she couldn't remember exactly what.'

'I'd have taken a gun to the back of the boy's head, if Rose had let me,' Dennis grunted. 'Bloody pervert.'

'Dennis!' exclaimed Rose, casting him another warning look. 'That's enough. It was a schoolboy crush, no more. At least, that's what we thought.'

Priest nodded and took a sip of tea. *That might have been wishful thinking, but what else were they supposed to do?*

'Anyway,' Rose continued. 'The diary that Ellie was writing was a very sensitive subject for us, obviously. We kept all her work, she was keen to show us and she could write very well; we encouraged her to do more but persuaded her not to try and publish it, thank goodness. Anyway, everything was kept on our computer – all her work, all her medical notes, so we had everything safe.'

'Or at least we thought it was safe,' Dennis added.

Rose continued, 'We don't know what happened. But when the computer kept crashing we took it to be repaired and the man said there was a virus on there. I don't know what it was called, can you remember, Dennis?'

'Trojan, or something.'

'Anyway, he said the computer had been hacked and all of the data stolen.'

'We didn't know who did it,' Dennis growled. 'But my money has always been on Karl.'

Priest nodded. *Turned out to be a good bet.*

Karl Jones had the key to everything. He had launched himself into a delusional crusade for a girl who hardly knew he existed. *What a pathetic waste.*

'Can I ask, Mr Priest,' Rose began, 'how did Alexia and Dominque die?'

Priest bit his lip, exhaling deeply.

'In the end, Rose, they got what they deserved.'

Chapter 64

Priest leant against the wall, one foot up, arms folded, whistling a tune that had stuck in his head. 'The Drugs Don't Work' by The Verve. Police officers bustled past, some cast him a wary look but otherwise no one paid much attention to him. It was late – they'd come here straight from visiting Rose and Dennis – and the station was quiet. Things wouldn't begin to get rowdy until past midnight when the drinkers would start to pile in.

The door to interview room four opened and Rowlinson appeared, shaking his head.

'She needs proper help, Priest,' he said, closing the door behind him. 'I mean professional help.'

'She has dissociative amnesia. The trauma of her childhood is partially suppressed, but you're right: she needs help.'

Rowlinson looked down. 'I can't let you see her. You know that.'

'Five minutes.'

'No.'

'Three.'

'Priest—' Rowlinson looked back up, the disapproval was embedded deep in his face. Priest waited until he finally relented, as they both knew he would.

'Two.'

*

Priest sat down carefully in the seat opposite Elinor Fox. She looked like an injured bird, terrified at not being able to fly. Half a plastic cup of tea in front of her and a blanket over her shoulders. There were bags under her eyes and her skin was deathly pale.

He remembered the church, the sound and smell of burning. And the last moment before he had passed out. His last memory had been of Jessica. He wondered if somehow Fox knew that.

'What happened to Michael?' she said, soft and croaky, her throat was swollen from the smoke inhalation.

'Karl Jones is dead.'

She nodded, relieved. 'And what about . . .'

'Georgie Someday is still very much alive. No thanks to you.'

'I just wanted to scare her.'

'We both know that isn't true. You knew she is susceptible to venom.'

Fox shook her head. 'No. The fish would have died straightaway. She was never in any danger.'

'Then why?'

She looked at him, and for a moment the old Fox was back. The bright, penetrating eyes and the seductive smile. 'For you, honey.'

'Because I mentioned a red-haired girl?'

She nodded, sadly. The brightness faded. Priest got up.

'It wasn't Georgie,' he said. 'It's never been Georgie.'

She looked up, startled. 'Then wh—The woman who came in when you stole the note from me.' She paused. 'But you came back for me, to the church. To save me.'

He didn't reply, but made for the door, all the while not taking his eyes off her. He had intended it to be a warning. He wanted her to see his disapproval; he wanted her to feel as ashamed as he was for sleeping with her.

But she just stared back, nonplussed. When he got to the door, she called out. 'Charlie, this isn't over.'

He looked at her one final time.

'Yes. It is.'

*

Georgie breathed a sigh of relief. Watching Charlie through the CCTV monitor interact with the woman who had tried to kill her had been electrifying. The tension between them was . . . was inescapable. Then the reference to another red-haired girl.

She swallowed hard. Of course. Jessica Ellinder.

Mixed feelings clouded her thoughts. Anger that Elinor had put her through so much trauma, but dreadful pity about her upbringing. What was ten minutes of fear compared to five years of systematic abuse?

She was just a child, Georgie thought. *She still is, in many ways.*

Georgie wasn't clear what the deal was between Fox and Charlie. Maybe just a little mutual attraction, nothing more. It wasn't important now. Nothing was, except that she was safe, and Karl Jones was dead, Alexia was dead, Dominique was dead. If anyone ever deserved to die, it was those three. That was, in a weird way, a form of justice.

'Miss Someday?'

She jumped. Hadn't heard Tiff Rowlinson come in.

'Sorry, didn't mean to startle you. But your boss is asking if you want a lift home.'

'Yes,' she said automatically. 'Coming.'

'Are you sure you don't want to press charges against Fox?'

Georgie hesitated. They had enough for attempted murder, although there were extensive mitigating circumstances; there might even be the question of diminished responsibility. But in the end, it was a straightforward choice.

'I'm sure. I think she's suffered enough, don't you?'

Chapter 65

Priest sat at Sarah's kitchen table trying to decipher the drawing Tilly had handed him. It looked like a monkey eating a bus.

'It's lovely,' he said, handing it back. 'Probably the best picture I have ever seen.'

'It's a golf course,' she said with absolute conviction.

He looked at it again.

'Hey,' he said to her, while Sarah sat opposite. 'Wanna come with me to the pet shop at the weekend. I need a new fish.'

'I can help you name it?' she asked, her eyes wide with the possibility.

'Sure.'

She grinned, jumped down from the kitchen table and skipped back into the lounge.

'Why do you need a new fish?' Sarah asked.

'Long story.'

In the background, the television was on low. *Channel 4 News* was showing footage of Dominque Elias confessing to paedophilia. The footage had been cut, although there would probably still be complaints. The full version was on YouTube. It was already viral. A reporter standing outside the Elias Foundation headquarters was asking Jack Oldham to comment on the 'extraordinary' story of how the footage was sent anonymously to every media outlet in the UK and in countries where the Elias Foundation had outreach centres. He was struggling to explain.

She put Jack's business card on the table in front of him.

'Thank you.'

'Ah,' said Priest, pleased. 'You got the job then.'

'The Elias Foundation is rebranding and I've got all the PR covered. It's a great gig, Charlie.'

'They'll pay you well.'

She winked and he got up, ready to leave. He had dropped in to see how the interview had gone but in truth Jack had called him five minutes before he arrived to tell him what a fantastic presentation Sarah had done and the Board had unanimously agreed to appoint her.

'What happened to the court case?' she asked.

'It turns out that Alexia had professional executors. She didn't have any family that we know of, other than Dominique. So two partners of a local law firm had been appointed. They took one look at the litigation and decided there wasn't enough money in the estate to indemnify them, especially if what money there is happened to be proceeds of crime. So they discontinued, meaning that *The Real Byte* won. They'll be more litigation over costs probably, but that's for another day.'

'All's well that ends well then.'

Priest looked away, thinking of Elinor. Rose and Dennis had called Priest earlier to say that they had taken her 'back to hospital' because they were worried about her mental health.

'At least it's over, for now.' He popped his head around the door to the lounge and shouted bye to Tilly, who waved back lazily, then turned to Sarah. 'Got to run. Bit of paperwork to catch up on.'

She raised an eyebrow. 'Who is she?'

Priest smiled. 'See you soon.'

She led him to the door, brushed a hair off his jacket.

'It'll take a long time but the new charity will be up and running eventually,' she said. 'You wouldn't believe the money people have come forward with.'

'Really?'

'One benefactor alone put in over a million pounds.'

'You're kidding,' he said, smiling internally. 'Who'd have thought it?'

*

It was early evening and the air was heavy. Rain was coming. The sky was a dark, hazy blue, blemished with ethereal clouds. The smoke from the small bonfire drifted high above the back of the allotment before dissipating into nothing.

'What happened to the fish in the end?' asked Li, tearing a page from one of the folders and casting it into the flames.

'Hemingway didn't make it,' Georgie replied, doing the same.

They had found two old deckchairs stacked around the back of a shed and, at this time of night, it seemed unlikely that anybody else would need them. So they sat, enjoying the warmth of the fire, feeding the flames with the Martin papers.

'I think you owe me an introduction,' Li said, with a wink.

'I'll see what I can do.'

'It's OK,' Li laughed. 'In your own time.'

Georgie smiled and threw on another piece of paper.

'How did – what was his name? DCI Rowlinson get your boss out of the church, by the way?'

'There was a side door. Rowlinson kicked it down and luckily Charlie was hunched up in the corner.'

'And the boy? What was his name? Julian?'

'Safe and back with his mother, although I'm not sure what he remembers of it.'

'Cool. What a fucked-up story.'

They sat for a while with nothing but the crackle of the fire and the sound of paper tearing to accompany them. Georgie glanced at the sheets occasionally. Two years' work. How quickly each sheet disintegrated into ash and with every toss she felt a little bit of Martin was also burning away.

After a moment, Li said, 'Why are we burning these again?'

'I don't think I need them anymore.'

'Ah-ha.' Li was quiet for a while. Then, 'You never went to the police.'

It was a simple statement, not a challenge, or even a question, but she still felt something twinge in her stomach. Nobody knew, except her, Martin and Li. As much as she didn't like it, that bound them together somehow.

'I know the system,' she said softly. 'I went into the room voluntarily, I kissed him voluntarily. He has no previous. I was alone with him. There was no chance of a prosecution.'

'I see.'

Li nodded, and for a moment there appeared the slightest fragment of a tear forming at the corner of Li's eye. Georgie caught sight of it glinting in the firelight and, in that moment, she felt relieved. *Somebody knows. Somebody cares.*

'Too much time has passed now,' she said at last.

'You should have told someone, if not the police.'

'I know.'

Georgie looked at Li again. The tear had been wiped away, but something had been left behind. Anger. Georgie recognised it immediately. She had seen it on her own face.

She shivered, despite the fire. Then it occurred to her. She was destroying the papers and giving up on any hope of natural justice. But she wasn't giving up everything. She would never give up the way she felt.

'I was up late last night,' Li said quietly after a while.

'Oh?'

'I walked past your room.'

'And?' Georgie turned to look at her. The light of the fire shimmered in her hair as she stared ahead, transfixed by the flames.

'Your light was off.'

She nodded, looking down at the folder. Most of the pages were torn up but a few remained. *I'm not going to be afraid of the dark anymore.*

She tossed the whole folder into the fire and they watched it burn together.

Chapter 66

Jessica took another sip of red wine then cupped her hands together on Priest's breakfast bar. He had his back to her but he was very aware that she was watching him as he rummaged through his cupboards, searching for something – *anything* – that he could make a meal out of. The television fixed to the back wall was on, the sound low; they were testing more missiles in North Korea. There had been repeats of Dominique's confession and a statement by Jack Oldham. Priest already recognised Sarah's spin on the words.

The text she had sent him had been clear enough: *Dinner, your place. Tonight*. It hadn't given him any time to prepare something and, by the look of things, his cupboards were pathetically bare.

'Do you like tuna sandwiches?' he called back over his shoulder.

She shrugged and continued to challenge him with her stare. He suspected that his panicked attempt to cook her something was also a source of great amusement.

'Did I ever tell you,' she said, touching the wine glass to her lips, 'that women hate men who pretend not to know how to cook or clean because they think a girl would like to mother them?'

Priest stopped and looked back at her. She was smiling. Her eyes were spellbinding.

'You don't strike me as the mothering type,' he observed.

'No. I'm not.'

'Then it's clear that I'm not pretending. I'm genuinely shit at cooking.'

She nodded, like an accord had been reached, before pushing her phone across the table at him. 'I'll have Chinese. Beef with green peppers and black bean sauce.'

He took the phone gratefully.

She had listened attentively to the details of his encounter with Karl Jones and the incident at Devil's Point and the church, raising her eyebrow occasionally and letting the odd gasp escape her mouth. But otherwise, just listening, like any other new story.

He was about to dial but she cut in with, 'I don't understand the confession. Why did Dominique just blurt it all out?'

'Karl had threatened him,' Priest explained. 'We found out afterwards that Karl had sent Dominique pictures of what he had done to Alexia. He had made the choice clear: confess your sins and have a clean death or Julian would be next.'

'Mm. And it made no difference. Jones was going to kill Julian anyway. It was always part of his sick endgame, whatever the outcome.'

'That's right, though I think Dominque was ready to spill anyway; the years of guilt had built up inside him. Old age was creeping up on him. He was ready to be judged for what he had done.'

'He deserves whatever punishment awaits him in the next life. And Jones wanted you to see it all, as long as you could prove to him you weren't a meddler, by passing his strange test. So you could attest to his work.'

'He wanted to be a victim, along with Julian and Elinor, and for everyone to know that he had martyred himself.'

She poured herself more wine, and topped up his glass. For the first time, he felt relaxed in her company and hoped that there might even be a possibility that she was feeling relaxed in his, as strange as it seemed.

The news had moved on.

'I wanted to say I'm sorry about telling you I knew about your medical condition,' she said. 'I should have been more . . . tactful.'

Priest was surprised, the apology was sincere. *Jessica Ellinder is sorry.* 'I don't really keep it a secret.'

'Nonetheless, I wish I hadn't said it.'

'It's under control now, sort of.' He lowered the phone, realising that she was still watching him, waiting for him to tell her about it. About the panic attacks, the hallucinations, the sudden intense awareness of *himself*. In truth, he had never really spoken about it. His ex-wife, Dee, had never been receptive to it, had never tried to understand it. In the end, it had destroyed them. But then, had he ever tried? Had he *wanted* to try? Maybe that was the difference. Now, he *wanted* to talk about it. But whether that was because of the passage of time or because it was Jessica, he wasn't sure.

'I had depersonalisation disorder, a type of dissociative disorder, for several years but, over time, the symptoms have faded. Now, it comes back on occasion but most of the time I'm fine.'

'What's it like?'

He waited a few moments, arranging the words in his head. It wasn't something that was easy to articulate; it was something that you could only really understand if you had it. 'Imagine suddenly realising – *knowing* without doubt – that your mind and your body are two separate beings, independent of each other. You are your mind but you no longer have control over your body. Sometimes you even see it from afar, like a real life out-of-body experience. You immediately question your own existence. Am I really here? Have I died? Then this detachment is accompanied by an overwhelming and irrepressible feeling of dread; you realise that your own existence is a facade. The cell you inhabit, your body, is nothing more than a collection of chemicals and organs, disgusting and unnatural. Then you question: is this the real world and the times when I'm normal the dream?'

Jessica nodded slowly, thoughtful. She didn't seem shocked, like when he had told her he had almost died in the church, she didn't flinch. Just nodded. Then she said, 'You must feel like you're going insane.'

'No. It's the very opposite. You feel like you are *too sane*. You can see everything with enhanced clarity, objects change size, you hear distinctly. Everything is suddenly exposed for what it really is and you realise that it's all fake, everything. Then you realise that you're the only one that knows that, and no one will believe you.'

'Must be pretty lonely in your world.'

You have no idea. 'Kind of is, but some people make it bearable. People like you.' She drank more wine, apparently with no intention of easing the conversation along. 'Did you mean what you said earlier? About starting again?'

'If that's what you want.'

'Is that what *you* want?'

'I really want you to be less awkward and less obtuse.'

'Likewise.'

She laughed, leant across the table. 'Maybe that's as good a basis for a relationship as any. A mutual desire for us both to be less like we actually are.'

She studied him, as she often did. But whereas her appraisal would ordinarily baffle and frustrate him to wondering what the hell she wanted, what she was thinking, it was pretty clear this time. This time, he could read Jessica Ellinder like a book.

'How about we skip the Chinese for now and go straight to bed?' he suggested.

'There now,' she replied. 'That wasn't so difficult, was it?'

EPILOGUE

Nurse Marie picked up the clipboard from the bedside table and checked the paperwork associated with the new admission. Marie was new to Fen Marsh, although she'd done some agency work for them last year. The turnover of staff was high, but this was an easier wing. The real creeps were across the courtyard – some of Britain's most notorious serial killers were held there. Marie was lucky to be on this side of what the staff called the Twilight Zone.

The woman was lying in bed, staring at the ceiling. She hadn't said much. Just mumbled her name and confirmed a few details. She knew why she was here, but she didn't want to be here. She wanted to go home. Usual story. The pills had quickly calmed her down. She had history. Nurse Marie hadn't seen this woman before but others had. Last stay was ten weeks, a year ago. She'd come full circle, but it wasn't clear what had caused the relapse. The consultant was on her way, typically taking her time.

Marie stared at the woman's face, her soft features, blonde hair. She was attractive, not like the usual sort they brought in under the Mental Health Act. This one was going to be trouble, Marie could feel it.

'Hello, Elinor.'

Elinor turned her head. Stared right through Marie. It sent a shiver down her spine.

'Would you like some water, Elinor?'

No response.

Marie made a note on the paper.

'Your mother is—' She checked the pad. 'Rose? She'll be here to see you later today. She's bringing a few of the things you wanted.'

Still no response. Not verbally anyway; but there was something in her eyes that worried Marie. Something that made her anxious.

Marie took out the photographs the doctor had given her. They had been found tucked into Elinor's bag on admission. They must be important to her but they were strange. Not like family photos of a loved one but more like the paparazzi shots Marie was used to seeing in the magazines that adorned the waiting room.

They were photographs of the same man, impersonally taken, without him knowing.

Marie picked one out and showed it to her new patient. 'Who's this, Elinor?'

Elinor cocked her head to one side, ruffling the pillow.

'That's my husband. His name is Charlie.'

ACKNOWLEDGEMENTS

Writing isn't a solitary business. OK, it starts with me, a laptop and a few loopy ideas but there's a host of people without whom this book, much like the first Charlie Priest novel, would never have made it to print.

Huge thanks go to the team at Bonnier Zaffre for your endless support and belief, but particularly to Katherine Armstrong, whose insightful and intelligent editing was invaluable and added an extra dimension to the story.

To Oliver, Grace and Archie, the people who live with me, and have to put up with my deeply flawed personality on a daily basis, thank you for being there and for being who you are. You probably don't realise, but you're a constant source of inspiration for me and I mean it when I say I'm deeply proud of you all.

Thanks and applause to Mum, not in an obligatory thanks-for-giving-birth-to-me kind of way, but genuinely your work on *The Ash Doll* was really helpful and your attention to detail is second to none. I'm still getting over the fish tank comment from *The Mayfly* – only you can notice minutiae to that level.

To Denise (MIL) and Rick (FIL), thanks for taking us in for those few weeks when we were less like a family and more like a nomadic tribe. Special thanks also to MIL for your read through of an early draft; it was great to see the book unfold through your comments.

To you, the reader: thank you for picking up this book and reading it. If you read *The Ash Doll* because you liked *The Mayfly*, then welcome back and I hope you enjoyed Priest's latest outing. If you're new to the series, thanks for giving a new author a try. There are so many talented writers out there, so many amazing books, I'm humbled to know that you gave up your time to read my work.

Finally, to my wife, Jo. Where the hell do I begin? As well as being my best friend, you've been my companion on this journey from day one and my most important adviser in everything. Your belief alone has seen me through the hard times and I can't stress enough how fundamentally important your input is. Priest just wouldn't be Priest without you to steer me. Look how far we've come since those days sat in the Sicilian sun listening to the tapping on the keyboard! Love you always.

Dear Reader

Firstly, congratulations and thank you, you made it to the end. I tried to tie everything together for you and hopefully you felt that the baddies were suitably punished and the goodies were suitably triumphant.

For me, it was a journey and a half to get there. It's not the hundred thousand words in the book that's the problem, you see. It's the four hundred thousand other words in the bin that are the killer.

So, thank you. Because now my book is finished. Not when I wrote the last few words, or my editors straightened out the last few kinks. When you finished reading it – that's when the book was properly complete.

After all, a book without a reader is just . . . well, paper with symbols on it.

As I write, I've almost finished the first draft of the third Charlie Priest novel, which I'll pass to my wife to read for the first time and point out where I've gone wrong. Like *The Ash Doll*, I've loved seeing it unfold; can't wait to see what you think of it.

For now, if you want to hear more, then you could join the James Hazel Readers Club. You can do so by emailing me at james.hazel@myreadersclub.co.uk. It only takes a moment to register and, to say thanks, I'll send you a free short story. There'll be important updates about forthcoming titles and some exclusive VIP content.

It's also a really great way to get in touch. I'd love to hear from you and get to know what you liked and what you didn't like.

Your data will never be passed to a third party and I'll only be in touch now and again. You can unsubscribe at any time. I hope you stay with me, though, because we've started this adventure together, you and me, and it's going to be a great ride!

I'd also love it if you were able to spend a few moments leaving a review on Amazon or GoodReads, or anywhere else that supports reviews. All authors appreciate fair and constructive reviews but new writers like me live or die by them, so anything you can do would be fantastic. If you liked Priest, spread the word, people value a good book recommendation.

Once again, thank you for reading.

With best wishes,

James Hazel

If you enjoyed *The Ash Doll*, read on for an
extract from James Hazel's debut novel,

THE
MAYFLY

Available now

December. Post-festivities. The frozen earth was veiled in a thin covering of snow that crunched under Detective Chief Inspector Tiff Rowlinson's boots. In a glade, the log cabin looked as though it had come out of a fairy tale, complete with a tall stone chimney and heart-shaped etchings above the door. A local landowner had built it for his daughter as a summer house sixty years ago, but it had long since been abandoned, and was now swathed with climbing plants and moss. A sanctuary built out of love and innocence, defiled in the most grotesque manner.

Rowlinson slowly circled the little wooden structure, his hands behind his back and his coat collar turned up inside the white plastic overall. The crime scene investigators mingled uncertainly, watching where they trod. They had established a perimeter with reams of blue-and-white plastic tape around the glade. Rowlinson had been here before, too many times. He had seen too many bodies, too many weeping loved ones and too few prosecutions. He didn't feel much anymore. The endless cycle had anaesthetised him.

Except in these woods.

In these woods, Rowlinson felt again.

He approached the entrance to the cabin and ducked through the doorway. Inside, the air was stale and heavy. He fumbled for the inhaler in his coat pocket. Felt a little relief at feeling the familiar plastic tube and the tip of the metal canister. He no longer noticed the bitter cold.

The room was empty, save for the victim. And the flesh-eating flies swarming around what was left of him. The victim's head was slumped over the back of a wooden chair, mouth and eyes wide open. His skin was yellow and withered. A reaction to the poison, Rowlinson had been told, but he now understood a comment one of the SOCO team had made a short while ago – 'Poor bastard looks like someone sucked his soul clean out.'

He was naked and his arms were covered with deep lacerations, but that was nothing compared to his chest. The flesh was hanging off, exposing a crimson network of muscle and tissue. There were similar wounds on the lower half but everything was so saturated in blood, it was hard to make out which parts of him remained intact and which didn't.

'Jesus,' a voice behind Rowlinson gasped.

He turned to find Hardwick in the entrance, hand over his mouth.

'What the hell have we got here, guv?'

DS Hardwick was a foot shorter than his superior but still managed to fill the little cabin with his portly frame. He was a city boy with a swaggering gait, but a decent copper despite his lack of charm.

'The damage is self-inflicted,' Rowlinson said quietly.

'He tore his own skin off, boss?'

Rowlinson peered more closely. Ptyalism – excretion of foamy saliva, but to such an extent that the victim had been unable to control it by swallowing alone. At some point, he had introduced his fist into his mouth in order to induce vomiting but had ended up biting down so hard that he had almost taken his hand clean off.

'The alkaloid caused unimaginable pain for many hours. To combat it, the victim attempted to fillet himself.'

'Why?'

'To get at his heart, Hardwick. It was the only way to end the pain.'

∽

Three hours earlier, Sir Philip Wren had been sitting in the study of his Kent home, his belly full of port and chicken, and his mind full of gushing phrases to use during his acceptance speech for an OBE. He had received the phone call only yesterday in the strictest confidence – the Honours Committee had resolved to acknowledge the incumbent Attorney General's services to the legal profession and Her Majesty's Government in the New Year's Honours list. Finally, a lifetime's commitment to public service was to be recognised and Wren had spent the last twenty-four hours in a state of euphoria.

But his jubilation had been short-lived and he was now in south Wales, cold and anxious, and with a sharp pain in his head.

The scene was as he had expected – a glade swarming with a forensic team. Blue flashing lights. A feeling of uncertainty hanging in the air. And in the centre, a little wooden cabin with hearts carved above the door.

It's happening again.

He had been told that the detective in charge, Rowlinson, was competent. He had no doubt that this was true, but a local detective couldn't possibly keep this case. Not if Wren's fears were realised. He found Rowlinson standing with another man by the cabin door, looking at him with the same expression of uneasiness as all the detectives he had seen over the years. He didn't blame them. If he could have it any other way, he would leave them to get on with their job – but he couldn't. Not this time.

He walked across the glade, conscious of the questioning eyes following him.

'Philip Wren.' He offered his hand and received a firm grip in response.

'DCI Rowlinson. We weren't expecting the Attorney General, sir. Is there a jurisdictional issue I should be –'

'Not at all. No one wants to tread on any toes here, Chief Inspector. Your authority is not in question.'

It was a lie. There was a task force already in place to take over the investigation, a sub-division of the National Domestic Extremist Unit. A covert, specialist Met unit.

'Then I don't see –'

'May I see the body, DCI Rowlinson?'

Rowlinson shifted his weight from one foot to the other. The Attorney General had arrived in a Jaguar XJ accompanied by a small company of dark-suited men. These men had gathered the bewildered SOCO team together and were issuing them with confidentiality agreements to sign. After a further moment's hesitation, Rowlinson stood aside.

Wren inhaled the cold air greedily before stepping inside the log cabin. His stomach churned. He didn't want to see that chicken again.

Rowlinson stood in the doorway watching him curiously, hands wedged in his pockets.

He cleared his throat.

'The poison was administered through a catheter in his wrist, probably while he was unconscious. The poison takes over the whole body, arrests every single nerve. The pain is excruciating, but the brain is too overloaded to shut down. The sensation apparently lasts for hours, during which, as you can see, the victim mutilated himself.'

'Is there anything in his mouth, Chief Inspector?'

Rowlinson faltered. 'What?'

Wren felt a lump in his throat, something restricting his airway. 'His mouth, Chief Inspector. Is there anything in his mouth?'

Rowlinson looked behind him, as if he thought it might be a test, before taking two strides across the floorboards to within touching distance of the victim. The foam around the victim's gaping mouth had begun to congeal but some of the froth dripped down the side of his face like egg white. Wren watched as Rowlinson peered in.

'There's nothing there.' Rowlinson straightened up.

'Check again.'

Rowlinson bent over the body again and looked closer. Wren balled his hands into fists. Perhaps Rowlinson was right. Perhaps there was nothing there.

'Hang on,' Rowlinson said, digging a pen and a pair of blue plastic gloves out of his pocket. 'There is something . . .'

Wren felt the tension in his body snap as Rowlinson repositioned himself, dipped the pen into the victim's mouth and gently eased it back out.

'What in God's name is that?' He held up a black object to the light.

Behind him, Philip Wren walked swiftly out of the cabin.